LEAVE HER TO HELL

Percy Hand is hired to locate Mrs. Markley—who supposedly ran off with another man two years ago. The soon-to-be-fourth Mrs. Markley, Faith Salem, doesn't want any loose ends before she weds Graham Markley. Percy doesn't want the case—what P.I. wants to track down a two-year-old elopement?—but the more questions he asks, the more he finds that there is something not right here. But if Constance and Regis are now living somewhere in connubial bliss, why doesn't anyone want them found... and where are they?

LET ME KILL YOU, SWEETHEART!

Guy Butler, Rex Tye and Ellis Kuder had all loved Avis Pisano that summer when she waitressed in Sylvan Green, each in their own way. But now Avis is pregnant and desperate, and so takes the train to Rutherford, where the father of her child lives. She calls him Curly. She doesn't realize that Curly will stop at nothing to keep her out of his life—not even murder. But who is this Curly—alcoholic Guy? Mama's boy Rex? Or cold-hearted Ellis? Who indeed...

TAKE ME HOME

Henry Harper first meets Ivy Galvin in the Greek's diner. The immediate dislike is mutual. But in spite of her caustic comments, he also feels a little sorry for her—broke, nowhere to go. Ivy asks Henry to take her home with him, and for some reason, he agrees. But Ivy has no interest in Henry as a man. He understands. He knows that Ivy is different. He doesn't expect their relationship to be anything but plutonic. But there is something so appealing about Henry, and maybe Ivy can change...

FLETCHER FLORA BIBLIOGRAPHY (1914-1969)

Strange Sisters (1954)
Desperate Asylum (1955; reprinted as Whisper of Love, 1959)
The Brass Bed (1956)
The Hot-Shot (1956)
Leave Her to Hell (1958)
Let Me Kill You, Sweetheart (1958)
Park Avenue Tramp (1958)
Whispers of the Flesh (1958)
Lysistrata (1959)
Take Me Home (1959)
Wake Up With a Stranger (1959)
Killing Cousins (1960)
Most Likely to Love (1960)
The Seducer (1961)
The Irrepressible Peccadillo (1963)
Skulldoggery (1967)
Hildegarde Withers Makes the Scene [w/Stuart Palmer] (1969)

As Timothy Harrison

Hot Summer (1966)

As Ellery Queen

Who Killed the Golden Goose [aka The Golden Goose] (1964)
Blow Hot, Blow Cold (1964)
Devil's Cook (1966)

Leave Her to Hell

Let Me Kill You, Sweetheart

Take Me Home

By Fletcher Flora

Introduction by Bill Pronzini

Stark House Press • Eureka California

LEAVE HER TO HELL / LET ME KILL YOU, SWEETHEART / TAKE ME HOME

Published by Stark House Press
1315 H Street
Eureka, CA 95501
griffinskye3@sbcglobal.net
www.starkhousepress.com

ISBN: 1-933586-95-8
ISBN-13: 978-1-933586-95-3

Book design by Mark Shepard, shepgraphics.com
Cover art by Harry Schaare.

First Stark House Press Edition: March 2016
FIRST EDITION

M
FLORA

FLETCHER FLORA: MAN OF MANY TALENTS

BY BILL PRONZINI

Fletcher Flora was a talented writer whose work received regrettably little attention during his lifetime. His style was highly literate and sardonically (and sometimes farcically) humorous, and his range in both short stories and novels was remarkable – everything from hard-boiled to police procedurals to straightforward whodunits to light whimsy to historical fiction to probing examinations of 1950s and 1960s morals and mores.

Although his short stories earned him considerable stature among editors, fellow writers, and magazine readers of the period, his 21 novels – all but three of which were published as paperback originals – were mostly unsuccessful. Part of the reason for this was greater emphasis on psychological and psychosexual explorations than on plot; some of his books tend to be slice-of-life character studies and collections of incidents rather than fully realized novels. But the primary reason for his lack of success seems to have been poor professional advice and an indifferent agent who too often sold his books to the lesser paperback houses.

Born in Parsons, Kansas in 1914, Flora received a B.S. degree from Kansas State in 1938, did graduate work at the University of Kansas 1938-40, married in 1940 and was the father of two sons and a daughter. During World War II he served with the U.S. Army's 32nd Infantry Division in New Guinea, Leyte, and Luzon, attaining the rank of sergeant; in combat he received severe shrapnel wounds that plagued him for the rest of his life. After his discharge in 1945, he accepted a position as Education Adviser of the U.S. Disciplinary Barracks at Fort Leavenworth, Kansas – a job teaching military prisoners that he held until 1963.

He began writing fiction for publication in the late 1940s, and made his first few sales to pulp magazines beginning in 1950. His first published work, "Showdown for Death," appeared in the December 1950 issue of *Private Detective.* Over the next eighteen years he contributed more than 150 stories, the bulk of which were crime tales, to *Manhunt, Ellery Queen's Mystery Magazine, Alfred Hitchcock's Mystery Magazine,* most of the other digest mystery/suspense periodicals that flourished during that time, such men's magazines as *Escapade* and *Adam,* and the slick magazine *Cosmopolitan.* Two of his stories won special awards in *EQMM*'s annual short story contest. While most of his short fiction is of the standalone type, he created one series character for the magazine markets in the 1960s: Lieutenant Joseph Marcus, the protagonist of several police procedurals.

He turned to novels in 1954 with *Strange Sisters* (Lion), a mordant tale of lesbian love and the dire consequences of three abusive relationships; his second book, *Desperate Asylum* (Lion, 1955) also has a lesbian theme. Several novels on heterosexual themes followed over the next few years, among them *The Brass Bed* (Lion, 1956), *Whispers of the Flesh* (Signet, 1958), *Park Avenue Tramp* (Gold Medal, 1959; reissued by Stark House in 2007 as part of a triple volume with novels by Dan J. Marlowe and Charles Runyon), *Wake Up with a Stranger* (Signet, 1959), *Most Likely to Love* (Monarch, 1960), *The Seducer* (Monarch, 1961), and *Hot Summer* (Beacon, 1962, as by Timothy Harrison). Though sex is the central ingredient in all of these, the stories are earnest in intent and realistically, not pruriently, developed.

Flora also published one historical novel, *Lysistrata* (Zenith Books, 1959). A novelized version of Aristophanes' sex-based comedy concerning a plot to end the Peloponnesian war, it is probably the least known of all his longer works – a shame because it is both bawdy and amusing.

The first of his eleven mystery/detective novels, *The Hot Shot*, about a young man involved in a gambling syndicate's point-fixing of college basketball games, was published by Avon in 1956. *Leave Her to Hell!* and *Let Me Kill You, Sweetheart!* were 1958 Avon titles. His first hardcover, *Killing Cousins* (Macmillan, 1960), a witty, tongue-in-cheek story of a lethal lady named Willie, won the publisher's Cock Robin Award for best mystery of the year. Another light-hearted mystery, *The Irrepressible Peccadillo*, also appeared under the Macmillan imprint two years later.

In the mid-sixties, Flora ghosted three of the series of Pocket Books paperback originals that carried the Ellery Queen byline but were in fact written by other authors on consignment; these are *Blow Hot, Blow Cold* (1964), *The Golden Goose* (1964), and *The Devil's Cook* (1966). His last solo novel, *Skulldoggery* (Belmont, 1967), an excellent murderous farce in the same vein as *Killing Cousins*, was given such poor distribution by its third-class publisher that it, like *Lysistrata*, was read by few in its day.

Flora's final book, *Hildegarde Withers Makes the Scene* (Random House, 1969), was in effect a collaboration with Stuart Palmer, Flora having been commissioned to finish a manuscript left uncompleted when Palmer died in February of 1968. Tragically and ironically, Flora himself died less than a year later, at the too-young age of 54 not long after completing the novel. Thus neither author lived to see it published.

The three short novels collected in these pages are among his darker and most entertaining works. *Leave Her to Hell!*, a condensed version of which appeared in the August 1958 issue of *Manhunt* under the author's original title, "Loose Ends," features Percy Hand, a "poor, proud but honest" PI who resembles, in the view of one character, the actor Jack Palance. Hand, who has a weakness for beautiful women, is hired by one named Faith Salem to find out what happened to a friend of hers who, along with her paramour, disappeared without a trace two years previously. Although it contains many of the conventions of the 50s private eye novel, and perhaps suffers somewhat from an absence of geographical location (the city in which it takes place is neither named nor characterized), the story moves swiftly and not always in a conventional fashion. What sets it and its protagonist apart from others of its type is Hand's reliance on brainpower instead of violence, an abundance of barbed humor, and a solution that may well take the reader by surprise.

Let Me Kill You, Sweetheart! (another lurid, publisher-generated title) demonstrates Flora's sure hand with the tale of dark suspense. In the small Midwestern town of Rutherford, a promiscuous, pregnant young woman, Avis Pisano, is murdered by one of three men nicknamed Curly, all of whom had a brief affair with her the previous summer and each of whom harbors secret demons that render him capable of cold-blooded violence. Only one man stands between the murderer and a perfect crime – fat, clumsy, mild-mannered, train-obsessed Purvy Stubbs. Tension in the Woolrich manner, Flora's usual fine delineation of character, and revelation of the murderer's identity in a clever fashion at the very end, make this a particularly satisfying read.

Although *Take Me Home* (Monarch, 1959) contains an attempted rape and at least one instance of attempted murder, it is only marginally a crime novel. In design and execution it's another of Flora's penetrating, sex-based character studies – in this case of a troubled woman named Ivy Galvin involved in a destructive lesbian affair with her cousin Lila, and an unsuccessful but dedicated young writer, Henry Hunter, who falls in love with her. Powerful emotions drive the narrative and create an effective noirish atmosphere.

One can't help wondering, given the quality and broadening scope of Fletcher Flora's later work, what he might have accomplished had he lived and written several more years. More's the pity that we'll never know.

August 2015
Petaluma, CA

LEAVE HER TO HELL
by Fletcher Flora

CHAPTER 1

A woman wanted to see me about a job. Her name, she said, was Faith Salem. She lived, she said, in a certain apartment in a certain apartment building, and she told me the number of the apartment and the floor it was on and the name and the address of the building it was in. She said she wanted me to come there and see her at three o'clock that afternoon the same day she called on the telephone. I went and saw her, and it was three o'clock when I got there.

The door was opened by a maid with a face like half a walnut. You may think it's impossible for a face to look like half a walnut, and I suppose it is, if you want to be literal. But half a walnut is, nevertheless, all I can think of as a comparison when I think of the face of this maid. She wasn't young, and she probably wasn't old. She was, as they say, of an indeterminate age. Her eyes smiled, but not her lips; and she nodded her head three times as if she had checked me swiftly on three salient points and was satisfied on every one. This gave me confidence.

"I'm Percy Hand," I said. "I have an appointment with Miss Salem."

"This way," she said.

Following her out of a vestibule, I waded through a couple acres of thick wool pile in crossing two wide rooms. Then I crossed a third room with another acre of black-and-white tile that made me feel, by contrast, as if I were taking steps a yard high. Finally I got out onto a terrace in the sunlight, and Faith Salem got up off her stomach and faced me. She had been lying on a soft pad covered with bright yellow material that might have been silk or nylon or something, and she was wearing in a couple of places a very little bit of another material that was just as shining and soft and might have been the same kind, except that it was white instead of yellow. Sunbathing was what she was doing, and I was glad. Her skin was firm and golden brown, giving the impression of consistency all over, and I was willing to bet that the little bit of white in a couple of places was only a concession to present company. Nine times out of ten, when someone tries to describe a woman who is fairly tall and has a slim and pliant and beautiful body, he will say that she is willowy, and that's what I say. I say that Faith Salem was willowy. I also say that her hair was almost the identical color of the rest of her. This seemed somehow too perfect to have been accomplished by design, but it may have been. You had to look at her face for a long time before you became aware that she was certainly a number of years older than you'd thought at first she was.

"Mr. Hand has arrived, Miss Faith," the maid said.

"Thank you, Maria," Faith Salem said.

I stepped twice, and she stepped twice, and we met and shook hands. Her grip was firm. I liked the way her fingers took hold of my fingers and held them and were in no hurry to drop them.

"Thank you for coming, Mr. Hand," she said. "You must excuse me for receiving you this way, but the sun is on this terrace for only a short while each afternoon, and I didn't want to miss any of it."

"I'd have been sorry to miss it myself," I said.

She smiled gravely, getting my meaning, and then released my fingers and walked over to a yellow chaise lounge on which a white hip-length coat had been left lying. She put on the coat and moved to a wrought-iron and glass table where there was a single tall tumbler with alternating red and yellow stripes. The tumbler was empty. Holding it against the light, she stared through it wistfully as if regretting its emptiness, and I watched her do this with pleasure and no regrets whatever. There is a kind of legerdemain about a short coat over something shorter. It creates the illusion, even when you have evidence to the contrary, that it's all there is—there isn't any more.

"I like you, Mr. Hand," she said. "I like your looks."

"Thanks. I like yours, too."

"Would you care for a drink?"

"Why not? Its a warm day."

"I had a gin and tonic before you came. Do you drink gin and tonic?"

"When it's offered. A gin and tonic would be fine."

She set the red and yellow tumbler on the glass top of the table and turned slightly in the direction of the entrance to the black-and-white tiled room.

"Gin and tonic, Maria," she said.

I had thought that the indeterminate maid with a face like half a walnut had gone away, and I felt a slight shock of surprise to discover that she had been standing all the while behind me. Now she nodded three times exactly, a repetition of the gesture she had made at the door, and backed away into the apartment and out of sight. Faith Salem sat down in a low wicker chair and crossed her feet at the ankles and stared at her long golden legs. I stared at them, too.

"Please sit down, Mr. Hand," she said. "Maria will bring the gin and tonics in a moment. In the meanwhile, if you like, I can begin explaining why I asked you to come here."

"I'd appreciate it." I folded myself into her chair's mate, "I've been wondering, of course."

"Naturally." The full lower lip protruded a little, giving her face a suggestion of darkness and brooding. "Let me begin by asking a question. Do you know Graham Markley?"

"Not personally. Like everyone else who reads the papers, I know something about him. Quondam boy-wonder of finance. No boy any longer. If he's still a wonder, he doesn't work at it quite so hard. From reports, he works harder nowadays at spending some of what he's made. Unless, of course, there's another Graham Markley."

"He's the one. Graham and I have an understanding."

There was, before the last word, a barely perceptible hesitation that gave to her statement a subtle and significant shading. She had explained in a breath, or in the briefest holding of a breath, the acres of pile and tile in this lavish stone and steel tower with terraces that caught the afternoon sun for at least a little while. Delicately, she had told me who paid the rent.

"That's nice," I said. "Congratulations."

"It's entirely informal at present, but it may not remain so. He's asked me to marry him. Not immediately, which is impossible, but eventually."

"That'll be even better. Or will it?"

"It will. A certain amount of security attaches to marriage. There are certain compensations if the marriage fails." She smiled slowly, the smile beginning and growing and forcing from her face the dark and almost petulant expression of brooding. And in her eyes, which were brown, there was instantly a gleam of cynical good humor which was the effect, as it turned out, of a kind of casual compatibility she had developed with herself. "I haven't always had the good things that money buys, Mr. Hand, but I've learned from experience to live with them naturally. I don't think I would care to live with less. With these good things that money buys, I'm perfectly willing to accept my share of the bad things that money seems invariably to entail. Is my position clear?"

"Yes, it is," I said. "It couldn't be clearer."

At that moment, Maria returned with a pair of gin and tonics in red and yellow glasses on a tray. She served one of them to Faith Salem and the other to me, and then she completed the three nods routine and went away again. The three nods, I now realized, was not a gesture of approval but an involuntary reaction to any situation to be handled, my arrival earlier, or any situation already handled, as the serving of the drinks. I drank some of my tonic and liked it. There was a kind of astringency in the faintly bitter taste of the quinine. There was also, I thought now that it had been suggested to me, a kind of astringency in Faith Salem. A faintly bitter quality. A clean and refreshing tautness in her lean and lovely body and in her uncompromised compatibility with herself.

"Did you know Graham's wife?" she asked suddenly.

"Which one?" I said.

"The last one. Number three, I think."

"It doesn't matter. There was no purpose in my asking for the distinction. I didn't know number three, or two, or one. Graham Markley's wives and I didn't move in the same circles."

"I thought perhaps you might have met her professionally."

"As an employer or subject of investigation?"

"Either way."

"Neither, as a matter of fact. And if I had, I couldn't tell you."

"Ethics? I heard that about you. Someone told me you were honorable and discreet. I believe it."

"Thanks. Also thanks to someone."

"That's why I called you. I'm glad now that I did."

"I know. You like my looks, and I like yours. We admire each other."

"Are you always so flippant?"

"Scarcely ever. The truth is, I'm very serious, and I take my work seriously. Do you have some work for me to do?"

She swallowed some more of her tonic and held the glass in her lap with both hands. Her expression was again rather darkly brooding, and she seemed for a moment uncertain of herself.

"Perhaps you won't want the job," she said.

I nodded. "It's possible."

"We'll see." She swallowed more of the tonic and looked suddenly more decisive. "Do you remember what happened to Graham's third wife?"

"I seem to remember that she left him, which wasn't surprising. So did number one. So did number two. Excuse me if I'm being offensive."

"Not at all. You're not required to like Graham. Many people don't. I confess that there are times when I don't like him very much myself. I did like his third wife, however. We were in college together, as a matter of fact. We shared an apartment one year. Her name was Constance Vaughn then. I left school that year, the year we shared the apartment, and we never saw each other again."

"You mean you never knew her as Mrs. Graham Markley?"

"Yes. I didn't know she'd married. In college she didn't seem, somehow, like the kind of girl who would ever marry anyone at all, let alone someone like Graham. That was a good many years ago, of course, and people change, I suppose. Anyhow, it was rather odd, wasn't it? I came here about a year ago from Europe, where I had been living with my second husband, who is not my husband any longer, and I met Graham. After a while we entered into our present arrangement, which is comfortable but not altogether satisfactory, and then I learned that he had been married to Constance, whom I had known all that time ago. Don't you think that was quite odd?"

"It seems to meet the requirements of the term."

"Yes. The truth is, it made me feel rather strange. Especially when I discovered that she had simply disappeared about a year before."

"Disappeared?"

"Simply vanished. She hasn't been seen since by anyone who knew her here. You'll have to admit that it's peculiar. Numbers one and two left Graham and divorced him and tapped him for alimony, which he probably deserved, and this was sensible. It was not sensible, however, simply to disappear without a trace and never sue for divorce and alimony, or even separate maintenance. Do you think so?"

"Offhand, I don't. There may have been good reasons. Surely an attempt was made to locate her."

"Oh, yes. Of course. Her disappearance was reported to the police, and they made an effort to find her, but it was kept pretty quiet, and I don't think anyone tried very hard. Because of the circumstances, you see."

"No, I don't see. What circumstances?"

"Well, Constance had a baby. A little boy that got to be almost two years old and died. Constance loved him intensely. That's the way she was about anyone or anything she loved. Very intense. It was rather frightening, in a way. Anyway, when the little boy died, she seemed to be going right out of her mind with grief, and Graham was no consolation or comfort, of course. And then she met Regis Lawler. Psychologically, she was just ready for him—completely vulnerable—and she fell in love with him, and apparently they had an affair. To get to the point about circumstances, Regis Lawler disappeared the same night that Constance did, and that's why no one got too excited or concerned. It was assumed that they'd gone away together."

"Don't you believe that they did?"

"I don't know. I think I do. What do you think?"

"On the surface, it seems a reasonable assumption, but it leaves a lot of loose ends."

"That's it. That's what disturbs me. Too many loose ends. I don't like loose ends, Mr. Hand. Will you try to tie them up for me?"

"Find out where Constance Markley went?"

"Yes."

"I'm sorry."

"You mean you won't?"

"I mean I probably couldn't. Look at it this way. The police have far greater facilities for this kind of thing than any private detective, and they've tried without success. Or if they did find out where Constance Markley went, it was obviously not police business and was quietly dropped. Either way, I'd be wasting my time and your money to try to find her now."

"Don't worry about wasting my money."

"All right. I'll just worry about wasting my time."

"Is it wasted if it's paid for?"

"That's a good point. If you want to buy my time for a fee, why should I drag my heels? Maybe I'm *too* ethical."

"Does that mean you accept?"

"No. Not yet. Be reasonable, Miss Salem. If Constance Markley and Regis Lawler went off together, they might be anywhere in the country or out of it. The West Coast. South America. Europe. Anywhere on earth."

She finished her tonic, lit a cigarette, and let her head fall slowly against the back of the wicker chair as if she were suddenly very tired. With her eyes closed, the shadows of her lashes on her cheeks, she seemed to be asleep in an instant, except for the thin blue plume of smoke expelled slowly from her lungs. After a few moments, her eyes still closed, she spoke again.

"Why should they do that? Why disappear? Why run away at all? Women are leaving husbands every day. Men are leaving wives. They simply leave. Why didn't Constance?"

"People do queer things sometimes. Usually there are reasons that seem good to the people in question. You said Mrs. Markley was an intense sort of person. You said she'd suffered a tragedy that nearly unbalanced her mentally. You implied that she hadn't been happy with Graham Markley. Maybe she just wanted to go away clean—no connections, no repercussions, nothing at all left of the old life but a man she loved and the few things she'd have to remember because she couldn't forget."

"I know. I've thought of that, and it's something that Constance might possibly have done, as I remember her."

"How do you remember her?"

"Well, as I said, she was intense. She was always excited or depressed, and I could never quite understand what she was excited or depressed about. Ideas that occurred to her or were passed on to her by someone. Impressions and suggestions. Things like that. Little things that would never have influenced most people in the least. She was pretty, in a way, but it took quite a while before you realized it. She had a kind of delicacy or fragility about her, but I don't believe that she was actually fragile physically. It was just an impression. She didn't appeal to men, and I never thought that men appealed to her. In the year we lived together, she never went out with a man that I can recall. Her parents had money. That's why I lived with her. I had practically no money at all then, and she took a fancy to me and wanted to rent an apartment for us, and so she did, and I stayed with her until near the end of the school year. I married a boy who also had money. Never mind me, though. The point is, we went away from school, and I didn't see Constance again. She was angry with me and refused to say good-bye. I've always been sorry."

"How did she happen to meet and marry Graham Markley?"

"I don't know. Graham is susceptible to variety in women. Probably her particular kind of prettiness, her fragility or something, happened to appeal to him at the time they met I imagine their marriage was one of those sudden things that usually should never happen."

"I see. How did you learn so much about her? Not back there in the beginning. I mean after she married Markley. About her baby, her affair with Lawler, those things."

"Oh, I picked up bits from various sources, but most of it I learned from Maria. She was maid to Constance, you see, when Constance and Graham were living together. When I came along and moved into this apartment, I sort of acquired her. Graham still had her and didn't know what to do with her, so he sent her over to me. Isn't that strange?"

"Convenient, I'd say. Did Maria see Constance Markley the night of her disappearance?"

"Yes. She helped Constance dress. Apparently she was the last person that Constance spoke to."

"May I speak with her for a moment?"

"If you wish. I'll get her."

CHAPTER 2

She got up and walked barefooted off the terrace into the black-and-white tiled room, and I drank the last of my gin and tonic and wished for another, and in about three minutes, not longer, she returned with Maria. She sat down again and told Maria that she could also sit down if she pleased, but Maria preferred to stand. Her small brown face was perfectly composed.

"What do you want me to tell you?" she said.

"I want you to answer a few questions about Mrs. Markley," I said. "Constance Markley, that is. Will you do that?"

"If I can."

"Miss Salem says that you saw Mrs. Markley the night she disappeared. Is that so?"

"It's so. I helped her dress for the evening."

"Did she go out alone?"

"Yes. Alone."

"Do you know where she was going?"

"I assumed that she was going to see Mr. Lawler. She didn't tell me."

"Did she go to see Mr. Lawler often?"

"Twice a week, maybe. Sometimes three."

"How do you know? Did she confide in you?"

"More in me than anyone else. She had to talk to someone."

"I see. Were you devoted to Mrs. Markley?"

"Yes. She was very kind, very unhappy. I pitied her."

"Because of the death of her child?"

"Partly because of that. I don't know. She was not happy."

"Did you approve of her affair with Mr. Lawler?"

"Not approve, exactly. I understood it. She needed a special kind of love. A kind of attention."

"Mr. Lawler gave her this?"

"He must have given it to her. Otherwise, she wouldn't have gone on with him. That's reasonable."

"Yes, it is. It's reasonable. And so are you, Maria. You're a very reasonable woman. Tell me. What was your impression of her the night she disappeared?"

"Pardon?"

"Her emotional state, I mean. Was she depressed? Cheerful?"

"Not depressed. Not cheerful. She was eager. There's a difference between eagerness and cheerfulness."

"That's true. Besides being reasonable, Maria, you are also perceptive. Did she seem excessively agitated in any way?"

"Just eager. She was always eager when she went to see Mr. Lawler."

"Do you think that Mr. Markley was aware of the relationship between his wife and Lawler?"

"I don't know. He didn't show much interest in anything Mrs. Markley did. Not even when the child died."

"All right. Just one more question, Maria. What time did Mrs. Markley leave here?"

"About eight. Perhaps a few minutes before or after."

"Thank you, Maria."

Maria turned her still brown face toward Faith Salem, who smiled and nodded. The maid nodded in return, three times, and went away. Faith Salem stood up abruptly, standing with her legs spread and her hands rammed into the patch pockets of the short white coat.

"Well?" she said.

"It looks hopeless," I said. "You'd be wasting your money."

"Perhaps so. If I don't waste it on you, I'll waste it on someone else."

"In that case, it might as well be me."

"You agree, then? You'll take the job?"

Looking up at her, I was beginning to feel dominated, which was not good, so I removed the feeling by standing.

"Tentatively," I said.

"What do you mean, tentatively?"

"I'll make a preliminary investigation. If anything significant or interesting comes out of it, I'll go ahead. If not, I'll quit. You'll pay my expenses and twenty-five dollars a day. Are those terms acceptable?"

"Yes. I accept."

"Another thing. I'm to be allowed to talk with whomever I think necessary. Is that also agreed?"

"Yes, of course." She hesitated, her soft lower lip protruding again in the darkly brooding expression. "You mean Graham, I suppose. I'd prefer, naturally, that he not know whom you're working for."

"I won't tell him unless I think it's advisable. I promise that much."

"That's good enough. I have confidence in your word, Mr. Hand."

"Ethical. Someone told you, and you believe it, and that's what I am. I'll begin my investigation, if you don't mind, by asking you one more question. What are you afraid of?"

"Afraid? I'm afraid of nothing. I honestly believe that I've never been afraid of anything in my life."

"I'm ready to concede that you probably haven't. Let me put it differently. What disturbs you about Constance Markley's disappearance?"

"I've explained that. I don't like loose ends. Graham has asked me to marry him. For my own reasons, I want to accept. First, however, he has to get a divorce. He can get it, I suppose, on grounds of desertion. I only want to know that it really was desertion."

"That's not quite convincing. What alternative to desertion, specifically, do you have in mind?"

"You said you would ask one more question, Mr. Hand. You've asked two."

"Excuse me. You can see how dedicated I become to my work."

"I should appreciate that, of course, and I do. I honestly have no specific alternative in mind. I just don't like the situation as it stands. There's another thing, however. I knew Constance, and I liked her, and now by an exceptional turn of events I'm in the position of appropriating something that was hers. I want to know that it's all right. I want to know where she went, and why she went wherever she did, and that everything is all right there and will be all right here, whatever happens."

I believed her. I believed everything she told me. She was a woman I could not doubt or condemn or even criticize. If I had been as rich as Graham Markley, I'd have taken her away, later if not then, and I'd have kept her, and there would have been between us, in the end, more than the money which would have been essential in the beginning.

"I'll see what I can do," I said. "Do you have a photograph of Constance Markley that I can take along?"

"Yes. There's one here that Maria brought. I'll get it for you."

She went inside and was gone for a few minutes and came back with the photograph. I took it from her and put it into the side pocket of my coat without looking at it. There would be plenty of time later to look at it, and now, in the last seconds of our first meeting, I wanted to look at Faith Salem.

"Good-bye," I said. "I'll see you again in a few days and let you know if I intend to go ahead."

"Call before you come," she said.

"Yes," I said. "Certainly."

"I'll see you to the door."

"No. Don't bother. You'd better stay here in the sun. In another half hour, it'll be gone."

"Yes. So it will." She looked up at the white disk in the sky beyond a ridge of tooled stone. "Good-bye, then. I'll be waiting to hear from you."

She offered me her hand, and I took it and held it and released it. In the middle of the black-and-white acre, I paused and looked back. She had already removed the short white coat and was lying on her stomach on the yellow pad. Her face was buried in the crook of an elbow.

I went on out and back to my office and put my feet on the desk and thought about her lying there in the sun. There was no sun in my office. In front of me was a blank wall, and behind me was a narrow window, and outside the narrow window was a narrow alley. Whenever I got tired of looking at the wall I could get up and stand by the window and look down into the alley, and whenever I got tired of looking into the alley I could sit down and look at the wall again. And whenever I got tired of looking at both the wall and the alley, which was frequently, I could go out somewhere and look at something else. Now I simply closed my eyes and saw clearly behind the lids a lean brown body interrupted in two places by the briefest of white hiatuses.

This was pleasant but not of the first importance. It was more important, though less pleasant, to think about Graham Markley. Conceding the priority of importance, I began reluctantly to think about him, and after a few minutes of reluctant thinking, I lowered my feet and reached for a telephone directory. After locating his name and number, I dialed the number and waited through a couple of rings, and then a voice came on that made me feel with its first careful syllable as if I'd neglected recently to bathe and clean my fingernails.

"Graham Markley's residence," the voice said.

"This is Percival Hand," I said. "I'm a private detective. I'd like to speak with Mr. Markley."

Ordinarily I use the abbreviated version of my name, just plain Percy, but I felt compelled by the voice to be as proper and impressive as possible. As it was, in the exorbitantly long pause that followed, I felt as if I had been unpardonably offensive.

"If you will just hold the wire," the voice said at last, "I shall see if Mr. Markley is at home."

Which meant, of course, that Mr. Markley was certainly at home, but that it remained to be seen if he would be so irresponsible as to talk with a private detective on the telephone, which was surely unlikely. I held the wire and waited. I inspected my nails and found them clean. I tried to smell myself and couldn't. Another voice came on abruptly, and it was, as it developed, the voice of Graham Markley.

"Graham Markley speaking. What can I do for you, Mr. Hand?"

"I'd like to make an appointment to see you personally."

"About what?"

I had already considered the relative advantages in this particular instance of candor and deception, and I had decided that there was probably little or nothing to choose between them. In cases where deception gains me nothing, I'm always prepared to be candid, and that's what I was now.

"About your wife. Your third wife, that is."

"I can't imagine why my wife should be a point of discussion between you and me, Mr. Hand."

"I thought you might be able to give me some useful information."

There was a moment of waiting. The wire sang softly in the interim.

"For what purpose?" he said. "Am I to understand that you're investigating my wife's disappearance?"

"That's right."

"At whose request?"

"I'm not at liberty to say at the moment."

"Come, Mr. Hand. If you expect any co-operation from me, you'll have to be less reticent."

"I haven't received any co-operation from you yet, Mr. Markley."

"It was reasonably apparent to everyone, including the police and myself, why my wife went away. I confess that I can't see any use in stirring up an unpleasant matter that I had hoped was forgotten. Do you know anything that would justify it?"

Again I evaluated the advantages of candor and deception, and this time I chose deception. The advantages in its favor seemed so palpable, as a matter of fact, that the evaluation required no more than a second.

"I've learned something," I lied, "that I think will interest you."

"Perhaps you had better tell me what it is."

"Sorry. I'd rather not discuss it over the telephone."

"I can't see you today. It's impossible."

"Tomorrow will do. If you'll set a time, I'll be happy to call on you."

"That won't be necessary. I'll come to your office."

"I don't want to inconvenience you."

"Thank you for your consideration. However, I prefer to see you in your office. How about two o'clock tomorrow afternoon?"

"Good. I'll be expecting you."

I told him where my office was, and we said good-bye and hung up. Rocking back in my chair, I elevated my feet again and closed my eyes. Faith Salem was still lying in the sun. I watched her for a few moments and then opened my eyes and lit a cigarette and began thinking about Regis Lawler. I didn't accomplish much by this, for I didn't have much material for thought to start with. I had met him casually a few times quite a while ago, in this or that place we had both gone to, but most of what I knew about him was incidental to what I knew about his brother, who was older and generally more important and had more about him worth knowing.

The brother's name was Silas. After long and precarious apprentice years in a number of illegal operations, he had begun slowly to achieve a kind of acceptance, even respectability, that increased in ratio to the measure of his security. Now he was the owner of a fine restaurant. At least, it was a restaurant among other things, and it was that equally, if not primarily. When you went there, it was assumed that you had come for good food, and that's what you got. You got it in rich and quiet surroundings to the music of a string quartet that sometimes played Beethoven as well as Fritz Kreisler and Johann Strauss. The chefs were the best that Lawler could hire, and the best that Lawler could hire were as good as any and better than most. On the correct principle that good food should tolerate no distractions, the service was performed by elderly colored waiters who were artists in the difficult technique of being solicitous without being obtrusive.

If you wanted distractions, you went downstairs, below street level. This was known as the Apache Room, a little bit of the Left Bank transplanted, and it was phony and made no pretense of being anything else, and it was frankly for people who liked it that way. There were red-checked cloths on the tables, pretty girls with pretty legs who serviced the tables, and a small orchestra with the peculiar quality that is supposed to be peculiarly Parisian. Around the walls were murals of girls in black stockings doing the can-can alternating with other murals of other girls being maltreated by Apaches and always showing quite a lot of one white thigh above a fancy garter in the deep slit of a tight skirt.

On the floor above the restaurant, up one flight of carpeted stairs, you could go to gamble if you chose. In a series of three large rooms muffled in drapes and carpets, you could play roulette or poker or blackjack or shoot dice, and sometimes you might even win at one or the other or all, but more often, of course, you lost and were expected to lose graciously. If you did not, as sometimes happened, you were escorted outside by a brace of hard-handed gentlemen in evening clothes, and you were thereafter *persona non grata* until you received absolution and clearance from Silas Lawler himself. The games were reputed to be honest, and they probably were.

In the basement, you could dance and make moderate love and get drunk, if you wished, on expensive drinks. In the restaurant, you did not get drunk or dance or make love or look at naughty murals. In the game rooms, you gambled quietly with no limit except your own judgment and bank account, and you saved everything else for some other place and some other time. Patrons passed as they pleased from one level to another, but the atmosphere was never permitted to go with them. The basement never climbed the stairs, nor did the upper floors descend.

Silas Lawler was, in brief, not a man to be taken lightly, or a man who would take lightly any transgression against himself or his interests. It was, I reflected, wholly incredible that he would be indifferent to the disappearance of a brother. Whatever the reason for the disappearance, whatever the technique of its execution, Silas Lawler knew it, or thought he knew it, and he might be prevailed upon to tell me in confidence, or he might not. But in any event it would be necessary for me to talk with him as soon as I could, which would probably be tomorrow. I would see Graham Markley at two, and later I would try to see Silas Lawler. If nothing significant came of those two meetings I would go again to see Faith Salem, which would be a pleasure, and terminate our relationship, which would not.

Having thought my way back to Faith Salem, I closed my eyes and tried to find her, but the sun had left the terrace, and so had she. Opening my eyes, I lowered my feet and stood up. I had determined an agenda of sorts, and now there seemed to be nothing of importance left to do on this particular day. Besides, it was getting rather late, and I was getting rather hungry, and so I went out and patronized a steak house and afterward spent one-third of the night doing things that were not important and not related to anything that had gone before. About ten o'clock I returned to the room and bath and hot plate that I euphemistically called home. I went to bed and slept well.

CHAPTER 3

I woke up at seven in the morning, which is a nasty habit of mine that endures through indiscretions and hangovers and intermittent periods of irregular living. In the bathroom, I shaved and necessarily looked at my face in the mirror. I *like you, Mr. Hand,* Faith Salem had said. I *like your looks.* Well, it was an ambiguous expression. You could like the looks of a collie dog or a pair of shoes or a shoebill stork. It could mean that you were inspired by confidence or amusement or the urge to be a sister. Looking at my face, I was not deluded. I decided that I was probably somewhere between the dog and the stork. I finished shaving and dressed and went out for breakfast and arrived in due time at my office, where nothing happened all morning.

Two o'clock came, but Graham Markley didn't. At ten after, he did. I heard him enter the little cubby-hole in which my clients wait when there is another client ahead of them, which is something that should happen oftener than it does; and when I got to the door to meet him, he was standing there looking antiseptic among the germs. His expression included me with the others. "Mr. Hand?" he said.

"That's right. You're Mr. Markley, I suppose?"

"Yes. I'm sorry to be late. I was detained."

"Think nothing of it. In this office, ten minutes late is early. Come in, please."

He walked past me and sat down in the client's chair beside the desk. Because I felt he would consider it an imposition, I didn't offer to shake hands. I felt that he might even ignore or reject the offer, which would have made me indignant or even indiscreet. Resuming my place in the chair behind the desk, I made a quick inventory and acquired an impression. He sat rigidly, with his knees together and his hat on his knees. His straight black hair was receding but still had a majority present. His face was narrow, his nose was long, his lips were thin. Arrogance was implicit. He looked something like the guy who used to play Sherlock Holmes in the movies. Maybe he looked like Sherlock Holmes.

"Precisely what do you want to tell me, Mr. Hand?" he said.

"Well," I said, "that isn't quite my position. What I want is for you to tell me something."

"Indeed? I gathered from our conversation on the telephone yesterday that you were in possession of some new information regarding my wife."

"Did I imply that? It isn't exactly true. What I meant to suggest was that the available information isn't adequate. It leaves too much unexplained."

"Do you think so? The police apparently didn't. As a matter of fact, it was quite clear to everyone what my wife had done. It was, as you may realize, an embarrassing affair for me, and there seemed to be no good purpose in giving it undue publicity or in pursuing it indefinitely."

"Is that still your feeling? That there is no purpose in pursuing it any further?"

"Until yesterday it was. Now I'm not so sure. I don't wish to interfere with whatever kind of life my wife is trying to establish for herself, nor do I wish to restore any kind of contact between her and me, but since our telephone conversation I've begun to feel that it would be better for several reasons if she could be located."

"Are you prepared to help?"

"Conditionally."

"What conditions?"

"Are you, for your part, prepared to tell me who initiated this investigation?"

"What action would you take if I told you?"

"None. The truth is, I'm certain that I know. I merely want to verify it."

"You're probably right."

"Miss Salem? I thought so. Well, it's understandable. Under the circumstances of our relationship, she's naturally concerned. She urged me once previously to try again to locate my wife, but I wasn't inclined to reopen what was, as I said, an unpleasant and embarrassing affair. Apparently I underestimated the strength of her feeling."

"You don't resent her action, then?"

"Certainly not. I'm particularly anxious to settle any uneasiness she may feel. I'm even willing to assume the payment of your fee."

"That's between you and her, of course. Will you tell me why, in your opinion, your wife disappeared?"

"As to why she disappeared, I can only speculate. As to why she left, which is something else, I'm certain. She was having an affair with a man named Regis Lawler. They went away together. The relationship between my wife and me had deteriorated by that time to such an extent that I really didn't care. I considered it a satisfactory solution to our problem."

"Satisfactory? You said painful and embarrassing."

"Painful and embarrassing because it was humiliating. Any husband whose wife runs away with another man looks rather ridiculous. I mean that I had no sense of loss."

"I see. Did she give you any idea that she was leaving before she went?"

"None. We didn't see each other often the last few months we lived together. When we did see each other, we found very little to say."

"You said you could only speculate as to why she disappeared instead of leaving openly. I'd like to hear your speculation."

"You would need to have known her before you could understand. She was, to put it kindly, rather unstable. Less kindly, she was neurotic. She may have been almost psychotic at times. I don't know. I don't understand the subtle distinctions between these things. Anyhow, she had had a bad time when our child died. At first, after the initial shock, she became withdrawn and depressed, totally uninterested in living. Later there was a reaction. A kind of hysterical appetite for activity and experiences. It was then that she met Regis Lawler. It's my opinion that she disappeared because she wanted to cut herself off completely from the life that had included our marriage and the death of our child. It's difficult to believe, I know."

"I wouldn't say so. Not so difficult. I've already considered that motivation, as a matter of fact. It seems compatible with the little I know about her. There's another point, however, that bothers me. Was Regis Lawler the kind of man to fall in with such a scheme?"

"I can't answer that. If he was devoted to her, it's fair to assume that he would do as she wished, especially if she convinced him that it was something she desperately needed."

"Possibly. I didn't know Lawler well enough to have an idea. Miss Salem said that Mrs. Markley's family had quite a lot of money. Did Mrs. Markley herself have any?"

"No. Her mother and father were both dead when we married. If they had money at one time, which I believe was so, it had been dissipated. The estate, I understand, did little more than pay the claims against it."

"Then your wife had no personal financial matters to settle before she left?"

"Not to my knowledge."

"Was Regis Lawler a wealthy man?"

"I have no idea. His brother apparently is."

"Well, you can see what I'm getting at. It would not be a simple matter for a man of wealth to disappear. It would certainly entail the liquidation of assets—securities, property, things like that. He'd have to convert his wealth to negotiable paper that he could carry with him. If he wanted to assure his not being traced through it, he'd have to convert to cash. Do you know if Regis Lawler did any such thing?"

"No. But the police surely made such an obvious investigation. Since it was not an issue, it follows that Lawler did do something of the sort, or that he had no holdings to convert."

"Right. If Lawler had left much behind, the police wouldn't have quit investigating. They'd have smelled more than a love affair. As you say, he either converted or had nothing to convert. At any rate, he must have had considerable cash in hand. Running away with a woman, I mean, wouldn't be any two-dollar tour. Unless he had a job arranged somewhere, an assured income, he must have been, putting it mildly, damn well heeled."

"Oh, I think it's safe to assume that he had at least enough cash to last a while. I can't imagine that Regis Lawler was a pauper."

His tone implied that no one but a simpleton, specifically me, would waste time speculating about it. I was beginning to think he was right. That was okay, though. I had been convinced from the beginning that I was wasting my time on the whole case. That was okay, too, since I was doing it for a fee.

"How long ago was it that Mrs. Markley left?" I said.

"Two years ago next month."

"Did she take anything with her? Any clothes, for example? I know from talking with her maid that she took nothing when she left home that night, but I'm thinking that she might have taken or sent luggage ahead to be picked up later. She'd have done something like that, I imagine, if she was being secretive."

"No doubt. On the other hand, if you accept the theory that she intended to make a complete break, she might not have wanted to keep any of her old possessions, not even her clothes. I don't find this incredible in her case. Anyhow, I honestly don't know if she took anything. She had closets full of clothes, of course. If anything was missing, I wouldn't know."

"How about the maid?"

"She thought that nothing was missing, but she wasn't positive."

He looked at his wrist watch and stood up abruptly, his knees still together as they had been all the time he was sitting, and he had, looking down at me, a kind of stiff, military bearing and collateral arrogance. "I'm sorry to end this interview, Mr. Hand, but I have another appointment. You'll have to excuse me."

"Certainly," I said. "I was running out of questions, anyhow. Thanks very much for coming in."

"I'm afraid I haven't been very helpful."

"You never know. It doesn't sound like much now, but it may mean something later."

I walked around the desk and with him to the door. I didn't offer to shake hands, and neither did he.

"Please inform Miss Salem or me of any progress," he said.

"I'm not optimistic," I said.

The door closed between us, and I went back and sat down. As far as I was concerned, I was still wasting time.

CHAPTER 4

From street level I went up two shallow steps into a spacious hall. The floor was carpeted. The walls were paneled with dark and lustrous walnut. At the far end of the hall, a broad sweep of stairs ascended. To my right as I entered was the dining room. The floor was carpeted in there also, and the walls were also walnut-paneled. Tables were covered with snowy cloths and set with shining silver. A few early diners were dining. The string quartet was playing something softly that I remembered by sound and remembered after a moment by name.

"Stars in My Eyes," by Fritz Kreisler. A very pretty tune.

I looked right. A cocktail lounge was over that way, beyond a wide entrance and down a step. A number of people were drinking cocktails. There was no music. I recognized a martini, which was all right, a manhattan, which was better, and an alexander, which you can have. Everything was very elegant, very sedate. Maybe someone saw me, maybe not. No one spoke to me or tried to stop me. I walked down the hall and up the stairs.

The carpet went up with me, but the walnut stayed below. The hall upstairs ran a gauntlet of closed doors recessed in plaster. It was nice plaster, though, rough-textured and painted a nice shade of brown. Cinnamon or nutmeg or one of the names that brown acquires when it becomes a decorator color. It was too early for the games, and the rooms behind the doors were quiet. All, that is, except the last room behind the last door, which was the private room of Silas Lawler. Someone in there was playing a piano. A Chopin waltz was being played. I thought at first it was a recording, but then I decided it wasn't. It was good, but not good enough.

I opened the door softly and stepped inside and closed the door behind me. It was Silas Lawler himself at the piano. He turned his face toward me, but his eyes had the kind of blind glaze that the eyes of a man may have when he is listening to good music or looking at his mistress or thinking of something a long way off. A pretty girl was sitting in a deep chair on the back of her neck. She had short black hair and smoky eyes and a small red petulant mouth. She was facing the door and me directly, and her eyes moved over me lazily without interest. Otherwise, she did not move in the slightest, and she did not speak.

Lawler finished the Chopin waltz, and the girl said, "That was nice, Lover." She moved nothing but her lips, in shaping the words, and her eyes, which she rolled toward him in her head. She didn't sound as if she meant what she said, and Lawler didn't look as if he believed her. He didn't even look as if he heard her. He was still staring at me, and the glaze was dissolving in his eyes.

"Who are you?" he said.

"Percy Hand," I said. "We've met."

"That's right," he said. "I remember you. Don't you believe in knocking?"

"I didn't want to interrupt the music. I like Chopin."

"Do you? It's better when it's played right."

"You play it fine. I thought at first it was Brailowsky."

"If you thought it was Brailowsky, you've never heard him."

"I've heard him, all right. I went to a concert once. I've got a couple records."

"In that case, you've got no ear for music. Brailowsky and I don't sound alike."

"Maybe not. Maybe it was just the shock of hearing you play at all. I never figured Silas Lawler for a pianist."

"I was a deprived kid. I had secret hungers. I made some money and took lessons."

"So was I. So had I. I didn't."

"Make money or take lessons?"

"Both."

"You can see he's poor," the girl said. "He wears ready-made suits."

"Botany 500," I said. "Sixty-five bucks."

Lawler looked at her levelly across the grand. I could have sworn that there was an expression of distaste on his face. The deprived kid business was on the level, I thought. He remembered the time. He didn't like people who made cracks about the poor.

"This is Robin Robbins," he said carefully. "She's pretty, but she's got no manners. That isn't her real name, by the way. She didn't think the one she had was good enough. The man you're trying to insult, honey, is Percy Hand, a fairly good private detective."

"He looks like Jack Palance," she said.

"Jack Palance is ugly," I said. "God, he's ugly."

"So are you," she said.

"Thanks," I said.

"In a nice way," she said. "Jack Palance is ugly in a nice way, and so are you. I don't really care if you're poor."

"Just as long as you're good in bed," Lawler said. "Come over here."

I walked over and stood beside the piano. Now I could see the girl only by looking over my shoulder. Instead, I looked down at Lawler. His face was clean shaven and square. He was neither tall nor fat, but he must have weighed two hundred. His hands rested quietly on the piano keys. They looked like chunks of stone.

"Here I am," I said. "Why?"

"I want to be able to reach you in case you haven't got a good reason for busting in here."

"I've got a reason. You tell me if it's good."

"I'll let you know. One way or another."

"I want to talk about a couple of people you know. Or knew. Your brother and Constance Markley."

He didn't budge. His face stayed still, his body stayed still, the hands on the keys stayed still as stone.

"It's lousy. I'd be bored to death."

"Is that so? I'm beginning to get real interested in them."

"That's your mistake. While we're on mistakes, I'll point out another. He isn't my brother. Not even step-brother. Foster brother."

"That makes it less intimate, I admit. Not quite impersonal, though. Wouldn't you like to know where he is? How he is? Or maybe you already know."

"I don't. I don't want to."

"Well, I never heard the like. A man's wife disappears. He doesn't care. A man's foster brother disappears. He doesn't care. The indifference fascinates me."

"Let me figure this." His left hand suddenly struck a bass chord and dropped off the keys into his lap. The sound waves lingered, faded, died. "I've got a sluggish mind, and I think slow. Regis and Constance ran away. You're a private detective. Could it be you're trying to make yourself a case?"

"I'm not making any case. The case is made. I'm just working on it."

"Take my advice. Don't. Drop it. Forget it. It isn't worth your time."

"My time's worth twenty-five dollars a day and expenses. That's what I'm getting paid."

"Who's paying?"

"Sorry. I'm not at liberty to say."

"It's not enough."

"I get by on it."

"Not enough to pay a hospital bill, I mean. Or the price of a funeral, even."

The girl stood up suddenly and stretched. She made a soft mewing sound, like a cat. I turned my head and watched her over my shoulder. Her breasts thrust out against her dress, her spread thighs strained against her tight skirt.

"I think I'll go away somewhere," she said. "I abhor violence."

"You do that, honey," Silas Lawler said.

She walked across to the door, and she walked pretty well. She had nice legs that moved nicely. You could follow the lines of her behind in the tight skirt. I'd have been more impressed if I hadn't seen Faith Salem lying in the sun. At the door, before going out, she paused and looked back at me and grinned.

"You couldn't hurt his face much," she said. "You could change it, but you couldn't hurt it."

She was gone, and I said, "Lovely thing. Is it yours?"

"Now and then." He shrugged. "If you're interested, I won't be offended."

"I'm not. Besides, I'm too ugly. Were you threatening me a moment ago?"

"About the hospital, yes. About the funeral, no. It wouldn't be necessary."

"You never can tell. I get tired of living sometimes."

"You'd get tireder of being dead."

"That could be. The way I hear it explained, it sounds pretty dull."

"You're a pretty sharp guy, Hand. You've got a nose for what's phony. I'm surprised a guy like you wouldn't smell a phony case."

"I won't say I haven't. I'm open to conviction."

"All right. Regis and Constance had a real fire going. It didn't grow, it was just there in both of them at first sight. First sight was right here. Downstairs in the lounge. Don't ask me to explain it, because I can't. Regis was there, and Constance was there, and to hell with everyone else. Everyone and everything. They got in bed, and whatever they had survived. They ran away together, that's all. Why don't you leave it alone?"

"You make it sound so simple. I can't help thinking, though, that running away's one thing, disappearing's another. You see the difference?"

"I see. It wouldn't seem so strange if you'd know the woman. Constance, I mean. She'd had a bad time. She was sad, lost, looking for a way to somewhere. You get me? She was a real lady, but she had queer ideas. When she left, she wanted to leave it all, including herself. It's pathetic when you stop to think about it."

"I get the same picture everywhere. The same idea. I'm beginning to believe it. I'm skeptical about Regis, though. He doesn't seem the type."

"He wasn't. Not before he met Constance. Before he met her, he was a charming, no-good bastard. But then he met her, and he changed. Queer. You wouldn't have thought she'd have appealed to him, but she did. He'd have done anything she wanted. Very queer."

"Yeah. Queer and corny."

"I don't blame you for thinking so. You'd have to see it to believe it."

"Did Regis have an interest in this restaurant?"

"Regis didn't have a pot. Just what I gave him. Spending money."

"What did they use for cash when they left? What are they using now? And don't feed me any more corn. You don't live on love. Some people get a job and live in a cottage, but not Regis and Constance. Everything they were and did is against it."

The fingers of his right hand moved up the keys. It was remarkable how lightly that chunk of rock moved. The thin sound of the short scale lasted no longer than a few seconds. The right had joined the left in his lap.

"I'll tell you something," he said. "I don't know why. What I ought to do is throw you out of here. Anyhow, Regis had cash. Enough for a lifetime in the right place. See that picture over there? It's a copy of a Rembrandt. Behind it there's a safe. Regis knew the combination. The night he went away, I had seventy-five grand in it. Regis took it."

"That's a lot of cash to have in a safe behind a picture."

"I had it for a purpose. Never mind what."

"You let him get away with it? You didn't try to recover it?"

"No. To tell the truth, I was relieved. I always felt an obligation toward him because of the woman whose lousy kid he was. Now the obligation is wiped out. We're quits." He lifted both hands and replaced them gently on the keys of the piano. There was not the slightest sound from the wires inside. "Besides, I figured it was partly for her. For Constance. I liked her. I hope she's happier than she ever was."

I started to refer again to corn, but I thought better of it. Then I thought that it would probably be a good time to leave, and I turned and went as far as the door.

"Hand," he said.

"Yes," I said.

"Forget it. Drop it. You hear me?"

"I hear you," I said.

I opened the door and went out. After three steps in the hall, I heard the piano. What I heard from it was something else by Chopin.

CHAPTER 5

On the way in, no one had spoken to me. On the way out, someone did. The lower hall was the place, and Robin Robbins was the person. She was standing in the entrance to the cocktail lounge, at the edge of the shallow step, and although she was standing erect, like a lady, she somehow gave the impression of leaning indolently against an immaterial lamppost. Her voice was lazy, threaded with a kind of insolent amusement.

"Buy me a drink?" she said.

"I'm too poor," I said.

"Tough. Let me buy you one."

"I'm too proud."

"Poor and proud. My God, it sounds like something by Horatio Alger."

"Junior."

"What?"

"Horatio Alger, Junior. You forgot the junior."

"I'm sorry I didn't forget him altogether. What do you say we start trying?"

"I'm surprised you know anything about him to start trying to forget. He was a long time ago, honey. Were kids still reading him when you were a kid?"

"I wouldn't know. I was never a kid. I was born old and just got older."

"Like me. That gives us something in common, I guess. Maybe we ought to have that drink together after all. I'll buy."

"No. I've got a better idea for a poor, proud man. In my apartment there's a bottle of Scotch left over from another time. Someone gave it to me. We could go there and drink out of it for free."

"I don't care for Scotch. It tastes like medicine."

"There's a bottle of bourbon there, too. In case you don't care for bourbon, there's rye."

"No brandy? No champagne?"

"Anything you want."

"That's quite a selection to be left over from other times. Was it all given to you?"

"Why not? People are always giving me something. They seem to enjoy it."

"Thanks for offering to share the wealth. However, I don't think so. Some other time, maybe."

She opened a small purse she was holding in her hands and extracted a cigarette. I went closer and supplied a light. She inhaled and exhaled and stared into the smoke with her smoky eyes. Her breath coming out with the smoke made a soft, sighing sound.

"Suit yourself," she said. "It's just that I've got something I thought you might be interested in."

"You've got plenty I might be interested in, honey."

She dragged again and sighed again. The smoke thinned and hung in a pale blue haze between us. In her eyes was a suggestion of something new. Something less than insolence, a little more than amusement. Her lush little mouth curved amiably.

"That's not quite what I meant, but it's something to consider. What I meant was something I can tell you."

"Information? Is it free like the Scotch and the bourbon and the rye? Don't forget I'm a guy who wears ready-made suits."

"I remember. Poor and proud and probably honest. Right out of H. Alger, Junior. Don't worry about it, though. It's free like the Scotch and the bourbon and the rye."

"Everything free. No price on anything. I hope you won't be offended, honey, but somehow I got an idea it's out of character."

"All right. Forget it. You were asking questions about a couple of people, and I thought you were interested. My mistake, Horatio."

Her mouth curved now in the opposite direction from amiability. What had been in her eyes was gone, and what replaced it was contempt. I thought in the instant before she turned away that she was going to spit on the floor. Before she could descend the step and walk away nicely on her nice legs with the neat movement of her neat behind, I took a step and put a hand on her arm, and we stood posed that way for a second or two or longer, she arrested and I arresting, and then she turned her head and looked at me over her shoulder.

"Yes?" she said.

"Make mine bourbon," I said.

We went the rest of the way down the hall together and down the two steps and outside. Beside the building was a paved parking lot reserved for patrons, and I had left my car there, although I was not properly a patron. We walked around and got into the car and drove in it to her apartment, which was in a nice building on a good street. It was on the fifth floor, which we reached by elevator, and it didn't have any terrace that got the sun in the afternoon, or any terrace at all, or any of many features that the apartment of Faith Salem had, including several acres. But it was a nice enough apartment just the same—a far better apartment than any I had ever lived in or probably ever would. Besides, it was certainly something that someone had just wanted to give her. For a consideration, of course. An exchange, in a way, of commodities.

"Fix a bourbon for yourself," she said. "For me too, in water. I'll be back in a minute."

She went out of the room and was gone about five times as long as the minute. In the meanwhile, I found ingredients and mixed two bourbon highballs and had them ready when she returned. She looked just the same as she'd looked when she'd gone, which was good enough to be disturbing.

"I lose," I said.

"Some people always do," she said. "Lose what, exactly?"

"A bet. With myself. I bet you'd gone to get into something more comfortable."

"Why should I? What I'm wearing is comfortable enough. There's practically nothing to it."

I was facing her with a full glass in each hand. She approached me casually, as if she were going to ask for a light or brush a crumb off my tie. She kept right on walking, right into me, and put her arms around my neck and her mouth on my mouth, and I stood there with my arms projecting beyond her on both sides, the damn glasses in my hands, and we remained static and breathless in this position for quite a long time. Finally she stepped back and helped herself to the glass in one of my hands. She took a drink and tilted her head and subjected me and my effect to a smoldering appraisal.

"I've always wanted to kiss a man as ugly as you," she said. "It wasn't bad."

"Thanks," I said. "I've had worse myself."

"I'm wondering if it's good enough to develop. I think it might be."

"You go on wondering about it and let me know."

"I'll do that."

She moved over to a chair and lowered herself onto her neat behind and crossed her nice legs. From where I found a chair and sat, across from her, I could see quite a lot of the legs. She didn't mind, and neither did I.

"If you decide to develop it," I said, "won't Silas Lawler object?"

She swallowed some more of her highball and looked into what was left. Her soft and succulent little mouth assumed lax and ugly lines.

"To hell with Silas Lawler," she said.

"Don't kid me," I said. "I know he pays the bills."

"So he pays the bills. There's one bill he may owe that he hasn't paid. If he owes it, I want him to pay in full."

"For what?"

"For the murder of Regis Lawler."

She continued to look into her glass. From her expression, she must have seen something offensive on the bottom. I looked into mine and saw nothing but good whisky and pure water. I drained it.

"Maybe you don't know what you said," I said.

"I know what I said. I said he *may* owe it. I'd like to know."

"And I'd like to know what makes you think he may."

"Start with that fairy tale about Regis and Constance Markley running off together. Just disappearing completely so they could start a beautiful new life together. Do you believe it?"

"I don't believe it. I don't disbelieve it. I've got an open mind."

"Brother, if you'd known Regis Lawler as well as I did, you'd know the whole idea is phony. He just wasn't the type."

"I've heard that. I've also heard that he was in love with Constance. It's been suggested that he might have done for her what he wouldn't have done for anyone else."

"That's another phony bit. His being in love with Constance, I mean. He wasn't."

"No? This is a new angle. Convince me."

"Maybe I can't. I don't have any letters or tapes or photographs. Neither does anyone else, thank God. I could give you some interesting clinical descriptions, but I won't. Basically I'm a modest girl. I like my privacy."

"I think I get you, but I'm not sure. Are you telling me more or less delicately that Regis had love enough for two?"

"Two? Is that all the higher you can count? Anyhow, what's love? All I know is, he went through the motions of what passes for love in my crowd, and he seemed to enjoy it. Whatever you call it, he felt more of it for me than he felt for anyone else, including Constance, and I guess you couldn't have expected more than that from Regis."

Her little mouth had for a moment a bitter twist. The bitterness tainted the sound of her words. She did not have the look and sound of a woman who had been rejected. She had the look and sound of a woman who had been accepted with qualifications and used without them. Most of all, a woman who had understood the qualifications from the beginning and had accepted them and submitted to them.

"Excuse me," I said. "I always have trouble understanding anything when it gets the least complicated. You were having Regis on the side of Silas, and Regis was having you on the side of Constance. Not that I want to make you sound like a chaser or a dish of buttered peas. Is that right?"

"Damn it, that's what I said."

"And Silas killed Regis in anger because he found out about it. Is that what you mean?"

"It's a solid thought. I like it better than the fairy tale."

"I'm not sure that I share your preference. I don't want to hurt you, honey, but I doubt like hell that Silas considers you worth killing for. He just gave me permission to try my luck if the notion struck me, but maybe he didn't really mean it. Anyhow, you'll have to admit that it doesn't sound like homicidal jealousy."

"Who mentioned jealousy?" She shrugged angrily, a small gesture of dismissal. "He's proud. He's vain and sensitive. He's made a hell of a lot out of nothing at all, but he can't forget that he only went to the fourth grade and got where he is by doing things proper people don't do. He still feels secretly inferior and insecure, and he always will. The one thing he can't stand is the slightest suggestion of contempt. He'd kill anyone for that. Can you think of anything more contemptuous than taking another man's wife or mistress?"

I thought of seventy-five grand. It seemed to me that helping yourself to that much lettuce was a contemptuous act too, and I thought about discussing it as a motive for murder. But I couldn't see that it would get me anywhere in present circumstances, and so I decided against it.

"So he killed Regis," I said. "That was a couple of years ago. And ever since he's gone on with you as if nothing at all had happened. After murder, business as usual at the same old stand. Is that it?"

"Sure. Why not? Laughing like hell all the time. Feeling all the time the same kind of contempt for Regis and me that he imagines we felt for him. Silas would get a lot of satisfaction out of something like that." She stared down into her glass, swirling what was left of her drink around and around the inner circumference. Bitterness increased the distortion of her mouth. "He'll throw me out after a while," she said.

"You're quite a psychologist," I said. "All that stuff about inferiority and insecurity and implied contempt. I wish I had as much brains as you."

"All right, you bastard. So I'm the kind who ought to stick to the little words. So I only went to the eighth grade myself. Go ahead and ridicule me."

"You're wrong. I wasn't ridiculing you. I never ridicule anyone. The trouble your theory has is the same trouble that the other theory has, and the trouble with both is that they leave loose ends all over the place. I can mention a few, if you'd care to hear them."

"Mention whatever you please."

"All right. Where's the body?"

"I don't know. You're the detective. Work on it."

"Where's Constance? Did he kill both of them? If so, why? He had no reason to hate her. As a matter of fact, they should have been on the same team. You, not Constance, would have been the logical second victim."

"I know. Don't you think I've thought of that a thousand times? Maybe she knew he killed Regis. Maybe she learned about it somehow or even actually witnessed it. Damn it, I've told you something you didn't know. I've told you about Regis and me. I've told you he was not really in love with Constance and would never have run away with her for any longer than a weekend. I've told you this, and it's the truth, and all you do is keep wanting me to be the detective. You're the detective, brother. I've told you that, too."

"Sure you have. I'm the detective, and all I've got to do is explain how someone killed a man and a woman and completely disposed of their bodies. That would be a tough chore, honey. Practically impossible."

"Silas Lawler's been doing the practically impossible for quite a few years. He's a very remarkable guy."

"He is. I know it, and I'm not forgetting it. However, I can think of a third theory that excludes him. It's simpler and it ties up an end or two. You said Regis didn't love Constance. He just had an affair with her. Suppose he tried to end the affair and got himself killed for his trouble. She was a strange female, I'm told. Almost psychotic, someone said. Do you think she was capable?"

Robin Robbins stood up abruptly. She carried her glass over to the ingredients and stood quietly with her back to me. Apparently she was only considering whether she should mix herself another or not. She decided not. Depositing her glass, she helped herself to a cigarette from a box and lit it with a lighter. Trailing smoke, she returned to her chair.

"Oh, Constance was capable, all right," she said. "She was much too good to do a lot of things I've done and will probably do again and again if the price is right. But there's one thing she could have done that I couldn't, and that's murder. And if you think that sounds like more eighth-grade psychology, you can forget it and get the hell out of here."

"I don't know about the psychology," I said, "but I'm pretty sure that you don't really think she killed Regis. If you did, you'd be happy to say so."

"That's right." She nodded in amiable agreement. "I wouldn't mind at all doing Constance a bad turn, but she didn't kill Regis. That's obvious."

"I'm inclined to agree. In the first place, she couldn't have got rid of the body. In the second place, if she could have and did, why run away afterward? It wouldn't be sensible."

"Well, it's your problem, brother. I guess it's time you went somewhere else and began to think about it."

"Yeah. I'm the detective. You've told me and told me. You haven't told me much else, though. Not anything very convincing. You got an idea that Silas killed Regis because you and Regis made a kind of illicit cuckold of him, and you lure me here with free bourbon to tell me so, and I'm supposed to be converted by this evangelical message. It's pretty thin, if you don't mind my saying it. Excuse me for being skeptical."

"That's all right. I didn't expect much from you anyhow. I just thought I'd try."

"Try harder."

"I've got nothing more to tell you."

"Really? That's hard to believe. You're not exactly inexpensive, honey, and I'll bet you have to earn your keep. What I mean is, you and Silas surely get convivial on occasions. Even intimate. Men are likely to become indiscreet under such circumstances. They say things they wouldn't ordinarily say. If Silas killed Regis because of you, I'd think he'd even have an urge to gloat. By innuendo, at least."

She moved her head against the back of her chair in a lazy negative. "I'm a girl who knows the side of her bread the butter is on, and I earn my keep. You're right there. But you're wrong if you think Silas Lawler is the kind who gets confidential or careless. He's a very reserved guy, and he protects his position. He tends to his own business, and most of his business nowadays is on the three floors of the building we just left. To be honest, he's pretty damn dull. He works. He eats and sleeps and plays that damn piano, and once in a while he makes love. Once a month, for a few days, he goes to Amity."

"Amity? Why does he go there?"

"I wouldn't know. I guess he has interests."

"Do you ever go with him?"

"No."

"Why not?"

"I'm never invited, thank God. Who wants to go to Amity?"

I took a deep breath and held it till it hurt and then released it.

"That's right," I said. "Who does? Incidentally there's something else that nags me. It seems to me that you're trying to ruin a good thing for yourself, and I don't understand it. What happens to you and all this if Silas turns out to be a murderer?"

"Whatever it is, I'll try to bear it. I may even celebrate. In the meanwhile, on the chance that I'm wrong about him, I may as well be comfortable."

I stood up and looked down, and she stayed down and looked up. And because she was a shrewd and tough wench with looks and brains and queer attachments and flexible morals, I thought it would be pleasant and acceptable to kiss her once in return for the time she'd kissed me once, and that's what I did, and it was. It was pleasant and acceptable. It even started being exciting. Just as her hands were reaching for me, I straightened and turned and walked to the door, and she came out of the chair after me. She put her arms around my waist from behind.

"It's worth developing," she said. "I've been thinking about it, and I've decided."

"Sorry," I said. "My own mind isn't made up yet. I'll let you know."

I loosened her hands and held them in mine against my belly. After a few seconds, I dropped them and opened the door and started out.

"You ugly bastard," she said.

"Don't call me," I said. "I'll call you."

"Go to hell," she said.

I got on out and closed the door softly and began wishing immediately that I hadn't.

CHAPTER 6

The next morning I checked a couple of morgues—the newspaper variety. I turned the brittle bones of old dailies and disturbed the rest of dead stories, but I learned nothing of significance regarding Constance Markley. She was there, all right, briefly and quietly interred in ink. No one had got excited. No one had smelled anything, apparently, that couldn't eventually be fumigated in divorce court. I left the second morgue about noon and stopped on the way out of the building at the desk of a guy I knew. He was sitting hunched in a chair staring with bitter animosity at a silent typewriter, as if the typewriter were somehow an oppressor and an object of hatred. His name was Ludwig Anderson, and he was a good reporter as reporters go. He looked up at me sourly, brushing lank dun hair out of one eye with one hand, and I had the impression that I shared with the typewriter his repressed and sour hatred.

"Hello, Lud," I said.

"Hello, Percy," he said. "What's the occasion?"

"I been down in the morgue," I said. "I didn't learn much of anything."

He shrugged and made another pass at his intrusive hair. "What's in a morgue? Old paper. Old mistakes. You working on something?"

"More or less. You remember Constance Markley?"

"Sure. Graham Markley's third. She got tired of him and ran off with another man. They've been bedded down, now, a couple of years. I didn't know you took divorce cases."

"Nothing like that. I was just wondering who covered the story for your paper."

"A frustrated chicken farmer. He's bored sick by most of the odd balls and pretenders who make the news that people read, and most of all he's bored by the antics of a prowling wife."

"You?"

"That's right."

"You ever get any idea of where Constance Markley went?"

"No." He shrugged again and looked as if he were on the verge of a sour belch. "Who cares? She was doing extra-marital business with Regis Lawler. That was established. She and Lawler ran off together. The implication was clear. Why make a case of it?"

"You satisfied there was nothing more to it?"

"I was satisfied at the time. Nothing's happened to make me dissatisfied since. You know anything that might?"

"Not I. I'm just trying to earn a fee."

His expression soured again, the belch, this time, erupting.

"God-damn ulcer," he said.

Opening a drawer in his desk, he removed a quart thermos bottle and a paper cup that had seen much service. He poured milk from the thermos into the cup and drank the milk slowly. The sour animus that I had previously shared with the typewriter was now directed toward his ulcer and the milk and beyond the milk to a guilty cow. He seemed to have forgotten that I was there.

"Ulcers are hell," I said.

"God-damn milk," he said.

"I could never stand it," I said. "*I* weaned early."

"I hate all God-damn cows." He capped the thermos bottle and put it in the drawer with the paper cup. "Fee for what?" he said.

"Didn't I tell you? Trying to find out where she is."

"Who wants to know?"

"A client."

"What for?"

"Just assurance."

"It's two years old, Percy. Who's getting anxious for assurance after two quiet years?"

"I told you. A client."

"That won't do. You come in here and stir up my ulcer with questions, but you don't want to answer any. You ought to know better."

"All right. The client's name is Faith Salem. She's got an interest in Graham Markley, and she wants to give it legal status."

"Number four?"

"That's the project."

"Dames are nuts. Don't they ever learn anything from each other?"

"This one learns from herself. She knows what she wants and what she doesn't, but she's willing to take some of the latter with a lot of the former. She's realistic."

"That's one word for it, I guess. There are others. What's on her mind that would make her hire a detective?"

"Nothing specific. She wants things clarified, that's all. No complications. Did you know Constance Markley?"

"No. I never saw her. She did something that rated a few lines, and I wrote them. That's all."

"Did she have a reputation?"

"Everyone has a reputation of sorts."

"You know what I mean. Any escapades? Any notoriety? Any proclivity for doing crazy things?"

"None to my knowledge. She was a quiet dame who had an affair and left one man for another. That's what everyone thought, including the police, and that's what I think, too. It's something that happened yesterday and today and will happen sure as hell tomorrow."

"Sure. It's that kind of world. You're wrong about everyone, though. Thinking that way, I mean. You and the police and others, maybe, but not everyone, I know someone who thinks differently."

"Who thinks?"

"Never mind. It's not solid enough to quote."

"Thinks what?"

"Thinks, for one thing, that Regis Lawler wasn't the kind to commit himself to a romantic extravagance like disappearing with a woman at the price of a soft spot. Not with Constance, not with any woman at all. Not for any reason."

"Graham Markley thought he was. So did Silas Lawler."

"I know. And so did you."

"I didn't know anything but what I was told. When a man tells me his wife's run off with a certain guy, I'm inclined to believe him. When the guy's brother agrees, I'm inclined to consider the matter closed."

"You and the police."

"Right. Me and the police."

"Who handled it for the police, incidentally?"

"Matt Thurston."

"I know Matt. I think I'll have a talk with him."

"Suit yourself, but it probably won't do you much good. To tell the truth, he didn't waste much time on the investigation. Maybe Mart's biased. He's been married for thirty years and has ten kids, and he's got no more time than the minimum for a wife who won't stay home."

"I can understand why he wouldn't. Thanks, Lud."

"Sure," he said. "For nothing."

I left him hunched in his sour animus, full of milk and hatred for cows. In my old clunker I drove to police headquarters and found Matt Thurston, sergeant by rank, in the area assigned to the Bureau of Missing Persons. Matt was crowding sixty and going to fat. The skin of his face hung in folds from its bones, and his belly hung over his belt. I said hello and shook hands and asked him if he'd tell me what he remembered about the Constance Markley case.

"To hell with Constance Markley," he said. "Let's go get a beer."

I thought it was a good idea, and we went. In a dark and comforting little bar down the street in the next block, we crawled onto stools and sank to our elbows on mahogany. The bartender drew two without asking, on the grounds, I suppose, of Matt's established habits and known cronies. It was all right with me. I accepted one of the beers and paid for both. Behind us, someone put a dime in a juke box, and one of the rock-and-roll rash began to sing about sugar. He had it in the morning, he had it in the evening, he had it for supper. It was a silly and rather nauseous song—so much sugar all the time—but the machine was modulated, and it gave to the dark and quiet little bar a soft substance and sense of motion that were not unpleasant if you were not particular.

"How's the family?" I said.

"The family's fine," he said. "Ten kids and not a mistake in the litter."

"Litter means all born at the same time," I said.

"Don't be technical," he said. "Ten kids are a litter however they're born."

"Brought forth at one time by a multiparous animal," I said.

"What's a multiparous animal?"

"An animal that has a litter."

"That's my old lady," he said.

We finished our beers and had two more drawn. I paid again as a matter of course. A cop with ten kids is entitled to certain freeloading perogatives when he is in the company of a private detective with none, and this is an opinion almost always shared by the cop.

"Ten kids are quite an accomplishment even when you space them," I said.

"We wanted a dozen, but it doesn't look like we'll make it. The old lady wore out on me."

He swallowed some beer and looked reproachfully into the suds, as if he saw there the worn out old lady who would never make a dozen. "What's your interest in Constance Markley?" he said.

"I'm trying to locate her for someone who wants to know what happened to her."

"Nothing happened to her. She ran off with a man, that's all. Wherever she went, she went because she wanted to."

"So I keep hearing. Just disappeared. She and Regis Lawler. You'll have to admit it isn't the usual pattern of infidelity."

"Is there a pattern of infidelity? I never found one."

"All right. Maybe there's no pattern. Nothing consistently repeated except the infidelity itself. But at least it's possible to see some kind of bad sense afterward in whatever was done or not done. In this case, there are too many things that make no sense at all, not even bad. Why all the mystery? Why all the indifference of people who should have cared for one reason or another? Damn it, Matt, why not simply a separation and a divorce? I keep asking that question, and I keep getting answers, but the answers amount to speculation, and no one knows anything for sure."

Matt glared at his beer. A curious expression of diffused and hopeless anger began in his eyes and spread perceptibly through the folds of his face.

"Look," he said. "I've been in this business for a long time, more years by far than it should take a man to get where I am, which isn't very far from where I started. And the one thing I've learned, if I've learned anything, is that you don't look for sense where there isn't any. Every day people are disappearing for their own reasons, and there are always other people who want the people found who have disappeared, and sooner or later they usually turn up in one place or another. And the reasons they give for what they did are reasons you wouldn't believe, but they're reasons, just the same, that were good enough for the people who had them. What I mean is, people who disappear are people with problems, and they don't think straight. They're running away from something, or after something, or maybe they're just running, period. And most of the time they don't know themselves just which way it is. Take this Markley dame. You ask me why the mystery. You ask me why people didn't give a damn who normally should have. You ask me why not a separation and divorce, all open and sensible. My answer is, how the hell should I know? Everything suggested that she'd run off with a man. Nothing suggested anything else. Am I supposed to get all worked up over the cheap affair of a dissatisfied wife?"

"Not if that's all it was."

"That's all. What else you got in mind?"

"Nothing definite. It just seems to me that there are a lot of loose ends no one's bothered to tie up."

"There are always loose ends. The lives of people like that are littered with loose ends."

"Was there anything, anything at all, that seemed out of line the night Constance Markley and Regis Lawler disappeared?"

"Sure. A man's wife ran off with another man. That's out of line."

"Okay. Granted. Nothing else?"

"All right, all right." He lifted his glass and slammed it down in a sudden concentration and explosion of his diffused anger. "I know what you're thinking, and I've thought it all before. If it wasn't a case of a man and a woman running away together, what was it? Amnesia? One of these fancy fugue cases you read about in the psychology books? It might have been worth considering if it had only been one of them. But it wasn't only one. It was both of them disappearing together. A man and a woman who were having an affair. Did something happen to both of them together that made them lose their memories at the same time? This is something that is hard to believe, even for a private detective."

"Thanks. It is."

"So what's left? Murder? One by the other? If so, what happened to the body? And why run if the body was so well disposed of that no one could find it? Both of them by a third party? Two bodies disposed of with no clues, no mistakes, no trail at all to follow? Look, Percy, it bores me to talk about it. They're somewhere together, if they haven't traded each other off by this time, which wouldn't surprise me. And if you want to earn a fee by looking for her, it's all right with me, but don't try to find something in it that isn't there and never was."

"I appreciate the advice. Thanks very much. Did you ever learn how they left the city?"

"No. There are lots of ways to leave a city."

"Did Regis Lawler cash in on any investments before he disappeared?"

"Apparently he didn't have any. Guys like Regis Lawler don't have any confidence in anything but cash."

"Guys like me, too. Speaking of cash, did you know that Regis lifted seventy-five grand that belonged to brother Silas?"

"I didn't know."

'That's what Silas told me. He said he cut his loss and let it go."

"Maybe Silas can afford it. As for me, I can't even afford another beer. If you want to buy me one for my time, I'll drink it and say thanks and get back to work."

"Sure. Have another beer."

I had one with him and paid and said good-bye and stopped for a bowl of clam chowder and a sandwich on the way to the office.

CHAPTER 7

In the office, sitting, I elevated my feet and began to think.

Maybe thinking is an exaggeration. I didn't really have an idea. All I had was an itch—a tiny burr of coincidence that had caught in a wrinkle of my cortex. It didn't amount to much, but I thought I might as well worry it a while, having nothing else on hand or in mind. What I thought I would do specifically was go back and see Faith Salem again. And I would go, if I could arrange it, when Faith and the sun were on the terrace. She had said to call ahead of time, and so I lowered my feet and reached for the phone, and that's when I saw the gorilla.

He was a handsome gorilla in a Brooks Brothers suit, but a gorilla just the same. There's something about the breed that you can't miss. They smell all right, and they look all right, and there's nothing you can isolate ordinarily as a unique physical characteristic that identifies one of them definitely as a gorilla rather than as a broker or a rich plumber. But they seem to have a chronic quality of deadliness that a broker or a plumber would have only infrequently—in special circumstances, if ever. This one was standing in the doorway watching me, and he had got there without a sound. He smiled. He was plainly prepared to treat me with all the courtesy I was prepared to make possible.

"Mr. Hand?" he said.

"That's right," I said.

"I have a message from Mr. Silas Lawler. He would appreciate it very much if you could come to see him."

"I just went to see him yesterday."

"Mr. Lawler knows that. He regrets that he must inconvenience you again so soon. Apparently something important has come up."

"Something else important came up first. I was just getting ready to go out and take care of it."

"Mr. Lawler is certain that you'll prefer to give his business priority."

"Well, I'll tell you what to do. You go back to Mr. Lawler and tell him I'll be around this evening or first thing tomorrow."

"Mr. Lawler is most urgent that you come immediately. I have instructions to drive you there and bring you back. For your convenience, of course."

"Of course. Mr. Lawler is notoriously considerate. Suppose I don't want to go."

"Mr. Lawler hopes you will want to accomodate him."

"Let's suppose I refuse."

"Mr. Lawler didn't anticipate that contingency, I'm afraid. He said to bring you."

"Even if I resist?"

"As I understood my orders, Mr. Lawler made no qualifications."

"Do you think you're man enough to execute them without qualifications?"

"I think so."

"In that case," I said, "we'd better go."

I got my hat and put it over the place where the lumps would have been if I hadn't. Together, like cronies, we went downstairs and got into his car, which was a Caddy, and drove in it to Silas Lawler's restaurant plus. In the hall outside Silas Lawler's private room, we stood and listened to the piano, which was being played. What was being played on it this time was not something by Chopin, and I couldn't identify who it was by certainly, but I thought it was probably Mozart. The music was airy and intricate. It sounded as if it had been written by a man who felt very good and wanted everyone else to feel as good as he did.

"Mr. Lawler doesn't like to be interrupted when he's playing," the Brooks Brothers gorilla said.

"You can't be too careful with artists," I said. "They're touchy."

"Mr. Lawler's a virtuoso," he said.

He didn't even blink when he said it. It was obviously a word he was used to and not something special for effect. I wondered if they were granting degrees to gorillas these days, but I didn't think it would be wise to ask. There wouldn't have been time for any answer, anyhow, for the virtuoso stopped playing the music by Mozart, or at least not Chopin, and the gorilla knocked twice on the door and opened it, and I walked into the room ahead of him.

Silas Lawler got off the bench and walked around the curve of the grand and stopped in the spot where the canary usually perches in nightclubs. He didn't perch, however. He merely leaned. From the same chair in which she had sat yesterday, Robin Robbins looked across at me with a poker face, and I could see at once, in spite of shadows and cosmetics, that somebody had hung one on her. A plum-colored bruise spread down from her left eye across the bone of her cheek. There was still some swelling of the flesh too, although it had certainly been reduced from what it surely had been. She looked rather cute, to tell the truth. The shiner somehow made her look like the kid she said she never was.

"How are you, Hand?" Lawler said. "It was kind of you to come."

"Your messenger was persuasive," I said. "I couldn't resist him."

"Darcy, you mean. I can always depend on Darcy to do a job like a gentleman. He dislikes violence almost as much as I do. I'm sure you didn't find him abusive."

"Not at all. I've never been threatened half so courteously before." I turned my head and looked down at Robin Robbins. "Apparently you weren't so lucky, honey. You must have run into an inferior gorilla somewhere."

"I fell over my lip," she said.

Lawler laughed, and I could have sworn that there was a note of tenderness in it. "Robin's impetuous. She's always doing something she later regrets, and

I'm always prepared to forgive her eventually, although I sometimes lose my temper in the meanwhile. Isn't that so, Robin?"

"Oh, sure," she said. "We love each other in spite of everything."

"I won't deny that Robin's been punished," Lawler said, "but I'm afraid I must charge you with being partially responsible, Hand. You ought to be ashamed of yourself for taking advantage of her innocence."

"I am," I said. "I truly am."

"Well," he said, "I don't think we need to be too critical. Robin, I realize, is even harder to resist than Darcy. For different reasons, of course. She's told me what the two of you talked about yesterday after leaving here together, and she understands now how foolish she was. Don't you, Robin?"

"Sure," she said. "I was foolish."

"She wants me to ask you to forget all about it, don't you, Robin?"

"Sure," she said. "Forget it."

"You see?" Lawler shrugged and shifted his weight against the piano. "Robin and I are really very compatible. We are never able to keep secrets from one another for very long."

"That's sweet," I said. "I'm touched."

He was looking directly at Robin for the first time now. "Wouldn't you like to apologize to Mr. Hand for causing him so much trouble, Robin?"

"I apologize, Mr. Hand," she said.

"I liked it better when you told me to go to hell," I said.

Lawler stood erect and stopped looking at Robin in order to look at me. "That wasn't a very gracious response, Hand. However, let it pass. I also want to apologize to you."

"What for?"

"I'm afraid I was a little unreasonable yesterday. I understand now that you were hired to investigate the matter we discussed, and you're naturally concerned about your fee. I have no right to ask you to sacrifice that, of course. What do you think it will amount to?"

"That depends on how long the job lasts. I get twenty-five dollars a day and expenses."

"Very reasonable. I'll pay you five thousand to drop the case. That should be adequate."

"Bribery?"

"Don't be offensive. Compensation for the loss of your fee."

"It's not enough."

"Really? I figure that it comes to two hundred days' work. What do you think would be fair?"

"Make it a million, and I'll take it."

"Your joke isn't very funny, Hand. It's bad taste to joke about a serious matter."

"I'm not joking. You see, I've got to be compensated for more than the loss of a fee. I've got to be compensated for the loss of my integrity, such as it is. I don't figure a million's too much for that."

"Nonsense. You're wasting your time, anyhow. I assured you of that. Is it ethical to go on accepting a fee under false pretenses?"

"I explained to my client that it might not come to anything. Probably wouldn't, as a matter of fact. We're both satisfied."

"Perhaps I could persuade your client that he is making a mistake. Would you care to give me his name?"

"No, I wouldn't. The truth is, I don't particularly care for your methods of persuasion."

"No matter. If I really want to learn the identity of your client, I can do it easily enough. Now, however, I don't propose to discuss this matter with you any longer. I believe I've made you a fair proposition. Do you still refuse to accept it?"

"Sorry. I'm holding out for the million."

If there was the slightest sign between him and Darcy behind me, the lifting of a brow or the twitch of a tic, I never saw it. It could be, I guess, that they'd developed a kind of extra-sensory communication that functioned automatically when the time was precisely right. Anyhow, sign or not, Darcy grabbed me abruptly above the elbows from behind and wrenched my arms and shoulders back so violently that I thought for a moment I'd split down the middle like a spring fryer. At the same instant, Lawler made a fist and stepped forward within range.

"I regret this, Hand," he said. "I really do."

"I know," I said. "You dislike violence. You and Darcy both."

"It's your own fault, of course. You're behaving like a recalcitrant boy, and it's necessary to teach you a lesson."

"Don't you think you ought to teach me somewhere else? You wouldn't want to get blood on this expensive carpet."

"It's acrilan. Haven't you heard of it? One of these new miracle fabrics. Blood wipes right off."

"Is that a fact? Better living through chemistry. I'm impressed."

He was tired now of the whole business. I could see in his face that he was tired, and I believe that he actually did regret what he considered the necessity of having to do what he was going to do. It was only that he knew no other way to fight, in spite of Chopin and Mozart and the veneer of respectability, than the way of violence. He wanted to get it over with, and he did. He drove the fist into my face, and it was like getting hit with a jagged boulder. Flesh split on bone, and bone cracked, and darkness welled up internally. I sagged, I guess, and hung by my arms from the hands of Darcy, and after a while, I guess, I straightened and lifted my head and was hit again in the face. When I opened my eyes after that, I was lying on the carpet, and there was blood on it. In my mouth there was more blood, and a thin and bitter fluid risen from my stomach. I was sick and in pain, but mostly I was ashamed. I got up slowly, in sections, and looked at Lawler through a pink mist.

"Your carpet's a mess," I said. "I hope you're right about acrilan."

"Don't worry about it," he said. "You're a tough guy, Hand, and I like you. If you think I get any kicks out of pushing you around, you're wrong. There's a lavatory in there. Through that door. Why don't you go in and wash your face?"

"I think I will," I said.

I went in and turned on the cold tap and caught double handfuls of water and buried my face in them. The water burned like acid, but it revived me and dispelled the pink fog. In the mirror above the lavatory, I saw that a cut on my cheekbone needed a stitch or two. I found some adhesive tape in the medicine cabinet and pulled the cut together and went back out into the other room.

Lawler was seated at the grand again. Darcy was leaning against the wall behind him. Robin Robbins, in her chair, was still wearing her poker face. I thought I saw in her eyes a guarded gleam of something appealing. Compassion? Camaraderie based on mutual beatings? A raincheck? Who could be sure with Robin? I kept right on walking toward the door, and I was almost there when Lawler spoke to me.

"Hand," he said.

I stopped but didn't turn. I didn't answer either. It hurt to talk, and I saw no sense in it.

"One thing more," he said. "I made a reasonable offer, and you'd be wise to accept it. This is just a suggestion of what you'll get if you don't. I'll put a check for five thousand in the mail today. You'll get it tomorrow."

"Thanks very much," I said.

I started again and kept going and got on out of there.

CHAPTER 8

In a sidewalk telephone booth I dialed Faith Salem's number and got Maria.

"Miss Salem's apartment," she said.

"This is Percy Hand," I said. "Let me speak with Miss Salem."

"One moment, please," she said.

I waited a while. The open wire hummed in my ear. My head felt three times its normal size, and the hum was like a siren. I held the receiver a few inches away until Faith Salem's voice came on.

"Hello, Mr. Hand," she said.

"You said to call before I came," I said. "I'm calling."

"Is it something urgent?"

"I don't know how urgent it is. I know I just turned down five grand in a chunk for twenty-five dollars and expenses a day. Under the circumstances, I feel like being humored."

She was silent for ten seconds. The siren shattered my monstrous head.

"You sound angry," she said finally.

"Not at all," I said. "I'm an amiable boob who will take almost anything from anybody, and my heart holds nothing but love and tenderness for all of God's creatures."

Silence again. The siren again. Her voice again in due time.

"You'd better come up," she said. "I'll be expecting you."

"Fifteen minutes," I said.

When I got there, the sun was off the terrace, and so was she. She was waiting for me in the living room, and she was wearing a black silk jersey pullover blouse and black ballerina-type slippers and cream colored capri pants. On her they looked very good, or she looked very good in them, whichever way you saw it. She was lying on her side, propped up on one elbow on a sofa about nine feet long, and she got up and came to meet me between the sofa and the door. I thought I heard her breath catch and hold for a second in her throat.

"Your face," she said.

"It must be a mess," I said.

"There's a stain on the front of your shirt," she said. "Blood," I said. "Mine."

She reached up and touched gently with her finger tips the piece of adhesive that was holding together the lips of the cut that needed a stitch or two. The fingers moved slowly down over the swollen flesh and seemed to draw away the pain by a kind of delicate anesthetization. It was much better than codeine or a handful of aspirin.

"Come and sit down," she said.

I did, and she did. We sat together on the nine foot sofa, and my right knee touched her left knee. And this might have been by accident or design, but in either event it was a pleasant situation that no one made any move to alter—certainly not I.

"I'm so sorry," she said.

"So am I," I said. "I'm sorrier than anyone."

"Would you like to tell me about it?"

"It's hardly worth while. I took a job, and this turned out to be part of it."

"It's all my fault."

"Sure it is."

"But I don't understand. Why should anyone do this to you?"

"Someone wanted me to give up the job, and I didn't want to. We had a difference of opinion."

"Does that mean you've decided to go ahead with it?"

"That's what it means. At least for a while longer. When anyone wants so hard for me to quit doing something I'm doing, it makes me stubborn. I'm a contrary fellow by nature."

"You must be careful," she said.

She sounded as if it would really make a difference if I wasn't. She was sitting facing me, her left leg resting along the edge of the sofa and her right leg not touching the sofa at all, and she lifted her hand again and touched the battered side of my face as if she were reminding herself and me of the consequences of carelessness, and it seemed a natural completion of the gesture for her hand to slip on around my neck. Her arm followed, and her body came over against mine, and I was suddenly holding her and kissing her with bruised lips, and we got out of balance and toppled over gently and lay for maybe a minute in each other's arms with our mouths together. Then she drew and released a deep breath that quivered her toes. She sat up, stood up, looked down at me with a kind of incredulity in her eyes.

"I think I need a drink," she said. "You, too."

"No gin and tonic, thanks," I said. "Straight bourbon."

"Agreed," she said.

She walked over to a cabinet to get it. I watched her go and watched her come. Her legs in the tight capri pants were long and lovely and worth watching. This was something she knew as well as I, and we were both happy about it. She handed me my bourbon in a little frosted glass with the ounces marked on the outside in the frost, and the bourbon came up to the third mark. I drank it down a mark, leaving two to go, and she sat down beside me and drank a little less of hers.

"I liked kissing you, and I'm glad I did," she said, "but I won't do it again."

"All right," I said.

"Are you offended?"

"No."

"There's nothing personal in it, you understand."

"I understand."

"There are obvious reasons why I can't afford to."

"I know the reasons. What I'd like to do now, if you don't mind, is to quit talking about it. I came here to talk about something else, and it would probably be a good idea if we got started."

"What did you come to talk about?"

"About you and Constance Markley. When I was here before, you said you knew her in college. You said you shared an apartment that she paid the rent on. I neglected to ask you what college it was."

"Amity College."

"That's at Amity, of course."

"Yes. Of course."

"What was your name then?"

"The same as now. Faith Salem."

"You told me you'd been married a couple of times. I've been wondering about the Miss. Did you get your maiden name restored both times?"

"Not legally. When I'm compelled to be legal, I use another name. Would you believe that I'm a countess?"

"I'd believe it if you said it."

"Well, I don't say it often, because I'm not particularly proud of it. The count was attractive and quite entertaining for a while, but he turned out to be a mistake. I was in Europe with my first husband when I met him. You remember the publisher's son I married in college? That one. We were in Europe, and he'd turned out to rather a mistake too, although not so bad a one as the count turned out later. Anyhow, I met the count and did things with him while my husband was doing things with someone else, and he was a very charming and convincing liar, and I decided it would probably be a smart move to make a change. It wasn't."

"Wasn't it profitable?"

"No. The amount of his income was one of the things the count lied about most convincingly. Are you being rather nasty about it, incidentally? I hope not. Being nasty doesn't suit you somehow."

"Excuse me. You'll have to remember that I've had a hard day. The publisher's son and the count are none of my business. At your request, Constance Markley is. I'd like to know exactly the nature of the relationship that caused you to share an apartment."

"It was normal, if that's what you mean."

"It isn't." I lowered the bourbon to the first mark. My mouth was cut on the inside, and the bourbon burned in the cut. "I don't know just what I do mean. I don't even know exactly why I asked the question or what I'm trying to learn. Just tell me what you can about Constance."

She was silent, considering. Her consideration lasted about half a minute, and after it was finished, she took time before speaking to lower the level of her own bourbon, which required about half as long.

"It's rather embarrassing," she said.

"Come on," I said. "Embarrass yourself."

"Oh, well." She shrugged. "I liked Constance. I told you I did. But I wasn't utterly devoted to her. She was rather an uncomfortable girl to be around, to tell the truth. Very intense. Inclined to be possessive and jealous. She often resented the attention and time I gave to other people. At such times, she would be very difficult and demanding, then withdrawn and sullen, and finally almost pathetically repentant and eager to make everything right again. It was a kind of cycle that she repeated many times. Her expressions and gestures of affection made me feel uncomfortable. Not that there was the least sign of perversion in them, you understand. It was only that they were so exorbitant."

"Would you say that she admired you?"

"I guess so. I guess that's what it was."

"Well, I understand it isn't so unusual to find that kind of thing among school girls. Boys either, for that matter. Do you have anything left over from that time? Any snapshots or letters or anything like that?"

"It happens that I do. After you left the other day, I got to thinking about Constance, the time we were together, and I looked in an old case of odds and ends I'd picked up different times and places, the kind of stuff you accumulate and keep without any good reason, and there were this shapshot and a card among all the other things. They don't amount to much. Just a snapshot of the two of us together, a card she sent me during the Christmas holiday of that year. Would you like to see them?"

I said I would, and she went to get them. Why I wanted to see them was something I didn't know precisely. Why I was interested at all in this period of ancient history was something else I didn't know. It had some basis, I think, in the feeling that the thing that could make a person leave an established life without any trace was surely something that had existed and had been growing for a long time, not something that had started yesterday or last week or even last year. Then there was, of course, the coincidence. Silas Lawler wanted this sleeping dog left lying, and once a month he went to the town where Constance Markley had once lived with Faith Salem, who wanted the dog wakened. It was that thin—that near to nothing. But it was all there was of anything at all.

Faith Salem returned with the snapshot and the Christmas card. I took them from her and finshed my bourbon and looked first at the picture. I don't know if I would have seen in it what I did if I hadn't already heard about Constance Markley what I had. It's impossible to know how much of what we see, or think we see, is the result of suggestion. Constance and Faith were standing side by side. Constance was shorter, slighter of build, less striking in effect. Faith was looking directly into the camera, but Constance was looking around and up at the face of Faith. It seemed to me that her expression was one of adoration. This was what might have been no more than the result of suggestion. I don't know.

I took the Christmas card out of its envelope. It had clearly been expensive, as cards go, and had probably been selected with particular care. On the back, Constance Markley had written a note. It said how miserable and lonely she was at home, how the days were interminable, how she longed for the time to come when she could return to Amity and Faith. Christmas vacation, I thought, must have lasted all of two weeks. I read the note with ambivalence. I felt pity, and I felt irritation.

Faith Salem had finished her bourbon and was looking at me over the empty glass. Her eyes were clouded, and she shook her head slowly from side to side.

"I guess you've got an idea," she said.

"That's an exaggeration," I said.

"Why are you interested in all this? I don't understand."

"Maybe it's just that I'm naturally suspicious of a coincidence. Every time I come across one, I get curious."

"What coincidence?"

"Never mind. If I put it in words, I'd probably decide it sounded too weak to bother with. I think I'll drive down to Amity, and the trip'll hike expenses. You'd better give me a hundred bucks."

"All right. I'll get it for you."

She got up and went out of the room again. I watched her out and stood up to watch her in. From both angles and both sides she still looked good. She handed me the hundred bucks, and I took it and shoved it in a pocket and put my arms around her and kissed her. She had meant what she had said. She had said she wouldn't kiss me again, and she didn't. She only stood quietly and let me kiss her, which was different and not half so pleasant. I took my arms away and stepped back.

"I'm sorry," I said.

"So am I," she said.

Then we said good-bye, and I left. Going, I met Graham Markley in the hall, coming. We spoke politely, and he asked me how the investigation was getting along. I said it was getting along all right. He didn't even seem curious about the condition of my face.

CHAPTER 9

I stopped in a package liquor store and bought a fifth of Jim Beam. Carrying Jim, I climbed the stairs to my room. It was a long way up there—a long, long way. My head ached, and my legs ached, and my feet dragged on the treads. I was filled with a kind of ebullient and impotent anger, and the cause of the anger, aside from what had been done to me, was that I had come to a time and condition where I wanted to quit doing what I was committed to do, but I could not quit in good faith with myself. Not that I'm a hero. Not that I'm as ethical as I've been accused of being. It is only that I must, in order to live with him compatibly, sustain a certain amount of respect and fondness for Percy Hand.

Holding Jim like a suckling in the cradle of my right arm, I used my left hand to find a key and open the door to my room. Inside in the close and comforting darkness, I leaned against the door and took three long and leisurely breaths. Then I had the sudden feeling that the darkness was breathing too—had stirred and made the slightest sound—and it was as suddenly a threat and no longer a comfort. Straightening, pulling away from the door, I took Jim by the neck and made a club of the suckling. Tensed against the rush of darkness toward me, I felt on the wall with my free hand for a switch.

"Don't turn on the lights," Robin Robbins said.

Aware that I had not breathed for a while, I started again.

"What the hell are you doing here?" I said.

"At the moment, I'm standing here by the window looking at you. Before you came, I was standing here at the window looking down into the street."

"It's not much of a view. I can't imagine why you chose it."

"I didn't choose it. I was here, and so was it, and we got together. I was thinking. I always like to stand at a window and look down into a street when I'm thinking. It's somehow helpful. I guess it's psychological."

"Psychology again? The last time we got psychological, it ended badly for both of us."

"I know. I'm sorry."

I could tell from the sound and simplicity of her words that she meant them. She said she was sorry, and she was. Not for herself, but for me. Probably, in all her life, she had not wasted as much as an hour feeling sorry for herself. In her tough little psyche, whatever a psyche is, she had sheltered and somehow sustained a sense of fairness according to her notion, the capacity to regret the hurt she did and the trouble she caused. Robin Robbins was becoming a girl I was beginning to like.

"How did you get in here?" I said.

"I persuaded the janitor. By telling him I needed to see you on urgent business, I managed to convince him that I only wanted to spend the night for fun. He came up and unlocked the door for me, and it was clear that he was sympathetic and in favor of people enjoying themselves. He's very partial to you, incidentally. He thinks you're a fine fellow, and I think so, too."

"You're only trying to compensate for getting the hell beat out of me."

"And me. Not that it matters. It was my fault for being obvious, and I said I was sorry."

"Forget it. My pride was hurt, but otherwise nothing seriously. When looking out of windows to assist your thinking, do you always do it in the dark?"

"Whenever there is dark to do it in. I like the dark. Do you know that there are other things about the dark besides the look of it? You can feel it, too. It feels different from light, and you can close your eyes and feel the difference around you. If I were blind, I would always know whether it was day or night by the feel. It smells different too, and sounds are heard differently in it. Small sounds are bigger, and big sounds are smaller. In the dark it doesn't matter so much what has happened or what may happen. Nothing matters so much in the dark."

During the time of our conversation, the pupils of my eyes had dilated in adjustment to the darkness she liked, and I could see her by the window. Beside her and a little beyond her, the glass below the blind was thinly glazed by the soiled light of a lamp in the street below.

"Nevertheless," I said, "I think it would be better now if we had a light. Do you mind if I turn one on?"

"Wait a minute first. Do you know that you're being followed?"

"Yes. By you."

"Not by me. I came here ahead of you and waited. That isn't following. By someone in a small black sedan. He drove up a minute or two after you did, and he's now parked across the street. He went to the corner and turned and came back, and I'm sure he was following you, because he got out of the car and stood for a moment looking up at this window, and then he got back into the car.

Would you like to see?"

I walked across to the window and looked down into the street, and the small black sedan was there by the curb, as she had said, and I could see in the dense darkness of its interior the tiny glow of a bright coal when someone drew on a cigarette. I could smell Robin Robbins beside me. I could hear her breathing, and I had a notion that I could hear, if I listened intently, the beating of her heart. She smelled good, and the soft sound of her life, which breathing is, was at once comforting and exciting.

"Silas Lawler?" I said.

"No. If Silas were having it done, it would be Darcy doing it. That isn't Darcy."

"Who, then?"

"That's your question. You answer it."

"Sure. I'm the detective. You keep telling me and telling me. All right, honey. Wait for me. Don't go away."

"I'm not going anywhere. Not for a while."

I went back across the room to the door, and I had opened the door and had a foot in the hall before she spoke again.

"Play it cool," she said.

"Thanks," I said. "It helps to know you care." I went on out and downstairs and straight across the street toward the black sedan. I was half way there before the guy behind the wheel awoke to events and jammed his foot on the starter. Fortunately, it was an old car, a little tired, and did not come to life easily. By the time the engine had caught fire, I had jerked open the door and snatched the ignition key. The engine died with a cough and a twitch of a piston, as if dying were welcome and better than living. The guy behind the wheel cursed and slapped at the wrist of the hand that held the key. His nails raked flesh.

"What the hell!" he said.

I reached in and grabbed his tie and twisted and pulled, and he came out of the car like a grape from its skin. He was six inches shorter than me, forty pounds lighter. I could whip him easily if necessary, and I was glad, because I felt like whipping someone. His name was Colly Alder, and I knew him. He was a fair private detective, not so good as a lot and a little better than a few.

"Hello, Colly," I said. "We haven't met for a while."

"Cut it out, Percy." He pawed at the hand that twisted the tie that cut his wind. "God-damn it, you're choking me."

"Certainly I'm choking you," I said, "and after I get through choking you, I'm going to slap your chops and stand you on your head and kick you over your car. I'm going to do this, Colly, simply because I'm big enough and feel like it. I was worked over myself today by a couple of experts, and it hurt my face and my feelings, to say nothing of my professional prestige, and ever since it happened I've been looking for someone to work over in return, and you seem to be it. I admit that this isn't fair. I think it's psychological or something. I have a friend who is sharp about such things, and I'll ask her later."

His eyes were popping a little, as much from what I said, I think, as from his assaulted trachea. His voice, working under handicap, was hoarse and sporadic, issuing in short bursts.

"What the hell's the matter with you, Percy? You drunk or crazy or what?"

"I told you what's the matter. My feelings have been hurt, and I'm looking for someone to stomp. It doesn't help my feelings any to find myself being tailed by another private detective. There's something reprehensible about it, Colly. It's treason, sort of."

His face was getting darker than I liked, not liking homicide, and so I let him go. He slipped the knot of his tie and loosened his collar and began massaging his throat with his fingers. While doing this, he uttered plaintive little retching sounds that almost made me bleed.

"You think I'm tailing you?" he said finally.

"I know damn well you're tailing me."

"Honest to God, I'm not, Percy. I swear I'm not."

"Sure you do. You swear and swear, and you're a damn liar. I think I'll choke you some more, Colly. It's fun."

I reached for him, and he skipped backward, plastering himself against the side of the car.

"All right, Percy, all right. So I'm tailing you. It's legitimate, God damn it. A guy's got a right to take a case where he finds it."

"Sure he has, Colly. He can take the case, and he can take the consequences. That's something I learned a long time ago, and I started learning it all over again today. Who hired you?"

He looked sullen, shaking his head.

"That's privileged stuff, Percy."

"The hell it is. Private detectives don't receive privileged communications."

"Not legally, maybe, but we got to respect each other's privilege in the trade. You know that as well as I do, Percy, and you got no right to ask me."

He had me there, and I had to admit it. It was a privilege I'd exercised myself and would exercise again whenever it was necessary and I could get away with it. It had no legal status, as Colly said, but it was accepted and honored by honorable members of the trade, if by no one else. I was still hurting and still mad and still wanting to slap Colly around, but I decided under the circumstances that I'd better spit in his eye and let him go.

"All right," I said. "You've got a right to a case, and you've also got a right to turn one down. I didn't think you'd do this to me, Colly, and I'm disappointed. I'll respect your privilege to keep your client's name to yourself, and it doesn't matter a hell of a lot, to tell the truth, because I've got a good idea who he is, and you can go back to him tomorrow and tell him you loused up the job by getting caught and won't be any good to him any longer. Even if you decide to keep the job for the fee, you might as well go home and go to bed now, because that's what I'm going to do, and it would be a shame for you to lose your sleep for nothing. Good-night, Colly. I don't think, from now on, that I'm going to like you much."

Tossing the ignition key onto the front seat of the car, I started back across the street. Before I had reached the curb, the starter of the car was grinding, and the tired engine coughed and caught fire with a roar. By the time I had crossed the sidewalk to the entrance of the building, the car and Colly were half way to the corner under a full head. I went inside and back up the long, long stairs and into my room.

It was still dark in there, and this time I found the switch and flipped it. Jim Beam was still sitting on the table, where I'd put it before going down, but Robin Robbins had moved. She had left the window and was sitting in a corner of a sofa. She was wearing what she had been wearing when I had seen her earlier in Silas Lawler's office, and what this was primarily was a black sheath dress with a slit in the skirt to give leg room for walking. Her high-heeled sandals were black also, and the sandals and the dress and her hair and her eye made quite a lot of black altogether, but on her it all looked good and not in the least mournful, even the eye. The slit skirt of the tight sheath had slipped up an inch or two on her thighs, which is inevitable in a sheath in a sitting position, and this left quite a lot of pretty nylon out in the open.

"I watched from the window," she said. "You handled him nicely."

"He was a little guy," I said. "I had a notion to get real tough."

"Who was he?"

"One of the brotherhood. A private detective. His name's Colly Alder."

"You know him before?"

"Slightly. We'd brushed against each other in some connection."

"Who put him on your tail?"

"He didn't want to say."

"Couldn't you persuade him? As you said, he was a little guy."

"I guess I'm just a softy. The sight of blood makes me sick."

She tilted her head to one side and stared at me with a speculative expression. In accomplishing this, besides tilting her head, she closed her plain eye and stared with the one that had been decorated.

"That's partly a joke and partly not," she said. "You've got a soft spot, all right. Basically you're a tender slob. I've got a theory that ugly men tend to be tender."

"That's interesting. You're simply loaded with interesting theories about this and that. Do you mind if I take off my coat and stay awhile?"

"Not at all. Make yourself at home."

I removed the coat and tossed it into a chair that was already occupied by mink. The mink and worn tweed didn't look very compatible. They looked as if someone were slumming. Leaving them together in a state of precarious tolerance, I went into the bathroom and splashed my face with cold water. When I returned, Robin had shifted sidewise on the sofa and had drawn her feet up under her neat behind, leaving her nylon knees out. I went over and sat on the sofa beside her.

"You have nice knees," I said.

"Do you like them?" She bent over from the hips to examine them for a moment. "One of them has a dimple when I'm standing."

"Only one? That's tough."

"Oh, I don't know. I think it makes them rather intriguing for one to have a dimple and the other not."

"You're probably right. The next time you're standing, remind me to look and see."

Her plain eye and her decorated eye moved slowly around the room together. It was a homely room, even a shabby room, but it had in it a few things I liked. And sometimes, when I was reading at night or lying in bed, it seemed like home and a good place to be. Now, with her in it, it had color and light and warmth and a sense of excitement. To me, that is. To her it was palpably nothing much. Her eyes moved slowly from one thing to another and were finally arrested by a picture of some olive trees. I had bought it in a second-hand shop one rainy afternoon when I had felt the need of something pleasant to look at.

"What's that?" she said.

"It's a picture of some olive trees."

"Is that what they are? I like them."

"So do I. Maybe it's a sign that we have an affinity or something."

"It's possible. I admit that you appeal to me in a peculiar way. Is it supposed to be a good picture?"

"It's a bad print of a good picture. The original was painted by a Dutchman named Van Gogh. He was nuts. He cut off one of his own ears."

"He must have been nuts in a nice way to have painted such trees."

"Sure. In a nice way. The same way I'm ugly."

"That's right." She looked at me briefly with her black eye. "Your room is interesting as a change, but it's really a dump. Can't you actually afford any better?"

"I sort of like it," I said. "What can you expect from a guy who wears ready-made suits?"

"Aren't you sometimes depressed by living here?"

"I'd be sometimes depressed no matter where I lived. You're under no obligation to stay, incidentally, if you find it intolerable. As a matter of fact, you were under no obligation to come, and I wonder why you did."

If she heard me, she gave no sign of it. Her eyes moved away from the cheap Van Gogh print and hung up on Jim Beam.

"Are you saving that for something special?"

"Sure," I said. "For you."

"Good. I'll have some right now, if you don't mind."

"There's no ice."

"That's all right. I'll have it straight." I got up and went into the bathroom and got a couple of tumblers off the back edge of the lavatory. I rinsed them in hot water and carried them back into the room. Opening Jim Beam, I poured about three ounces into both tumblers and handed one of them to Robin. She took a stout swallow and held her breath for a few seconds afterward and released the breath slowly. I sat down beside her again, almost brushing the nylon knees, and she lifted the tumbler until it was touching her sulky mouth and looked at me levelly over the rim. She was a tough and accomplished little charmer, all right, and I enjoyed playing the casual game we were playing together. But I was also bruised and worried, if not scared, and I thought it was probably getting time for business.

"Look, honey," I said. "You're smart, and you're beautiful, and any man in his right mind would be tickled to death to have you break into his room any old time, and that's what I am. I'm tickled to death. I'd like to believe that you did it because I'm a guy you just can't resist. But I'm not, and you didn't, so there's no use wasting time on that one. Suppose you tell me the real reason in simple words, and I'll listen and maybe understand. I might even believe you."

Her petulant little mouth curved slowly and slyly in a smile that was reflected in her smoky eyes, and she leaned forward deliberately from the hips and put the mouth on mine, and it was soft and inciting and still smiling all the while. I didn't retreat or advance or attempt to evade. For a few seconds I managed an overt passivity that was a covert lie, but a reasonable limit is placed on passivity by glands and such, and finally I reached for her and held her and felt in my hands the vibration of her body in its thin black sheath. Her mouth opened and stopped smiling. Her breath caught in her throat. She forgot her glass and spilled bourbon on the rug. After a while, with a pleased little mew, she leaned back in her corner and closed her eyes and began again smiling slyly.

"Maybe you underestimate yourself," she said. "Maybe you're a guy I just can't resist."

"Really? How do I compare with Regis Lawler?"

"Regis was a handsome heel. You're an ugly touch. In time, I think, I could learn to like you better."

"I know. It's worth developing."

"That's it." She opened her eyes and looked at me through the lashes. "I told you that, and you walked out on me. You hurt my feelings."

"Sorry. I thought you were trifling with me. I'm a lad who doesn't like being trifled with."

"Sure. Poor and proud. We've been through that."

"So we have. There's something else we've been through, too. Both of us. It happened right after the other time we got together, and it was painful. Do you suppose this little session will have the same result? I wouldn't want it to become a habit."

"Don't worry. Silas was still in the office when I left, and Darcy was tailing you. No one knows where I went. Do you have a cigarette?"

I gave her one and lit it. She inhaled deeply and blew out a long thin plume through pursed lips.

"Did you know that Darcy was tailing you?" she said.

"That's one of the reasons I came. To tell you that."

"Thanks. If that's true, aren't you running quite a risk being here? It poses a problem."

"I don't think so. How could he have followed me if he was following you? Even Darcy can't be two places at the same time."

"I didn't mean when you came. I meant when you leave. If he's got the place under observation, how the hell do you expect to get away without being seen?"

"Oh, it isn't likely that he'll spend the night in the street. Once he's certain you're bedded down, he'll probably go home and pick you up again tomorrow. However, I admit there's an element of risk, and I've been thinking about it. In order to take no chance at all, I've decided to stay here until morning. If Darcy's waiting outside then, he'll follow you away when you leave, and I can leave later without any risk whatever."

I drained my tumbler of Jim Beam and walked over for more. My legs felt rubbery, and there was in my head a peculiar lightness. It was not Jim that caused this. Nor bruises nor fatigue nor the cumulative effect of a long and difficult day. It was Robin who caused it. Her casual assumptions and propositions demanded quick and tricky adjustments, and she was, too frequently, too much in effect like a sharp inside belt to the belly.

"You seem to have thought this out very carefully," I said.

"It didn't require much thought," she said. "To be honest, it's something I want to do anyhow, so it worked out naturally."

"You took it for granted, I suppose, that I'd be agreeable."

"Do you object?"

"I've got an idea I'd be smart if I did, but I don't. Maybe we owe it to each other. It'll give us a good chance to find out if it's worth developing."

"That's true. Anything worth developing will certainly develop now. Would you please pour a little more of that into my glass?"

I gave her more Jim and sat down again beside her. More of the nylon knees were showing than had shown before, and her short black hair had acquired a tousled look that may have been no more than a blur in my eyes. Her own eyes were warm and filled with smoke and an utterly amiable solicitation. I had a strong conviction that business would soon be waiting, and there was still before pleasure a point of business that I wanted to bring up. I took a drink and a deep breath and summoned endurance.

"Did you know that Regis Lawler took seventy-five grand out of the safe in Silas Lawler's office the night he disappeared?" I asked.

Behind the haze of smoke in her eyes there was for an instant a brief bright flare of genuine surprise.

"Nuts," she said. "Who told you?"

"Silas himself. Don't you believe it?"

"No. It's out of character. Not for Regis, but for Silas. Regis would have been capable, all right—the heel—but Silas would never have let him get away with it. He'd have hunted him down if it had meant never doing another thing for the rest of his life. Not just for the money, you understand. The loss of seventy-five grand wouldn't mean too much to Silas. For the sake of his precious pride, the essential principle that no one on earth makes a sucker of Silas Lawler. Silas hasn't been trying to find Regis. He hasn't been trying because Regis is dead, and Silas knows he's dead. He knows he's dead because he killed him."

"That's your opinion. I remember your telling me. Why would Silas want to improvise a lie like that? What does it gain him?"

She swallowed some Jim and looked at me levelly while she held her breath and released it slowly in the little ritual of drinking straight. Her black head moved from side to side.

"Cut it out," she said. "You're ugly, but you're not dumb. He did it to patch a hole in the fairy tale that Regis and Constance ran away together. It would take money to do something like that, and Regis didn't have any. He had some kind of crazy scheme to make a bundle in a hurry, but it wasn't to steal it from Silas, I'm sure of that. And I'm also sure that it never came to anything, whatever it was."

"What kind of crazy scheme?"

"I don't know. I said I didn't. I only know that it was something that would have been very unpleasant to someone."

"What makes you think so?"

"He was at my place one night. He was cocky drunk and talking a lot. He was different from Silas that way. Silas keeps a tight lip, but Regis always talked too much. He had a newspaper clipping folded into his wallet. He showed it to me and said that it was going to be worth a fortune to him, but I thought it was just Scotch talking, and I still think so. He had me in heat, damn him, but I knew he was a phony just the same."

"What was the clipping about?"

"I didn't read it all. Just the head. It was about some woman getting killed by a hit-and-run driver out in one of the counties."

"Blackmail?"

"I got the idea."

"Nice lovers you have, honey."

"I told you he was a heel. Can a girl turn off her glands? Besides, as you see, I'm trying to do better."

Standing abruptly, she walked over and set her glass on the table beside Jim Beam. Business, I felt, was finished for the night.

"Where do you sleep?" she said. "On a sofa? On the floor? Or do you stand yourself in a corner?"

"The bed's in the wall," I said. "It unfolds."

"I had one of those once. It wasn't very comfortable."

"Neither is this one. The springs sag, and you roll toward the center from either side."

"Really? It sounds interesting. Is that the bathroom there?"

"Yes."

"I'll use it for a minute, if you don't mind."

"Not at all. Use it for as many minutes as you wish. There's a clean toothbrush in the cabinet above the lavatory."

She went into the bathroom, and I had another short drink and heard water running. Pretty soon she came back carrying the black sheath and a couple of black trifles, and after that a lot of things happened in some kind of order, and somewhere in the order of things that happened, the bed got unfolded from the wall.

CHAPTER 10

I awoke in the morning at the bottom of the slope on my side. Robin was still asleep at the bottom of the slope on hers. There was very little room between the slopes, and no room at all between us. Reluctantly and very gently, I removed myself and gathered clothes and went into the bathroom to dress. I shaved and dressed quickly, skipping a shower to avoid the noise, and then returned to the bedroom on my toes. The notion I had was to get out and away before she awakened, giving her and the night, in the day after, time to assume for each other their proper relationship. If the relationship was sick or sour or nothing much, then we could pretend, if we met again, that we were two other people. If it was better than that and good enough, we could take it, if we met, from where we were.

I might as well have saved the effort and the good intentions. When I came into the room, she was sitting up watching me. Her short black hair was a tousled mess, and her mouth was smeared, and her eyes were heavy with the dregs of sleep. She was, I mean, the loveliest woman in the world at that moment, except one.

"What time is it?" she said.

"Seven o'clock."

"Don't be absurd. No one wakes up at seven o'clock."

"Lots of people do. Including me."

"Whatever for?"

"It's a nasty habit. It's especially prevalent among poor men who wear ready-made suits and live in dumps."

"Are you going somewhere?"

"Yes. To work."

"What a dull thing to do under the circumstances. Come back to bed instead."

So it wasn't sour, and it wasn't sick. How much it would amount to in the long run was a question, but at least it was worth repeating, and I wished I had the time. I went over and sat down on the bed beside her. The sheet that had covered her had slipped down to her hips, and she left it there.

"Do you want me to?" I said.

"Naturally. I said so, didn't I? Do you need a written invitation?"

"No. I need a raincheck."

"It's not raining."

"On me it is. Someone's got me shut out in the wet, honey, and I'm beginning to feel the cold."

"What do you mean?"

"Never mind. I'm not sure myself."

"Come off it, you big ugly chump. You spend the night with a girl in bed, and all of a sudden next morning you've got secrets. What's more, you've got the nerve to ask for a raincheck. This is Robin, Horatio. You'll have to do better."

"I'm doing the best I can. It's just that I'm playing this thing by ear."

"What are you going to do?"

"I'm going to Amity."

"Amity?" The surprise in her voice was immediate and real. "What the hell's the idea in going to Amity?"

"No idea. It's not that solid. It isn't even as solid as a hunch. Call it an itch."

"What's itching?"

"Amity's a place that keeps coming up. Constance Markley went to school there. Her best friend at the time was a girl who now has an arrangement with Graham Markley and wants Constance found. Silas Lawler makes trips there. You told me that yourself. All these things together make an itch."

"It's pretty weak. What do you expect to learn?"

"I don't know. Probably nothing. I told you it was just an itch. I'll go to Amity to scratch it, and maybe then it'll quit bothering me."

She reached up and took my face in her hands and pulled it down to hers. Her lips under mine were warm and alive, and her tongue was quick and clever. My tensile strength was low and getting lower, and I was on the shaky verge of letting Amity and good intentions go to the devil for another day, but then the instant before I cracked she pushed me away and dropped her hands.

"Go on," she said. "Go on to Amity."

Gulping air, I stood up and got a bag from the closet. She sat quietly and whistled softly through her teeth while I packed the bag with a couple of clean shirts and a change or two of socks and shorts. At the door on the way out, I stopped and looked back at her, and she was still sitting there in the bed with her shoulders against the headboard and her black eye on the near side watching me from a corner.

"There's a hot plate and a pot and some coffee," I said.

"Thanks very much."

"Make yourself at home for as long as you like."

"This dump a home? Don't be ridiculous."

"Do I get the raincheck?"

"I'll think about it. Call me the first fair day."

"The very first. If you see the janitor, give him my regards."

"Are you going," she said, "or not? If you are, please hurry and get the hell out of here."

I got out, followed by the black eye, and went downstairs to my clunker at the curb. On the way to the office, I stopped at a drug store for a cup of black coffee, which I needed, and it was approximately a quarter after eight when I reached my desk in time to answer the telephone, which was ringing.

"Hello," I said. "Percy Hand speaking."

I was answered by a measured voice I had heard before. It seemed to imply a careful calculation of effect in even its simplest remarks.

"Good-morning, Mr. Hand," it said. "Graham Markley here. Excuse me for calling so early, but it's urgent that I see you."

"Can't it wait? I'm getting ready to leave town."

"I know. That's one of the things I want to talk with you about."

"What are the others?"

"Not now. When I see you."

"All right. I'll wait for you in the office."

"I'd rather you'd come here."

"To your home?"

"No. I'm in Miss Salem's apartment. Can you come immediately?"

"If not sooner," I said.

After hanging up, I opened a couple of pieces of mail left over from yesterday. One was an offer from a finance company to loan me up to a grand on my signature, which I dropped in file thirteen. The other was a check for a hundred dollars from a client, which I tucked in my wallet and stuck in a pocket. The check from Silas Lawler had not had time to arrive yet. When it did arrive, I'd file that in thirteen too, in small pieces.

Desk work concluded, I locked the office and went back to my clunker and drove to the apartment house in which Faith Salem lived, sometimes in the sun. When I pressed the button beside her door, the hour was pressing nine. I had to wait a minute before Maria opened the door. She retreated backward before me, nodding three times, one nod for each backward step.

"Miss Salem and Mr. Markley are having coffee on the terrace," she said.

"They would be pleased to have you join them."

"Thanks," I said. "I know the way."

I waded the pile and crossed the tile and came out onto the terrace. Faith Salem and Graham Markley were sitting at a glass-topped table on which there was a silver tray on which there was a silver coffee service. I could smell the coffee as I approached, and it smelled good. Markley heard me and saw me and stood up to meet me. He was wearing a soft blue sport shirt with a square tail hanging casually outside a pair of darker blue trousers. His feet were shoved into comfortable brown loafers. He didn't look like a man who had come from somewhere else after getting up in the morning. Although he didn't offer to shake hands, he smiled without any apparent effort.

"It was good of you to come so promptly, Mr. Hand," he said. "Will you have coffee with us?"

"Thanks," I said. "I don't mind if I do. Good-morning, Miss Salem."

My claim, as I recall it, was that tousled Robin, sitting up in bed, was the loveliest woman in the world, except one. I was now looking at the exception. She smiled and extended a hand, which I took and held and released after a moment. The cool light of the morning had gathered in her golden hair, and her golden skin had a light that was all its own.

"How are you, Mr. Hand?" she said. "I hope you had a good night."

"As a matter of fact, I did. I had an exceptionally good night. And you?"

It was an innocent enough question, a small courtesy in return for one, but it startled her in reference to the particular night, and after being startled, she was quietly amused. Her smile was now confined to her eyes, and the eyes flicked swiftly to Markley and back to me. I don't know *if* I intended the reference as she took it or not. Maybe I did and didn't realize it. Maybe, as Robin would have said, it was psychological.

"Quite pleasant, thank you," she said. "I was afraid your face might pain you and keep you awake. It looks much better this morning. Won't you sit down?"

I sat down in a wicker chair away from the table, and she poured coffee from the silver pot into a cup of white Bavarian china.

"Do you take cream or sugar?" she said.

"Just coffee," I said.

She passed the cup, and I took it and drank some of the coffee, and it was hot and strong and as good as it smelled. I wondered if Robin had made coffee on the hot plate and was possibly drinking some of it at this moment. Not that it was a possibility of importance. It was just something I happened to wonder.

"Miss Salem tells me that you're planning a trip to Amity," Graham Markley said.

"That's right," I said.

"I would like to know why."

"I'm tired of being poor and ignorant. I intend to matriculate in the college there."

His face, which had maintained a kind of neutrality between amiability and animus, froze all of a sudden in lines of the latter. He lifted his coffee cup and drank from it and set it carefully down again, and the action was obviously a deliberate exercise of control—or a diversion until control had been secured.

"I hope you won't try to entertain me, Mr. Hand. I'm never amused by evasions and clever remarks."

"I'm not trying to entertain you. It's just my awkward way of telling you that you're asking questions about something that's none of your business."

"That's better. I much prefer the direct treatment. However, I disagree with you. You are engaged in a case that involves my wife. Your trip to Amity is connected with this case. This makes it my business."

"Is that so? I wasn't engaged by you. The single fact that the subject of the investigation is your wife doesn't necessarily give you any prerogatives. Moreover, since you prefer the direct treatment, I might add that you've shown an almost incredible indifference to your wife's disappearance up to this time. Why the sudden interest?"

"I'll let that pass. You're clearly a crude man with few sensibilities, and you wouldn't understand the difference between indifference and reticence. I know you better than I want to, Mr. Hand, but that's really not very well. I don't know if you're competent. I don't know if you're honest. I don't know what you will make, or try to make, of a rather delicate matter which concerns me vitally. In brief, I don't trust you, and I intend to establish jurisdiction over this investigation whether you like it or not."

"You're at liberty to try, of course. Along that line, incidentally, you'd just as well get rid of Colly Alder. We had a little understanding last night, Colly and I, and I don't think he'd be of much value to you from now on. Colly's even more incompetent than you suspect me of being. He hasn't bothered to learn the fundamentals of his trade."

He stared in my direction with eyes gone blind in his frozen face, and I could see that he was deciding whether to acknowledge Colly or deny him. He decided finally to acknowledge him. Vision returning to his eyes, he shrugged.

"Thanks for the information. I'll dismiss him at once. Actually, I didn't have a very high regard for him from the first. I suspect that it would be difficult, if not impossible, to find a reliable private detective. Are you ready now to tell me your purpose in going to Amity?"

"Not yet. I was hired by Miss Salem. I'm responsible to Miss Salem. I'm obligated to report my purposes and results to no one but Miss Salem. She hasn't instructed me to report to you, and until she does, I won't."

"That's very commendable of you. I can see that you're devoted to your duty, if not to Miss Salem personally. We've decided, however, that our interest in this is mutual. You may consider that you have been working for both of us equally."

I looked at Faith Salem, and Faith Salem looked back. Her eyes were clear and cool and untroubled, and it was someone besides me who had held her in his arms and kissed her and felt for a few moments the tremor of her passion. She nodded her head gravely.

"Please try to answer any of Mr. Markley's questions," she said.

"All right." I turned back to Markley. "As I've said before, I'm playing this by ear, and the vibrations, such as they are, tell me that it might be profitable to go to Amity. On the other hand, other vibrations tell me that it might not. If I go down there, I may find out which vibrations are right."

"You're still being evasive. You must have a more definite reason."

"No. I'm not being evasive, but I don't intend to commit myself to any position until it's justified. Right now, none is."

"Do you expect to find Mrs. Markley in Amity?"

"I don't expect anything. She was in Amity once, and anywhere she was might be a place to give us a clue where she is."

"That's too tenuous. You're wasting your time and our money."

"I told Miss Salem in the beginning that I'd probably be. She insisted that I take the case anyhow, so I did, and I'm doing the best I can."

"I'll concede that. Nevertheless, it's not good enough. At any rate, something has happened to make Miss Salem change her mind. She feels now that it would be better if you dropped the whole thing."

"Better for her or for you or for me?"

"For you, as a matter of fact. Miss Salem is a generous person. She's very considerate of the welfare of others."

I looked again at Faith Salem and kept on looking at her. Her expression was grave but serene. If she had been subjected to pressure or persuasion or was in the least concerned for herself, it was not apparent. Or was there, perhaps, a mute suggestion of urgency for the merest moment?

"Even mine?" I said.

"Under the circumstances," she said, "especially yours."

"What circumstances?"

"I had a visitor last night. Mr. Markley had dropped in earlier, just after you had gone, but he had to leave for a while to keep another engagement. It was while he was gone that I had the visitor. He told me that I was doing you a disservice by hiring you for this job. He said that something unfortunate would surely happen to you if you kept on with it. He was very convincing, and I believed him."

"Darcy?"

"That was his name. He claimed to be representing Silas Lawler. He gave me Silas Lawler's assurance that Constance and Regis Lawler are all right. It seems that Silas Lawler is devoted to Constance and feels an obligation to his brother. He wants us to quit molesting them."

"Who's molesting them? We can't even find them."

"He wants us to quit trying."

"My face testifies to that. You used a plural pronoun a couple of times. Us, you said. Did Darcy threaten you too?"

"I have the impression that he did, but not directly. He was quite subtle and polite about it."

"That's Darcy. Darcy is probably the politest and most subtle hood on record. He admires virtuosity."

"What do you mean by that?"

"Skip it. It's just a private understanding between Darcy and me. I don't blame you, however, for not wanting to annoy him. Defacing me is one thing. Defacing you would be another, and I can't imagine a greater shame. I'll consider myself dismissed."

"If you think I'm worried about myself, you're mistaken. I told you that I've never really been afraid of anything in my life, which is true, and I'm not afraid of anything now. It's you I'm worried about, if you will only believe me."

"I do believe you, and I wish you'd stop. It makes me uncomfortable to have someone worrying about me."

"Well, since we're dropping the investigation, I can stop, and you can get comfortable. Will you have another cup of coffee before you go?"

I didn't want it, but I said I would. The reason I said I would was because it was a reason for staying there a little longer. As a dismissed detective, I wasn't likely to see her again in proximity, if ever again at all, and I thought it would be pleasant this pleasant morning to look at her while the looking was good. She filled my cup and returned it, and at that moment Maria came out onto the terrace and pointed herself at Markley. He was wanted, she said, on the telephone. Whoever wanted him had said that it was important. Markley hesitated, undecided whether to take the call or not, and then he decided that he would. Standing, he excused himself and went inside.

"I'm glad we've been left alone for a moment or two," Faith Salem said. "It saves me the trouble of contacting you later."

"As I remember," I said, "I've been dismissed. Why should you want to contact me?"

"You're not dismissed, of course. That was only to humor Graham."

"You mean you want me to go on with the investigation?"

"Yes. I still want to know where Constance is."

"Isn't this a pretty fancy piece of deception? It doesn't seem to suit you."

She smiled slowly, the smile spreading upward from her mouth into her eyes, and I was aware again, as I had been the first afternoon on this terrace, of an effect of astringency, an uncompromised compatibility she sustained with herself.

"If you assumed that I'm incapable of deception, you made a mistake. Deception is sometimes necessary."

"True enough. I'd be the last one to deny it. I guess I'm suffering from deflation, to be honest. It appears that you're not worried about my welfare after all."

"I'm not excessively. You impress me as a man who can look after himself."

"Thanks for your confidence. I'll work hard to deserve it."

"Are you being sarcastic about it? You're not dismissed, but you can quit, of course. Do you want to?"

"In a way I do, in a way I don't. Anyway, I won't."

"I didn't think you would."

I stood up and put the white Bavarian cup on the glass-topped table. She stood up beside me, very close, and for an instant I had a dizzy notion that she was going to lean against me, and that I was going to put my arms around her and hold her, and that everything was somehow going to be suddenly different from what it was. But nothing like that happened, and nothing was different. I thanked her for the coffee and said good-bye, and she let me hold her hand again briefly.

"Are you still going to Amity?" she said.

"Yes," I said.

"Call me when you get back," she said.

"I will," I said.

I met Graham Markley in the middle of the black-and-white acre. He turned around and walked with me to the door and held the door politely as I went out.

"No bad feelings, I hope," he said.

"None at all," I said.

He didn't look as if he really cared, one way or the other.

CHAPTER 11

As it turned out, I didn't go to Amity that day. I intended to go, and I kept thinking that I'd surely get started pretty soon, but I was diverted by a couple of things that kept nagging me in the head. The first of these things was a hit-and-run accident that probably didn't have anything to do with anything that concerned me; but it was, nevertheless, another loose end and bothersome. Once, over two years ago, it had played a part in the plans or the fantasy of Regis Lawler, if the story of Robin Robbins could be taken as true. And the story had been told so casually and briefly, as something no more than incidental to something else, that it had the smack of truth.

Robin had discounted it, however. To her, she'd said, it was only Scotch talking, and I was inclined to accept this as being what Robin thought was true, whether it was, in fact, the truth or not. To be sure, Robin was a sly character when it suited her; but I couldn't credit her with the accomplished duplicity it would have taken to make such a beautifully casual reference with some kind of deliberate intent.

I went back to see Lud Anderson again. He wasn't at his desk when I arrived, and it wasn't known when, if ever, he'd be back. I sat down and began waiting and smoking, and it was six cigarettes and thirty minutes later when I saw him flapping toward me in a kind of modified version of the lope once affected by Groucho Marx. He flopped in his chair and opened the drawer of his desk and poured himself a paper cup full of milk. It seemed to me to be the same cup he'd used the last time, and I wondered if it were possible to be fatally poisoned over a period of time by an accretion of old butterfat. After a large swallow and an ulcerous face, he pulled up to his typewriter and rolled paper under the platen.

"How are you, Lud?" I said.

"I see you," he said.

"I wasn't sure. I don't remember hearing you say hello."

"I didn't say it. I was ignoring you in the hope that you'd get the hell away."

My inclination was to spit in his eye and go, but a man looking for a favor can't afford sensitivity, so I pulled on my elephant hide and stayed. Along with his ulcer and his evil disposition, Lud had one of the most cluttered minds in existence among upper bipeds. And I wanted, with his permission and assistance, to poke around for a few minutes in the fabulous accumulation of odds and ends in his long skull.

"I won't stay long," I said. "I thought you might be willing to give me a little information."

"About what?"

"A hit-and-run accident."

"Come off it, Percy. How many hit-and-runs do you think happen in this city?"

"This one was out in a county. About two years ago. Probably longer. A woman was killed, and I don't think it was ever solved."

"Which county?"

"I don't know. Not too far out. I'm hoping you can tell me. Just try to remember where a woman was killed about the time I said."

He finished his milk and leaned back and closed his eyes, and in the enormous transformation that is sometimes worked by such small changes, he looked completely at peace and almost dead. He was really only sifting and sorting the clutter, however, and after a while he raised his lids and fixed me with a baleful eye.

"I remember the one you probably mean," he said. "Woman's name was Spatter. Perfectly mnemonic. Impossible to forget. Can you imagine any name more appropriate for anyone who gets knocked seven ways from Sunday by a speeding automobile?"

"It would certainly be difficult. You remember when it happened?"

"About when you said. Over two years ago, less than three. It wasn't my job, and it's vague."

"Were there any suspects?"

"Not to my knowledge. Someone hit her and killed her and got away, that's all."

"You think the morgue would tell me anything?"

"Why should the morgue tell you anything? There were no witnesses. No clues. Nothing to tell."

"Maybe I'll go down and check it just the same."

"It's your time. If you want to waste it, go ahead."

"Didn't I tell you the other time I was here? Wasting time is what I'm getting paid to do. I suppose the state troopers investigated the thing."

"Sure. And the sheriff. Good old Fat Albert."

"Fat Albert Gerard?"

"Who else? Fat Albert's been sheriff off and on since then. All he has to do is put his name on the ballot, and that's just about all he *does* do. Rakes off a little here and there. Gets a little fatter on the gravy. Don't expect Fat Albert to know anything."

"I used to know Fat Albert when I was a kid. I was born in his county seat, as a matter of fact. I guess it wouldn't hurt to talk with him."

"What could it hurt?" Lud looked at me through slits, as if he could not bear the sight of me full view, but I saw in the slits a bright gleam of interest. "Yesterday you were in here asking about the Markley dame. Today you're back asking about an old hit-and-run. You working two jobs or trying to make a connection?"

"No connection. Not with Markley. Thanks, Lud. I'll send you a quart of milk."

"Go to hell," he said.

Instead, I went down to the morgue, but it didn't pay. About all I learned that I didn't know was the exact date of the accident, which was no more significant than the approximate date, which I'd known already. If it was a loose end of anything that I was trying to put together and make tidy, it was still loose, and I was still wasting time for pay. I left the morgue and walked down the street toward my car.

In a phone booth, I used the directory but not the phone. All I wanted was an address, and the address I wanted was Colly Alder's. Specifically, Colly's office. I was curious about something I frequently get curious about.

Why, I mean, does a person who wants a private detective hire one particular private detective instead of another particular private detective? I suppose the same question could be raised relative to doctors and dentists and lawyers. But there are more people who hire doctors and dentists and lawyers, and there are, therefore, more and easier ways to find out about the ones they hire. Very few people hire detectives, relative speaking. And how do the relative few who do, decide which one? Do they just shop around until they find one with good references? Do they just pick a name they like from the yellow pages? It's an interesting speculation in which I've indulged, and right now I was speculating as to why Graham Markley, who could have afforded anybody, had hired Colly, who was practically nobody. The answer was something I wanted to get, and I thought that I might even be willing to pull Colly's nose to get it.

The office was in a better building in a better block of a better street than I had expected. The office itself, congruously, was also better. It was, as a matter of fact, a suite of offices, if you can call two rooms a suite. There was an outer office and an inner office, and the inner office had a door with a nice pane of frosted glass and Colly's name on the glass above the word PRIVATE. The outer office was small, as was the inner; but both were nicely appointed, and one of the nicest appointments in the outer was a small-sized secretary-receptionist. If I had to describe this small-sized secretary-receptionist in a word, I would say that she was cute. She had curly titian hair and sassy eyes and a pert nose and alert breasts and agreeable legs. She had, besides, an indefinable air of being more than merely employed.

"How do you do?" she said.

"How do you do," I said, as polite as anybody. "Is Colly in?"

"Mr. Alder?"

"Excuse me. Mr. Alder."

"Do you have an appointment?"

"Not I. I just dropped in."

"Would you care to state the nature of your business?"

"I'm not sure. I may only ask Colly a few questions, and I may pull his nose."

She flushed and looked at once hostile and wary, which led me to believe that others had dropped in to pull Colly's nose and that she resented it. She was, definitely, more than merely employed.

"Who shall I say is calling?" she said coldly.

"Percy Hand. Tell Colly I'm determined."

She stood up and smoothed her skirt over her hips and walked on her agreeable legs into Colly's private office. In a couple of minutes she came back, leaving the door open behind her.

"Mr. Alder will see you," she said.

"That's generous of Mr. Alder," I said.

I went in and closed the door that she'd left open. Colly was sitting in a swivel chair behind a desk that was big enough to emphasize his runtiness. He didn't bother to get up and welcome me, but neither did he look as if he wished especially that I hadn't come. As a matter of fact, he looked rather friendly.

"Hello, Colly," I said. "What a fancy den you've got here. I didn't dream you were so prosperous."

"Business is good," he said smugly. "Sit down and have a cigar, Percy."

"Cigars even! I'll just have a cigarette, though, if you don't mind." I sat down in an upholstered chair beside his desk and lit the cigarette and looked around the room. "You must have quite a bit of overhead here, Colly."

"Quite a bit."

"Everything nice and fairly expensive. Even that little red-headed item in the outer office. I'll bet she's fairly expensive, too."

"Rosie? I never counted the cost. Anyhow, you get what you pay for."

"Sure. It's a sweet sentiment. It's fine as long as you keep a good set of values."

"What's that supposed to mean?"

"I've got no idea. I had an idea it might sound profound or something."

He shifted his weight in the swivel and stuck one of his cigars in his mouth. It was long and fat, king-size, and it looked almost ludicrous in the middle of his midget mug.

"You didn't come here to moralize and make an inventory, Percy. What's on your mind?"

"Well, I got to thinking about our little encounter last night, and the more I thought, the curiouser and curiouser I got. Like Alice."

"Like who?"

"Never mind. It's an allusion. Incidentally, you aren't sore about what happened, are you, Colly?"

"It's all in the business." He shrugged and rolled his cigar from one corner to the other. "Why should I be sore?"

"Has Markley called you today?"

"No. Why?"

"He's going to fire you. I told him he might as well, and he agreed."

He sighted me over the unlit tip of the cigar, and for the merest instant his little eyes turned yellow, but then he shrugged again and managed what might have been a laugh.

"I couldn't care less, Percy. I was ready to give it up anyhow."

"That's a sensible attitude. Let me congratulate you. What I've been curious about, though, is how you got on the job in the first place."

"It was a job. It was offered to me. Like you said, I've got quite a bit of overhead."

"But why you? Colly Alder specifically?"

He looked at me in silence for a few seconds, and I began to feel that there was something turning over and over in his mind. I'm pretty sure that he was wondering whether to lie or tell the truth or simply to invite me to go to hell, and I was also pretty sure, when he finally answered, that he'd decided for his own reasons to tell me the truth.

"We'd had a previous contact," he said. "I did some work for him."

"What kind of work?"

"I tailed his wife when she was on the prowl with Regis Lawler. Back before she and Lawler broke loose and ran."

"Why did he want her tailed? According to my information, he wasn't much concerned with what she did."

"True enough. He wasn't. But it doesn't hurt to have evidence on your side in case it's needed. It might save some alimony."

"I see. So you tailed Constance Markley. What did it come to?"

"Nothing. I did the job and made a few reports, and then she and Lawler made their break. That was the end of it."

"Were you on her tail the night she disappeared?"

"I started on it, but I fell off. I lost her."

"Where'd you lose her?"

"At Lawler's apartment. She went in, but she didn't come out. Not the way she went in, I mean. They must have left together by a back way or something."

I was pretty sure, as I said, that Colly had started telling the truth, but I wasn't so sure at all that he was keeping it up. Somehow, I had lost my conviction.

"No wonder Markley's firing you," I said. "It seems like every time he's given you a job, you've fumbled it."

If he was raw, he didn't show it. He leaned back and closed his eyes, and his face had in repose the kind of dry and bloodless and withered look that I have seen in the faces of aging midgets. Not that he was a midget, of course. He was just a runt.

"It makes no difference," he said. "I'm sick and tired of the racket anyhow. I'm thinking of giving it up."

"Is that so? What are you thinking of doing instead?"

"I don't know. I been thinking about going south. Out of the country south. Maybe Mexico. Maybe South America. I've got a yen to lie on a beach and soak up some sun. I been thinking about taking Rosie and going."

"How does Rosie feel about it?"

"Agreeable." He opened his eyes and stared at me with an odd kind of quiet assurance. "Rosie'd go anywhere with me, and I wouldn't go anywhere without Rosie. She's the only person in the world I've ever trusted, and I guess that's because she's the only one who's ever trusted me."

I had again the conviction that he was levelling. Colly and Rosie forever. One of those odd and dedicated pairs that sometimes stick together in the attrition of things that happen. There was a kind of pathos in it that made me, for a moment, feel almost partial to them.

"You and Rosie at Acapulco," I said. "It sounds like fun, and it sounds like money."

"Could be I've got money." He leaned forward earnestly. "How'd you like to earn a little of what I've got?"

"I wouldn't. Why do I have to keep repeating to people that I'm poor but honest?"

"This is honest, Percy. All you have to do to earn a century is one simple thing. One simple thing."

"Nothing doing."

"Maybe you'd do it as a favor."

"Why the hell should I do you a favor?"

"Look, Percy. I know how you feel about me. You don't like me, and you don't trust me, and I don't give a damn. You've got a reputation for being honest, and I need an honest, dependable guy for one hour to do one honest, simple thing."

There was something compelling in the runt's earnestness. He had something on his mind, that was certain, and whatever it was, whatever piece of sordid craft for the sake of Colly Alder, it was something big by the dimensions of Colly's world.

"What one honest, simple thing?" I said.

He took a deep breath and released it in a long sigh that seemed exorbitant as a reaction to my slight concession of asking for information that committed me to nothing.

"This is it. You go to your office tonight at nine and stay until ten. Just an hour. If I haven't called by ten, you go see Rosie in her apartment. She'll have something interesting to tell you. I promise it'll be interesting."

"Nix, Colly." I shook my head and stood up. "I can smell this thing already. Do I look like the kind of cheap crook who'd get himself involved in one of your shady operations just to do a favor or earn a lousy century?"

He popped out of his swivel and came around the desk and put a hand on my arm. I looked down at the hand without moving or speaking until it dropped away. In his voice when he spoke was a peculiar mixed quality of entreaty and sincerity and tiredness.

"You won't get involved in anything, Percy. I swear to God you won't. If I call before ten, you'll never hear anything more about it. If I don't call, you'll hear something you'll be glad to know."

"From Rosie?"

"That's right. From Rosie."

I looked down at him and wondered what it is that makes a man agree in the end to do something he feels he shouldn't do. Maybe it's because he's a fool or avaricious or curious or riding his luck or whatever may be in accordance with the man and the circumstances. In my case, I think, it was because I had this odd conviction of Colly's sincerity and need and something more. Was it fear? I thought it was. He was, I thought, a bad little egg involved with something bigger and worse, and what he wanted to make of me at most was a kind of precarious insurance against some kind of threat. Besides, he had been connected in at least a minor way with Constance Markley, and he knew that I was trying to find her, and he had now appealed to me to do this one honest and simple thing—me of all persons to whom he might have appealed or might have bought. And why would he have chosen me if there were not a connection between the two that might or might not become clear later?

"All right," I said. "From nine to ten. One honest, simple thing."

"Thanks, Percy," he said. "You won't be sorry."

I hoped I wouldn't, but I wasn't sure.

"Give me Rosie's address," I said.

He wrote it on a piece of paper and handed it to me, and I folded it four times into a small square and stuck it in the watch pocket of my pants. Then I went out of the better office and the better building and down the better street.

CHAPTER 12

Since I was not going to Amity that day, I decided that I might as well run out to Fat Albert's county seat. It was the middle of the afternoon when I got there, and it was like coming home. I had, as I'd told Lud Anderson, been born there, and I had lived there until I was old enough to move away. Afterward, until my mother and the old man were dead and buried, I had gone back now and then for a few hours or a day; but now I hardly ever went if it could be avoided, and I was saddened and depressed when it couldn't and I did. The reason for this, I think, was that the town reminded me too clearly of what a particular kid there had planned largely to do, and of how little of it had been done by a particular man.

The county jail was on the east side of town and sat in the middle of a square block of blue grass and crab grass and oaks and maples and catalpa trees. There were lots of catalpa trees in the town. Long green beans come on them in the spring, and in the summer the beans ripen and dry and turn black. They burn as well as a cigarette or a cigar, only faster and hotter; and they give off, when drawn upon, great and satisfying clouds of hot, oily smoke. I guess I smoked, when I was a kid, at least a thousand altogether.

I parked on one side of the square and walked up across the front yard beneath the oaks and maples and catalpas to the jail. A couple of trusties were working in the yard. One of them was pushing a mower, and the other was trimming along the front walk with a pair of grass clippers. Inside the building, a central hall ran straight ahead for about twenty-five feet and terminated at a steel grill. There were cells at the back, I knew, and a flight of narrow stairs ascended to a second floor, where there were more cells. There were a couple of doors on the left side of the hall. One was closed and one was open, and I went through the open one into a littered office.

Fat Albert was standing beside a water cooler with a paper cup in his hand. He had shed his coat and was wearing a faded blue shirt and bright yellow tie. The tie had been loosened and the collar of the shirt opened to free the particular chin it entrapped when fastened. Although it was not a hot day, the shirt was soaked with sweat beneath the arms and around the open collar and under the heavy galluses that crossed it to suspended seersucker pants, and the pants were settled comfortably under the maximum bulge of a monstrous belly. I had known Fat Albert in the old days, and he had been fat enough then to deserve the name, but he had continued to grow more gross by the year until now, I judged, he must surely weigh well over three hundred pounds and possibly closer to four. His eyes were hardly more than twin glitters in an encroachment of flesh.

"Hello, son," he said. "Come on in. You want a drink of water?"

"No, thanks."

He moved over to a desk and sank into a chair that must have been specially made, or at least enlarged and reinforced. His movement, for a man so monstrous, was incredibly easy and light.

"Sit down," he said. "Tell me what's on your mind."

I sat in the chair he indicated and held my hat in my lap.

"I guess you don't remember me," I said.

"Can't say I do."

"Percy Hand. Miller Hand's kid."

"Well, Jesus Christ," he said. "Didn't I have you in jail once for swimming naked in the creek behind the country club?"

"That's right," I said. "You did."

"I remember. I was a deputy at the time. Jailed half a dozen of you kids that day." His laugh was an asthmatic wheeze. "God-damn women used to sit on the veranda of the club house and watch you kids swim naked until they got tired of it, then they'd call here and want us to put you in jail for indecent exposure or something. I finally had to do it to get them off my back."

"We all understood how it was. You only kept us a couple of hours."

"Sure. You can't keep a kid in jail for swimming naked in a creek. I tried to tell those God-damn women that, but they wouldn't listen to reason." He laughed again and peered at me with his little twin glitters. "Didn't I hear that you're a private dick?"

"I try to be."

"Thought so. That's what I heard. Why the hell would anyone become a private dick?"

"I don't know. I've often asked myself the same question."

"Any money in it?"

"It's a living."

"I suppose you run into lots of interesting stuff."

"Once in a while."

"I mean divorce cases. Stuff like that."

"I don't take divorce cases."

"Murder?"

"Not very often. Mostly routine investigations. Pretty dull on the whole."

"That's not the way it is in the books."

"I know. I read the books myself to see how it ought to be."

He leaned back in the massive chair and laced his fingers in front of his belly. His arms, in accomplishing this, were extended almost to their limit. Staring at me, he shook his head slowly from side to side and sucked his lips audibly.

"Miller Hand's kid," he said. "I never dreamed you'd turn into a private dick."

"Neither did I."

"You here on business or just for old time's sake?"

"A little of both."

"What's the business?"

"A hit-and-run accident that happened in your county. I wonder if you can tell me anything about it."

"Hit-and-run? Haven't had one for quite a time. When did it happen?"

I gave him the exact date and watched him close his eyes and suck his lips and cogitate.

"The victim was a woman named Spatter," I said. "She was killed, and the driver was never found."

He raised his lids, exposing the glitters, and blew moist air between his lips. I had the notion that a mountain of flesh was about to collapse in front of me.

"It's coming back to me. The way it looked, this Spatter woman started across the highway just below the crest of a rise. Car came over the rise and hit her. Probably killed her instantly. You're right about no one ever finding the driver. I tried and the troopers tried, but it wasn't any good. No witness, no evidence, nothing at all we could ever get hold of. Why you interested?"

"I'm not sure. There seems to be a connection with someone else I'm interested in."

"You think you may know who the driver was?"

"No. Not that. I guess that's something we'll never know."

"You can't tell. It might come sooner or later. If it does, though, it'll be plain good luck and nothing else. The guilty guy may get drunk and talk too much in a bar. It's happened before. Someone who knows who he is and what he did may get sore for some reason and squeal. That's happened before, too."

"I admit it's possible, but it doesn't seem likely."

"You're right. It's not likely."

"You never did learn anything that wasn't published, then? Some bit of evidence that wasn't enough for a charge but still might be significant?"

"No. Not a thing. In my opinion, you're at dead end fooling around with that old case. Like I said, it'll be plain good luck if it's ever solved."

"I don't doubt it. I wasn't really expecting to learn anything new."

"In that case, let's forget the business and go have a cold beer for old time's sake. I been owing you one for a long time for those two hours I kept you in jail."

"A cold beer sounds good," I said.

We drove in my car to a neighborhood tavern and took turns buying beers while we talked old times, and then I took him back to the jail and left him and drove on alone to the city, and it was about six when I got there, and about seven when I got home after having a steak in a steak house.

The room was neat and lonely. The bed was made, and the litter was cleared, and the room was neat and lonely.

Jim Beam was on the dresser, and I poured a couple of fingers and drank them. There was a note on the dresser beside Jim, and I read it. I *left some coffee in the pot in case you might come back and want it,* the note said. I went over to the hot plate and looked in the pot, and the cold coffee was there. I turned on the plate and waited, and pretty soon the coffee began to get hot and smell like old coffee reheated. I didn't really want any of it, but I drank a cup for the principle of the thing. It was getting dark, but I didn't turn on a light. I don't know that I've ever sat by myself in a neater and lonelier room.

After a while I turned on a light and consulted the telephone directory to see if Robin had a listed number. She had one, and I dialed it, and she answered after the phone had rung three times at her end.

"Hello," she said.

"Thanks for the coffee," I said.

"Whom did you want?" she said.

"I'm satisfied with what I've got," I said.

"Sorry," she said. "You have a wrong number."

The line went dead, and I hung up and sat down on the edge of the bed, which she had not folded into the wall after making, and it seemed to me that one of two things was true. Either she had not wanted to talk in the hearing of someone who was present, or the night before had turned sour in the day after, and the polite pretension was established that the night had never been. I hoped it was the former, but I had a depressed feeling in the neat and lonely room that it was the latter, and pretty soon I got up to see what two more fingers of Jim Beam could do about the feeling.

It didn't do much. After drinking it and waiting for the lift that didn't occur, I took off my shoes and put out the light and lay down on my back on the bed in the darkness. She was only, I thought, a classy little tramp who shouldn't matter much to anyone on earth, just as Faith Salem was only a slightly classier tramp in the sun or out of it, and a man was much better off to make his own coffee and his own bed and to lie alone and uncommitted in his own neat and lonely room. It was then about seven-thirty, an hour and a half before I had to be in my office in faith with Colly, and I guess it was about eight, after a fine half hour of wonderful rationalizing, when the telephone rang and I answered it.

"Hello, ugly," Robin said.

"Whom did you want?" I said. "I think you have a wrong number."

"Don't be silly. I had to say that because Silas was here."

"It occurred to me that he was. On the other hand, I considered the possibility that maybe you'd decided it wouldn't develop. I was lying here thinking about it when you called."

"I thought you were going to Amity."

"I thought I was too, but something kept getting in the way."

"What was it?"

"Several things. I got fired and rehired, and then I went to see a couple of people about an accident, and finally I got an honest and simple job for an hour tonight."

"I don't believe I quite understand all this."

"Neither do I, honey. I'm just moving along with things, and I don't have much of an idea where, if anywhere, I'll wind up."

"Are you still going to Amity?"

"Tomorrow, if nothing else gets in the way."

"I'm sorry I can't come to see you tonight, but it's impossible."

"All right. I'll hang onto the raincheck."

"You do that. Did you like the way I left your room?"

"It was very neat and empty. Do you always leave a room so empty?"

"I have a feeling that you've just paid me a great compliment. Did you?"

"I tried."

"You know something? I'm beginning to like you quite a lot. You're ugly and comfortable and sentimental and capable at times of being exciting. I hope nothing unfortunate happens to you as a result of this case you're on. I think I'd regret it."

"No more than I."

"Well, you'll have to be careful, that's all. Is Darcy still following you?"

"I don't know. I haven't spotted him."

"It isn't likely that you would. Darcy's competent. He's good at anything he undertakes."

"I have evidence of Darcy's competence, and I've already conceded it."

"Maybe you'd better give up."

"I don't think so. Not yet."

"Didn't Silas offer you five grand? It would make you not so poor, and I'd enjoy helping you spend it."

"Don't be so mercenary, honey. The best things in life are free."

"If you're thinking about what I think you're thinking about, it might not be as free as you're thinking it is."

"That's a pretty complex statement, but I get the idea."

"It's just something to consider. How long will you be gone?"

"I don't know. As long as it takes."

"What takes?"

"I don't know that, either. Whatever it is."

"Will you call me when you get back?"

"The first fair day."

"All right. Good-bye, ugly."

"Good-bye," I said.

I hung up and lay down on my back on the bed again. I felt much better than I had, and the room, although still neat, did not seem so lonely. I kept on lying there with my mind pleasantly still and stagnate and unconcerned with pressing problems, and when it got to be eight-thirty I put on my shoes and went to the office.

CHAPTER 13

The glass in the hall door was glazed by the low light in the hall. The light passed on a narrow path through the tiny waiting room and into my office and touched a chair and the corner of the desk, but other objects were no more than deeper shadows in the shadowed room. I stood by the narrow window and looked down into the narrow alley. Above the door of the building opposite, a bulb was burning in a dirty round globe. It cast a soiled perimeter on old brick, and within the perimeter as I stood looking down were two empty cans and a broken bottle and a piece of newspaper, stirred by the draught between buildings, that moved slowly across the area of light and passed into the outer darkness beyond. I had the notion, watching, that I could hear the dry rustle of the paper as it moved. But this was only a trick of imagination in silence and shadows, and I heard nothing, actually, but the sighs and soft complaints of old wood and brick and steel and stone and mortar, the worn substance of old buildings.

I hadn't ignored the possibility that I might be waiting in a trap. Turning away from the window, I sat down behind the desk out of reach of the faint light. In the belly drawer of the desk was a loaded .38 automatic. I opened the drawer and removed the automatic and laid it on the desk in a position convenient to my right hand. Besides the narrow window overlooking the alley, the only way into the room was the door from the hall. I sat and watched for a sudden shadow on the glaze of glass, but there was no shadow and no sound, except the tired sounds of the old building in the night, and I continued to sit there in the expectation of anything or nothing from a little after nine until a little after nine-thirty, about twenty years altogether.

I stood up and stretched and lit a cigarette and sat down again, and all at once I became intensely conscious of the telephone. It crouched on the desk like a black and breathing miniature monster, exploiting in malice its constant threat to shatter the silence with its shrill bell, and tension and malice gathered and grew between us as I waited and waited for another twenty years for the bell to ring, but it never did. At ten o'clock exactly by the luminous dial of the watch on my wrist I stood up again and put the .38 into the pocket of my coat on the right side and went out through the little waiting room and beyond the glazed glass into the hall. After locking the door behind me, I read the address on the scrap of paper Colly Alder had given me, and then I went down to my car and started through the streets toward the street of the address.

I was driven now by a growing sense of urgency. I didn't know why precisely. I only knew that Colly had not called, and that his not calling was somehow of ominous significance to him and possibly to me. It took me almost half an hour to reach the apartment building in which Rosie lived. I ignored the elevator and climbed the stairs to the right floor and the right door. I knocked three times with intervals between, but no one came, and I had a feeling that no one would ever come if I knocked at intervals forever.

Made wary by a premonition of trouble, I used a handkerchief in handling the doorknob. It turned smoothly and silently under pressure, and I slipped into a tiny foyer and took two steps into a living room. A light was burning in a wall bracket and another on a table at the end of a sofa, and I saw immediately by the light that my premonition had been solid. Someone was in trouble, bad trouble, and it might turn out to be Percy Hand, or person or persons unknown, but whoever it was, it wasn't little Rosie the redhead, for Rosie was out of trouble for good and all. I could see her bare feet and ankles and about six inches of green velvet lounging pants projecting beyond the end of the sofa opposite the table with the lamp, and from the position of the scarlet-tipped toes, pointing at the ceiling, it was apparent that she was lying on her back on the floor, and the odds were enormous against her having lain down there for a nap.

I walked across the room and around the sofa and looked down at her. She was not as cute as she had been a few hours ago when she had given me the formal treatment and stared her resentment of my casual threat to pull Colly's nose. Her eyes were open and fixed in anguish and terror, and her slender throat was bruised and crushed by the pressure of fingers. There is, I think, something especially terrible in a killing by hands. A knife or a gun or a bludgeon seem, somehow, to come between the killer and the victim and to share the guilt of the killing. But there is nothing to share the guilt of naked hands. A hands killing has an incomparable quality of cruelty.

In a gesture of futile formality, I knelt beside the body and felt for a pulse, but there was none. The flesh, however, was still warm and pliant, and I was shaken by the anger and pity that were elements of my futility. Rosie the redhead had probably been an avaricious little wench, surely no better and probably not so good as she should have been. But she had at least been faithful and important to one odd and insignificant runt. Most of all, she had been warm and alive and full of juice, and it was wrong and ugly and pitiable that she was now dead by hands. After perhaps thirty seconds beside her, I stood up and went out the way I had come in, using my handkerchief on the knob as I went.

At first I thought I'd call the police, but then I thought I wouldn't. Not yet. Behind the wheel of my car, I lit a cigarette and tried to think logically. What I tried logically to determine was why Rosie had died, and it seemed to me pretty apparent. Colly had said to go see Rosie at ten if he had not called before. Rosie would have, he had said, something interesting to tell me. This meant, no doubt, that Rosie had been possessed of certain dangerous information she was under instructions to divulge if a certain questionable and perilous venture in which Colly was certainly engaged went wrong. In brief, Rosie and I together had been Colly's insurance, and the insurance, like the venture, had gone wrong. Ten o'clock was long past, and Rosie was dead, and Colly had not called, and why hadn't he? Well, it didn't take any genius to answer that one. He hadn't called, I was sure, for the same reason that Rosie hadn't answered the door.

Starting the car, I drove to the good block of good street where Colly had his office, but the street door to the lobby was locked, and I could see, looking up the face of the building, not a single light in any window. I considered rattling up the watchman, if any, but decided against it. Instead, I found a telephone booth in a cigar store and looked up Colly's name in the white pages of the directory. He had a private residential phone, all right, and the place of his residence was a fair hotel on the south side of town. While I was in the booth, on the long chance of better luck than I expected, I spent a dime and dialed his number, but luck was not better, and no one answered, and after three long rings I hung up and returned to my car and drove to the hotel.

The small lobby was empty, and no clerk was in evidence behind the desk. I'd have preferred climbing the stairs unseen, and that's what I'd have done if I'd known the number of Colly's room, but I didn't know it, and so I couldn't. There was a call bell on the desk, and I slapped it with a palm and waited and slapped it again, and pretty soon after the second slap a tousled character came out of a back office digging the sleep out of his eyes. I thought that he might be annoyed and slightly recalcitrant because of being wakened, but he didn't seem to be. He seemed to be no more than anxious to dispose of me and to get back to his cot. I gave him Colly's name, and he checked a file and gave me Colly's number, and I went up to the number while he went back to the cot.

There was a crack of light under Colly's door, and the knob of the door turned easily in my hand. I went into the room and closed the door behind me, and there was no one there but me. A magazine was lying face down on a lumpy sofa. A small radio on a small table was playing softly a current tune. As I looked and listened, the tune ended and a clever deejay announced another tune that was to follow. And in a few seconds, sure enough, it followed. There were two doors in the wall of the room to my left as I stood by the door to the hall. One of the doors was partly open to disclose a closet. The other was tightly closed, and I went over and opened it. Beyond was a bathroom, and Colly was in it. Besides being dead, he was in extremely bad condition.

He was lying in the bathtub with his mouth stuffed full of a handkerchief gag and his head propped against the rise of porcelain beneath the water taps, and his face was swollen and stained by tears. His shirt had been torn open at the throat, and his tie was missing, and the reason the tie was missing was because it had been used to bind his wrists together behind his back. The belt had been removed from his trousers to secure his ankles, and the shoe and sock had been stripped from his left foot. The sole of the foot was deeply burned in three places where something very hot, probably the coal of a cigarette, had been applied. Besides all this, there was a neat small-caliber hole in his forehead just above the bridge of his nose, and a trickle of blood had run down from the hole to add its stain to the stain of tears.

Colly had obviously been tortured in the first place and murdered in the third place, and what had happened between in the second place was surely the telling of a secret that Colly had wanted to keep. It was a competent job of practical sadism, in the general sense of sadism without sex; and the first name that came into my mind was the name of Darcy. But why it should have, what the connection could possibly have been between Darcy and Colly, was something I didn't know and couldn't guess.

I backed out and closed the door and used Colly's private phone to get Homicide at police headquarters. A Sergeant Dooley answered, and I told him who I was and where I was and why I was calling. I also told him the location and condition of Rosie. He told me to wait, and I said I would and hung up and started. It looked, I thought, like a long, long night, and while I was waiting for the police to come in the beginning of what was left of it, I went back in my mind to where I'd left Colly earlier and tried to think on from there.

Colly had been living off the fat—that was apparent—and such affluence was not commensurate with his ability, which was scant, and his practice, which was negligible. He had surely, in brief, been tapping for some time a source of revenue that had nothing to do with what he earned as a somewhat legitimate operator. Moreover, he had been dreaming of points south and Rosie on a beach, and this suggested strongly, if it did not establish, that he had planned a quick and considerable killing and a sudden exit. So he had made the definite arrangements for a dangerous meeting, and Rosie and Percy Hand had been essentials in the arrangements. The name of the person with whom Colly had met had been known to Rosie, and the purpose of the meeting had been known, and it had been her assignment, if anything went wrong for Colly, to see that justice, or at least retribution, was accomplished. I had been picked, or had as a result of a combination of circumstances presented myself, as the agent of the justice or the retribution, whichever you could call it. And maybe, just maybe, there was an association of Colly's interests and mine of which I was still innocent.

Colly hadn't really expected anything to go wrong, of course, because Rosie was supposed to prevent it. To secure his safety, as he thought, he had only to make clear to his blackmail victim that a third party was informed and would take appropriate action if anything happened out of order. But it was imperative to keep the identity of the third party secret, and Colly had, with the natural tendency of a petty operator to evaluate everyone in terms of himself, grossly underestimated his victim. And so he had died, and before he had died he had suffered, and between suffering and dying he had betrayed the one person on earth he had trusted because she had been the only one who trusted him. Colly was dead, and Rosie was dead, and one person had killed both. In the grim urgency of very little time, he had taken Colly's keys and gone to Rosie's apartment to eliminate the remaining threat to his security, and he had been gone from there, at the longest, only a little while before I had arrived.

This was speculation, of course. But it conformed to the facts and Colly's character, and I was satisfied that this was substantially the way that Colly and Rosie had come to die. Somehow or other, in this deal or that, he had got onto a good thing, and so long as he'd exploited it with discretion he'd been tolerated and paid off. But then he'd got greedy—he'd got hot for the big killing—and the killing for his greed had been his own and Rosie's. I sat there organizing the few facts that I had and formulating the theory that I believed so that I could offer them clearly to the police when they came. After what seemed like an inordinate time, but in fact wasn't, they did come; and the one in charge was a Lieutenant Haskett.

I knew Haskett. We were not exactly friends, but there existed between us at least a tolerance based on a mutual moderate respect, and I admit that I was relieved to see him on the job. The night ahead still looked like a very long night indeed. But it might not, after all, be otherwise so bad as it might have been.

Haskett came into the room and spoke curtly, but not harshly, and went past me into the bathroom, where he remained for about twenty minutes with a couple of his men. Then he came out and straddled a straight chair and sat staring at me with his chin resting on the chair's back. His hat was pushed back off a high bald forehead, and his glum expression seemed to indicate that his disposition was calm enough, if not cheerful.

"By God, Percy," he said, "you're finding bodies all over town tonight. How come?"

"Two bodies," I said, "with connections."

He nodded. "Keep on talking. I'm ready to listen."

That's what I did and what he did. I talked and he listened. I told him about Colly's request and how I'd agreed to it. I told him how I'd waited from nine to ten in my office for a call that hadn't come. I told him how I'd gone as per agreement to the apartment of Rosie to find her dead. I told him how I'd then gone to Colly's office and found the building locked. I told him, finally, how I'd come to Colly's room and found him as dead as Rosie, although by a different method. These were facts, the things that had happened. Afterward I told him my theory of why they were facts that had happened, and I had a notion that his generous ears were quivering as he heard me out.

"Let me get this straight," he said. "You think Colly was blackmailing someone. You think he got dissatisfied with a steady but small income and tried for a big bundle. You think his redheaded girl friend was a kind of passive partner in this and was killed because Colly had set her up as a threat to the victim and then, under torture, gave away her identity. Is this right?"

"That's my theory."

"Well, it's a pretty good theory. Try to be just as convincing when you tell me why it happened to be you that Colly got involved in this savory little operation."

"I don't know. I guess it was because I happened to be suitable and convenient. I had some contact with Colly on another matter and had come here to see him earlier today. Or is it yesterday now? Anyhow, that's when he appealed to me."

"What other matter?"

"A private case. It's got nothing to do with this business."

"Okay. I'll find out later if it begins to look important. Now tell me if you've got any idea of the identity of this theoretical blackmail victim and murderer."

"I haven't."

"I didn't think you would." He shook his head without lifting his chin from the back of the chair. "All you've got are a few facts and a lot of notions. Well, I've got some more work to do here, and then I'd better run over and see how Sergeant Dooley and his crew are coming with Rosie. It's sure as hell that there's a connection, one way or another, and it might even turn out to be the way you've said."

He stood up, and I said, "Look, Lieutenant. I ought to go to Amity tomorrow on a case. I won't be gone more than a few days at the most, and if you want me in the meanwhile you'll know where to find me. Okay?"

He looked at me with professional skepticism, but finally he grunted and nodded and took me on faith and my record.

"Okay, I guess. Right now, though, you'd better stick around and go over to Rosie's with me. I might think of some questions for you after I get there. After that, you'll have to go with me to headquarters and sign a statement."

"Sure," I said.

I sat and smoked and waited until he'd finished his work, which took about an hour. Then we went to Rosie's, where everything had been taken care of efficiently by Dooley and his crew, and finally we went to headquarters, where I dictated and signed a statement. I got home around three-thirty.

CHAPTER 14

After the long night and a sluggish morning, I didn't get out of town the next day until ten o'clock. It was three hundred and fifty miles by highway to Amity. In my cold clunker, allowing time for a couple of stops, I did well to average forty miles an hour. Figure it for yourself. It was almost exactly eight and a half hours later when I got there. About six-thirty. I was tired and hungry, and I went to a hotel and registered and went up to my room. I washed and went back down to the coffee shop and got a steak and ate it and went back to the room. By then it was eight. I lit a cigarette and lay down on the bed and began to wonder seriously why I was here and what the hell I was going to do, now that I was.

I thought about a lot of things and people. I thought about Robin Robbins looking like a tough and lovely kid with her beautiful shiner. I thought about Faith Salem lying in the sun. I thought about Silas Lawler and Graham Markley and Regis Lawler and Constance Markley. The last pair were shadows. I couldn't see them, and I couldn't entirely believe in them, and I wished suddenly that I had never heard of them. I thought about Colly Alder and Rosie the redhead, and I wondered if anything could possibly be worth dying for the way Colly and Rosie had died.

I did this thinking about these people, but it didn't get me anywhere. I lay there on the bed in the hotel room for what seemed like an hour, and I was surprised, when I looked at my watch, to learn that less than half that time had passed. The room was oppressive, and I didn't want to stay there any longer. Getting up, I went downstairs and walked around the block and came back to the hotel and bought a newspaper at the tobacco counter and sat down to read it. Tomorrow, I thought, I would begin making inquiries of certain people in an effort to discover, as a beginning, why Silas Lawler came to Amity once a month. But in the meanwhile I would read the paper. I read some of the front page and some of the sports page and all of the comics, and started on the classified ads.

Classified ads interest me. I always read them in the newspapers and in the backs of magazines that publish them. They are filled with the gains and losses and inferred intimacies of classified lives. If you are inclined to be a romantic, you can, by a kind of imaginative interpolation, read a lot of pathos and human interest into them. Someone in Amity, for instance, had lost a dog, and someone wanted to sell a bicycle that was probably once the heart of the life of some kid, and someone named Martha promised to forgive someone named Walter if he would come back from wherever he'd gone. *Someone named Faith Salem wanted to teach you to play the piano for two dollars an hour.*

There it was, and that's the way it sometimes happens. You follow an impulse over three hundred miles because of a thin coincidence. And right away, because of a mild idiosyncrasy, you run into another coincidence that's just a little too much of one to be one. And then the first one, although you don't know why, no longer seems like one either.

I closed my eyes and tried to see Faith Salem lying again in the sun, but I couldn't. I couldn't see her lying in the sun because she was in another town teaching piano lessons for two dollars an hour. It said so in the town's newspaper. I opened my eyes and looked again, just to be certain, and it did. *Piano lessons,* it said. *1828 Canterbury Street, call LO-3314,* it said. *Faith Salem,* it said.

I stood up and folded the newspaper and stuck it in my coat pocket and looked at my watch. The watch said nine. I walked outside and started across the street to the parking lot where I'd left my car. But then, because it was getting late and I didn't know the streets of the town, I turned and came back to the curb in front of the hotel and caught a taxi. I gave the driver the address, 1828 Canterbury Street, and sat back in the seat. The driver repeated the address after me and then concentrated silently on his driving. I didn't try to think or make any guesses. I sat and listened to the ticking of the meter that seemed to be measuring the diminishing time and distance between me and something.

We hit Canterbury Street at 6th and went down it twelve blocks. It was an ordinary residential street, paved with asphalt, with the ordinary variations in quality you will find on most streets in most towns. It started bad and got better and then started getting worse, but it never got really good or as bad in the end as it had started. 1828 was a small white frame house with a fairly deep front lawn and vacant lots between it and the houses on both sides, which were also small and white and frame with fairly deep front lawns. On the corner at the end of the block was a neighborhood drug store with a vertical neon sign above the entrance. It would be a place to call another taxi in case of necessity, and so I paid off the one I had and let it go. I got out and went up a brick walk and across a porch. There was a light showing at a window, but I heard no sound and saw no shadow on the blind. After listening and watching for perhaps a minute, I knocked and waited for perhaps half of another. While the half minute was passing, a car, a Caddy, drove slowly down the street and turned left at the corner.

Without any prelude of sound whatever, the door opened and a woman stood looking out at me. The light behind her left her face in shadow. She was rather short and very slim, almost fragile, and her voice, when she spoke, had an odd quality of detached airiness, as if it had no corporeal source.

"Yes?" she said.

"I'm looking for Miss Faith Salem," I said.

"I'm Faith Salem. What is it you want?"

"Please excuse me for calling so late, but I was unable to get here earlier. My name is Percival Hand. You were referred to me as an excellent piano teacher."

"Thank you. Are you studying piano, Mr. Hand?"

"No." I laughed. "My daughter is the student. We're new in town, and she needs a teacher. As I said, you were recommended. May I come in and discuss it with you?"

"Yes, of course. Please come in."

I stepped past her into a small living room that was softly lighted by a table lamp and a floor lamp. On the floor was a rose-colored rug with an embossed pattern. The furniture was covered with bright chintz or polished cotton, and the windows were framed on three sides by panels and valences of the same color and kind of material. At the far end of the room, which was no farther than a few steps, a baby grand occupied all the space of a corner. Behind me, the woman who called herself Faith Salem closed the door. She came past me into the room and sat down in a chair beside the step-table on which the table lamp was standing. It was apparently the chair in which she had been sitting when I knocked, for a cigarette was burning in a tray on the table and an open book was lying face down beside the tray. The light from the lamp seemed to gather in her face and in the hands she folded in her lap. The hands were quiet, holding each other. The face was thin and pretty and perfectly reposed. I have never seen a more serene face than the face of Constance Markley at that moment. "Sit down, Mr. Hand," she said.

I did. I sat in a chair opposite her and held my hat and had the strange and inappropriate feeling of a visiting minister. I felt, anyhow, the way the minister had always appeared to be feeling when he called on my mother a hundred years ago when I was home.

"What a charming room," I said.

"Thank you." She smiled and nodded. "I like bright colors. They make a place so cheerful. Did you say you are new in Amity, Mr. Hand?"

"Yes. We arrived just recently."

"I see. Do you plan to make your home here permanently?"

"I don't know. It depends on how things work out, Miss Salem. Is that correct? I seem to remember that you're single."

"That's quite correct. I've never married."

"I'm surprised that such a lovely woman has escaped so long. Do you live here alone?"

In her face for a moment was an amused expression that did not disturb the basic serenity, and I wondered if it was prompted by the trite compliment or the impertinent question. At any rate, she ignored the first and answered the second simply.

"Yes. I'm quite alone here. I like living alone."

"Have you lived in Amity long?"

"Many years. I came here as a student in the college and never left. I wouldn't want to live anywhere else."

"Forgive my asking, but don't you find it difficult to live by giving private music lessons?"

"I'm certain that I should if I tried it. I give private lessons only in my off hours. Evenings and weekends. I'm also an instructor in the Amity Conservatory. A private school." She hesitated, looking at me levelly across the short space between us, and I thought that she was now slightly disturbed, for the first time, by my irrelevant questions. "I understand that you should want to make inquiries of a teacher you are considering for your child, Mr. Hand, but yours don't seem very pertinent. Would you like to know something about my training and qualifications?"

"No, thanks. I'm sure that you're very competent, Miss Salem. I'm sorry if my questions seemed out of line. The truth is, I know so little about music myself that I hardly know what to talk about."

"Do you mind telling me who sent you to me, Mr. Hand?"

"As a matter of fact, it was the Conservatory. They recommended you highly, but they didn't mention that you were an instructor there."

"I see. Many students are directed to me that way. The ones who are unable to attend the Conservatory itself, that is."

I looked down at my hat, turning it slowly in my hands, and I didn't like the way I was beginning to feel. No one could accuse me fairly of being a particularly sensitive guy, and ordinarily I am conscious of no corruption in the dubious practices of my trade, dubious practices being by no means restricted to the trade I happen to follow. But now I was beginning to feel somehow unclean, and every little lie was assuming in my mind the character of a monstrous deception. I was suddenly sick of it and wanted to be finished with it, the whole phony case. I had been hired for twenty-five and expenses to find a woman who had disappeared two years ago, and here she was in a town called Amity, living quietly under the name of Faith Salem, which was the name of the woman who had hired me to find her, and it had all been so fantastically quick and easy, a coincidence and an itch and a classified ad, and now there seemed to be nothing more to be done that I had been hired to do.

But where was Regis Lawler? Here was Constance, but where was Regis? Well, I had not been hired to find Regis. I had been hired to find Constance, and I had found her, and that was all of it. Almost all of it, anyhow. All that was left to do for my money was to get up and get away quietly with my unclean feeling after my necessary deceptions. Tomorrow I would drive back where I had come from, and I would report what I had learned to the woman who was paying me, *and* then she would know as much as I did, and what she wanted to do with it was her business and not mine.

There were still, however, so many loose ends. So many mental itches I couldn't scratch. I did not know why Constance had come to Amity. Nor why she had assumed the name of Faith Salem. Nor certainly why, for that matter, the real Faith Salem wanted her found. Nor why Silas Lawler did not. Nor where in the world was Regis Lawler. Nor if, in fact, he was. In the world, that is.

Suddenly I looked up and said, *"Mrs. Markley, where is Regis Lawler?"*

Her expression was queer. It was an expression I remembered for a long time afterward and sometimes saw in the black shag end of the kind of night when a man is vulnerable and cannot sleep. She stared at me for a minute with wide eyes in which there was a creeping dumb pain, and then, in an instant, there was a counter-expression which seemed to be a denial of the pain and the pain's cause. Her lids dropped slowly, as if she were all at once very tired. Sitting there with her hands folded in her lap, she looked as if she were praying, and when she opened her eyes again, the expression of pain and its denial were gone, and there was nothing where they had been but puzzlement.

"What did you call me?" she said.

"Mrs. Markley. Constance Markley."

"If this is a joke, Mr. Hand, it's in very bad taste."

"It's no joke. Your name is Constance Markley, and I asked you where Regis Lawler is."

"I don't know Constance Markley. Nor Regis Lawler." She unfolded her hands and stood up, and she was not angry and apparently no longer puzzled. She had withdrawn behind an impenetrable defense of serenity. "I don't know you either, Mr. Hand. Whoever you are and whatever you came here for, you are obviously not what you represented yourself to be, and you didn't come for the purpose you claimed."

"True. I'm not and I didn't."

"In that case, we have nothing more to discuss. If you will leave quietly, I'll be happy to forget that you ever came."

I did as she suggested. I left quietly. She had said that I was in bad taste, and I guess I was—because the taste was in my mouth, and it was bad.

CHAPTER 15

I turned left at the street toward the drug store on the corner, and I had walked about fifty feet in that direction when a man got out of a parked car and crossed the parking to intercept me. The car was a Caddy I had ridden in before, and the man was Silas Lawler.

"Surprised?" he said amiably.

"Not especially," I said. "I thought it was probably your Caddy that crawled past when I arrived."

"Mine? Not mine, Hand. You were in the house when we got here. Otherwise, you never would have got in at all."

"Well, no matter. I heard you've been coming out here pretty regularly the last couple years."

"I was afraid that might have been one of the things you heard. Robin has a bad habit of knowing things she's not supposed to. Not that it matters much. You've just made me make an extra trip, that's all. Darcy's really annoyed, though. He's the one who's had to tail you since you got into this business, and Darcy doesn't like that kind of work. He figures it's degrading."

"Poor Darcy. I'll have to apologize the next time I see him."

"That could be right now. Just turn your head a little. He's sitting over there behind the wheel of the Caddy."

"I'll do it later. Right now I'm on my way to the corner to call a cab."

"Forget it. Darcy and I wouldn't think of letting you go to all that trouble. We've been waiting all this time just to give you a lift."

"I hope you won't be offended if I decline."

"I'm afraid I would. I'm sensitive that way. I always take it personally if my hospitality's refused. You wouldn't want to hurt my feelings, would you?"

"I wouldn't mind."

"That's not very gracious of you, Hand. I offer you a lift, the least you can do is be courteous about it. What I mean is, get in the Caddy."

"No, thanks. The last time we got together, you didn't behave very well. I don't think I want to associate with you any more."

"It won't be for long."

He took a gun out of his pocket and pointed it at me casually in such a way that it would, if it fired, shoot me casually through the head. I could see, in a glimmer of light, the ugly projection of a silencer.

"Now who's not being gracious?" I said. "It seems to me a guy with any pride wouldn't want to force an invitation on someone."

"Oh, I won't force it. You don't want a lift, have it your own way. I'd just as soon kill you here."

"Wouldn't that be rather risky?"

"I don't think so. Odds are no one will hear anything. You probably wouldn't even be found for a while. Anyhow, I'm not here. I'm in my room at the restaurant. So's Darcy. If it got to be necessary, which it probably wouldn't, we could find half a dozen guests who are with us."

I thought about it and decided that he could. Maybe even a full dozen. And so, after thinking, I conceded.

"I believe you could," I said, "and I've decided to accept the lift after all."

"Thanks," he said. "I appreciate it."

I crossed the parking to the Caddy, and while I was crossing, Darcy reached back from the front seat and unlatched the door, which swung open, and I got in like a paying passenger, with no effort, and Silas Lawler got in after me and closed the door behind him.

"Good-evening, Mr. Hand," Darcy said.

"I'm beginning to doubt it," I said.

He laughed softly and politely and settled under the wheel of the Caddy and started the engine and occupied himself with driving. He drove at a moderate rate of speed, with careful consideration of traffic regulations, and where he drove was out of town on a highway and off the highway onto a country road. I admired the erect and reliable look of the back of his head. He looked from the rear exactly like a man whose vocabulary included virtuoso.

"You're a very stubborn guy, Hand," Silas Lawler said. "You simply won't take advice."

"It's a fault," I said. "All my life I've been getting into trouble because of it."

"You're through with that," he said. "This is the last trouble you'll ever get into."

This was not merely something he was saying. It was something he meant. I began trying to think of some way to change his mind, but I couldn't, and so I began trying then to think of some way to get out of the Caddy and off in some dark field with a sporting chance, but I couldn't think of that either. In the meanwhile, Darcy drove most of another mile and down a slope and across a culvert, and it was pitch dark down there in the little hollow where the culvert was. Silas Lawler leaned forward slightly and told him to stop the Caddy and turn off its lights, and Darcy did. The window beside Darcy was down, and I could hear clearly the infinite variety of little night sounds in the hollow and fields and all around.

"It's a nice night to die," I said.

Lawler sighed. He really did. A long soft sibilant sound with weariness in it. "I'm sorry, Hand. I rather like you, as I've said before, and I wish you hadn't made this necessary."

"I fail to see the necessity," I said.

"That's because you don't know enough about something you know too much about."

"Is that supposed to make sense?"

"It is and it does."

"Excuse me for being obtuse. I don't know much of anything about anything that I can see. I know that Constance Markley is alive and teaching piano lessons in Amity at two bucks per. I know she's calling herself Faith Salem. So what? She's got a right to be alive, and to teach piano lessons, and what she calls herself is her business. I was hired to find her, and I found her. That's a capital offense?"

"Murder is. Murder's capital almost everywhere."

"You've got the wrong guy. I haven't commited any murder."

"I know you haven't," he said. "But Constance has."

I sat and listened to the sounds of the night from the hollow and fields and all around. For a few moments they were thunderously amplified and gathered in my head, and then they faded in an instant to their proper dimensions and places.

So that's where Regis is, I thought. *Regis is where I almost am.*

And I said, "I don't know anything about that. I haven't got a shred of evidence."

"Sorry." He shook his head and took his gun out of his pocket again. "You know where Constance is, and that's enough. You'll tell the client who hired you, and your client will tell others, and the cops will know. Everyone thinks she and Regis ran away together. And when they learn that Regis isn't with her and hasn't ever been, they'll wonder where he is, and he's dead. It wouldn't take them long to find that out. She couldn't hold out against them for an hour. So you see? So you know too much to be trusted. So you've got to die. I'm glad for your sake that it's a nice night for it."

I didn't try to convince him that I'd swap silence for life. The risk in a deal like that would have been all his, and he was too good a gambler to consider it. I sat and listened some more to the sounds in the nice night to die, and I was thinking pretty clearly and understanding a number of things, but there were some other things I wanted to understand and didn't, and they were things that Silas Lawler could explain. Moreover, the longer we talked, the longer I lived, and this was important to me, if not to him.

"All right," I said. "Constance killed Regis, and for some reason you want her to get away with it. Why? After all, Regis was your brother."

"Foster brother."

"Okay. Foster brother. It's still in the family."

"Regis was no damn good. Dying was the best thing he ever did, and he had to have help to do that. He wasn't fit to touch Constance, let alone sleep with her. Why she ever loved him is something I'll never understand. But she did. She loved him, and she killed him."

"It sounds paradoxical, but it's possible. It wouldn't make her the first woman to kill a man she loved. Anyhow, I'm beginning to get a picture. You're on her side, maybe because you both play the piano, and you helped her get away after she killed Regis. I'm guessing that you disposed of the body too, and that poses a puzzle I've been trying to figure. No body, no murder. Why should Constance run? And why, since she did, only to Amity? With your collusion, which she had, why not to Shangri-La or somewhere?"

He stared past me out the window into the audible night, and he seemed to be considering carefully the questions I'd asked. After a while he sighed again, the sibilant weariness with the job he had to do, or thought he had to do. Either way, unless I could prevent it, it would come to the same end for me.

"I guess it won't hurt to tell you," he said. "It'll take a little time, but I've got plenty, and you've got practically none, and maybe it won't hurt to allow you a little more."

"Thanks," I said. "That's generous of you."

"Don't mention it. And you'd better listen close because I'm only going over it once lightly. The night it happened, I went up to Regis's apartment to see him about something personal. I punched the bell a couple times, but no one answered, so I tried the door, and it wasn't locked. I went in, and there they were. Regis on the floor and Constance in a chair. Regis was dead, and she was gone. What I mean, she was in a state of shock. She was paying no more attention to Regis than if he'd just lain down for a nap. She hardly seemed aware that I'd come into the room. I checked Regis and saw that he'd been shot neatly between the eyes. She just sat there and watched me without moving or saying a word, her eyes as big and bright and dry as the eyes of an owl. I asked her what had happened, but she only shook her head and said she didn't understand. She said she was confused and couldn't seem to get things clear in her mind. I wanted to help her. I held her hands and kept talking to her, trying to get her to remember, but even a dumb guy like me could see pretty soon that it wasn't any use. She was gone, not home—and it wasn't any act. She kept insisting she didn't understand. She didn't understand where she was, or why, or who Regis was, or I was, or a damn thing about anything. She said her name was Faith Salem. She said she lived in Amity. She said she just wanted to go home.

"That's the way it was. Whatever I did to help her, I had to do blind. So it was a big chance. So I was an accessory after the fact. To hell with all that. What I finally did, I took her to my room at the restaurant and made her promise to stay there, and then I got Darcy and went back for Regis. Darcy's a guy I trust. About the only guy. We got the body out of the building the back way between us. I've got a place in the country I sometimes go to, and we took Regis there, and Darcy put him in a good deep hole in the ground with a lot of quicklime, and I went back to the restaurant, and that was all for Regis. It was good enough. I haven't lost any sleep because of Regis."

He said all this quietly and easily, without the slightest trace of anger or excitement. He said it in exactly the same manner in which he would kill me in a little while, in his own time when he was good and ready, and I sat and waited for him to finish the story, whatever was left of it. I had a strange and strong sense of revelation—a kind of gathering of loose ends in an obscure pattern.

"She wasn't there," he said. "She had simply walked out of the restaurant and was gone. I went looking for her. I beat the whole damn city, but I never found her. It was two weeks later before I saw her again. I remembered what she'd called herself: Faith Salem. I remembered where she'd said she lived: Amity. I went to Amity and tried to find her, but she wasn't there, and so I waited and kept looking, and finally she came. About two weeks later. I don't know where she'd been in the meanwhile, or how she got there, but she was dressed differently, in a plain suit, and she seemed to be in perfectly good condition. She'd had money in her purse the night she left. I know because I checked. Almost seven hundred dollars. Anyhow, I let her alone and kept watching after her, the same as I've done ever since, waiting to see what she'd do. What she did was rent that little house she lives in and start giving piano lessons.

"She advertised. She called herself Faith Salem. She got along all right, and finally she started teaching at a private conservatory. The point is, she wasn't acting or consciously hiding. *She really thought she was someone named Faith Salem.* I'm pretty ignorant about such things, but I did some reading and fished a little information out of a medico who had a debt in my game rooms, and I finally I got an understanding of it. She was in a kind of condition that's called a fugue. Same name as a kind of musical composition. Unless something happened to shock her out of it, she might go on in this condition for years. Maybe the rest of her life. I figured it was safer for her to leave her as she was. As long as she was in the fugue state, she'd act perfectly normal in the identity she'd assumed and would never give herself away.

"There were obvious dangers, of course. The thing I worried most about was that she'd come out of the fugue. She wouldn't remember anything since the murder, because the fugue period is entirely forgotten after recovery. But the murder was before the fugue, and she'd remember it as the last thing that happened to her, and if I wasn't around to help her then, she'd be done for. God knows what she'd do. So I've been keeping watch over her the best I can, and everything's been all right, except now you've come along and made like a Goddamn detective, and I've got to kill you. And now's the time for it."

That was Darcy's cue. He got out of the front seat and opened the door to the back seat on my side, and I was supposed to get out quietly into the road to save the cushions, but I didn't want to do it. What I wanted to do was live, and in the growing sense of revelation and gathering ends, I thought I could see a faint chance.

"You're making a mistake," I said, "and if you go ahead and finish making it, it won't be your first, but it may very well be your last and worst."

Darcy stood erect by the open door and waited patiently and politely. Silas Lawler made an abrupt gesture with his gun and then became utterly still and silent for the longest several seconds there have ever been. Finally he sighed, and the tension went out of him.

"All right," he said. "Another minute or two. What mistake?"

"Assuming that Constance Markley killed Regis Lawler," I laid.

"She was in the room with him. He was dead."

"Conceded. But you said you checked her purse and saw seven hundred dollars. Did you see a gun?"

"No. No gun."

"Was it in the room? Anywhere in the apartment?"

"I never found it."

"You think maybe she shot him with her finger?"

"I've wondered about that. You explain it."

"I already have. She didn't shoot him."

"You're just guessing."

"Maybe so. But I've got better reasons for my guess than you've got for yours. You think she went off the deep end and killed him because he was getting tired of her. Is that it?"

"She'd had troubles. Things had piled up. Regis was more than a lover. He was a kind of salvation."

"I'll tell you something I've learned. The night Regis died, Constance Markley's maid helped her dress. According to this maid, she was eager. She wasn't angry or depressed or particularly disturbed in any way. She was only eager to see her lover. Does that sound like a woman betrayed and ready to kill? It sounds to me more like a woman who was still ignorant of whatever defections her lover was committing."

"Say she was ignorant. She learned after she got there."

"Sure. And shot him with her finger."

Again, for the time it took to draw and release a long breath. Silas Lawler was silent. At the open door, Darcy shifted his weight with a grating of gravel.

"You got anything else to say?" Lawler said.

"Only what you're already thinking," I said. "Constance Markley didn't kill Regis. Neither did you. *But someone did.* Pretend for a minute that it *was* you. You murdered a man, and the night of the murder the man's mistress vanishes. No one knows where she went. No one knows why. In your mind these two things, the murder and the disappearance, are inevitably associated. It's too big a coincidence. There must be a connection. But what is it? Does she know something that may be placing you in jeopardy every second of your life? Or every second of hers? You must learn this at any cost, and you must learn it before anyone else. You may pretend indifference, but in your mind are the constant uncertainty, the constant fear. They're there for two long years. Then a garden variety private detective stumbles onto something. Maybe. He makes a trip to a town named Amity where the vanished mistress once lived with the same woman who has hired the detective to find her. Several people, in one way or another, learn of this trip. Including you, the murderer. What do these people do? They stay at home and mind their own business. Except you, the murderer. You don't stay at home and mind your own business because your business is in Amity. I keep thinking about the Caddy that crawled past the house while I was on the porch. I *wonder whose it was?*"

That was all I had. It wasn't much, but it was all, and I had a strong conviction that it was true. Silas Lawler was still, and so was Darcy. In the stillness, like a living and measurable organism, was a growing sense of compelling urgency. I could hear it at last in Lawler's voice when he spoke again.

"Darcy," he said, "let's go back."

Darcy got under the wheel, and we turned and went. We went as fast as the Caddy's horses could run on the road and highway and streets they had to follow. On Canterbury Street, in front of the small frame house in which Constance Markley lived, Silas Lawler and I got out on the parking and looked up across the lawn to the house, and the light was still on the blind behind the window, and everything was quiet. Then, after a terrible interval in which urgency was slowly becoming farce, there was a shadow on the blind that was not a woman's, a scream in the house that was.

The scream was not loud, not long, and there was no shadow and no sound by the time Lawler and I reached the porch. I was faster than he, running on longer legs, and he was a step behind me when I threw open the door to see Constance Markley hanging by the neck from the hands of her husband.

Interrupted in murder, he turned his face toward us in the precise instant that Lawler fired, and in another instant he was dead.

Constance Markley began to scream again.

She screamed and screamed and screamed.

I had a notion that the screams were two years old.

CHAPTER 16

It took a week to get things cleared up. I stayed in Amity that week, and then I went home, and the first thing I did after getting there was to go see Lieutenant Haskett.

"Hello, Percy," he said. "I've been expecting you."

"Sorry to keep you waiting."

"It's all right. I hear you've been pretty busy. Sit down and explain the connection between that mess at Amity and the mess you called me into up at Colly Alder's."

"What makes you think there's a connection?"

"Isn't there?"

"Yes."

"That's what makes me think so."

I sat down and fished for a smoke, and he patiently rubbed his bald head with the knuckles of one hand while I found the smoke and a light and got them together.

"Graham Markley killed Colly and Rosie," I said. "It was the result of a situation that developed from his killing of Regis Lawler two years before."

"You can skip the Lawler killing. I'm briefed on it."

"Okay. The point is, Colly knew Markley had killed Lawler, and he lived comfortably off the knowledge for a couple of years. He was discreet in his demands, and Markley apparently preferred to tolerate a nuisance rather than risk another murder at that time. Besides, Colly was incriminated himself, and probably Markley thought he might be useful in certain ways. Then I got on the trail of Constance Markley, and Graham Markley put Colly on mine, and Colly got his wind up. Like Markley himself, he was afraid that Constance knew all about the murder of Lawler, and Colly had made himself, besides a blackmailer, a kind of accessory. He could see the possibility of a long prison term ahead of him if Constance was found and the truth came out. So he decided to go for a big bundle and get out, and that was his mistake. Markley could be pushed only gently, and only so far. He went to his meeting with Colly, and he killed Colly and killed Rosie, and I think it happened just about the way I told you that night."

"A very savory character. Lovable. How did Colly learn about the murder of Lawler?"

"He'd been gathering evidence for Markley concerning Constance and Lawler. Apparently Markley planned to use the evidence to beat an alimony rap if it became necessary. Alimony and blackmail seem to have been the big problems in Markley's life. Besides murder, I mean. Anyhow, the night Markley went to Regis Lawler's apartment and killed him, Colly was outside and saw him arrive and saw him leave later. Colly was supposed to be tailing Constance, I think, and I don't know certainly how he happened to be waiting outside Lawler's place. Maybe he'd lost Constance and intended to pick her up there if and when she came that night. Maybe he knew she'd show up eventually and just came on ahead to short-circuit the job of following her. However it happened, he was there and saw Markley, and you can imagine the jolt it gave him. Right away, being Colly, he began to sniff something. As soon as Markley left, Colly went up to Lawler's apartment. He found Lawler dead, just as Constance was to find him later, and that was the beginning of Colly's affluence. The beginning of his own death, too."

I took a breath, and Haskett knuckled his skull and squinted at me dourly.

"You got any evidence to support this?"

"No. But it fits. It's neat."

"It is. Convenient, too. It's always a help if you can hang several murders on one guy. Sort of tidies things up in a hurry. Well, it won't hurt Markley to take the rap. You can only execute a man once at the most, and you can't even do that if he happens to be dead."

There wasn't a lot to say after that was said, and after a while, being very tired, I went home and went to bed, although it was still daylight, and I slept with only a few bad dreams until the next day, when I went up to the apartment of Faith Salem. I made a point of going when the sun was on the terrace. Maria let me in, and I crossed the acres of pile and tile and went out where Faith was. She was lying on her back on the bright soft pad with one forearm across her eyes to shade them from the light. She didn't move the arm when I came out.

"Good afternoon, Mr. Hand," she said.

"Good afternoon," I said.

"Excuse me for not getting up. Will you please sit down?"

"It's all right," I said. "Thanks."

I sat down in a wicker chair. It was very warm on the terrace in the sun, but the warmth was pleasant, and after a few minutes I began to feel it in my bones. Faith Salem's lean brown body remained motionless, except for the barely perceptible rise and fall of her breasts in breathing, and I suspected that her eyes were closed under her arm.

"So it was Graham after all," she said.

"That's what you suspected, wasn't it?"

"In a way. I had a feeling, but it was a feeling that he had done something to Constance. I can't understand why he killed this man."

"Not because of the affair. He didn't care about that."

"Why, then?"

"As I told someone yesterday, there seemed to be two big problems in Graham Markley's life. Alimony and blackmail. They both happened to him more than once. As for the blackmail, Regis Lawler was the first to try it. It went back to something that happened about three years ago. Graham Markley and Constance were driving back from the country. They'd been on a party, and Graham was drunk. He hit a woman on the highway and killed her and kept right on driving. It was a nasty business. Constance isn't a strong person, nor even a very pleasant person, and she agreed with Graham that it was better to keep quiet about the incident. It's easy for some people to rationalize that kind of position. Then, in due time, after the death of her child, she met Regis Lawler, and she wanted to do with Regis just what everyone actually assumed she had done. She wanted to run away from everything—her marriage, her guilt, everything associated with her child's death, all the unhappiness that people like her seem doomed to accumulate.

"Apparently Regis let her believe that he might be willing to go along with this, but he had no money. Silas Lawler told me that Regis stole seventy-five grand from a wall safe at the restaurant, but it wasn't so. It was only a rather clumsy lie Silas used to make their running away plausible. What really happened was that Constance told Regis about the woman's death on the highway, and Regis tried the blackmail, although he actually had no intention, it seems, of going anywhere at all with Constance. The blackmail didn't work. Whatever passes for pride in an egoist like Markley would never let him hand over a small fortune to his wife's lover, although he could and did submit to blackmail for a while under other circumstances. He went to Lawler's apartment and killed him.

"When Constance went there later the same night and found his body, she knew immediately what had surely happened. Her own burden of guilt was too heavy to bear in addition to everything else, and so she escaped it by becoming another person to whom none of this had ever happened. It was something that could only have happened under certain conditions to a certain kind of person. She became you, the one person she had ever known that she completely admired and envied, and she went back to the place where she had, for a time, been happier than she had ever been before or since. She became you, and she went back to Amity.

"With a break or two and a couple of hunches, I got the idea that she might be there, and I went there to see if I could find her, and Graham Markley learned from you where I was going. He was terribly afraid of what Constance might know and tell if she was found, and it was imperative, as he saw it, to get rid of her for good and all. And so he followed me and found her and tried to kill her, but it didn't turn out that way."

"I'm sorry I told him," she said. "It was a mistake."

"Not for me," I said. "It made me a smart guy instead of a corpse."

"What do you mean?"

"Nothing," I said. "It's not important."

The sun in the sky was nearing the tooled ridge of stone. I wished for a drink, but nobody brought one. Faith Salem's breasts rose and fell, rose and fell. Her long brown legs stirred slightly in the sun. I wondered if I should tell her about Colly and Rosie and decided not. Maybe, if I didn't, she would never know, depending on whether the police broke the case wide open or closed it quietly on a theory.

"Did Constance tell all this?" she said.

"The part about the accident and the blackmail and the murder. Not the rest."

"How strange it is. How strange simply to forget everything and become someone else."

"Strange enough, but not incredible. It's happened before. People have gone half around the world and lived undetected in new identities for years."

"Is she all right now?"

"She remembers who she is and everything that happened until she found the body of Regis Lawler in his apartment. She doesn't remember anything that happened in the time of the fugue. That's a long way from all right, I guess, but it's as good as she can hope for."

"Why become me? Why me of all people?"

There was honest wonderment in her voice. Looking at her, the lean brown length of her, I could have told her why, but I didn't. I had a feeling that it was time to be going, and I stood up.

"I think I'd better leave now," I said.

"Yes," she said. "I think you'd better."

"I'll send you a bill."

"Of course. I'll be here as long as the rent's paid. That's about three months."

"Are you going to look at me before I leave?"

"I don't think so. Do you mind letting yourself out?"

"I don't mind."

"Good-bye, then, Mr. Hand. I wish you had a lot of money. It's a shame you're so poor."

"Yes, it is," I said. "It's a crying shame."

She never moved or looked at me, and I went away. The next day I sent her a bill, and two days after that I got a check. I saw her her twice again, but not to speak to. Once she was coming out of a shop alone, and once she was going into a theater on the arm of a man. I learned later that she married a very rich brewer and went to live in Milwaukee.

Robin? I see her every now and then on a fair day.

THE END

LET ME KILL YOU, SWEETHEART!

by Fletcher Flora

CHAPTER 1

Late in the summer of the year in which Avis Pisano was murdered in the fall, there were three young men from Rutherford who stayed for short periods at different times at the lake resort where Avis worked as a waitress. Avis was a pretty girl but not very bright. The three young men were bright enough but not on the surface exceptional. The lake resort, called Sylvan Green, was not exceptional either. It consisted of the small hotel in which Avis worked and a dozen cabins scattered among the trees along the shore. From Rutherford to Sylvan Green was about two hundred miles. Rutherford was a small town, a railroad division point, and it was even less exceptional than Sylvan Green.

Besides living in Rutherford and going that summer to the same resort, the three young men had three significant things in common:

In the first place, they were all determined, each for his own reasons, to marry the same girl;

In the second place, and in spite of the first, they all went to bed with Avis Pisano, who was extremely enthusiastic about making love;

In the third place, they were all called Curly at times by people who knew them well. In the cases of two of the young men, the nickname was applied because it was a fair description of the character of their hair. In the case of the third, by the kind of suitability one finds in calling a fat man Skinny and a skinny man Fatty, the nickname was applied because it was an exact opposite description of his hair, which was straight and cropped close.

In addition to these significant things which these three young men of Rutherford had in common, there was another significant thing, which they did *not* have in common.

One of them had murdered Avis Pisano.

He murdered her in November, about a week before Thanksgiving, and he had made love to her in the preceding July, three days before August. Immediately after loving her and long before murdering her, he lay and listened to the summer night, and he could hear many sounds. He could hear the breathing of the girl beside him, and he could hear the lapping of the water of the lake outside, and he could hear an owl mourning among the trees on the lake's shore and he could hear the voices of a man and a woman in a boat on the water, and he could hear over and under and beyond all these the thousands of tiny unidentifiable sounds in a kind of integrated whole that was the total sound of the night.

It was hot in the little cabin. He could feel the perspiration gather in the hair in his armpits and trickle down across his flesh onto the damp sheet on the bed. The perspiration seemed scalding hot, though it actually wasn't. But it stank. He could smell his own body, and he could smell the body of the girl. The two bodies, his and hers, were hot and adherent at points of contact. In the violation of his normal fastidiousness, he felt for himself a deep disgust that was almost nauseous. For the girl, the easy conquest, he felt intense contempt. He had cultivated her with contempt and taken her with contempt, and the contempt in satiety was swollen and gross. Rolling over abruptly, he lay on his side with his back to her.

At first it had seemed amusing enough, an interlude of no consequence, and it had begun without any particular intent. As a matter of fact, now in the hot night, he could not remember how it had begun exactly, the first significant word or look that had initiated everything that was to follow. Her name was Avis, and she was a waitress in the dining room of the small hotel up the slope, a pretty girl with long legs and a long, calculating look, and it was apparent to him in the beginning of their relationship, while it was still casual, that she considered him much more significant materially than he actually was, that she was weighing concessions against possible profits. This had amused him, being so exorbitantly evaluated, and he had slyly contributed with small lies to the perpetuation of her mistake. It served her right for being so transparently calculating, the damned little fool, but he had been conscious tonight, a little while ago in the time of the ultimate intimacy, that the element of calculation seemed to be gone from her. He was surprised and alarmed and a little sickened by the honest intensity of her immediate response, and it was all so adherent and hot and fetid, and all, in the end, so goddamned easy.

The breathing of the girl Avis was softer and smoother now, punctuated at intervals with little sounds like whimpers. The whimpering sounds caused him to remember the coarse moans she had made in her orgiastic excitement, and remembrance made him nauseated again, and even as he remembered and was nauseated, she reached out and touched his hair and trailed her fingers down his back.

"Curly," she whispered. "Sweet Curly."

He had acquired the nickname as a boy, and he had never resented the use of it by anyone before, but now he resented it fiercely, and he wished he had not told her about it. Perhaps it was because of the way she spoke it, with a kind of plea in the whisper, as if she were begging him to be kind and tender and to go on making love to her. It was bad enough to have become involved with her in a tangle of perspiring passion, and to touch her now or to commit himself to tenderness in the aftermath would be utterly intolerable. He thought all at once of the girl he wanted to marry, and he had in the instant an irrational and terrifying feeling that she was standing beside them in the darkness of the small hot room and had been standing there from the beginning to witness with revulsion his carnal performance. With terror came anger for the girl responsible, the girl beside him in the sticky bed, and the terror would have been multiplied and the anger deadlier if he had known then, as he did not, that she had played the percentages once too often and had lost. To remove himself from her entreating fingers, he rolled off the bed and stood up in the darkness beside it.

"What's the matter?" Avis Pisano said.

"Nothing," he said. "I thought I'd have a cigarette, that's all."

"Light one for me, too, and come back."

He lit a cigarette and handed it to her, but he did not light one for himself nor resume his place beside her. He walked across the room to a window and looked out across the lake. The moon cast upon it a silver shadow of light. Beyond the window the night air stirred and crept inside to dry his body and cool its fever. Behind him from the bed, he could smell the smoke of the cigarette and hear the long whispers of breath that expelled it from her lungs.

"Come back," she said. "Please come back."

"It's too hot," he said. "It's cooler here by the window." He wished she would go. He wished she would get up and dress and go away and that he might never see her again or remember again what they had done. Anger and impatience must have edged his words, for she did not speak for a full minute, and when she did speak again, it was again with the suggestion of pleading in her voice.

"You're angry," she said. "What have I done to make you angry?"

"I'm not angry. As I said. I only want to stand here by the window for a while."

"Didn't I please you? Is that why you are angry?"

"Goddamn it, I am not angry. Why must you keep insisting that I am?"

Her bald reference to their intimacy revolted him and increased the anger that he denied. Now that they were finished, why in hell couldn't she simply get up and go away and leave him alone? He could feel her behind him in the bed, staring at his back through the darkness and trying to decide in her rather dull mind what it was that she had done to offend him. As a matter of fact, he did not know precisely himself, for she had only been agreeable and ardent in a function to which she was obviously no stranger, and now afterward it was certain that she wanted only a little consideration and tenderness in return. It was merely a casual relationship, cheap and sordid but no more, and there was surely no rational reason for his feeling that he had somehow imperiled himself, that he had in the last half hour started everything going wrong that had before been going so beautifully right.

"If you're worried," she said, "you needn't be. I don't expect anything from you."

"Of course not. I didn't imagine that you did."

He forced himself to turn away from the window and approach the bed. He took her cigarette from her fingers and crushed it in a tray. Proceeding now under a compulsion to go ahead with whatever was necessary to get the whole business finished with as little emotion as possible, he sat down beside her and began to stroke her shoulders and forearms with his hands.

"I'm sorry," he said. "Honestly, it's only that it's so hot in here."

"That's all right. I just didn't want you to spoil everything."

She sighed and began to breathe unevenly again. Feeling the response of her flesh to his fingers, he stood up abruptly.

"Why don't we go outside and walk along the lake for a while?" he said.

"Do you want to?"

"Yes. It will be much cooler there."

"All right. I'll go if you want to."

She got up and began to dress, and he sat down again on the edge of the bed and lit a cigarette and kept his eyes averted.

He thought that he would go away in the morning. He would get up early and go away.

CHAPTER 2

The conductor did not see Avis Pisano when she boarded the train, but later, when he went through her car checking tickets, he noticed her particularly because he thought she looked ill.

It was cold in the coach in which she rode. Huddled in her seat with her cheap fur coat pulled closely about her, she shivered and stared through the window at the gray countryside slipping drearily past under a dull steel sky. Ordinarily, her face would have been prettier than most faces are, but now it was livid and lax and gave an effect of pathetic futility to the cosmetics that tried to brighten it. She looked very tired as well as ill and her lips were stretched tight on her teeth and turned down at the corners in an expression of ugly bitterness.

She presented her ticket without speaking, and he punched it and went on about his duties, but a long time later, when he came through the car again, she looked up at him and said, "How long will it be before we reach Rutherford?"

He stopped and consulted his massive silver watch. Looking down at her, thinking again that she looked really quite ill, he felt for her a thin but genuine compassion that did not disturb him greatly but was sufficient to lift her in his mind above the gray, collective anonymity of his other passengers.

"We're due in fifty-five minutes," he said.

"Thank you."

She began looking again at the back of the seat ahead of her, seeming as she did so to shrivel and grow smaller inside the cheap fur coat, and he remained for a moment looking down at her, unconsciously replacing the massive silver watch in its assigned pocket to complete a routine action that had become long ago the ritual of his peculiar dedication.

"Are you all right?" he said.

"Yes, thank you."

"Well, it won't be long now. Just fifty-five minutes to Rutherford."

He moved on down the aisle and out of the coach and did not return until forty minutes later when the train was stopping at the last station before Rutherford.

The train ground to a halt through a series of diminishing jerks. Through her window, the girl was looking down upon the rough, red brick of a small platform washed with watery yellow light, and the conductor also looked out past the reflection of her impaired face in the glass. A man passed along the platform, pulling behind him a four-wheeled baggage truck on which there was no baggage. The man was dressed in striped overalls and a short, blue, heavy jacket. On his head was a black-and-red plaid cap with flaps turned down over his ears. The train started again with another series of jerks, gathering momentum as it labored into the night.

"Rutherford in fifteen minutes," the conductor said.

Avis Pisano glanced up and down. "Thank you," she said.

Fifteen minutes later when the train stopped finally at Rutherford the conductor was standing on the station platform as Avis descended from the car with the assistance of the porter. It was very cold on the platform, the wind sweeping across from north to south, between the station and the tracks. The station was really quite large for a small town, because Rutherford was a division point. The center section of the building, smoke stone and stucco, was obviously the main waiting room. North of the waiting room in the same structure was the baggage room. South of the waiting room was a restaurant with steamed-over windows. Standing just outside the entrance to the restaurant, leaning back with his shoulders braced against the wall of the building, was a man in a too-short topcoat that reached not quite to his knees. He looked across at the girl Avis, the only passenger to descend from the train, with what seemed mild curiosity, and she, the conductor noticed, seemed to be looking with a kind of quiet desperation for someone who should have met her but apparently hadn't. Then, following the direction of her gaze down the length of the platform into the darkness beyond the reach of the yellow light, he saw dimly, as she did, the shifting and separation of a shadow, the lifting of an arm in a gesture of beckoning.

Carrying her bag, she hurried down the wind in response.

CHAPTER 3

It was no later than half-past-six when Purvy Stubbs went down to the station to watch the seven o five come in from the north. It wasn't much of a train, only a local and hardly worth watching, but to Purvy a train was a train, and any one you cared to mention was worth watching any time you cared to choose. This was because trains were in his head and blood.

Something is always getting in someone's head and blood and this can be good or bad, depending upon circumstances. If it's something a person can do something about, quite a bit can frequently be made of it. Beethoven did this with music, for instance, and Van Gogh with painting. On the other hand, if it's something a person can't take advantage of, it's very likely to become eventually a bitterness and a frustration. Thereafter, everything the person does in his life, no matter how commendable, will be to him of little importance simply because it seems so insignificant compared with whatever it was that had got into his head and blood earlier to torment him all his days. There was a poem written about a fellow in this condition. His name was Miniver Cheevy, and he was miserable.

With Purvy Stubbs, it was trains. As a kid, Purvy was shy and awkward, and he never grew out of it, but he had remarkable things in his head. Besides the trains, that is. Among these remarkable things were little scraps of poetry about this and that. These scraps of poetry were all delicate little bits of pretty sound, and you'd have thought that merely saying them aloud would have shattered them completely. Not that Purvy often said them aloud. They were just there in his head with the trains, left over from the reading he'd done, and every now and then with the proper association one or another of them would get into his consciousness and he'd think about it for a while.

It's impossible to say just how and when the trains got into Purvy's head but he was certainly very young when it happened. This in itself was nothing unusual for lots of kids like trains and plan to be engineers when they grow up. In most cases they change their minds and become farmers or grocers or doctors or something else, and there is no trauma in the change at all. It's just that wanting to be an engineer is something they grow out of painlessly. It's not even very unusual when a kid wants to be an engineer and actually grows up to be one. It's often done and is a satisfaction to both the kids and the people who own railroads. What made Purvy's case different and rather sad was that he could never accomplish either of these two alternatives. He never got to be an engineer and he never quit wanting. He stayed shy and he stayed awkward, and the trains stayed right in his head.

He was born and had lived all his life in the town of Rutherford. Except for being a division point on the railroad, Rutherford was not much of a town, and no matter where you lived in it, you were not far from the tracks. You could hear the long sad sound of whistles at all hours of the day and night, and possibly this was the way the trains got into Purvy's head in the beginning. Possibly they got into his head through his ears, for the whistling of a train is a seductive sound, and it is a sound that would quite likely stick around in the kind of head that was inclined to retain scraps of poetry and things of that sort.

Purvy's devotion to trains made his Old Man wild. The Old Man was president of the Rutherford Commercial Bank, and he was determined that Purvy was going to be president after him. For a long time he was as patient as he could be with Purvy's deviation, thinking that it was just kid stuff that Purvy would grow out of in good time, but as Purvy grew older he only seemed to become more and more set in his deviant devotion. He slipped off to the station to meet every train that he possibly could, sometimes cutting classes at school to do it, and at the sound of a whistle he'd quiver like an old hound scenting game. Old Man Stubbs privately wondered if he'd given issue to some kind of unclassified maniac, and as time went on and Purvy got worse instead of better, he very nearly lost all patience entirely.

The situation broke wide open the summer after Purvy graduated from high school. One day he went into his Old Man's office at the bank, and it was pretty apparent immediately that he had screwed up his nerve and had come to get something off his chest.

"Well, Dad," he said, "I want to tell you that I've decided to take a job with the railroad and try to work my way up to being an engineer."

The Old Man just sat and looked across his desk at Purvy for a few seconds, and then he stood up and walked over to the door of the office and closed it quietly. After that, he turned and gave Purvy a terrific kick in the ass. It was a kind of sneak attack, and Purvy wasn't braced for it. It catapulted him into a chair, and he fell sprawling all the way to the floor. Rolling over, he sat up on the floor and kept sitting there for a while, looking up at his Old Man as if he couldn't believe what had happened to him.

"Well, Purvy," his Old Man said quietly, "I'm bound to tell you that you aren't going to do any such thing, and if there's one thing I'm determined about, it's that there isn't going to be any goddamned engineer jockey in the Stubbs family. What you'll do, you'll either go off to college in the fall like a reasonable person, or you'll come into the bank and work like a dog until you know the banking business inside out. You have a choice of either one of these two prospects, and that's all the choice you have, and if I hear any more hocus pocus about working for the railroad, I'll kick your ass up and down Main Street."

Purvy stood up slowly and rubbed his bruised butt.

"I'm not going to college," he said. "I'm sure as hell certain of that."

"All right," his Old Man said. "Then you'll come to work in the bank, and you can count on it."

That's what Purvy did. He went to work in the bank. The truth is, he was a nice big lubber, but he didn't have the guts to face up to his Old Man over an issue. He didn't learn much about banking, however, because he wasn't particularly bright and didn't have his heart in it, and he never got the trains out of his head. Now that there was no hope of his ever becoming an engineer, the trains took on for him a kind of bittersweet, antebellum-like quality that made them more seductive than ever. Whenever he went to the station and saw an engineer bringing in one of the big steam jobs or a diesel, he felt like a fellow thinking of someone else in bed with a girl he wanted to be in bed with himself. He learned to hate his Old Man in a quiet way that never showed, and every single chance he got, he went to the station to watch the trains. He knew the time schedule of arrivals and departure by heart, and if his Old Man didn't watch him like a hawk, he was apt to walk right out of the bank during business hours. After business hours, unless a most critical contingency prevented it, you could depend on his being at the station for every train without exception, excluding only the few that passed while he was sleeping. He was almost always pretty early, and he was early this night, as has been said, the night that Avis Pisano came to Rutherford.

He went first into the warm waiting room and saw by the large electric clock above the ticket agent's window that he had fully thirty-five minutes to wait. Then he went into the men's toilet and relieved himself. It was like that in cold weather, it seemed. He had to relieve himself much oftener than was necessary in warmer seasons. Coming out of the toilet, he stood and looked slowly around the waiting room, feeling for the hard oak benches something that was very much like reverence, as if they were pews in a chapel, listening with a rather sorrowful contentment to the friendly staccato sound of the telegraph in the ticket agent's office. There was no one in the room except himself and an old man in a ragged black overcoat who was asleep in a sitting position on one of the benches. The old man's jaws, surmounting sleep, worked slowly and rhythmically at a cud of tobacco. Beside his feet on the floor was a squat brass cuspidor. Seeing the cuspidor, Purvy thought suddenly of one of those little scraps of poetry that were always moving in and out of his head according to associations.

A bright bowl of brass is beautiful to the Lord, he thought.

He held the scrap in his head for a minute and then let it go. Crossing the waiting room, his too-short topcoat flapping around his knees, he went out onto the windy brick platform beyond which the parallel pairs of steel tracks lay shining in yellow light to the edge of darkness. The wind sliced through his clothing and threatened to tear his hat from his head. Turning his back to it, he went down to the entrance of the restaurant in the south end of the depot. Inside, the warmth was as sudden and almost as shocking as the cold had been on the platform. It was a steamy kind of warmth, heavy with the rich aroma of hot coffee. There was an oval counter in the middle of the room with stools all around the circumference, and inside the oval, the only other person present when Purvy entered, was the waitress, Phoebe Keeley. She was pouring water into one of a pair of polished coffee urns.

Purvy sat down on one of the stools at the counter and said, "Hello, Pheeb."

Phoebe finished pouring the water into the urn and replaced the cap. When she was finished, she smoothed her starched white uniform over her broad hips and walked slowly, with a swaying of the hips, down to where Purvy was sitting. She was a big girl, easily five-ten in the flat heeled shoes she wore to work in, and she carried quite a bit of weight even for so much height. It was firm weight, however, nothing flabby, and satisfactorily distributed. Beneath thick blond hair done in a bun on her neck, her face was broad and not pretty, but it possessed, nevertheless, a heavy attractiveness that was somehow primitive in its effect. As a matter of fact, the total effect that Phoebe created was so substantial that it seemed tangible, something that could be touched and contained in the hands and turned over and over for inspection. A lot of the fellows around Rutherford thought Phoebe would be really something to have, and a couple could have testified to the truth of it, but Purvy wasn't one of them and wasn't likely to be. He was too busy thinking about trains.

"Hello, Purvy," Phoebe said. "Come down to see the seven-o-five in?"

"That's right."

"You want a cup of coffee?"

"I wouldn't mind."

Phoebe returned to the urns and drew a cup and brought it back. Purvy watched her broad hips going and coming under the white uniform, but he didn't get the pleasure out of it that most fellows would have got. He stuck his nose into the steam rising from the coffee and took a couple of long sniffs.

"Smells good, Pheeb," he said. "Thanks a lot."

He didn't offer to pay for it, because it was understood that it wasn't expected. Free coffee was a kind of tribute to his long devotion to the trains. Sometimes he bought a sandwich or a couple of doughnuts or something of the sort, and for these he was expected to pay, but never for coffee.

"Is it getting colder outside?" Phoebe asked.

"It's pretty cold. The wind's come up."

"Well, it's about time for it, I guess. Almost Thanksgiving."

"You're right, at that. Next Thursday. Time sure gets away, doesn't it, Pheeb? It only seems like a little while ago that it was Thanksgiving last year."

"Oh, I don't know. Seems to me that time usually drags in this dump. I get awfully damned bored sometimes."

"Dump? Rutherford, you mean? Rutherford isn't so bad, Pheeb. There are lots of worse places than Rutherford."

"All I can say is, I'd hate like hell to live in a worse one. I wonder why it's always on Thursday. Thanksgiving, that is. Did the Pilgrims start it or something?"

"Hell, no, Pheeb. The Pilgrims didn't start it at all. Not as a regular holiday, anyhow. Lincoln started it with a proclamation right after the Civil War or sometime around then."

"Is that a fact? I thought the Pilgrims started it."

"Well, they didn't. They didn't have a damn thing to do with it. Not as a regular holiday."

She stared at him silently for a moment, shaking her head slowly from side to side.

"You're an odd ball, Purvy," she said.

Purvy looked surprised, almost shocked, as if it were entirely beyond his understanding that anyone would consider him in any way unusual.

"Me? What's so odd about me?"

"Well, take those lousy trains for instance. Why are you always hanging around to watch the lousy trains come in and go out?"

"I like trains. Ever since I can remember, I've liked trains. When I was a kid I wanted to be an engineer. I wanted to be an engineer more than anything else in the world."

"Why didn't you be one, then? It seems to me that almost anyone could be an engineer."

"My Old Man wouldn't let me. He made me go into the bank."

"How the hell could he make you go into the bank if you didn't want to?"

Purvy thought about this for quite a while, as if he were wondering himself, for the first time in ten long years, just how his Old Man had managed it.

"I don't really know," he said. "I just sort of gave up on the trains and went into the bank like he wanted."

"Well, I'll be damned! Did you tell him how *much* you wanted to be an engineer?"

"Sure. I told him, all right."

"What did he say?"

"To tell the truth, he didn't say anything right off. First thing he did, he kicked my ass. He kicked it so hard I fell over a chair and landed on the floor. Then he told me I couldn't be an engineer and would have to go into the bank, and I went."

"I'd be ashamed to admit it, if I were you. Damned if I wouldn't. A great big lubber letting his Old Man kick his ass and boss him around like a baby. Not that I'm ready to say he was wrong. Personally, I can't see why anyone who could work in a bank and maybe someday be president of it would want to be a crummy engineer."

"People aren't alike," Purvy said. "It's all a matter of how you feel about different things."

He drank some of his coffee, listening already for the first sound of the whistle of the seven-o-five, and Phoebe looked at him and started shaking her head again.

"I'll bet you're lonely," she said, a note of surprise in her voice, as if this were a sudden flash of insight, a kind of revelation.

"I guess everyone is lonely sometimes," he said.

"What you need is to forget these goddamned trains and how you wanted to be an engineer and go find yourself a nice girl. A fellow whose Old Man is president of a bank could find all kinds of interesting girls if he wanted to."

"I don't think so," Purvy said. "I've never much liked girls to tell the truth."

"Oh, crap, Purvy. A girl with anything on the ball could *make* you like her. I'll bet I could make you like me plenty if I took the notion. Besides, I heard you been going to Phyllis Bagby's every once in a while, and that doesn't sound to me like a fellow who doesn't like girls. The way I get it, you've got to like Phyllis about twenty dollars worth before she'll give you any time at all."

"Well, Phyllis isn't exactly a girl. She's thirty-five, thirty-six if she's a day, and I only go there once in a while to talk."

"*Talk*! You go to Phyllis Bagby's to *talk*? Purvy, you're a big liar, that's what you are."

"It's the truth, just the same," Purvy said, "whether you believe it or not."

"Well, you can bet I don't believe it," Phoebe said, "unless talk is a new word for what fellows go to Phyllis Bagby's for." At that moment, two men came in from the platform and sat on stools at the oval, and Phoebe departed to wait on them. Left alone, Purvy began to think, now that Pheeb had brought her up, of Phyllis Bagby. The way Pheeb had referred to her, you'd think Phyllis was a common whore or something, but that wasn't true. It was a long way from being true. The truth was, Phyllis didn't have anything at all for sale except the services of her nice beauty parlor on Main Street, and those were for women, naturally, and she took in more than enough money from the beauty parlor alone and had no need whatever to supplement her income from other activities. The reason Phyllis had a kind of reputation around town, the kind just intimated by Pheeb, was because she was a real looker who made you think of a regular professional model or something, being a beauty operator and knowing just how to accomplish it. She liked men and wanted them, but she didn't want them around her neck. Anything she gave them or got from them she was given and gained in free exchange, without commitments from either side. She was a widow whose husband had died young in an automobile accident out on the highway, and she had a nice brick house on Locust Street with a colored girl to take care of it. The colored girl's name was Lutie, and when you went to the house in the evening, Lutie was sometimes there to let you in, if you were let in at all, but afterward she went off and was not seen again.

It was a joke how Purvy got acquainted with Phyllis. It happened one night when Purvy was especially depressed from thinking about how the only life he would ever have was being misspent in a bank while fine big steamers and diesels were running free on the rails of the American continent. As a consequence, he was hating his Old Man with even more intensity than usual and was unconsciously wanting to get even for everything by doing something he knew his Old Man would disapprove of. Dropping into the taproom of the Division Hotel, he drank a couple of beers and got to talking with Guy Butler, who was drinking bourbon in water and had been at it for quite a while before Purvy arrived.

Guy was a dark, thin-faced fellow with a bitter mouth and a crippled left hand. The hand had been smashed up in the war almost twelve years before, when Guy was just barely twenty, and it was a particular misfortune in his case because he had been a kind of genius at playing the fiddle, a child prodigy, and had already, before the war, been a soloist a couple of times with the philharmonic orchestra up in the city. When he had returned from the war with the smashed hand, the one he fingered the fiddle with, he had tried to learn to play all over again with his left, but it hadn't worked out. He had tried desperately and for a long time, in a sort of feverish agony, and often in the middle of the night, if you passed the house he lived in with his folks, you could hear him working and working and working and getting slowly a little better. As a matter of fact, he got damn good, but damn good is not good enough for someone who has been superb, and one afternoon he walked into the living room of his house and quietly laid his fiddle and bow on the fire in the fireplace, and that was the end of it. His mother was there having some tea with a couple of ladies at the time, and after Guy had put the fiddle and bow on the fire and walked out, she sat and watched them burn and began to cry silently with the tears rolling down her face.

Purvy liked Guy. He liked him and felt sorry for him and was of the opinion that they had quite a bit in common because of the fiddle in Guy's case and the trains in his. He had to admit, though, that Guy's trouble had distorted his personality to some extent. Ordinarily he was friendly and kind and generous, but sometimes, when he got to floating his bitterness in bourbon, he became cruel. It was as if he were slashing out in retaliation at anyone handy, and that's the way it was the night he sent Purvy to Phyllis's. It was a cruel kind of joke on Purvy and Phyllis both, either one of whom would have given almost anything in the world to make Guy's hand good again.

Talking with Guy in the taproom, Purvy couldn't help letting his depression show, and he even said a few hard things about his Old Man, which was something he seldom did. He thought them frequently, but he seldom said them. Guy listened silently, staring into his bourbon and water with a twist to his thin lips, and after a while he looked up at Purvy with a shine in his dark eyes that should have been sufficient to warn Purvy to back off.

"What you need," he said, "is to go see Phyllis Bagby."

"Phyllis Bagby?" Purvy said. "What good would that do?"

"You'll be surprised at the good Phyl can do you. The least you can do, anyhow, is to give her a chance. I'm always going to see Phyl when I need pepping up."

Purvy had heard a few of the things that were said about Phyllis, of course, and it crossed his mind right then that his going to see her would be something that would infuriate his Old Man. Tomorrow he would remark rather casually that he had been around to Phyllis's, and then he would have the pleasure of listening to the Old Man fume and call him names. Once it had disturbed him to be called things like a bum and a fat, lubberly fool by his Old Man, but it didn't disturb him any longer, and in fact it gave him pleasure because he had come to understand that the names applied to him as a defective son were a reflection in consanguinity upon the father, and that this reflection was also understood and detested by the Old Man. For this reason, the Old Man's vulnerability to his own abuse, the idea of going to Phyllis Bagby's appealed to Purvy, but he was afraid that it wouldn't work out. Actually, he was simply afraid, period. Phyllis was a damn attractive woman with a smooth sophistication about her, downright beautiful in Purvy's eyes, and therefore formidable. He was afraid of all women, except his mother and a few elderly relatives and maybe Pheeb Keeley at the depot restaurant, and he was particularly afraid, because of his awareness of his own homeliness, of beautiful women. Moreover, the area of his fear was excessively enlarged by the fact that he considered any woman who was even vaguely pretty to be beautiful. Now, entertaining Guy's suggestion, he simply couldn't believe that Phyllis would have anything whatever to do with him, and she might even have him hauled in by a cop for trying to molest her or something.

"I wouldn't have the nerve to go," he said.

"Why not?"

"I don't know anything about women to tell the truth."

"Anything you need to know, Phyllis can teach you. Phyllis is the greatest little teacher you could hope to find."

"Well, she's so beautiful and sophisticated and everything. She must have all kinds of men who want to go to see her, and it isn't like that she'd have anything to do with me."

"Oh, hell. You walk in and lay twenty bucks on the table and she'll have something to do with you, all right."

"Really? No kidding, Guy?"

"Sure. Why the hell should I kid you? It's nothing to me if you go or not."

"I know, but Phyllis has her beauty parlor and makes plenty of money, and I can't understand why she'd have to do anything like that on the side."

"Don't ask me. Maybe she gives it to charity."

"Anyhow," Purvy said, "I couldn't do it. I just haven't got the nerve."

Guy shrugged and finished his bourbon and water and went away. Purvy stayed at the bar and had another beer, and after that, without quite knowing precisely when or how the decision was made, he found himself outside walking toward the street Phyllis Bagby lived on. When he reached her house, he hung around on the front walk for quite a while, his decision wavering, but finally he hurried up in a moment of resolution and rang the doorbell. Lutie wasn't on duty that night, and Phyllis herself answered the bell. She was dressed in a brown woolen dress that looked expensive, simple and perfectly fitted, and she smiled at Purvy in a friendly way. "Hello," she said.

He said hello and stood there awkwardly in the light from inside as she looked him up and down.

"Well?" she said.

"Guy Butler said I should come," he said.

"Guy? Come for what?"

"Well, he just suggested it. You know."

"I'm afraid I don't." She smiled at him, and the smile was still friendly. "You're Purvy Stubbs, aren't you?"

"Yes, I am. That's who I am, all right."

"Maybe you'd better come in and explain. Would you like to come in?"

"Yes, I would. Thank you very much."

He went in, and she closed the door after him. The living room of the brick house was conservatively and comfortably furnished, softly lighted, and there was a fire in a brick fireplace at the far end of the room. He stood just inside the door, turning his hat around and around in his hands, and after a moment she took the hat with a little laugh and tossed it into a chair.

"You seem to be upset about something," she said. "Maybe it would help if you'd just tell me directly what it is you want. It might make you feel better."

He didn't know how to tell her. As a matter of fact, he was wishing desperately that he hadn't been such a fool as to act upon Guy's suggestion. Maybe Phyllis sold it, but she surely didn't look or act like someone who did, and he had an uneasy feeling, in excess of the unease he would have felt in any event, that he was in an extremely precarious position. Suddenly, with an imperious compulsion to get it settled one way or another, he walked forward to a small table at the end of a sofa and laid a twenty dollar bill on it. Then he stood looking at it, feeling like more of a lubberly fool than his Old Man had ever said, and Phyllis stood looking at it too. After a while she said softly, "What's that for?"

"You know," he said. "To pay."

He didn't have the nerve to look at her, and it was a good thing that he didn't, for she had gone deathly white with fury, and it would have terrified him if he'd seen the way she looked at that moment. However, she could see very well that Guy had duped him, and she felt sorry for him, and in the end the compassion transcended the fury. She walked past him and picked up the twenty and handed it back to him.

"Put it in your pocket," she said. "Go back and tell Guy Butler never to come to my house again so long as he lives. Tell him never to speak to me or look at me or suggest in any way that we are in the same world."

That was enough for Purvy. Even he was capable of understanding then that Guy had played a wicked joke on him, one of those cruel things Guy would do when bitterness and bourbon collaborated. He took the twenty, still without looking at Phyllis, and turned and started stumbling across to the door. He was almost there when Phyllis spoke again.

"Wait a minute," she said.

He stopped, standing with his back to her, waiting.

"Don't tell him that," she said. "I'd be sorry if Guy never came again. He can't help being cruel now and then, and we must both forgive him. You and I. Tomorrow he'll be sorry and will come to tell me so."

He agreed with her, knowing Guy, but was unable to say it. He swallowed painfully and remained silent.

"If you knew him as I do," she said, "you'd know I'm telling the truth."

"I know him pretty well," he said, "and I know it's true. I won't hold it against Guy, but I'm sorry I did what I did."

"Well, never mind, so long as you understand."

Before he could think better of it, because it got into his head so suddenly, he said, "*All places shall be hell that are not heaven.*"

"What?" she said.

"Nothing. It's something someone wrote. I was thinking how it kind of fits Guy. Sometimes, anyhow. When he's feeling particularly bad and does things like this. He can't ever be what he wants, and he knows he can't be, and so nothing else is any good at all, and it's like being in hell, and he does things to people."

"You're right. It certainly fits him." She paused, looking at his broad back. "Maybe there are times when it fits all of us. Tell me, Purvy, would you like to stay a while?"

After she said that, he had the nerve to turn and look at her. He could see plainly that she wasn't angry, more sad than anything else, and he smiled at her sheepishly.

"If you don't mind," he said.

"All right. Come and sit with me in front of the fire, and we'll talk."

They sat there for quite a long time, a couple of hours all told, and he told her about the trains and his frustration and his quiet hatred for his Old Man, and afterward he felt remarkably relieved and good, and inexpressibly happy that he'd come, even though it had meant showing, in the beginning, what a fool he was. During the two hours. Phyllis had three calls on the telephone, and it was apparent from the way she talked that at least two of them were from men who wanted dates, and she turned them down, and it made him very proud that she should do this for him. The truth was she truly liked him, and she felt sorry for him because he was an ineffectual fellow with a simple dream that was already dead, and this made her feel warm and generous toward him. A generous and kindly woman by nature, when Phyllis felt sorry for someone the extent of her generosity was incredible.

At last she said, "What you came for. You really didn't want it, did you?"

"I don't think so," he said.

She laughed. "I really didn't think you did. Even in the beginning. I don't know whether to feel respected or scorned."

"It's not you," he said, getting red in the face. "It's me."

"Why did you come in the first place, really?"

"I don't know. I guess I thought it was something my Old Man wouldn't like, and that's why."

"I see. Well, anyhow, I hope you haven't been disappointed."

"Oh, no. It was fine talking to you."

"Thanks. When you feel like talking again, give me another try."

"I'll do that. You bet I will."

And he did. Sometimes it was possible for her to see him, and sometimes it was not possible, and sometimes he went and stayed all evening, and sometimes he went and stayed for a little while and left when someone else came later, but in the beginning and always afterward there was nothing between them but talk, and this was the simple truth whether Pheeb Keeley or anyone else believed it or not. It was one of the good things in his life, a partial compensation for the abortive and still-born engineer.

The whistle. The seven-o-five.

Hearing faintly the sorrowful, seductive sound, he got off the stool in the restaurant and hurried outside, taking up a position on the cold platform beside the door. The laboring local puffed in and stopped, blowing off steam as if it were panting with exhaustion. The porter and the conductor came down the steps from one of the coaches and stood waiting. Soon a single passenger, a young woman, appeared at the top of the steps and handed down her bag. She followed it herself and stood beside it on the platform. In her cheap fur coat, she seemed, somehow, abandoned and wretched and on the verge of a definitive defeat. Suddenly, after looking down the platform toward the south, she picked up her bag and moved quickly in that direction.

Turning his head to follow her progress with, mild curiosity, Purvy saw for an instant in the darkness beyond the platform a shadowy figure that receded and disappeared. In the instant that he saw it, there was something that struggled for recognition, a vague familiarity of shape or size or distinctive motion, but then it faded as the figure faded and could not later be recalled.

CHAPTER 4

Curly stood and waited in the cold darkness and cursed the winter and the remembrance of summer. He had left his car parked near the tracks almost two blocks away in a place where the odds were great that it would not be seen and had walked up along the tracks to his present position in the darkness at the south end of the station platform. He was standing in a very small park, an aesthetic effort to relieve the raw ugliness that was natural to the environment of a railroad yard the grass dead under his feet but the surrounding upright and Pfitzer Junipers living and green and rustling in the wind that swept down across the platform from the north. Near him in the little park was a stone bench, but it was too cold to sit down. He stood well back from the edge of yellow light, waiting for a train and a girl on it, and he wished with all his strength that the train would wreck, pile up in a mass of distorted steel, and that the girl would die swiftly in the cold night and be out of his life forever.

He remembered the summer and cursed it. He remembered the fool he had been in the summer, and he cursed the fool. It had been late summer, really, almost the end of July, and he had gone by himself to this small resort called Sylvan Green. Two weeks were all he had for a vacation, besides being all that he could afford, and he had intended to spend them quietly in fishing and loafing and, most of all, in making plans for a girl named Lauren Haig, cool and golden and wanted. He had already made a remarkably careful study of this girl before going to Sylvan Green, and he had cataloged precisely and exploited deliberately her vulnerabilities, which were many, and he was certain at last that she was in love with him and almost ready to do whatever he asked, but now it was all in jeopardy, the entire precise and beautiful conquest, because of a cheap little bitch in a summer resort who was had too easily.

He had left Sylvan Green the morning after the consummating night in the hot little cabin, and it was not until quite some time later that he had received in Rutherford the first of the notes. And that was the beginning of fear and hate and the threat of ruin, his precise and beautiful plans in sudden jeopardy, and it was all the result—oh, damn, damn, damn the cursed luck!—of a cheap little glandular episode at a third-rate little resort with a rotten little bitch who was at this moment coming through the night in a train to ruin him utterly.

The last of the notes had come that afternoon, and it had been lying on the table in the hall when he got home in the evening. With a rising feeling of sickness, he had recognized it immediately for what it was. The pastel envelope whose pretensions could not hide its cheapness. The cramped, childish script on the front of it. The absurd green ink with which she always wrote. He had picked it up and carried it upstairs with him to his room. In previous notes, exactly three of them, there had been nothing more than entreaty, a desperate supplication that he had known how to appease without explicit concession or denial. Reading this one, he had been struck by its quality of bitter determination, the expression of a decision reached in a manifestation of unsuspected strength.

You must help me, she had written. *It's the least you can do, and you've got to do it. I won't listen to any more lies or anything, because I know very well you've been lying to me, and I'm coming to see you on the train that will arrive in Rutherford at five minutes after seven Saturday evening. I hope you will meet me, but if you don't I will go to a hotel and make you see me later. I'm not mad or anything, and I know everything is as much my fault as yours, but none of that makes any difference now, and it's just that I need help, and you've got to help me. If you don't do it willingly, I'll go to a lawyer or someone like that and make you, and I will also go to this girl you say you want to marry and tell her all about it and maybe spoil everything for you. I'm sorry this happened, and I'm sorry I have to be this way about it, but it's partly your fault because you don't seem to want to help me.*

That was all, and it had terrified him. And after the terror had come an interval of icy fury. Tearing the note and the envelope into fragments, he had sat on the edge of his bed and pounded a fist into a palm and cursed her to hell in a whispered monotone for what must have been five full minutes. Following the fury and the cursing was the final phrase of his adjustment to the emergency, and hour or more of calm, almost impersonal calculation that had pleased him greatly as a sign of his own immense potential and had filled him with a kind of singing sense of dark immeasurable power. In that hour he decided that the simple and complete resolution of his difficulty was for Avis Pisano to die.

Now, suddenly from far down the tracks, came the whistle of the seven-o-five. Almost immediately, within seconds, the door of the restaurant in the depot opened, and Purvy Stubbs came out and stood waiting on the platform with his shoulders braced against the wall of the building. Unconsciously, though it wasn't necessary, Curly shrank back a little into the darkness of the park. It was imperative, of course, that he not be seen. It was absolutely imperative that he never be significantly connected in anyone's mind with the girl on the train who was going to die. Watching Purvy, that lubberly, lonely man at his incredible devotions in the coal-smoked chapel of his dead, ridiculous gods, Curly smiled with derision, feeling in the uplifting magnitude of his own design a cold contempt for lesser destinies and commitments.

The train had come into the station now and stopped. Avis descended from her coach and stood alone on the platform, and he was gratified to discover, now that the necessity of her dying was established, that he was able to look at her with practically no emotion whatever, neither anger nor fear nor even futile regret. Aware all at once that she was looking directly at him down the lighted length of the platform, he stepped forward three paces and raised an arm and stepped quickly back again in shadows. But she had seen him. Lifting her bag from the platform at her feet, she hurried toward him.

In the dark little park among the rustling Junipers, she stopped and set her bag on the dead grass and said tiredly, "Hello, Curly."

"Hello, Avis," he said evenly.

"Are you angry with me?"

"No. Not at all. I'm not at all angry."

"I thought you might be. I dare say I'd be, if I were in your place."

"I'm not angry, but you shouldn't have come here. I told you not to come."

"I'm sick and frightened, Curly. I don't know what to do, and I had to come. I couldn't help it."

"I suppose so. Does anyone know you came to see me? Have you told anyone who you are?"

"No. I didn't think you'd want me to. Honestly, Curly, I don't want to cause trouble, but you've got to help me. You've simply got to."

"All right. Anyhow, there's no use standing here in the cold. Come on. I've got a car parked down here by the tracks."

They walked south along the tracks to his car, and if she wondered why he had left it in such a distant and secluded place, she asked no questions. Perhaps she was by then too tired and ill to wonder about anything, or too relieved that he had come to meet her at all. After they had walked a short way, she placed a hand on his arm to steady herself, and he could feel her trembling.

The distance he had driven to the station had not been sufficient to start warm air coming through the heater, and it was very cold in the car. He put her into the front seat, and she sat huddled against the door, hugging her coat about her. Getting in on the other side, he could hear her teeth chattering. He started the engine and drove away parallel to the tracks, turning right at the first crossing.

"You're going away from town," she said. "Where are you taking me?"

"Only for a drive. It will give us a chance to talk."

"I'm very tired. I want to go to a hotel."

"I'll take you to a hotel soon."

"I'm cold. I think I'm going to be sick."

"We'll have some warm air in a minute. It won't take long."

He continued to drive west on the street, and in ten minutes they had reached the edge of town and turned south on a farm-to-market road. After the turn, he reached down and switched on the heater, and the small fan began to hum and force warm air into the interior of the car. Avis sighed and let her head fall back against the seat, and he could almost feel in his own flesh and bones the sudden, sensuous relaxing of her tired body. After a minute, when the warmth had increased, she turned her head and looked at him with dry, entreating eyes. She opened her coat and he saw she wore a short sleeveless evening dress. She saw with a queer little catch of pain that was not related to parasitic life the fine line of his boyish profile touched and softened by the tiny lights on the dash. Her evaluation of masculine appeal was still basically adolescent, substantially as superficial as it had been ten or fifteen years ago, and seeing him now and feeling the pain, she succumbed at once to the same emotion that had already made her a fool and had destroyed vague plans and was now threatening to destroy her life.

Impulsively, she said, "Do you remember the night in the cabin? Do you ever think of it?"

He turned his head to look at her quickly, immediately looking away again. Remember? He remembered, all right. Good Christ, the remembrance made him sick to his stomach. The hot adherence, the soft swift surrender, the utter idiocy that had put everything he really wanted in its present peril.

"How could I forget?" he said. "It's the reason we're in all this trouble, isn't it?"

"Yes," she said tiredly, "I guess it is."

They had now traveled several miles down the graveled road and had not passed a single car. Suddenly, scarcely decreasing their speed, he turned left, east, and descended a grade on a frozen dirt road, crossing at the bottom a stone culvert that spanned a dry slough. Beyond the culvert, he pulled over onto the shoulder of the road and stopped. Turning off the lights but leaving the engine idling to continue the heat, he twisted on the seat to face her.

"Now," he said.

"What?"

"Now let's talk. You want to settle this, don't you?"

"I want you to help me, that's all."

"How? Tell me how I can help you."

She raised her eyes, still dry and entreating, and lowered them again.

"The simplest way would be to marry me. I don't suppose you'd consider marrying me?"

"No. It's impossible. I've explained all that to you."

"I know. The other girl you're in love with."

"That's right."

"Then you must give me some money."

"I've already given you some."

"A hundred dollars."

"It was all I had."

"Just the same, it wasn't enough. A hundred dollars doesn't go very far."

"Maybe I can give you some more later. How much will you need?"

"I've been thinking about it, and I've decided that I ought to have at least a thousand."

"A thousand! Goddamn it, where would I get a thousand dollars?"

"You could borrow it. You could get it from a bank or something."

"Don't be insane. Banks don't loan that much money without some kind of security. Besides, how could I explain what I wanted it for?"

"I don't know. I'm not clever about such things, but I'm sure you could think of something if you really wanted to."

"I can't do it, and that's that. Why should you need so much?"

"Well, I won't be able to work for quite a while, and there will be the doctor and the hospital, and I'll have to have something for the baby."

"You needn't worry about that. There are plenty of places that take unwanted babies. Homes and places like that where they hold them for adoption."

"I'm going to keep it."

"Oh, Jesus! Have you lost your mind completely?"

"No. I've thought and thought about it, and I'm going to keep it."

"How can you possibly take care of it?"

"I'll work. I won't be the first woman who's taken care of a child by herself."

"What if you have trouble? You might get sick or lose your job or something like that. Will you expect me to go on helping forever?"

"Not unless it's absolutely necessary. I promise you that. But if it's necessary, I'll expect it. It's your responsibility too, and you can't deny it. It's only right that you should help if it's necessary."

Up to that moment, there may have still existed for her some hope of living. Afterward, there was none at all. He could see very clearly that she was an impossible fool and that she would be a menace, or at best a burden, so long as she lived. She seemed perversely determined to ruin him, and even if he could buy a reprieve now with something less than she demanded, there was no assurance at all that it would be more than that, any more than a reprieve, and she would probably return later with her miserable little bastard to destroy everything that he might accomplish in the meanwhile. Lauren and all that Lauren entailed, the beautiful precise plans. This was suddenly a terrible certainty in his mind, and he was shaken again by the fury that had succeeded the terror in his room. Slowly, with his right hand, he removed the blue nylon scarf that he wore under the collar of his topcoat.

"It's getting too hot in here," he said.

"Do you think so? I don't. I was so terribly cold. I don't think I've ever been colder in my life."

He watched her closely, twisting and twisting the scarf in his hands, transforming it slowly into a long, tough cord. "Are you tired?"

"Yes. I'm tired and I need something to eat."

"Would you like to go to a hotel now?"

"Yes."

"You're not looking very well. Do you feel as if you were going to be sick to your stomach?"

"No. Not now. I feel better than I did on the train."

"I thought you might like to get out and breathe some fresh air before we start back."

"I don't think so. Thank you, just the same."

She slumped down a little farther on the seat, resting her head on the back drawing her almost bare legs up under her and closing her eyes with a long sigh that had almost the sound of a whimper. Then, with the cold purpose that followed his fury, he leaned toward her swiftly and slipped the twisted scarf around her neck and jerked it tight.

And in the end, though she struggled some and tried a little to live, she died with such readiness that she may have accepted it, after all, as a reasonable solution to everything.

CHAPTER 5

The town of Rutherford rises gently east of its tracks to the minor eminence of a kind of low ridge, and to this ridge, perhaps as a symbol of their social position in relation to the rest of the population, Rutherford's rich withdrew to build their homes. It is not a very long ridge, but it does not need to be, for the rich in Rutherford are few, and so, consequently, are the homes of the rich. The homes are all built on the same side of the concrete street that runs down the ridge's spine, all facing the town that sprawls below, and affording from the rear a bucolic view of the valley beyond. The view of the town is quite pretty at night, when darkness hides the scars and brings out the lights, and the view of the valley is even prettier in the day with its scattered red and white farm buildings and multicolored parallelograms of crops and grass and turned earth, and so the privileged inhabitants of the ridge are not deprived at any hour of something charming to look at.

Among the big rich houses, the biggest and richest by quite a bit was the house of Gordon Haig. There are many places, of course, where it would not have seemed so much, but in Rutherford it seemed like very much indeed, and it was. It was natural and proper that Gordon Haig should have had the biggest and richest house by quite a bit, for he was by quite a bit the biggest and richest man. Unlike most of the other wealthy or at least prosperous men of Rutherford, he was not associated with the railroad. He owned a shirt factory that provided employment for nearly a hundred people, and he was actually a millionaire, which was something that no one in Rutherford was. It was rumored that he was worth about five million dollars, but this was not true. He was really worth a little over one million, which was plenty, and he had in addition to all those dollars and the accumulation of things that dollars bring, a wife, who does not count, and a daughter who does. The daughter's name was Lauren, and she was pretty.

The night that Avis Pisano came to Rutherford on the seven-o-five and was murdered, Lauren was sitting alone in her room in the biggest, richest house on the ridge. She was sitting there when the train came in, and she was still sitting there several minutes later when Avis and Curly were driving west out of town. She was sitting in her panties and bra and was doing nothing, which was something, if nothing can be something, that she did quite often. She was a tall girl with hair almost precisely the color of the valley parallelograms in which wheat had been planted and stood ready to harvest, and she had a beautiful willowy body that she herself admired in a narcissistic sort of way but hadn't made much use of. She was twenty-six years old and single. The reason she was single, in spite of being attractive and rich, was not because she had lacked chances, but simply she had never in her life been able to take a definitive step about anything important, and marriage is certainly a definitive step, if nothing else. This night, the Saturday before the Thursday that would be Thanksgiving, she was thinking about this, about marriage, and about three young men of Rutherford who wanted to marry her.

Rex, she thought.

Ellis, she thought.

Guy, she thought.

Rex or Ellis or Guy, she thought.

Of the three images that the three names invoked, one elicited a stronger response, a warming and stirring of the blood in her body, and of this one she began to think exclusively. Remembering his voice and the trespassing of his hands, she felt in remembrance an itch of desire that was as close to passion as she ever came. Passion had always seemed to her a kind of degradation, impossible in herself and ugly in others, the acts that incited it being violations, and she could not understand how this one person, this one young man of Rutherford, could cause her to feel as she had never felt before and had never wanted to feel. She did not understand it, but at last she accepted it. When he called her darling and stroked her body, or even when she thought of it after the time, as she now thought of it in her room this Saturday night, she felt submissive, if not responsive, and she was certain then, with only the slightest uncertainty afterward, that he was the one she wanted and would marry. When they were married, they would live in a fine house that her father would build, and she would reign coolly and quietly among expensive and gracious accoutrements that her father would buy, fabrics and silver and shining crystal, and perhaps now and then, only occasionally, there would be the times of desire and necessary submission.

Curly, she thought, *Oh, Curly*, giving him in her mind the warmth of affection his warm, affectionate name.

She had, as a matter of fact, a date with him at eight o'clock, and it was surely getting late, pretty close to the time, and it was necessary to get up and begin dressing if she was to be ready when he came. Looking at the electric clock on the small table beside her bed, she saw that she had indeed been sitting and doing nothing—unless you counted thinking, which was, after all, a kind of doing—for much longer than she had thought, and that she would have to hurry now to make up the lost time.

Standing, she went into the bathroom and turned on the shower, adjusting the flow of hot and cold water until she had the proportion precisely as she liked it, just slightly less than intolerably hot. She would have much preferred a bath to the shower, but the shower was quicker and must therefore be had in concession to time, or the lack of it, and she kept reminding herself while she was having it that it was time to stop and get on with her dressing, but it was very pleasant under the hot stinging spray, almost as pleasant as it would have been to lie in the tub, and she remained there, as she had remained sitting previously in the bedroom, much longer than she intended.

Out of the shower and dried at last, she returned to the bedroom and began selecting the clothes she would wear, and she was conscious all the while of the pressure of time and the necessity to hurry, and she actually thought that she was conforming to the necessity, but it was only the consciousness of the pressure that made her think so, and really she did not hurry at all. Before beginning to dress, holding the first sheer trifle in her hand, she stopped for a moment to consider herself, to feel the cool, aesthetic pleasure she had in sole possession, and she thought sadly, with a kind of abortive nostalgia, that this would be lost when she was married, or at least it would be impaired, and she would never again belong to herself in quite the same way that she now did. But she understood that this was a way of thinking and feeling that was bad for her and that must be abandoned once and for all for her own good, and so she began deliberately to think again of Curly, of Curly's voice and Curly's hands, and she began at the same time actually to hurry at last. Telling herself that he would surely arrive at any moment, and might even be in the house already, though no one had come to tell her so, she finished dressing and went downstairs into the living room, but he wasn't there yet, after all her unnecessary concern, and it was then almost ten minutes past eight.

There was no one in the living room but her, and there seemed to be no one but her in the whole house. At any rate, though she stood quietly and listened intently, she could hear no sound, and the house had suddenly the feel of an empty house. She remembered then that her mother and father had driven up to the city and would not be back until morning at the earliest, but there should be servants in the house, the maid and the cook, and she wondered where they were. Going back into the hall into which the stairs descended, she walked past the stairs to the rear of the hall, and then she could hear, beyond a closed door to the kitchen, the sound of movement and after a few seconds the sound of one voice saying something followed by the sound of another voice saying something else in reply. Relieved to learn that she was not alone in the house, but not quite knowing why she was or should have been, she returned to the living room, and it was by then a quarter past the hour, and she was a little angry. This was foolish too, however, as foolish as having been disturbed by the empty feeling of the house, and if Curly was a little late, if he had been delayed for one reason or another, it was certainly nothing to get upset or angry about, and what she would do, since it was necessary to wait, was watch television or listen to some music. She would listen to the music, that's what she would do, because music was something you could select and play according to your own taste, while television had to be taken as it came and could be pretty awful, which it almost invariably was.

At the record cabinet, she read through the index of recordings, which was on a card fastened to the inside of the cabinet door. She did not want anything too somber, nor did she feel in the mood for anything that was, on the other hand, particularly gay, and so she finally selected Tchaikovsky's *Pathetique*, which was both. The part she especially liked and wanted to hear was the second movement in 5/4 time, the strange and haunting rhythm that seemed to her a kind of deviation or distortion, and the movement had just ended and been succeeded by the march-scherzo when the front door bell sounded in the hall. Leaving the recording playing, she went out into the hall and intercepted the maid, who was coming up from the kitchen.

"I'll get it, Martha," she said.

The maid stopped and turned and retreated to the kitchen, and Lauren went on to the front door and opened it, and it was, as she expected, Curly at last. His face had assumed already, when she opened the door, a small-boy smile of contrition and entreaty. "I'm late," he said, "but I have a good reason. Really I have. Do you forgive me?"

"Of course," she said. "It doesn't matter in the least. I was playing some music and hardly noticed. It's quite safe for you to come in."

He laughed and came into the hall and removed his coat. "Well, please don't be *too* indifferent. I think it would be more flattering if you were a little angry."

"All right. At first I was a little angry, but now I'm happy. Is that satisfactory?"

"Would you object to showing me how happy you are?"

"Not in the least. I admit that I've been anticipating it." She put her arms around his neck and raised her face, which was something that always required in the very beginning an inner effort, a small conquest of reluctance, but then he was kissing her, and his hands were on her body, and she felt the familiar quickening of blood that was now accepted and even wanted, and in the living room the march-scherzo came to an end and was followed after a moment of silence by a swelling symphonic cry of deepest sorrow, *Adagio lamentoso*.

He raised his head abruptly in an attitude of listening, and she felt in his body a sudden rigidity. Looking up across the set, flat planes and almost classic projections of his face, she saw a shadow across his eyes that seemed in that instant to be a shadow of the music itself, as if sound had substance that could block the light. He was staring over her head into the room from which the music came, and it was perfectly apparent that he had been caught and fixed and profoundly affected, and she wondered mildly why this should be so, but it was easily understandable, after all, for it was surely profoundly affecting music.

"What is that?" he said. "What are you playing?"

"It's the *Pathetique*," she said. "The last movement."

He gave a sigh, a prolonged whisper of released breath, and his body shivered and grew still as rigidity left it. "It's a dismal thing, isn't it?"

"It is, rather. Do you want me to stop it?"

"No, no. Let it play out."

"I put it on in the first place only to hear the second movement. The 5/4 part, you know. Someone said once that it's like a waltz for a three-legged man. I admit that it's very queer, but I like it."

He laughed again and kissed her again, and the music ended in the second kiss as it had begun in the first, and afterward they went into the living room, and the night went on from there.

The night grew a little older, and after a while, after quite a while, in the softest of light that was hardly more than a shadow of light, she submitted to the subtle, persuasive hands and the strong, seductive word said softly and softly and softly again, *darling, darling, darling*. And she would then have agreed to anything he asked. He could then have done with her whatever he chose.

But he couldn't be sure, and now in his delicate and precarious game he would certainly be the greatest of fools to risk by imprudence what he had sustained by murder. And so, thinking so, he attempted less than he could have accomplished, and he left early.

It was, when he left, exactly ten-thirty.

CHAPTER 6

An hour later, at eleven-thirty, the taproom of the Division Hotel was almost deserted. The only persons present were Bernie Juggins, the bartender, and Purvy Stubbs. Purvy sat on a stool and stared moodily into half a glass of Miller's High Life that was going flat. He hadn't drunk from the glass for quite a long time, and it looked like he sure as hell was never going to drink from it again, and for all Bernie could tell from looking at him, the fat bastard might be dead. Bernie wished he would drink his goddamned beer and go home, that's what Bernie wished, because then he could put out the lights real quick, before anyone else drifted in, and beat the lousy closing hour by a good thirty minutes. A guy got tired tending bar. Tending bar was long hours and hell on the feet, and if some slob like old Purvy didn't have a damn thing to do but play dead on a stool with a glass of flat beer under his nose, that didn't mean that some other guy like Bernie didn't have anything else to do, either. He had a home, Bernie did, and in the home was a bed, and in the bed was a wife, and he could think of just a hell of a lot of things he'd rather be doing than what he was, but there was no use thinking about that now, about his wife or sleeping or anything else, because here came Guy Butler, and it was just too damn late to beat the last thirty minutes, as he'd hoped, thanks to that damn Purvy, the big dope.

Guy crawled onto the stool next to Purvy, and Bernie drifted along behind the bar and stopped opposite him. He was a damn nice fellow, as a matter of fact, in spite of hanging around in the taproom until the very last lousy minute and keeping a guy from getting a little break once in a while, and if he was a mean son of a bitch sometimes, it was something you could understand, because of what had happened to his hand and all, and you couldn't blame him a hell of a lot. Still, he certainly could do some mean things if the notion struck him. Like the time he'd told old stupid Purvy that Phyllis Bagby was a whore and had sent Purvy around to Phyllis's house with twenty bucks to buy a piece. That was mean to Purvy, and it was even meaner to Phyllis, because Phyllis really liked Guy, better than anyone else in the world, which was something everyone knew perfectly well, and she was ready any old time to sleep with him or marry him or do anything he wanted anytime he wanted to do it. That was all finished now, though, Bernie supposed, since Guy had started going out with that rich bitch on the ridge, that snotty Lauren Haig, and it sure as hell looked like Guy was deadly serious about it, it sure did, even including orange blossoms and all that crap. You couldn't blame him, of course, because the bitch would be coming into a million bucks at least when her old man and old lady died, besides being a real fancy looker that no guy in his right mind would feel inclined to kick out of bed, but you couldn't tell how it was going to come out in the end, because Guy didn't have any clear track with her like he had with Phyllis, and Rex Tye and Ellis Kuder were working at it just as much as he was and just as hard. What Bernie secretly hoped, which he admitted freely to himself, was that she'd pop off and marry someone else entirely, none of the three, and he thought it would be a hell of a good belly laugh and just what they had coming.

"What's it gonna be, Guy?" Bernie said.

"Straight bourbon," Guy said.

Bernie set up a double-shot glass and poured in a jigger of Jim Beam, which was what he always used if the customer didn't specify, and Guy took it and downed it with a little shudder and pushed it back for the same. While Bernie was pouring the second time, Guy turned to Purvy.

"How's it going, Purvy?" he said.

Purvy roused from the dead and shifted his eyes with a grin from the flat beer to Guy's face.

"All right, Guy," he said. "Can't complain too much. How's it with you?"

"Well, I'll get by as long as Bernie's bourbon holds out. You been out to see Phyllis lately?"

"I go out there now and then. Matter of fact, I was there tonight for an hour or so. Between the seven-o-five and the ten-twenty. Phyllis was asking about you. She's wondering where the hell you been keeping yourself."

"I've just given up, that's all. When you started seeing Phyllis, I quit. I knew damn well I didn't have a chance any longer with you in the picture, so I just quit."

"Oh, damn it, Guy, cut out that crap. You know damn well that Phyllis hasn't got any time for anyone else when you're around. She feels real bad because you been staying away, she really does. You ought to go out and see her."

"Well," Guy said, "to hell with it."

He picked up the double-shot glass and drank from it, a single quick gulp, but this time he downed only half the whiskey instead of all of it, and he used his left hand to lift the glass and to hold it afterward, the crippled one, but it didn't really look so bad, in spite of the scars, only a little stiff, with the fingers drawn down in the slightest suggestion of a claw when they were relaxed. The fingers were long and slender and sensitive, the kind of fingers that could draw the soul out of a fiddle, and maybe out of a woman. The reason he used the hand for everything, like eating and drinking and everything, was because it was a kind of habit left over from the days when he used it and exercised it constantly in the hope of getting it perfectly flexible again, as it had been before being hurt, and now that he'd given up the hope and had no purpose, he still did it as a kind of habit. In the opinion of Bernie, though, there was something more to it than that. Bernie liked to study people and try to figure out why they did things, and Bernie figured that Guy was deliberately throwing the hand in your face, so to speak, as a kind of bitter gesture or something—as a kind of epitaph, when you came to think of it, as if he were saying in his own special way, *Here lies Guy Butler*.

Well, Bernie thought, he was an odd son of a bitch, pretty twisted and fouled up inside, but you had to like him in spite of that, and you had a lot of sympathy for him too, not so much for what had happened to him, because a lousy bunged-up hand wasn't such a hell of a tragedy in itself after all, but because of what he had lost because of what had happened, which was something else again and a hell of a lot more. He'd been on his way to being something really big, not just fat and prosperous like old man Haig up on the ridge, who made shirts and was a millionaire, but who hadn't ever been heard of except right around close, or by the people who bought and sold his lousy shirts. Guy had been on his way to being famous and admired all over the country and in Europe and all such places, and then his hand got loused the way it was, and Uncle Sugar said thanks and dropped a pension on him, and it was over, just all over and done and nowheres to go. Well, hell, you felt a lot of sympathy for a guy like that, but you didn't tell him so, of course, because he'd spit in your eye if you did, and you liked him and wished it hadn't happened to him, but at the same time you wished it didn't sometimes make him quite so goddamned mean, either.

For instance, telling old lubberly Purvy just now that he'd quit going out to Phyllis Bagby's because he knew he didn't have any more chance after Purvy started going. That was just a way of breaking it off in Purvy for being a fellow that no sensible woman would take seriously, and it was pretty damn mean and nasty, even if Purvy was just naturally the kind of fellow you were constantly tempted to break it off in. You just absolutely couldn't understand why Purvy didn't do something about himself, though God only knew what it was he could do, running all the time to the depot to watch the lousy trains come in and go out, and it was common knowledge around town that he'd wanted to be an engineer, but his old man had kicked his ass and wouldn't let him. Look at him now. Just look at him. Sitting there like a sack of something on the stool, and just looking and looking into his flat beer as if there were a naked female swimming around in it or something. Why the hell didn't he go home like a sensible person? And why the hell didn't Guy Butler go home, too? It was a quarter to twelve now and time that everyone was going the hell home, including Bernie Huggins, who was damn well ready.

At that moment in Bernie's weary reflections, Ellis Kuder came into the taproom from the lobby and crossed to the bar, and Bernie took an angry swipe at the mahogany with his rag and watched him sourly as he got onto a stool beside Guy. He didn't like Ellis very well under the best of circumstances, and he liked him less than ever at this moment, the arrogant bastard, blowing in this way at a quarter to twelve as if he owned the crummy joint and never thinking or caring a damn that somebody might want to close up and go home. He didn't know exactly why he didn't like Ellis, when you came right down to it, and he'd tried to figure it out to his own satisfaction, because there's always a reason for everything, of course, and it's sort of comforting to know what it is, but all he could figure in the end, no matter how hard he tried, was that he didn't like Ellis very much simply because there was something about him that you couldn't like very much. It wasn't just that he was good-looking and conceited, which he certainly was, and maybe it was just a feeling he gave you that didn't have anything to do apparently with the way he looked and the things he said and did. It was a rather uneasy feeling, really, though it seemed pretty silly to feel uneasy about a guy you'd known forever, and what it was, it was a feeling that Ellis didn't care a damn bit more about you, or anyone else on earth except himself, than he cared about a horsefly or a cockroach or any kind of low life you cared to mention. You got this feeling in spite of his always being perfectly pleasant and friendly and everything, and that was the reason you didn't like him, as nearly as you could figure it.

"Hi, Guy," Ellis said. "How's it going, Purvy?"

Purvy looked up from whatever he saw in the beer, the naked female or something, and grinned without saying anything. Guy grunted and lifted the double-shot glass and drained off what was left in it. Ellis turned to Bernie, who had come up opposite.

"Thought I'd have one before I go home, Bernie," he said. "Have I got time?"

"You got ten, fifteen minutes," Bernie said.

"That's enough," Ellis said. "Rye and water."

"Same again for me," Guy said.

Purvy said nothing and Bernie poured. From the lobby, Rex Tye came into the taproom.

Well, here it was, Bernie thought, the final, culminating, absolutely last goddamned straw. No one but precious Rex himself, Mother's fair-haired boy in the flesh, and out all by himself at damn near midnight, too, and patronizing a nasty taproom where hard liquors were served, to make it worse, and keeping honest bartenders out of bed until all hours to make it as bad as it could get. A stinking spoiled brat, that's what he was, if you wanted Bernie Huggins' opinion. Even if he was a grown man. If you were a spoiled brat at ten, you were a spoiled brat at twenty or thirty or forty or any age you got to be, and that's the way it worked out. To give the devil his due, though, you had to admit that it was his mother's fault. Everyone in town knew how she'd always treated him like God and taught him that he was different from other people and a hell of a lot better, the other kids and later the other men, and the wonder was, to tell the truth, that he hadn't turned out to be a bigger stinker than he had. It was unhealthy, that's what it was, the way the damn woman hung onto him and tried to make him out to be something that he plainly wasn't, except in her own mind, and you wondered what kind of enormous ego or something she had, to keep it up that way all these years without getting wise to how phony she was and how phony she had made her brat, especially when she was as poor as Job's turkey and had to keep paying on back bills all the time, a little to one or two creditors this month and a little to one or two others next month, so she and precious Rex could keep on living like refined and cultured people and all that crap. It was like one of these lousy Freudian messes you heard about, mother and son all loused up with each other and stuff like that, and no girl had ever been good enough for precious Rex until he got after Lauren Haig, up on the ridge, and that was a horse of another color and perfectly all right, of course, because the daughter of a millionaire was good enough for anyone, even Rex, and if the truth were known, Bernie was willing to lay odds, Mother herself had probably been planning the whole thing for years, and had sicced Rex on when she thought the time was right and was goosing him along for all he was worth.

And speaking of Lauren Haig, or thinking of her, Bernie realized all of a sudden that all the competition was present, lined up at the bar at ten minutes to twelve like three night birds, with Purvy Stubbs thrown in for good measure, as a kind of extra or neutral, and it was pretty damn funny when you thought of it like that. Lined up there just like the best of cronies, the three guys who were trying to crawl into little old Lauren's bed and bankbook, and it really was funny, a real belly laugh, to see them acting like little gentlemen when they were probably trying to figure out a way to cut each other's throat. You couldn't exactly call it a triangle, like they were always making movies about, because you had to count Lauren as one of the points, which made four, and what it was, it was a regular goddamned rectangle or something. Bernie wondered which one would win out in the end, or if maybe it would be someone else entirely, which he hoped. He wondered if any one of them was maybe getting a little in advance from old Lauren, something on account, but he bet none of them was. He bet not a damn one of them was even getting a feel.

"You got eight, ten minutes," he said to Rex. "What'll it be?"

"Whiskey sour," Rex said.

He leaned forward over the bar and looked down the line to his right and said names in order.

"Ellis," he said. "Guy. Purvy."

Two heads were nodded in acknowledgement, Ellis' and Purvy's, and one hand was raised slightly, Guy's, but no word was spoken. Bernie mixed the whiskey sour, cursing mentally. You might have known that precious Rex wouldn't have something simple, like a straight whiskey or whiskey and water or a beer. Oh, no. It had to be some fancy damn thing like a whiskey sour that took a lot of time and trouble, and he wasn't fooling old Bernie a damn bit, either. The reason he ordered this kind of crap was because he couldn't stand the taste of whiskey and had to have it doctored up with sweet stuff in order to get it down in his delicate little stomach, that was the reason, and ordinarily it was all right with Bernie, he could drink what he damn well pleased, but it wasn't all right at eight, ten minutes to twelve, and if anyone was thinking he was going to stay even one minute after closing hour, he damn well had another think coming.

Bernie walked around from behind the bar and switched off the lights in the room, leaving only the ones behind the bar itself. He returned and made a few swipes at the bar with his rag and rattled some glasses. He took off his white jacket and put on his street coat. He yawned loudly and scratched his head and looked at his watch.

"Purvy," said Guy suddenly, "why the hell don't you drink your beer?"

"I let it get flat," Purvy said. "I don't intend to drink it."

"Well, for God's sake, why don't you at least quit looking at it like that? You think it's poison or something?"

"No. I was just thinking. I been trying to think who it was."

"Who was?"

"Well, I don't know. I said I didn't, damn it. Down at the depot, I mean. I was watching the seven-o-five come in, and a girl got off and looked around, and then she walked down the platform toward that little park at the south end, and there was someone waiting for her there, and I been wondering who it was. I guess what makes me wonder is why whoever it was didn't just wait on the platform like you'd expect."

There was a period of silence, which was nothing new or different. But it was a different kind of silence. It had a different feel, and even Bernie Huggins felt the difference. It was rather hard to understand, but it was something like the silence in the night when you were a kid in bed, and there was something terrifying off there in the dark that was about to jump and grab you by the throat. It was the silence before your scream.

"You mean it was someone you didn't know?" Guy said finally.

"No." Purvy shook his head. "It was more that I just didn't get a good look at him. He was in the dark down there, and I just got a glimpse of him, hardly more than a shadow, but there was something familiar about him, just the same, the way he moved or something, and it bothers me. You know how a thing gets in your mind and bothers you? I keep trying to think who it could have been."

Guy pushed his double-shot glass away with a kind of violence and stood up. The glass fell over on its side and rolled into the trough along the rear edge of the bar. Bernie picked it up and dropped it into the rinse.

"Well, what the hell difference does it make?" Guy said. "To hell with it. To hell with everything. I'm going home." He was loaded, all right, three shots in the last half hour, plus what he'd had before, but he carried it pretty well, you had to hand it to him, and he walked straight across the room without weaving to the entrance to the lobby. Purvy slipped off his stool and went after him.

"Wait a minute, Guy," he said. "I'll walk a piece with you." Ellis finished his rye and water and spoke to himself, or to whomever wanted to listen.

"That Purvy," he said. "Purvy and his goddamned trains." He got up and walked out, and that left Rex. Rex drank his whiskey sour. At one minute to twelve, he ate the cherry and left also.

Don't anyone bother to say good-night, Bernie thought. *Don't any of you snotty bastards bother to say good-night to old Bernie.*

CHAPTER 7

Purvy caught up with Guy on the sidewalk outside. Turning left on the sidewalk, Guy walked along rapidly with Purvy panting beside him in the effort to keep up. Guy walked with what seemed to be a kind of desperate purposefulness, his shoulders hunched up and his head drawn down inside the upturned collar of his topcoat and his eyes fastened to the sidewalk about two yards in front of his feet.

"Jesus, Guy," Purvy said, "what the hell's the big hurry?" Guy glanced at Purvy with an expression of surprise and impatience, as if he hadn't been aware of Purvy's presence and wasn't very pleased to discover it. He shrugged and slowed his pace.

"Purvy," he said, "what in God's name makes you so damn clumsy? A guy as big as you ought to be able to make a little time without panting like a dog in heat. Don't you ever get any exercise?"

"Well," Purvy said, "the truth is, the men in my family are just bound to be sort of awkward in spite of anything. Take my Old Man, for instance."

"You take him," Guy said. "I don't want him."

"So far as that goes," Purvy said, "I don't want him either, but I'm sure as hell stuck with him."

Guy didn't comment, and the pair of them reached the intersection and crossed it, and Purvy said, "You got your car, Guy?"

"Sure. It's parked down the street at the curb. Why?"

"I thought you might give me a lift home. It's a pretty cold night, what with the wind and all, and it's a hell of a long walk up to the ridge."

"Why don't you get yourself a car, Purvy? Doesn't your Old Man pay you anything for working in the bank?"

"He pays me, all right, but not very damn much. That's not the reason, though. I'm just no good with cars. I get nervous and scared every time I try to drive one. The last time I drove the Old Man's car, I drove it right smack into a tree."

"Hell's fire, Purvy, I thought you always wanted to be an engineer. How the hell did you expect to drive one of those big engines when you can't even drive a car?"

"An engine's different, Guy. You know that as well as I do. It runs on rails, for one thing, and for another, I'd have my heart in it. I wouldn't be scared at all of an engine."

"Well, I'll drive you home, if you want me to, but you'll have to wait a little. I'm going in the Owl Diner down here and have a cup of coffee."

"That's all right. I'll go in there with you. I'm sure as hell in no hurry to get home."

The Owl Diner was a small white stucco building standing next door to a used car lot. Along one side was a short counter with eight stools fastened to the floor at intervals in front of it. It was warm inside, the air fragrant with the scent of coffee and chili and fried onions. With the exception of the proprietor, a thin fellow with a sour expression who was called Cheerful, Guy and Purvy had the place to themselves. They crawled onto stools and sat hunched over the counter, braced on elbows, in the traditional lunch-counter posture. Cheerful, who had been napping in a cane chair behind the counter, roused himself and approached.

"Curly," he said. "Purvy."

"Coffee," Guy said. He rubbed his bad hand across his close-cropped black hair in a sort of reflexive response to the nickname.

"Not for me," Purvy said. "I drink coffee this late, it keeps me awake the rest of the night."

"That's all right, Purvy," Cheerful said. "You don't have to explain why the hell you don't want coffee. Just tell me what you *do* want, that's all."

"Well, I'll have a glass of milk and a piece of butterscotch pie, that's what, and you can go to hell. No wonder they call you Cheerful, you're so damn cranky."

"Sure." Cheerful grinned with sour pride, pleased with Purvy's reaction.

Purvy turned his head toward Guy as Cheerful turned his back to both Guy and Purvy in the execution of his orders.

"What you fellows been doing with yourselves?" Cheerful asked in a tone of voice that made clear his basic indifference.

Guy kept looking into his coffee, which he had not yet touched, and Purvy, prompted by the question, remembered the episode at the station when the seven-o-five came in. He saw again the girl descend to the platform, clearly saw her stand there in her cheap fur coat and look around with that kind of desperate intentness for someone who wasn't there, saw her finally look down the platform toward the south end and move at once in response to a beckoning shadow among the Junipers. That shadow itched Purvy. It itched and itched him, and he couldn't help it.

"I met the seven-o-five," he said to Cheerful. "A strange girl got off, and someone met her. They come in here, by any chance?"

"Here? Why the hell should they come in here?"

"Well, damn it, why not? People get hungry on train rides, don't they? I just thought they might have come in for a bite."

"Seems to me, if she was hungry, she'd have gone in the restaurant at the station. Who was it met her?"

"I don't know. What I mean, I almost know, but not quite. Point is, he was standing in the little park at the end of the platform, and I just barely got a glimpse of him."

"Why the devil would he wait down there in the park?"

"That's a funny thing, isn't it? It doesn't seem like a natural thing to do, does it?"

"Oh, I don't know, come to think of it. It could be natural enough. Maybe it was a guy had a girl coming in to shack up a few days or something. A married guy or someone like that. A guy shacking up sure wouldn't want to parade himself around with the girl on the station platform." Purvy shook his head dubiously, and Guy stood up abruptly. There was in his movement a suggestion of restrained violence.

"You want me to drive you home, Purvy? Come on, if you do."

"You haven't drunk your coffee."

"To hell with the coffee."

He dropped a coin on the counter and went out. Purvy had to wait for the change from a dollar, and when he reached the sidewalk, Guy was getting into his car about twenty yards down the street. Hurrying, Purvy trotted down after him, feeling that his arms and legs were somehow flying in all directions. He wished Guy hadn't made that remark about his being clumsy. Damn it, it was bad enough to be clumsy without having someone always making remarks about it. In the car beside Guy, he sat back and closed his eyes and breathed deeply; When he opened his eyes again, the car was already ascending the tilted street to the ridge where the favored folk of Rutherford lived, which included the president of the Commercial Bank. Looking out across the lawns at the dark houses, he felt sad and impoverished, nagged by a sense of accelerated Time and irreparable loss.

"Time sure goes right along, doesn't it, Guy?" he said, aware that he had made substantially the same remark to Pheeb Keeley earlier in the station restaurant.

Guy shrugged. "It's not Time that goes, Purvy. It's us." Purvy twisted his head around to look at Guy, his eyes popping a little in an expression of surprised delight.

"Say, Guy, that's damn good, you know. How'd you happen to think of that?"

"I didn't. I read it somewhere."

Purvy smiled sheepishly. "I guess I sounded pretty silly about that. You know how those things are, Guy. Something like that just gets in your mind and keeps itching and itching." Guy didn't answer. He pulled into the drive beside Purvy's house, and Purvy got out and said good-night, and Guy backed into the street again and started down the ridge the way he had come. Passing the Haig house, he slowed his speed and looked up across the deep lawn to the dark windows of the second floor, the corner windows of the room where Lauren slept, and he wondered if she were asleep now, or if she were lying awake in the night, and what, if anything, she wore to bed. It was almost certain that she wore something, for it was somehow impossible to imagine that she did not, and it was also almost certain, at least in his own mind, that she would wear the sheerest of pale gowns over the shadow of her body. Cool, cool Lauren. Cool as moonlight, cool as rain, cool and ever so slightly detached even in response to his advances. Cool and ever so slightly stupid. Cool and more than slightly rich.

Well, he did not object to the coolness of flesh and emotions. He rather preferred it that way, to tell the truth, because it demanded less of him who had given too much too soon to something else. One who quit living to any purpose in his twenties wants in his thirties little more than to live to no purpose comfortably, which entails money, which can, with luck and guts, be acquired by marriage. He could not remember exactly when he had decided to marry Lauren Haig. Neither could he quite remember how he had come to the decision. But however he had come to it, at whatever instant, it was held from inception with abnormal ferocity, and the marriage had become in his mind a kind of desperate alternative to a deadly life of being and having nothing. There were other things he could have done, of course, after the crippling of his hand and the destruction of his precocity. He could have played in minor musical organizations, for which he was more than adequate, or he could have given private lessons, or he could have got a few hours in Education at the University and gone into teaching into some school or other. But it was intolerable to be mediocre in an area where he had excelled, something he could in no way bear. It was better, much better, to be nothing at all—a lousy clerk in an insurance office.

It was not fair, of course, to be forced to such a cruel choice. It was criminally unfair, a monstrous divine crime, but you did not, because of that, overtly cry and whine at God. You merely hated and festered and became cruel in ways that you sometimes regretted. Eventually you merely decided quite coldly to make the best of nothing by marrying a rich girl, a cool and lovely and acceptable rich girl you did not love, and this became established after a while in your mind as more than your privilege. It was your right, your compensation, something God owed you. And nothing would deprive you of it, nothing. Not love. Not conscience. Not God. Certainly no person on earth.

The car descended from the ridge to the level of lower Rutherford, and he began to think of Phyl Bagby and wish that he could go to see her, but this was not possible, or at least not advisable, because of Lauren and of everything that might be lost by imprudence. He regretted Phyl and missed her, far more than she or that clown Purvy Stubbs dreamed or would ever know, and he supposed that he loved her in spite of understanding perfectly well that she had done a lot of sleeping around, which did not really disturb him at all. She had, in fact, a marvelous potential for being a fine friend, as well as a fine lover, and there was in her avid abandonment to pleasure a kind of dry white heat that was clean and consuming and somehow redeeming. She was far removed from Lauren's cool detachment, but on the other hand she was also far removed from the sticky agitation of an Avis Pisano, whom he had taken in the summer in a fetid prelude to disgust and contempt. Yes, he regretted Phyl, her loss, and he missed her, and it was a measure of his commitment to his design on Lauren that he had, without showing the regret or any sign of compunction, excised Phyl from his life.

In a little while, after descending from the ridge, he reached the house in which he still lived with his parents. Leaving the car parked at the curb in the dark street, he went up across the porch and inside.

From the east, over in the railroad yards, came the immense and labored breathing of a slow freight gathering speed.

CHAPTER 8

Ellis Kuder's car was parked down and across the street from the hotel, about a hundred feet at an angle from the entrance. Ellis crossed to it on the angle and got in and drove west through the Main Street underpass. On the other side of the tracks, after another block of business houses, he turned south and again west into the area of town in which he lived. He felt relieved to be away from his recent companions of the Division Hotel taproom, and this relief, depending on cases, was an effect of different causes. In the case of Purvy Stubbs it was merely the relief of being rid of a clown, a dunce, a clumsy fool and a bore. In the case of the other two, however, Rex and Guy, the cause was something else. He saw Rex and Guy as threats, agents of possible ruin at worst or inconvenience at best, and he began to think now, as he had thought at the bar while being outwardly congenial, that it might become necessary to remove them, and he wondered how, if it came to this, he could accomplish the removal most effectively. That he had known Rex and Guy practically all his life and was ostensibly their friend seemed to have no influence on his thinking. He knew quite well that he was perfectly capable of doing them any dirty or deadly trick that he considered essential to his own ends.

When, he thought, did you first clearly understand yourself, and when, after that, did you finally accept yourself as you really were without rationalization? But this was nonsense, certainly a manifestation of weakness, the idea that there must be between understanding and acceptance a period of squeamish rejection and sickly readjustment. If you were sensible and had any guts at all, understanding and acceptance came simultaneously and without trauma, and you did not create within yourself a futile conflict over what naturally was and could in no way be helped or changed. He did not remember precisely his own first instant of insight, or exactly the incident which prompted it, but probably it was the time he killed the cat. At any rate, though there may have been something earlier, it was the killing of the cat that assumed precedence in his mind. He was a little kid, eight or nine, and he was teasing the cat, a rangy yellow Tom with a temper, and the Tom reached out with a hiss and clawed him. He looked down at the back of his hand, at the thin parallel lines drawn in blood, and there was little or no pain, and the commanding thing suddenly inside him was enormous and icy fury that this filthy beast had the effrontery and the nerve to do this to him, *him*, and there was no retaliation that he was not capable of making. He seized the Tom by the hind legs as he turned scornfully to leave, and he beat the cat's head methodically against the cement walk that ran from the back porch to the garage. When the animal was dead, his proud Tom's head a pulp of blood and matted hair, he, Ellis, carried him back to the alley and lay him on the ash pile and stood looking at him, and all he felt, now that the fury had passed, was a cold and quiet satisfaction and sure conviction that the Tom had damn well got what he deserved. No regret, no compassion, no sense of guilt. Above all, even so early, understanding and acceptance of himself as he was, his potential for deadly retaliation for the slightest affront or threat. Also, deep in his mind, the awareness that this was a menace to himself as well as to others, something which must be controlled and directed for his own security.

Security was, he learned, no more than a matter of developing patience and an alert sense of caution and of being, when the time came, clever enough to avoid exposing himself. Sometimes it was even possible to accomplish what he wished by omission, without taking any overt action whatever, as it had in fact worked out in the case of the boy who had humiliated him and later drowned. At this time he was in high school, a junior, eight years after the killing of the imprudent Tom, and there was this girl whose name no longer mattered that he wanted for himself, as his steady girl, for as long as it might please him to want her. He was proud, as he had the right to be proud, and it didn't occur to him that the girl would reject him on his own terms, not really, and when she did foolishly reject him, it was a shameful thing that could not pass, and what made it even worse was that he was rejected in favor of the other boy, the one who later drowned. It was very foolish of this boy to be preferred. It was just too goddamned bad.

He, Ellis, could not handle this as he had handled the Tom, by means of sudden and satisfying reprisal, and so he waited and waited and lived patiently with his shame and the unsettled score that survived his interest in the girl, which had not lasted long anyhow, and eventually reprisal was secured quite adequately by accident and by omission. A group of them was on this wiener roast at the small lake seven miles north of Rutherford, and it was dark, and everyone was across the lake in the picnic area except him and this boy, and since it was late and after dark, the pair of them decided to swim across, rather than walk around the end, which would save time. They started out together, and it was quite a long way to swim, and about three quarters of the way across, something happened to the boy. A cramp or something. The boy called for help, but he, Ellis, simply swam away and left him, and so he was even at last without any investment in danger to himself, and no one ever knew or guessed what was done or not done or for what reason. He went on to the picnic area in the low region beyond the dam and reported that the boy had drowned in spite of his efforts to reach him and save him, and he watched the girl who had started it all go into the ugly antics of hysteria, and he wondered why in God's name he had ever thought he wanted her in the first place. Other than that, his only feeling was one of requital.

There was never, in short, any particular pleasure in ruthlessness for its own sake. The pleasure was in the awareness of the grand potential to accomplish without remorse or excessive emotion whatever might be required by condition. As in the war. As in the instance, which was only one among many, when he climbed the slope to the ridge from which the enemy had recently withdrawn under fire. The dead were around him, the scattered remnants of men, and among the dead remnants were three living, the deserted wounded. They lay together at the base of a tree, their breathing labored and harsh with suffering and terror, and one of them opened his eyes and looked up with irises fevered and supplicating in enormous whites. He stood holding his BAR in his hands and considered objectively what should be done about the three wounded men, and it was obviously a convenience and a precaution against possible treachery from behind to kill them, and so he raised the BAR, and the wounded man who was looking at him closed his eyes, and he shot the three of them as methodically as he had once killed the Tom, but this time there was no rage, and on the other hand neither was there any particular excitement or regret or aftermath of depression.

He was, in fact, scornful of excessive demonstration of any kind in the business of killing and trying to escape being killed in which he and the other men in his outfit were engaged. With those who showed a kind of adolescent savagery in the moratorium on the sixth commandment, keeping score as if they were playing in some kind of new and exciting and bloody game, he despised equally those who were shaken and disturbed and brooded on their guilt. As for him, he killed in necessity without compunction, and he was not fool enough to waste time afterward in either exultation or regret. In the meanwhile, in accordance with his early understanding, he took all possible precautions to avoid putting some individual among the enemy in the position of exulting or brooding over Ellis Kuder.

Now, over a decade later, in a dark street in the southwest part of Rutherford, he stopped his car in front of a large old house with a porch running completely across the front and half way to the rear on one side. The house was constructed of clapboard, elaborately decorated with gingerbread. Once it had been the private residence of a prosperous merchant who had built it before prosperity's general trend to the ridge to the east, but the merchant was now dead, his family dispersed, and the house was the property of a real estate dealer who rented it out as two small apartments on the lower floor and four sleeping rooms above. Ellis had one of the rooms. Although his father was dead, his mother still lived in her own home in town, but he preferred not to live with her. He had discovered immediately after the war that living with her was scarcely tolerable any longer, and so he had moved away, and he had remained away in spite of entreaties to return. His mother was a dull woman, full of platitudes and engaged in good works. He hardly ever saw her.

Upstairs in his room, he dropped his topcoat and suit coat onto a chair and went into a small private bathroom, which was something the other second floor rooms did not have, and for which he paid a small premium. After turning on the light above the lavatory, he removed his shirt and washed his face and hands and brushed his teeth. In the cloudy mirror on the door of the medicine cabinet, he examined briefly the good lines of his face, the shining curly hair that was so dark a red that it seemed at times actually to be black with red highlights. His reflection gave him a feeling of satisfaction that was, besides being a tiny part of his total enormous vanity, a simple recognition of the value of appearance as a tool. Turning away from the mirror, he returned to the bedroom, leaving the door partly open behind him to permit the entrance of a swath of light that cut diagonally across the floor below the foot of the bed. Outside the swath, in the shadows beyond it, he stripped to his shorts and lay down on the bed. It was warm in the room, much too warm for sleeping, and it would be necessary after a while to get up and cut off the radiator and open a window, but now he did not want to sleep, could not have slept had he wanted to. Lying quietly on his back and looking up at the bathroom light striking diagonally across the dark ceiling, he began to think of Lauren Haig and to wish that she were beside him on the bed in the dreary rented room. His desire for Lauren was strong and genuine and would have existed even if she had been poor instead of rich. He did not feel love, for there was no tenderness in his feeling, which was something he felt for no one and was incapable of feeling for anyone, but it had endured for a long time and would continue to endure.

It was only Lauren who now kept him in Rutherford, which was, God knew, a miserable hole of a town. He had returned to it after the war only because he was familiar with it and had thought that he could manipulate it easily to his own advantage, especially as a war hero, but he had been unable to do it and had grown sick to his belly of it long ago, the ugliness and frustration and enervating dullness of it, and he would have gone away for good if it had not been for Lauren, whom he desired, and Lauren's wealth, which he also desired. His desire for both antedated only slightly the calculated determination to possess them, Lauren and what Lauren had, the beginning fully four years ago of a careful scheme of conquest which now, he felt, was approaching a successful end if only some goddamned emotional cripple like Guy Butler or some mother-smothered ass like Rex Tye did not in some way cut him out and louse things up for keeps. Or if he did not louse it up himself by damn fool carelessness such as he had been guilty of, for instance, in the sordid little gonadal episode with that panting bitch at Sylvan Green last summer. Thinking of Avis, he felt sick, and thinking of Guy and Rex, he felt a rising cold resentment that approached the quality of fury. Though he did not consciously think so, he reacted to their encroachment as if it were deliberate insolence, a kind of intolerable violation of his person, as the Tom's had been, as later the boy's had been in the matter of the girl who was, in herself, not very significant.

But Lauren was significant. In herself and in what she stood for, she was vastly the most significant individual on earth, excepting Ellis Kuder only, and her significance was based on both his genuine desire and his realization that he could never in the world by the exploitation of his own assets, even shored by his almost perfect ruthlessness, escape from the terrible mediocrity that was in him and around him and was slowly smothering him from within and without. A million or so dollars, or the prospect of them, did not alter mediocrity, but they made it possible to live with it compatibly. They made it possible to bear the whole vast encroachment and corruption of a life otherwise unbearable.

He lay on his bed in his rented room, and Lauren lay beside him. He reached out in the darkness and touched her body, her cool taut flesh, and he felt in her flesh the quivering of passion against restraint, the agony and excitement of capitulation.

After a while he got up and went into the bathroom and turned off the light and came back into the dark bedroom. He cut off the radiator and opened a window and lay down again, now under the covers. Lauren was no longer in the bed with him. He was completely alone. He heard in the railroad yards the same laboring freight that Guy Butler heard.

CHAPTER 9

Rex Tye closed the front door of the house carefully. There was only the faintest click when the latch slipped into place behind him. A small table lamp, left burning by his mother, spread its weak light thinly on wall and floor, and the shadows beyond the perimeter of light seemed to press upon it and wait and wait with infinite patience for the time when they could close in. Quietly, for several full minutes without moving, Rex stood by the door with one hand still on the knob. He listened to the house, the whispers of the house, the stirring and breathing of wood and fabric and the immaterial residue of things said and done and felt. A tiny night-light was burning in the wall at the head of the stairs, and he lifted his eyes to it and looked at it steadily for quite a while, and he thought that the light on the table in the hall and the light in the wall at the head of the stairs were somehow symbolic of his mother, of his mother and him and their relationship, and everywhere he had ever gone, or went now, or would ever go, he would find little trails of weak light that she had left in the darkness to show him the way.

There would be a light in his room, too. The last thing she had done before going to bed, he knew as certainly as if he had witnessed it, was to go into his room and light the lamp which was now there burning for him, the last of the three to show him the way. She had left the light and gone to bed, but she had not gone to sleep, and she was lying and waiting for his return now in the darkness of her room upstairs, and he believed that there was no sound in the night too soft for her to hear, not even the rush of air into the place his body vacated in movement, and quite possibly she had already heard the tiny snick of the latch which even he, right next it, had hardly been able to hear.

He wondered why he hated his mother so utterly. It was easy to understand why a clown like Purvy Stubbs hated his Old Man, for one was a coward and the other was a bully, and so hatred was natural between them, but it was by no means so easy to understand why he, Rex, hated his mother, and there were many obscure forces involved in it. Not that he really wanted to understand it, or tried seriously to analyze it. It was so enormous and virulent inside him that it justified itself in its simple enormity, and far more astonishing that its existence was the incredibly natural cunning with which he had all his life concealed it. He had always been a courteous and considerate child, and he was a courteous and considerate man, and he performed the superficial functions of devotion with a kind of consummate ease, so that they could, though it was not suspected, be as naturally the expression of animus as otherwise. In a minute, for example, he would go upstairs and open his mother's door and speak to her, and she would be awake and would respond, and he would go in and sit on the edge of her bed, as he always did, and they would talk for a while, and he would kiss her good-night, as she would never in the world suspect that he wished she were dead for no other reason than that it was the only way she would ever leave him, while it was somehow impossible for him to leave her. And this was something else he could not understand: that he could not desert her, though he wished each time they parted never to see her again.

Moving abruptly with a suggestion of effort, as if against a compulsion to remain indefinitely where he was, he walked over to the hall table and turned off the lamp and went upstairs. In the upper hall, he stopped at the head of the stairs and looked at the floor outside his mother's door, which he had to pass in order to reach his own, and there was no sign of a light yet, but he knew that she was awake and waiting and perhaps even at that instant reaching for a switch, and as he watched and anticipated it, the light appeared in a thin bright line at the door's bottom edge. Promptly, responding to an invitation that had the authority of a command, he went to the door and knocked and entered.

His mother was sitting up in bed with her pillow bunched behind her back. Her gray hair had been undone and brushed and brought over her shoulders in two parts, but it was not otherwise disarranged and had obviously not touched the pillow that supported her back, and it was clear that she had been sitting erect in the darkness awaiting the sound of his return. There were blue shadows in the gray hair, and blue shadows under the eyes that looked at him levelly across the room with an expression of adoration that was a kind of refined and subtle wickedness. It possessed, he thought, the ugly narcissism of a cultist who had created his own esoteric deity in his own image.

"Hello, Mother," he said, closing the door of the room behind him.

"Hello, darling." She patted the bed beside her with a thin, blue-veined hand. "I was hoping you'd stop to chat with me. I've been quite unable to sleep."

He walked over and sat on the bed in the precise place the hand had indicated. He held the hand in one of his and began stroking it softly with the other. It was somehow essential to their relationship to sustain the fiction that this was all charmingly casual and unplanned, with nothing demanded or conceded, although he always stopped, and she never slept, and everything was done and said almost with the practiced precision of a ritual.

"Have you had a pleasant evening?" she said.

"All right," he said. "Nothing exceptional."

"Perhaps you would like to tell me about it. I'm always so interested in hearing about your affairs, you know."

He hesitated before answering, and there was, after the hesitation, a thin edge to his voice.

"It's hardly worth telling, Mother. The evening was really quite dull."

This was a deviation from the ritual, and he felt her hand stiffen in his. The hand was very cold, he thought. Why was her flesh always so cold when she kept her room so warm?

"I'm sure I'd not find it dull," she said, "but it is unnecessary to tell me about it, of course, if you don't wish. How is Lauren?"

"Lauren? Lauren's fine."

She was silent again, clearly waiting for him to tell her whether or not he had seen Lauren tonight, but he looked down at her hand, tracing with his eyes its blue veins, and volunteered nothing. She was not certain, but she thought she detected in him a hint of deliberate recalcitrance, and it disturbed her and made her a little angry, and she was forced to prolong the silence until she was quite sure that the anger would not be apparent in her voice.

"She's a sweet girl," she said. "Quite unspoiled, in spite of her family's wealth. I was very pleased when you and she became such close friends, darling."

"I know, Mother. You want me to marry her, and I am more than willing, in spite of her family's wealth."

Irony was something he had never used against her, and it was cruel and terrifying in its implications of what might develop between them, or might be secretly between them at this moment, and she felt suddenly tired and venomous and exceedingly old. But she ignored his remark, waiting again for the assurance of control, for it was imperative that nothing he brought into the light that might grow there. In the dark, things withered and decayed and did not grow.

"You look tired," she said. "Would you like to go to bed?"

"I think I would, if you don't mind. It's rather late, really. I stopped in at the taproom of the Division Hotel at the last minute."

"Do you think the taproom is really a proper place to go?"

"There's nothing wrong with the taproom, Mother. I met Guy Butler and Ellis Kuder and Purvy Stubbs there tonight."

"Really? That's nice. They're all quite acceptable friends, I'm sure."

Oh, Jesus, Jesus, Jesus, he thought. *Because Guy was precocious and almost famous, and because Ellis Kuder's mother is a dull woman involved in good works, and because Purvy's Old Man is president of a bank and lives on the ridge, it follows with some kind of odd logic that they must necessarily be acceptable to anyone, and it does not matter or refute the logic in the least that Guy is a psychic cripple and near-alcoholic, or that Ellis is capable of committing any atrocity that suits his purpose without jeopardizing his security, or that Purvy is a frustrated incompetent, festering with hate and guilty of mental patricide at least. It is quite acceptable to associate, even in a taproom, with these honorable young men of Rutherford, even though I am, of course, superior to all of them, in spite of their superior advantages, and this is something taught to me by my mother that I believe. I believe in my own superiority as something that does not have to be demonstrated or proved, the result of a sort of laying on of hands or spiritual visitation, and whether the hands and spirit were of God or the devil is also something that does not matter in the logic of my mother.*

Leaning forward, he brushed his mother's forehead with his lips. The perfunctory kiss was like a touch of dry ice, and he caught from her thin blue nylon bed jacket a faint scent of nauseous lavender. Abruptly, he stood up.

"Good-night, Mother. I hope you will be able to sleep now."

"I don't feel that I shall. I'm sure I shall lie awake all the rest of the night."

"Have you taken anything?"

"No. I don't want to develop a dependence on soporifics. They become a habit, I understand."

"I doubt that one tablet would do you any harm. Would you like me to bring it to you?"

"Do you mind? The box is in the medicine cabinet in the bathroom."

He went into the bathroom and found the box, a shiny green cardboard container with a pharmacist's label pasted on the top. Closing the cabinet door, he caught a glimpse of his reflected face below shimmering pale curls. It was a face that gave the impression of delicacy without actually being delicate in the structure of bone or the molding of flesh. His mother had told him once that he looked like pictures of Percy Bysshe Shelley, and he had thought himself, after finding a picture of Shelley in an anthology, that there was a resemblance. His mother had told him also that she regretted not having thought of Shelley as a Christian name for him, which was a regret he shared. It seemed to him much more appropriate than Rex, his father's name, and when he was quite young he called himself Shelley secretly and sometimes in school wrote it over and over in his notebook.

After filling a water tumbler about a quarter full from the tap of the lavatory, he carried the tumbler and the barbiturate into the bedroom. Handing the tablet to his mother, he stood watching while she swallowed it, and then he handed her the tumbler and waited again until she had drunk the water, which she did quite slowly in small sips. Taking the tumbler from her hand when it was empty, he set it on her bedside table.

"Are you ready to lie down now, Mother?"

"Yes. I think so. Perhaps I shall sleep after all."

"If you'll just lean forward a little, I'll arrange your pillow."

"Thank you, darling. You're very considerate."

She leaned forward as he suggested, and he arranged the pillow in its proper place, and smoothed it with his hands and helped her to lie down with her head upon it.

"Good-night, Mother," he said again. "Shall I put out the light?"

"Yes, please."

He turned out the light and bent over from the waist in the exaggerated immediate darkness to kiss her a second time, the dry ice touch and scent of lavender, and then, without speaking, he went out of her room and down the hall to his own. He undressed at once and put on his pajamas and sat down in a chair beside his bed and stared across the room at the wall, and for a while he saw nothing whatever, because his eyes were blinded by the thoughts behind them, but then he became aware of a large photograph of a man and a woman and a child. The photograph was hanging on the wall, where it had hung for as long as he could remember, and the man was his father, the woman his mother, the child himself. He had been about seven, he thought, when the picture was made, and his father had died during the winter following, and it was a long time ago. He did not remember his father very well, and he would not have been able to recall the father's appearance at all if it had not been for the picture. He had learned, however, from things said and suggested and perceived dimly in the shadows of old conflicts in his mother's mind, that his father had been a timid, introverted man, a material failure, the worst possible kind of man to have been married to the woman he was married to, a woman of velveteen arrogance and fierce ambition. He had learned from his mother to despise his father, the memory of him. Most of all, he had learned that he was somehow dedicated to compensating the mother for the father's inadequacy. He had not so far, however, been or done anything exceptional at all, and he had, like his father, been deprived in his turn of his proper position. There seemed always to be a kind of conspiracy against him, the right combination of qualities and circumstances never quite falling out together, and it was not fair, it was simply not fair.

But now the conspiracy had collapsed. Now he saw that he would actually achieve the position that had been withheld, and it was as simple as a seduction, although a polite and proper and subtle seduction. He would marry Lauren Haig. This was an objective to which he had for a long time been dedicated, except for the single insane lapse last summer at Sylvan Green, and the vanity which was essential to his survival did not for an instant permit him to doubt that he would in the end be chosen over Guy Butler or Ellis Kuder or anyone else who wished to compete. For he was Rex Tye. On him had been laid the hand.

Thinking of Guy and Ellis, he smiled thinly. He knew perfectly well that they didn't like him, though they treated him with courtesy and accepted him with reservations. This did not disturb him, however. On the contrary, it rather pleased him. They disliked him because of his air of fastidious superiority, and their very recognition of it gave it validity.

He heard the freight that Guy heard, that Ellis heard, and he went to bed.

CHAPTER 10

The one who murdered Avis Pisano fell asleep and slept for almost two hours and awoke suddenly for no particular reason that he could isolate and identify.

Murderer, he thought. *Murderer.*

The thought was like a whisper coming from a dark corner of the room into the darker cavity of his skull. It moved like the merest breath of air in the deep night over the contour of his brain.

Murderer, murderer, murderer.

He was not afraid of the darkness or of what the darkness held, for that fear springs from a sense of distinction, of being apart and alien and vulnerable, and he and the darkness were one. He lay on his bed and listened to the slow and cadenced breathing of the night, which was also his own breathing, and the pulse of the night was in his throat and was measuring time behind his eyes. In his mind, with a precise and exceptional clarity, he began to recall the chronology of the night, and he was standing again in the little park among the Junipers, and it was cold, and the Junipers rustled in the wind. The cold penetrated his clothing and his flesh and crept into his bones. He cursed the cold and beat his hands, and from far down the parallel shining rails came the thin and distant cry of the seven-o-five. The cold now diminished by an intense and rising sense of hot excitement, he watched Avis Pisano descend from the train and peer about her in the yellow light, and he stepped forward among the rustling Junipers and raised an arm, and then there was instantly a dissolution and reassembling of time and action, and he was walking slowly over the frozen ground of the shallow slough with her dead weight in his arms, and her hair hung down and swayed with his walking as if it possessed a separate and continuing life of its own.

Bending his knees with the right foot forward of the left, he descended into a kneeling position, as one might kneel to receive an accolade, and then bending the trunk of his body forward from the hips, he laid the body he carried upon its back on the frozen ground, and afterward arose and brought his left foot up even with his right and stood for a moment looking down with bowed head in a posture of prayer or mourning. Above him, the moon slipped silently into an unclouded space, and the light of the moon touched the eyes of Avis, and she stared upward into the light with wide-open eyes through a lacery of black branches to the moon itself. In spite of her facial distortion and visible tongue, she acquired in that moment of light an ethereal quality she had never had, a brief and capricious delicacy in death.

Turning away, he walked back up the dry slough to the road, and there was another dissolution and reassembling, and he was back in an instant at the railroad station, in the windswept park among the Junipers, and there was a fat fool standing in the yellow light on the platform beside the restaurant door, and the fool was a deadly menace.

Purvy. Purvy Stubbs. That odd obstructed clown to whom striped overalls and a striped cloth cap were as much a fetish as the cloak of Christ. Recapitulated now, leaning like a bloated adult child against the station in the windy cold, he possessed a gross and obscene quality that was like the innocent evil of an idiot. He was not a joke, as he had always been, no longer despicable and fit for contempt, for he had become by chance, or perhaps design, a potential agent of ruin. How much had he seen? Well, very little. That was apparent from his comments in the taproom at the Division Hotel tonight. But how much significance was attached to the little? That was the threat and the essence of terror. Perhaps it would be, then understood, a clear clue to identity. If so, how long would it be before Purvy's tumbling brain recovered the clue and achieved understanding?

Fear probed the sheltering darkness and touched him and made him cold. He had felt no remorse, and felt none now, and would feel none ever, and what he had felt primarily, almost to the exclusion of other emotions, was an enormous exhilaration and pride that he had accomplished decisively so monstrous much. Avis Pisano had been a cheap little fool with the temerity to threaten him, and she had received nothing that she had not deserved and made necessary by stupidity, but now he was threatened again by another fool, and what made it worse, what made it utterly infuriating, was that the threat this time was not the conscious action of a directed intelligence, however inadequate, but the intolerable meddling of an inferior who had been placed by accident in a position to destroy him. Anger came, the cold fury with the cold fear, and he tightened the muscles of his body and lay rigidly looking up into the darkness, but he could not control the trembling which had seized him, and this was degrading and humiliating and took the fine edge off his sense of pride and power.

Suddenly he got up and stood beside the bed, and the icy air from the open window cut at his flesh and was like a blow above the diaphragm. In a gesture of defiance, as if it were imperative now to show his contempt for everything that threatened him or tried to hurt him, he walked directly to the window and stood there looking down at an angle to the street until he was numb, and then it occurred to him that his display of defiance was in itself a form of weakness, a concession to amorphous beings, and so he closed the window and returned to the bed and sat down on the edge of it.

Lauren, he thought. *Lauren*.

Thinking of her, forming in his mind the shape and sound of her name, he tried also to see her as she might be at that instant, and for a moment he succeeded. Lying in a softer, warmer darkness, she slept and breathed, and her breath stirred sweetly on her lips. Her breasts, with the breathing, rose and fell, and her white legs moved in sleep to a need she would not remember.

She receded, returned and was changed.

She lay on her back and stared blindly at the moon.

She was gross and obscene in a too-short coat in a wash of yellow light.

The murderer pounded a fist into a palm and cursed the gross image.

He lay down under covers and closed his eyes, but he could not sleep, and the night in time became day.

CHAPTER 11

Purvy Stubbs was an early riser. There were two reasons for this, neither of them indicating on Purvy's part any particular addiction to industry or the homely wisdom of Poor Richard. In the first place, by rising early and breakfasting at once, he was able to avoid the company of his Old Man at table, which was more than compensation for the loss of a little sleep. In the second place, he liked to go down to the station and watch the eight-ten come in from the south, and it was necessary to allow sufficient time for dressing and eating and the walk to town. For the first two hours of the day, as a matter of fact, he functioned on a schedule that was almost as precise as that of the trains. He set his alarm for six-thirty, rolled out immediately, shaved and dressed and was downstairs at seven, allow a minute or two either way. He took a full half-hour for breakfast, being a hearty eater, and he always had three scrambled eggs, six slices of crisp bacon, three cups of coffee with sugar and cream, and biscuits with jam, or toast with jam, depending upon which was served to him by Verbenia, the Negro cook, who loved him far more than anyone else on earth.

The second morning after the murder of Avis Pisano, which was the morning of Monday, he entered the dining room at two minutes before seven. His breakfast was ready and piping hot, a pleasure to see, as well as to smell and taste, white and yellow and shades of brown, and he wondered if anyone had ever written a poem about scrambled eggs and bacon, but he couldn't think of any. Then he tried to think if something of the sort had been written in prose by Thomas Wolfe, who had written quite a lot about food in general, but he couldn't remember anything like that either. He ate his breakfast slowly, left the house at seven-thirty, and reached the station at seven-fifty-five.

The wind had died in the night, but it was still pretty cold. Purvy went through the waiting room onto the platform and directly down to the restaurant. To his surprise, Phoebe Keeley was still inside the oval counter. She looked tired and cross.

"Hello, Pheeb," he said. "What the hell you doing here this hour? I thought you worked six to six."

"That's what I thought, too," Phoebe said. "The truth is, Madge Roney is working six to six days, or's supposed to be, but she called in and said she couldn't make it till eight and would I stay on. What can you do when someone calls and asks will you stay on?"

"Well, I guess you have to stay, when you come to think of it. Tough luck, Pheeb."

"Oh, it comes out all right. Madge'll stay on till eight tonight, so it all comes out all right."

"Still, twelve hours is a hell of a long shift, especially at night, and fourteen's just too damn long to expect. I bet you get pretty tired, Pheeb. Along about three, four in the morning, it must get pretty tough."

"It's not so bad, to tell the truth. Matter of fact, six to six nights is a hell of a lot better than six to six days, in my opinion. Days are busier, and your feet catch it. You're always on your feet without even any chance to sit down more'n a minute or two at a time, and your feet ache and all. Nights, especially after midnight, it gets pretty quiet usually, just a few customers now and then, and you can sit around quite a bit without being disturbed, and I've even been known to catch forty winks, but don't tell the boss. I got seniority over Madge and could have the day shift if I wanted it, but the simple truth is, I won't have it."

"I can see your point of view, at that, come to think of it. There sure are advantages to the night shift, Pheeb, there's no question about it."

"Of course it ties you down a lot. Concerning dates and things like that, I mean. You only get one night off a week for dates and all."

"That's right. There are advantages and disadvantages, sure enough. I guess that's the way it is with everything."

"I guess so. You want a cup of coffee, Purvy?"

"No, thanks. I had three cups at home. Fact is, I'm floating."

"Well, why didn't you stop in the men's room? You came through the station, didn't you?"

"I came through, all right, but it hadn't struck me yet. You know how these things are. Pheeb. It just now struck me."

"You better go on back while you got time."

"Oh, it's not that bad yet. I can hold it until the eight-ten comes in."

Phoebe leaned on one elbow on the counter and looked at Purvy, who had seated himself on a stool, with an expression of affectionate tolerance. She shook her head slowly from side to side.

"Purvy," she said, "you're the goddamndest fellow I know anything about, if you don't mind my saying so. I'd give a good tumble to know what it is you see in these lousy trains."

"I've tried to tell you, Pheeb, but I can't seem to get across."

"That's right. That's damn sure right, Purvy. I'm ready to say that I'll simply never understand it. I guess it would take one of these psychologists or someone like that to see what's really behind it."

"Well, it's sort of interesting. Pheeb. You'll have to admit that."

"The hell I will! What's interesting about a train?"

"Oh, the people coming and leaving, going places and all that. You wonder where and why, I mean. It's interesting to wonder. You take Saturday night, for instance. A girl got off the seven-o-five, Pheeb."

"Really? Now, that's really interesting, Purvy. That's about as fascinating a piece of news as I've ever heard. A genuine live girl with two legs and everything?"

"You needn't be so sarcastic, Pheeb. She got off, and she was wearing this fur coat, and looked around like she was expecting someone, and then she saw this person down in the little park at the south end of the platform, and she went down there and disappeared."

"In the park? That little patch of grass with the Junipers growing in it? Why would anyone wait down there?"

"Well, that's what's interesting about it. It looks to me like whoever it was would have waited out on the platform."

"You mean you didn't see who it was?"

"No. Just a sort of shadow. I was telling Cheerful Forbes about it Saturday night, and he said it was probably someone who had this girl coming in to shack up or something."

"That sounds reasonable. Whose wife is gone? You know anyone?"

"No, I don't, Pheeb. I haven't heard of anyone. It could have been someone from another town close by, as far as that goes. It would be smart to have her get off at another town than the one you lived in."

"Purvy, I do believe you'd be real good at having some sneaky affair with someone. It sounds to me, as a matter of fact, like you've got it all figured out how to do it."

"Oh, come off, Pheeb. You just get to wondering and figuring, and things like that come into your head, that's all."

"Well, you ever decide to lead a life of sin, you let me know, Purvy. I might be interested."

"You oughtn't talk like that, Pheeb. Someone who didn't know you might think you were serious."

Purvy looked at his wrist watch, more to avoid Phoebe's eyes than to read the time. Then he stood up suddenly and walked over to the big plate-glass window.

"Say, Pheeb," he said, "the eight-ten's late. It's eleven after already."

"Lord God!" Phoebe said. "The world's coming to an end!" At that moment, as if to refute her, the whistle of the eight-ten drifted up faintly from the bend of the tracks to the south, and Purvy, since it was so cold outside, stayed standing by the window to watch it arrive and depart. While this was being accomplished, Madge Roney arrived and took over in the oval, and when Purvy finally turned away from the window, the train gone, Phoebe was standing beside him with her coat on.

"Purvy," she said, "you got a car here?"

"No, I haven't, Pheeb," he said. "I don't drive. Didn't you know that?"

"You don't drive? Why the hell not?"

"I just don't have the knack for it."

"Damn it, Purvy, anyone can drive if he tries."

"I can't. I've tried and tried, but I keep running into things."

"Oh, well, never mind. It's just that I'm pretty tired after fourteen hours, and I thought you might drive me home."

"I'd sure be glad to, Pheeb, if I had a car and could drive it. If you want me to, I'll walk home with you, though."

"What the hell good would that do? Purvy, you do come up with the damnedest things sometimes. I'll just go in the station and call a taxi."

"Okay, Pheeb. I guess I'd better be getting on down to the bank, myself."

"So-long, Purvy. See you when the trains come in."

"Sure, Pheeb. So-long."

She went out onto the platform and walked north toward the waiting room doors, and Purvy stood and watched her through the glass. He liked Pheeb a lot, even though she ribbed him and sometimes got sarcastic. The nice movement of her big hips was pretty much concealed by her coat right now, but it didn't make any difference to Purvy one way or another. He went out into the cold himself and started for the bank and got there about twenty-five after eight, which was twenty-five later than he was due, and thirty-five before the doors opened.

Purvy worked as a teller, but he wasn't very good at it. He made far more mistakes than a teller was ordinarily allowed. Every once in a while his Old Man, when he was particularly aggravated by something Purvy had done, would come out of his office and say in a loud voice for everyone to hear that he was damn well tired of tolerating endless stupidity and was damn well having Purvy's hands measured for a broom handle. This had disturbed Purvy at first and had caused him to feel humiliated and ashamed, but the Old Man killed the effect by over-doing it, the same way he killed all his effects, and after a while Purvy didn't pay much attention to it, and neither did anyone else. It was all bluff and bluster, anyhow. The Old Man wouldn't really have put Purvy to sweeping the floor and polishing the brass on the front door, which work was now done by a fellow named Wendell who had eaten some lye as a baby and had his mind affected by it, for it would have been a reflection on the Old Man himself to have Purvy doing such menial work around the bank. He just bluffed and blustered and threatened, and all the other employees were secretly on Purvy's side.

The morning went by pretty pleasantly, once the doors opened and it got started, and the one thing about being a teller that Purvy liked was the opportunity it gave him to exchange little bits of talk with all the different people who came in to deposit money or take it out or to see about having Purvy's last mistake corrected. Between eleven and noon there was quite a rush, which was usual, for it was then that the business places up and down Main sent someone in to do their banking for the day, and at noon, when things slacked off, Purvy went to lunch. He didn't go home, because his Old Man would be there. Most of the time he went to the coffee shop at the Division Hotel, and that's where he went this particular day. He didn't go directly into the coffee shop, however, but into the lobby, where he stopped at the desk to exchange a few words with Chick Jones, the day clerk.

"Hello, Chick," he said. "Let me have a package of those Kools and a package of Black Jack chewing gum."

"Jesus, Purvy," Chick said. "Menthol and licorice! You sure got peculiar tastes."

"Oh, I don't know. You get used to mentholated cigarettes, you don't want anything else. At least, that's the way I find it. As for the Black Jack, I been chewing it ever since I was a kid. When I was a kid, I thought a stick of Black Jack was about the best treat there was, and I guess I've just never gotten over it. Matter of fact, my Old Man says I've never gotten over most of the things I liked when I was a kid. How are things going, Chick?"

"Okay, Purvy. Everything quiet."

"No wild parties in the rooms, or anything like that?"

"Nope. Maybe a little quiet fornication, but no wild parties."

Chick laughed, and so did Purvy. Purvy opened his pack of Kools and offered it to Chick, who declined. Purvy lit one himself and puffed up a little cloud of mentholated smoke. He never inhaled. He just drew the smoke into his mouth and blew it out through pursed lips, just exactly as he had smoked dried grape vine and catalpa beans years ago. It was something else he had never gotten over.

"You happen to remember the guests who checked in Saturday night?" he said.

"Not exactly. Man and his wife, I remember. Half a dozen salesmen."

"Oh. No strange girl?"

"Nope. No girl at all, strange or otherwise. Why, Purvy? You fixing up one of these assignations or something?"

He laughed again, clearly considering this too ludicrous to be taken seriously.

"Nothing like that, Chick," Purvy said. "You know damn well I don't have anything like that to do with women. The truth is, I'm just curious. I saw this girl in a fur coat get off the seven-o-five down at the station Saturday night, and

I'm just wondering who she is and where she went and all. You know. Just curious about it."

"Well, she didn't check in here, and if she got sneaked up without registering, someone owes the balance on a double, that's all I can say. I don't give a damn who sleeps with who, but they can't do it for the price of a single."

"All right. Chick. I was just asking out of curiosity, that's all. Guess I'd better go in and get some lunch now. See you later."

"Sure, Purvy. Take it easy."

Purvy went into the coffee shop and had sweetbreads for lunch, and afterward, about twenty to one, he came back into the lobby and looked into the taproom and saw Guy Butler sitting on a stool at the bar. The taproom opened at twelve-thirty, and Guy was probably the first customer. He would probably, at midnight, be the last. Looking at him, Purvy remembered the bit from Housman about malt doing more than Milton can to justify God's ways to man. Guy didn't drink beer, of course, only bourbon, but the principal was the same. Purvy went in and sat beside him at the bar.

"Hi, Guy," he said.

Guy didn't look at him. He swallowed some bourbon and said hello. Bernie Huggins came up opposite, and Purvy said he guessed he'd have a short beer.

"What you mean, guess?" Bernie said. "You want a short beer or not?"

"Goddamn it, Bernie," Purvy said, "gimme a short beer."

Bernie drew it and shoved it across the counter. Purvy picked up the glass and looked at it. He didn't really want the beer, but he felt that he had to order something to justify his presence. As a matter of fact, he didn't even know exactly why he was present. He didn't have anything in particular to say to Guy, but somehow he always felt impelled to be friendly whenever he saw Guy around, even though Guy couldn't always be said to be responsive.

"How are things going, Guy?" he said. "You're starting early, aren't you?"

"This is breakfast," Guy said.

Purvy understood that this was Guy's way of telling him to mind his own damn business, but Purvy didn't resent it because he deserved it, and it seemed that he was always saying something innocently that had the sound of meddling.

"I asked Chick Jones if that girl who got off the train checked in Saturday night," he said, "but Chick says she didn't."

Guy turned his head then and looked at him for the first time. He looked at him levelly without any expression whatever for thirty seconds at least, and he didn't say a word. Then he turned away and took another swallow of bourbon and looked into his glass, still not saying a word, and Purvy realized that he had done it again, given the impression of meddling when he didn't really mean it that way at all. He gulped his short beer, wiped his mouth, and slid off the stool.

"Well," he said, "I got to get back to the bank. Be seeing you, Guy."

"Chances are," Guy said.

Purvy went back to the bank and got into his cage, and the afternoon drifted along uneventfully and was generally pretty dull until ten minutes to three, the closing hour, when Mrs. Brisket came in to deposit her pension.

"Hello, Mrs. Brisket," Purvy said.

"Hello, Purvy," Mrs. Briskett said. "I've simply never heard of anything so terrible."

"What?"

"I say it's simply terrible, isn't it?"

Purvy remembered to look to make sure that Mrs. Brisket had endorsed her check, which was something she usually forgot to do and he forgot to check, but since he had remembered this time, so had she, of course, and he thought that she sounded like she was thoroughly enjoying the most terrible thing she had ever heard of.

"What's terrible, Mrs. Brisket?"

"You mean you haven't heard?"

"I guess not. At least I haven't heard anything that struck me as being particularly terrible."

"That young woman being murdered, I mean. Hadn't you heard?"

"No, I hadn't. I hadn't heard."

Purvy made a neat entry in Mrs. Brisket's little black account book. His hand was steady, and he felt quite calm, and it crossed his mind that this was something he had a right to be proud of.

"Someone found her in a slough southwest of town," Mrs. Brisket said. "Her body, that is. It was a farmer, I think, who found her. Or maybe someone hunting rabbits. Anyhow, whoever found her, she had been strangled to death and left there in the cold for heaven knows how long, poor thing, and Sheriff Lonnie Womber went out and brought her into town to Haley's Funeral Parlor, and she's lying there this instant."

"Who is this young woman?"

"No one seems to know, Purvy. Anyhow, as I heard it, no one has been able to identify her yet. Seems she was a perfect stranger around Rutherford."

"Did you hear how she was dressed?"

"Dressed?"

"I mean her coat. Did you hear what kind of coat she was wearing?"

"Oh, yes. Now that you ask, I did. It was fur. Some kind of fur."

"Thanks, Mrs. Brisket. Do you need any blank checks today?"

"I don't think so, Purvy. I'm sure I have plenty, thank you very much."

Purvy pushed her account book through the aperture, and turned and walked right out of the cage and out of the bank without even bothering to put on his hat or topcoat. Haley's Funeral Parlor was on Main Street, a couple of blocks beyond the edge of the business district, and he walked directly there and went inside into the little hall outside the chapel, and Lonnie Womber was standing there talking to Mr. Haley.

"Hello, Purvy," Lonnie said. "If you came to see the girl, you can't."

"If she's the one I think she is," said Purvy, "I could tell you something about her."

Lonnie looked at Purvy for a few seconds. He had a long face with a long droopy nose and squinty eyes. His hair was the color of straw and straight as string and hung over his forehead almost into one eye. He looked shrewd, and folks said he was shrewd, and probably he was. For a county sheriff, anyhow.

"In that case," he said, "you better look and see if she's the one."

"It's all right," said Mr. Haley. "We haven't started to work on her yet."

They went into one of the back rooms, and the body was lying on a long table under a sheet. Lonnie pulled the sheet back a little, and Purvy looked at the distorted face of Avis Pisano.

"It's her, all right," he said.

He had thought she looked cold and lonely on the station platform night before last, and now he thought she looked colder and lonelier than ever. He felt all of a sudden like crying.

CHAPTER 12

The county jail was a yellow stone building sitting on a corner among a grove of walnut trees. In the fall, when the walnuts dropped, the kids in the neighborhood came and gathered them and took them home to spread out for drying. The juice in the hulls stained like dye and had to wear off, and for a long time afterward you could tell the kids who had gathered walnuts by the brown stain slowly fading to yellow on their fingers.

Inside, in Lonnie Womber's office, the air smelled of strong soap and men's bodies and sweeping compound. Overhead, suspended from the ceiling at a point determined by drawing diagonals from opposite corners, was one of those old-fashioned fans that beat the air slowly in the summer and made a kind of sleepy, satisfying sound that is not quite comparable to any other sound in the world. The fan was now still and had acquired a cobweb between its blades. Looking out a high, narrow window from his position in a chair in front of Lonnie's desk, Purvy could see a brown branch of ivy extending from the vine that climbed the yellow stones out of view to the right. The branch of ivy shivered in the wind and sometimes scratched at the glass.

"All right, Purvy," Lonnie said. "Now tell me what you know about this girl who was killed."

He was sitting behind his desk in a swivel chair. He rocked back in the chair and lifted his feet onto an open drawer of the desk. He acted as if this were all just pleasant conversation that didn't mean anything in particular one way or another.

"Well," Purvy said, "the only thing I know, as a matter of fact, is that she got off the seven-o-five Saturday night, and someone met her."

"Is that so?"

Lonnie found a cigarette paper in a vest pocket and a can of Prince Albert in his coat pocket. He shook a little tobacco into the paper and rolled it up and ran his tongue along the gummed edge of the paper. Some people said it was an affectation for Lonnie to smoke roll-your-owns instead of tailor-mades, that he did it because it made him seem more in the character of an old-school sheriff, and others said maybe not, maybe he simply preferred them, and the truth was, he smoked them because they were cheaper. He lit this one with a paper match and let it hang from the corner of his mouth. Smoke ascended from it in a very thin blue line.

"Well," he said, "it might not seem like much at first thought, but when you stop to consider it, it's quite a lot. We can find out where the train came from, the towns it stopped and all, and we ought to be able to find out where the girl got on it. Chances are we can find someone to identify her without too much trouble. Who was it met her? That's the important thing right now, as I see it."

"I don't know."

"You mean it was a stranger?"

"No. I didn't actually see whoever it was, that's what I mean."

"Then how the hell you know *anyone* met her?"

"Damn it, I mean I just got a glimpse of whoever it was. He was waiting down in the little park with the Junipers in it. It's dark down there at night, and I just saw a kind of shadow or movement or something, and the girl saw it, too, and went down there. That's the last I saw of her until a while ago in Haley's."

"You used the third person masculine singular." Lonnie looked rather proud of this bit of erudition which might not have been expected from a county sheriff. "How do you know it was a he?"

Purvy looked surprised, not so much as a result of Lonnie's knowledge of pronouns as of the question itself. Now that he was forced to think of it, he didn't know why he assumed that it was a man who had waited in the cold and windy darkness among the Junipers, but he just knew damn well it was, that was all. Still, there must have been a reason. A reason, that was, for the assumption. Something seen, something almost registered, something slipping in an instant into the shadows. His brain began to itch again, and it was simply the most aggravating feeling in the world to be unable to scratch it.

"I don't know, Lonnie," he said. "I don't know how I know, but I'm damn sure, just the same, that it was a man."

"Well, considering developments, it's likely that it was, at that. Did this girl have a bag or anything when she got off the train?"

"Yes. One bag. She picked it up and carried it with her when she went down the platform to the little park."

"All right. We haven't been able to find it, so someone took it away. Whoever killed her, no doubt. Buried or burned by now, probably. We may find a trace of it later, but I doubt it like hell." Lonnie removed the roll-your-own cigarette from his mouth and looked at it sourly. It had gone out, so he threw it into a number 10 can on the floor and stood up. "Confidentially, Purvy, I never had a murder on my hands before, except the one couple years ago when that crazy half-breed killed the farmer over his hay-pitching wages, which was all cut and dried, with witnesses and everything, and damned if I know just what to do to get started. I guess I ought to try to get this girl identified, first off. What do you think?"

"That's what seems logical to me," Purvy said. "Seems to me you can't do much of anything at all until you know who she was."

"The seven-o-five's a local, isn't it?"

"That's right."

"Well, that's a break, at least. It ought to be easy to check back on the passengers in a dinky little local. Maybe the conductor would remember something. I guess the railroad could tell me who the conductor was, and where he lives. If he can remember where the girl got on, we got a big jump on things. I really got no confidence in its turning out so nice and easy, though. I got a feeling the conductor won't remember a damn thing about anything."

"Even if he doesn't, you could check the towns on the line. There can't be so very many on a short run like that."

"That's true. You got a good head on your shoulders, Purvy."

"Another thing. If the girl's got a family or something, they'll probably report her missing after a while. If they don't hear from her or anything, I mean."

"Sure. If she's got a family. If she was the kind who kept in touch with her family, if she had one. If her family's the kind that would worry if she didn't. If to hell and back."

"Well, damn it, you can publish a picture and description and all, can't you?"

"Purvy, damned if you don't make me completely ashamed of myself. By God, maybe you ought to be sheriff instead of me, and I ought to go down to the station and watch the trains come in and go out. Well, I guess we can't arrange a shift like that, though, because the people elected me to this office, and I got to do the best I can, and that's all there is to it."

While talking, Lonnie had come around the desk and put an arm around Purvy's shoulders, and all of a sudden, without quite understanding how it had been accomplished, Purvy found himself at the office door and being guided through into the hall. He felt proud that he had been able to contribute something valuable to Lonnie in the matter of the murdered girl, but he didn't swallow Lonnie's bull about his own inadequacy, not by a long shot, and he knew perfectly well that Lonnie had already thought of all the things that he, Purvy, had mentioned—like being able to check the towns, and publishing a picture and description and all—long before Purvy had thought of them himself. It was part of Lonnie's character to belittle himself, except at election time, and a lot of smart guys around the county had taken it at face value and gotten careless and were a hell of a lot sorrier and wiser afterward.

"Well, I haven't done much, really," Purvy said. "I just happened to see the girl get off the train, that's all."

"I'm damn glad you did." Lonnie gave Purvy's shoulder a pat that was also enough of a shove to get Purvy all the way through the door into the hall. "You've been a big help, and I appreciate it. Good-bye, now."

He closed the door, and Purvy went down the hall and outside and started back to town, and he kept thinking about the dead girl and feeling terrible about her, worse and worse as he walked, and he decided he would go to the taproom at the Division and have a drink and see if there wasn't someone around to talk with. It helped make things a little lighter inside you if you could talk about them with someone. He wondered how it would be, watching the seven-o-five come in after this. He was certain his pleasure in it would be spoiled a little, at least for a while, and this was added to his sorrow for the girl and made him feel even more terrible than before.

It was a few minutes after five when he reached the hotel and went into the taproom, and the bar was doing a modest business. Guy Butler was there, on the same stool, in the same position, over a different glass. From appearances, he seemed not to have moved since noon, but this was not so. He had gone through the routine of his job, at least, and had just returned to the taproom. Next to him sat Ellis Kuder, and down the line, two Pabst Blue Ribbons intervening, Rex Tye sipped a whisky sour and seemed, between sips, to be inordinately preoccupied with the cherry. Purvy claimed an empty stool somewhat removed from all three. He climbed on and specified a shot of bourbon when Bernie Huggins got around to him. Bernie, who had been reaching for a short beer glass, looked at Purvy in amazement, his body posed in a position of arrested motion.

"Purvy," he said, "if I didn't know damn well better, I'd swear you said you wanted a shot of bourbon."

"That's what I said," Purvy replied, "and you know it."

"Okay, okay. It just requires a little adjustment, that's all." Bernie set out a glass and poured from a bottle. "What's the matter, Purvy, you had a bad experience or something?"

"As a matter of fact, I have. I been down to Haley's Funeral Parlor looking at that girl who was murdered." Conversation died down the bar. A focal point and feeling suddenly uneasy about it, Purvy gulped his shot, gagged, took a quick swallow of water. Then he felt more assured, a little important. Bernie Huggins leaned across the bar and peered closely into Purvy's eyes to see if he was telling a whopper. Purvy plainly wasn't.

"The hell you say!" Convinced of Purvy's sincerity, Bernie straightened and continued to stare across the bar with a great deal more interest than Purvy ordinarily elicited. "How come you been doing that? You acting as Lonnie Womber's deputy or something, Purvy?"

"You know I'm not any deputy, Bernie. It just happened that I knew something that turned out to be helpful."

"Is that a fact? Can you tell us about it, or is it a secret among you sleuths who are working on the case?"

This was meant to draw a laugh along the bar, but everyone was concentrating on Purvy and missed the humor. As a matter of fact, the only one who got it at all was Purvy himself, who didn't appreciate it. He flushed and looked at all the faces turned in his direction. All but two, that was. Ellis Kuder looked straight across the bar into the mirror at his own reflection. Guy Butler looked into his glass as if he hadn't the slightest awareness of what was going on around him. Rex Tye stared steadily at Purvy down the length of the bar, but his face was no more than a white blur in the dim light that did not touch it directly.

"You needn't try to be funny about it, Bernie," Purvy said, "because it's a long way from a joke. The way it happened, I was at the station Saturday night when the seven-o-five came in, and this girl got off. She was all alone, and I had a feeling, when Mrs. Brisket told me in the bank about a girl being murdered, that they might be the same. It was just a kind of feeling, I mean. I went down to Haley's to see, and they were, and that's all there is to it."

"Did you know her, Purvy?"

"No, I never saw her before. Before Saturday, that is. The first time I ever saw her was when she got off the train alone and stood there looking around like she was expecting someone who had forgotten to come. I felt sorry for her for some reason or other, and that's a fact, and I guess that's the reason I looked at her close enough to be able to recognize her a little while ago at Haley's."

"Where did she go, Purvy? Which way from the station, I mean. Did you notice?"

"Well, she walked south down the platform, but I don't know which way from there. There was someone waiting for her, and they must have gone away together."

"I thought you said she looked around like she was expecting someone who had forgotten to come."

"That was before she saw him, and that's the queer part of it, seems to me. Someone was waiting for her, all right, but he was down there in the dark in that little park where the Junipers grow, and he never did come out into the light. I just got a glimpse of him. Just a kind of movement, if you know what I mean."

"You mean someone was actually waiting for her? She went off with someone?"

"That's right. That's what I mean."

Purvy looked at his empty glass and wished it were full, and Bernie, as if reading his mind, immediately fulfilled the wish. Bernie seemed hardly conscious of what he was doing, and all along the bar there was no sound or movement from any of the early drinkers as the full significance of Purvy's words became apparent. Into the warm taproom crept the cold of the little park, and it was suddenly as if the murderer sat among them.

Which, of course, he did. He sat in the cold and said nothing and listened to the whispering Junipers.

"Jesus," Bernie said. "Jesus."

CHAPTER 13

The man standing beside Lonnie Womber in the back room of Haley's Funeral Parlor plainly wished that he were elsewhere, but he was as plainly resigned to the doing of his duty. He stood looking down at his pot belly like some sort of odd philosopher seeking peace in the contemplation of his navel. Across the belly, threaded through a button hole of the vest and stretching on either side to opposite pockets, was a massive silver chain. Automatically, although he was not now on schedule and had no particular place to be at a certain time, the man removed from one of the pockets the heavy watch that was attached to one end of the chain. This was a gesture of habit, and he did not even read the time. Replacing the watch, he resumed the contemplation of his belly and did not look up immediately when Lonnie coughed and nudged him gently with an elbow. It was apparent that it required some effort to do what was required of him, and he was not to be hustled into doing something he would have preferred not doing at all.

"All right, Mr. Craddock," Lonnie said. "If you'll just have a good look at her and tell me what you think."

Mr. Craddock lifted his eyes then to the exposed face of Avis Pisano, and after the initial shock, it wasn't quite so bad as he had anticipated, and there was even a kind of quietude in the face, a suggestion of release that was less disturbing than the drawn look of illness that it had worn on the train. He stared at the face for almost a full minute without stirring, and he thought that there was really no sign that the girl had died violently, murdered, except the marks on her throat. This surprised him a great deal. He hardly knew what he had expected to see, but certainly something. Some ineradicable mark of evil and terror to indicate the enormity of this death.

"Yes," he said. "Yes."

"Yes, what, Mr. Craddock?"

"This girl was on the train, all right. I remember her particularly because she looked ill, and I felt sorry for her, and asked her if I could be of any help, but she said no. I remember that she kept looking out the window with this blind look in her eyes that people get sometimes. Not seeing anything. Just looking. I thought she was ill."

"Probably she was."

"Sort of nauseated and feverish, that is. As if she might be taking flu or something."

"She was pregnant."

"Pregnant? You say she was pregnant?"

Mr. Craddock looked slowly around at Lonnie, and then reluctantly back at the face of Avis, dreadfully certain now that the indicative mark of monstrous evil would surely be there, and he was surprised again to see that it was not. Only the suggestion of quietude and release.

"That's right, Mr. Craddock," Lonnie said. "Post-mortem showed it up."

The thought of the post-mortem was extremely unpleasant to Mr. Craddock, although he was uncertain as to what exactly was done in one, and he had for one moment the terrible feeling that he was going to humiliate himself by being sick to his stomach. He turned abruptly, standing with his back to the body, and assumed the same briskness of tone that he might have used with the porter on his train.

"What do you want me to tell you, Sheriff? I hope that I won't be detained much longer."

"After a couple of questions you are free to go, Mr. Craddock. To begin, now that you have been good enough to verify that she was on the train, I'd like to know the name of the town where she boarded it. It will be a big help if you can remember it."

"There's no problem there. I collected her ticket just this side of Twin Springs. Therefore, since tickets are collected between each stop, that's where she boarded."

"Twin Springs, then. Thanks very much, Mr. Craddock. Twin Springs isn't a very big place, and it ought to be easy enough to get some information about her there. Tell me. Were you on the platform when she got off? Here in Rutherford, I mean."

"Yes. I was standing by the steps when she came down from the coach."

"Did anyone meet her?"

"I don't think so. I don't remember seeing anyone on the platform except that fellow who always hangs around. He was standing over by the restaurant door."

"Purvy. Purvy Stubbs. He meets nearly all the trains. He's a nut about it. Well, thanks again, Mr. Craddock. You've helped me out a lot, and I won't keep you any longer."

"You're welcome, I'm sure."

Mr. Craddock took two steps toward a door that opened onto the rear drive where he'd left his car, and then he stopped, stood motionless for a moment, and turned very slowly, as if under a compulsion he tried to resist, to look back a final time.

"I'm sorry," he said, "I'm truly sorry," and it was impossible to tell if he was speaking to Lonnie or to the body of Avis.

Under way again, he walked briskly to the door and out into the drive, and although Lonnie followed him immediately, he was in his car, the car in motion, before Lonnie arrived. Standing under a permanent awning that extended over the drive outside the door, Lonnie watched the car turn into the street and disappear, and he wondered if he had better drive to Twin Springs today, or if it could be postponed until tomorrow, and he decided reluctantly that it could not be postponed and that he would have to go.

First, however, he returned to his office in the county jail. From a drawer of his desk, he took a brown manila envelope that contained three photographs of Avis Pisano, all from different negatives and all taken in the back room at Haley's. Standing by the desk, he looked at the photographs one at a time slowly, the varied perspectives of the serene death mask. He felt a little sick, a little angry, but most of all he felt afraid, and what he feared was not what he knew, but what he might learn. After a few minutes, slipping the photographs back into the manila envelope and the envelope into the right side pocket of his coat, he went out and got into his Ford and drove through town on the Main Street to its intersection with a north-south highway. Turning north, he drove steadily for two hours, about a hundred miles, when he stopped at a highway restaurant for a cup of coffee. The coffee was inferior, and he smoked two cigarettes with it. This required altogether about fifteen minutes, after which he returned to the Ford and drove for slightly longer than two more hours and slightly farther than another hundred miles. It was just before two o'clock in the afternoon when he reached Twin Springs.

He was hungry by that time, eight hours removed from breakfast, and he was tempted to eat before doing anything else, but he resisted the temptation and drove first to the railroad station. The depot was wooden, painted an ugly mustard yellow, separated from the tracks by a narrow brick platform. He parked in a graveled area at one end of the platform and crossed the bricks to the entrance. Inside, in the small waiting room, along three walls, there were the kind of hard oak benches that are apparently designed for the purpose of making people prefer to stand. In the center of the room was a pot-bellied cast-iron stove with a scuttle of coal on the floor beside it. In the fourth wall, from left to right as it was faced, were a door marked Ladies, the agent's grill, a door marked Men. Lonnie went to the grill and peered into the room beyond. There was no one there, and so he waited patiently, leaning against the grill beside the aperture and utilizing the time to roll and light another cigarette. After a while, a door opened, admitting to the agent's office a gust of cold air and a small man who seemed to be propelled by it. The man took off a wool mackinaw and a wool cap that matched it, hanging the mackinaw on a hook in the wall and stuffing the cap into one of its pockets. Then, rubbing his hands, he approached the grill and peered through at Lonnie, who turned to face him squarely. The agent was wearing bifocals which had steamed over when he came inside, and he took them off, wiped the lenses on a blue bandana handkerchief, replaced them on his nose. He held his chin tucked in against his chest so that he could look easily above the insets in the lenses.

"What can I do for you?" he said.

Lonnie introduced himself and took the manila envelope out of his coat pocket. Removing the photographs, he pushed them through the aperture in the grill.

"You know this girl?" he said.

The agent studied the pictures carefully, holding them in a stack neatly and slipping the top one off and putting it on the bottom as he went through them. He looked at each picture a second time before he pushed them back to Lonnie through the aperture.

"She looks dead," he said.

"That's because she is."

"Why you interested in a dead girl?"

"She was murdered. Last Saturday night. In Rutherford or near it."

"Oh. That one. Remember hearing it on radio, now that you mention it. Didn't actually hear it myself, to tell the truth. My wife heard it and told me about it. Hardly ever listen to radio myself. You the sheriff, you say?"

"That's right."

The agent shook his head. "I don't know her."

"You sure?"

"Never seen her before. Not to my recollection."

"Maybe your recollection isn't so good. She came to Rutherford in the local the day she was murdered. Saturday. She boarded it here. Could someone else have sold her the ticket?"

"Nope. If she bought a ticket here Saturday, I sold it to her."

"But you don't remember? It was only three days ago."

"Can't help that. I still don't remember her. Maybe I sold her the ticket, and if what you say's true, I guess I did, but I got no recollection of it just the same."

"You'd probably remember her if she were familiar to you, wouldn't you?"

"Probably."

"I thought maybe she lived here in Twin Springs."

"Maybe she did. I don't know everyone who lives here, son.

"It isn't a very big town."

"Neither's Rutherford. You know everyone there?"

"Okay. I get your point. But tell me this. You remember selling a ticket on the local to *anyone* Saturday?"

"Seems I did. Two or three, it seems. But I couldn't say who. In the first place, I never pay much attention. Second place, I don't see so well. You're a little blurred yourself, son."

"You think you'll remember me three days from now?"

"Don't be sarcastic with me, son. If she lived here in town, you ought to find someone who knew her."

"Sure. No offense. Thanks for trying."

Carrying the envelope with the photographs in it, Lonnie went outside and got into the Ford. He started the engine so the heater would operate and sat thinking. He supposed he ought to contact the chief of police, as a courtesy if not for information, but first, he decided, he would go get something to eat. Having made the decision, he turned in the graveled area and drove up the main street of the town until he came to a short-order lunch room. Parking the Ford in front, he went inside and ordered two hamburger sandwiches with apple pie and coffee. The hamburger was greasy, the apple pie was too dry, but the coffee, unlike that in the highway place, was aromatic and hot and very good. He drank it and was grateful for it and ordered another cup. He was the only customer in the place at the time. The waiter, who was probably also the owner, was a beefy fellow with a heavy red face beginning to hang on its bones. He leaned against the back counter with his arms folded across his chest, a toothpick hanging from his mouth. Every once in a while, he made a soft sucking sound, and the toothpick was briefly agitated. The name of the lunch room, established by the identification painted on the front window, was Ed's Place, and it was therefore likely that the name of the man was Ed. This was also soon established.

"You the owner?" Lonnie said.

"That's right."

"Lived in Twin Springs long?"

"All my life."

"Business good?"

"Lousy. Lousy business, lousy town."

Looking into his coffee cup and sniffing the rich aroma, Lonnie had an idea. Not much of one, really. Just something that might, with good luck, pay off. The idea was that girls are sometimes waitresses, and Avis Pisano, for no particular reason that he could justify, had seemed to be the kind who might have been.

"You ever hire a waitress?" he asked.

"Sure. Got one now. Mornings and evenings. Afternoons are slow. After one-thirty or so. I handle afternoons myself."

Lonnie took the manila envelope out of his pocket, removed the pictures, spread the pictures on the counter facing Ed.

"You ever seen this girl?" he said.

Ed leaned forward from the hips, his backside maintaining contact with the back counter. He was very still, giving an effect of sudden rigidity, staring intently.

"It's Avis. Avis Pisano." He looked up abruptly, his eyes wary. "Who the hell are you?"

Avis, Lonnie thought. *Avis Pisano.*

So that was her name. That was the peculiar arrangement of symbols and sounds that had given her identity, and still did, and the sounding of it now gave her also an added substance, a reality she had somehow not quite possessed previously. For the first time since he had gone out to the dry slough and looked at her staring blindly at the sky through the black branches of trees, she was in his mind a person who had lived as well as died, who had been called something, by a name, had written it on school papers, at the end of letters, on the fly-leaves of books, in and on the thousands of perishable places where one identifies one-self for an instant of infinity.

Now, in response to Ed's question, he established again his own identity in his own instant. He told the beefy proprietor who he was, and what, and how Avis had died.

"Did you know her well?" he said.

"Pretty well. She worked here a couple of months last winter. Early this year, it was. January, February, maybe part of March. With spring coming, she quit and went out to Sylvan Green to work. It's a resort out on the lake, and she could make more money there, what with tips and all."

"Did she live here in town?"

"She did. Had a room at Mrs. Gorman's. Old place over on Sage Street, about three blocks from here. After the season was over at Sylvan Green, she came back there, I understand, but she didn't ask for her job with me back. I had another waitress, anyhow."

"When did she come back from this Sylvan Green?"

"End of September. Sometime around then. The hotel there is open year-round, but it doesn't do a hell of a lot of business in the winter."

"Does she have a family in town? Any relatives at all?"

"No family anywhere that I know of. Her folks used to live on a farm out west a piece, but they're dead. Avis had moved into town even before they died, when she was about fifteen, at a guess. She worked around, here and there, waitress jobs and the like." He hesitated, looking down at the spread of photographs as if he were reluctant to say what was in his mind. "She developed a kind of reputation," he said.

"Reputation?"

"Round heels."

"Oh." Lonnie gathered his pictures and returned them to the envelope. "I guess I better go see this Mrs. Gorman. Where did you say she lives?"

"On Sage. Three blocks north, straight over. It's a big house with gingerbread. Needs paint. You can't miss it."

"Thanks," Lonnie said.

He went out to the Ford and drove north and found the house that needed paint in a block of houses that needed it. He crossed a rickety porch and rang a bell and waited. Pretty soon the door was opened by a woman with a massive torso, sagging at breasts and belly, that seemed to be balanced precariously on thin, bird-like legs.

"Are you Mrs. Gorman?" he asked, removing his hat and allowing his hair to fall immediately over his forehead, almost into his eyes.

"Yes," she said. "What do you want?"

"Does an Avis Pisano have a room here?"

"She does, but she's not in."

"Where did she go?"

"Out of town. She left last Saturday, and I don't know when she'll be back."

"I know when. Never. She's dead."

"What?" The woman's mouth fell open, exposing unbridged gaps between remnants of teeth. "What happened to her? How did she die?"

Again Lonnie identified himself, offering proof. He explained everything he thought the woman ought to know, which was, at this point, practically everything he knew himself. Her flaccid face, as he talked, assumed a variety of expressions, including brief concessions to horror and compassion, and settled at last into the lines of a final judgment that encompassed neither.

"I can't say it's entirely unexpected," she said. "I always felt she might come to a bad end."

"Is that so? Why?"

"She was not a good girl. She permitted men to go to her room."

"Really? Did you permit her to have them there?"

"I disapproved, and said so, but she was past her majority and paid her rent. It was not my place to dictate her behavior."

"I see. Well, I don't mind saying that I admire a person with a tolerant attitude. May I see her room, please?"

"If you consider it necessary."

"It might be helpful. You never can tell about such things." He went into a dark hall and past an iron radiator that hissed at him. Following Mrs. Gorman upstairs, he had a closer look at the bird-like legs and wondered again how they functioned and survived. In an upper hall a few feet from the head of the stairs, he was admitted to the room in which Avis Pisano had lived, had washed and dressed and dreamed and slept and made love, and there was nothing there, no scrap of a thing, that made him feel that she had done any of those things, or had really ever been there at all. He went through her possessions in closet, in drawers, wherever they were found, and nothing spoke to him, nothing answered what he asked. Eventually he left and went back downstairs and said good-bye to Mrs. Gorman in the lower hall. Outside on the porch, he decided that it would be a futile gesture to see the chief of police. He would, instead, drive immediately to Sylvan Green, which he could reach, he thought, around dark.

He was accurate in his estimate, reaching the hotel minutes ahead of darkness. The water of the lake at the foot of the slope was still as glass, a sheet of burnished gray that glittered darkly in the fading light. The litter of cabins among the black trees along the shore were dark and obviously unoccupied. The rustic hotel, affecting unpeeled logs and heavy timbers, showed light at three upstairs windows and at the windows of the lobby below. The light from the lobby windows spilled out across a high, wide porch of thick planks. Mounting steps, Lonnie counted them. There were an even dozen. Crossing the porch, he entered the lobby.

When the spring and summer vacation season was over, guests were few at Sylvan Green. Hunters came now and then, alone or in small groups, to stay a few days and tramp the low hills covered with leafless scrub oaks, and there was a nominal amount of overnight patronage by transients who preferred the accommodations to those of inferior hotels in the towns of the area, but it barely paid to keep open after September, and affairs were managed by a skeleton staff. In the lobby now, a man in a wool plaid shirt was talking by the tobacco counter to a man in a red flannel shirt, and another man in a gray business suit was reading a city paper in an upholstered chair with maple arms and legs. Besides these and Lonnie, only the clerk was present. A blond young man of effeminate mannerisms, the clerk leaned on the counter with languid limpness and watched Lonnie approach with an expression that seemed to suggest that he would rather Lonnie didn't.

"I'd like to see the manager, please," Lonnie said.

Somewhat to his surprise, the languid blond claimed that distinction for himself, and once again, with increasing weariness in the routine, Lonnie explained who and what he was, the purpose of his visit. This time, for which he was grateful, there was no necessity to show his collection of pictures. That bit of his approach made him feel illogically surreptitious, as if he were somehow soliciting attention to obscenity. Besides, the clerk-manager was sufficiently shaken by the unadorned report of murder, and Lonnie did not wish to add the shock of the dead face.

"Avis Pisano was employed here last summer, I believe," he said.

"That's right. As a waitress."

"I wonder if I may see your register for that period. Say the months of July and August."

"Certainly. Would you care to step into the office?"

"I would, thanks."

Going around the counter, Lonnie crossed the small space behind and passed through a doorway into an office that was no larger. There was a desk and a chair, of which he assumed the use, and the clerk-manager placed in front of him a file box of registration slips approximately five by eight inches in size. Alone, the other having excused himself and returned to his desk, Lonnie went through the slips slowly, reading the meaningless signatures, and in the end there was still no meaning, and he was vastly relieved. Rocking back in his chair, he rolled a cigarette and lit it. Squinting through the thin blue smoke, he thought of something that destroyed in an instant his abortive relief, and after a few minutes he stood up reluctantly and crossed to the door and spoke to the blond.

"Do you have a separate file for the cabins?" he asked.

The manager said that they did. He came back into the office and got it. Again alone, Lonnie started through it, turning each slip with a feeling of dread that seemed to acquire more intensity in each instance, and when he was finished at last, the dread had been justified, and he sat back and closed his eyes and pressed against the lids until he was compelled to relax the pressure by unendurable pain. He felt sick, violated by a kind of odd anger that was partially inverted for no good reason, and he wished that he were not a sheriff and in no way involved in what he was. It had been, moreover, a long, long day, and he was suddenly bone-tired. It would be possible, of course, to take a room in the hotel for the night, but he had a desire to get away that was stronger even than the attraction of a bed, and the desire was actually a compulsion to be moving at once toward a necessary end. Getting up abruptly, he went out into the lobby. The manager and the three guests watched him in a hiatus of silence, and he understood that he had been reported and discussed. There was no justification for his resenting this, but he did, and he thought tiredly that he would have to guard his emotions. It wouldn't do at all to become excessively irascible just because he had a rotten job that he'd asked for.

"I'm finished now," he said to the manager. "Thanks for your help."

He crossed the lobby, followed by four pairs of eyes. Outside, he stood for a minute on the porch, listening to the night. The lake was so still that it made no sound. In the Ford, he began the long drive back to Rutherford.

CHAPTER 14

Purvy Stubbs didn't think very fast, and he knew it. He also knew that he talked too much. He had even learned from experience that slow thinking and excessive talking are an unfortunate combination that can often get a fellow into trouble, a condition to which Purvy was no stranger. It was no wonder, then, that it took him quite a while to understand that he might now be in danger because he was himself a danger to someone else. To a murderer. It was not pleasant, when you finally came to consider it properly, to be the only person on earth to have seen a particular murderer in damning circumstances. Of course, Purvy had not actually seen the murderer, not to recognize him, but he had got a glimpse of him, a shadow among shadows, and what was worse he had opened his big mouth frequently since to say that there had been something vaguely familiar about the shadow that itched his mind, something significant that he was trying to isolate and pin down.

Suppose the murderer was in town. Suppose he had even sat quietly in his personal hell and listened to Purvy talk like this. Purvy did suppose, finally, and he felt cold and miserable. He wasn't ashamed to admit that he was afraid, in fact, and when the fear really got powerfully into him was the afternoon that Lonnie Womber had him down to the office in the county jail for a talk, which was the afternoon of the day after Lonnie went to Sylvan Green. What made the fear somehow more terrible than it would otherwise have been was that it was inspired by someone, not precisely known, who was probably quite familiar and had never inspired fear before. It was like when you were a kid in the dark, and the friendly objects of your room betrayed your trust and became enemies, and even the room became a trap.

It was after two in the afternoon when Lonnie called Purvy on the telephone, and things were slow in the bank.

"That you, Purvy?" Lonnie said.

"Yes," Purvy said.

"Lonnie Womber here. You busy?"

"Not very. You know how it is in the bank in the afternoon, Lonnie. Things are slow."

"I was wondering if you could come down to the jail for a little talk."

"Well, damn it, Lonnie, I'm supposed to stay on the job whether we're busy or not. The Old Man doesn't like me to be running off before quitting time."

"This is pretty important, Purvy. I don't think your Old Man would object under the circumstances."

"What you want to talk with me about?"

"Telephone's no place, Purvy. I'll tell you when I see you."

"Is it about what I saw at the station?"

"Look, Purvy. Just get the hell down here to the jail, will you, please?"

Purvy could see then that Lonnie was determined that he was going to come, and so he said he would and hung up. After all, Lonnie was a sheriff, which is a kind of cop, and he probably had the authority to order you around if you were involved in something, and he might even be able to make trouble for you if you didn't do as you were told. The Old Man was in his office with his door closed, talking to a farmer about a mortgage or something, so Purvy didn't bother to report that he was leaving. As a matter of fact, he hadn't spoken to his Old Man about the girl at the station, and how he had got himself involved by just being around at the time, and if he had his way in the matter, he wasn't ever going to say anything about it, for his Old Man would sure as hell cuss him out and call him all kinds of a bumbling fool who couldn't manage to stay out of trouble even when he was standing around doing nothing. He got his hat and put on his too-short topcoat and walked across town to the jail.

Lonnie was in his chair with his feet on the half-open drawer. The door to his office was open, and Purvy stopped at the threshold, waiting for an invitation to cross. Lonnie looked at him sourly, looked away at the dead cigarette in his fingers. The cigarette was coming apart at the seam, and Lonnie threw it into the number 10 can on the floor with more force than was necessary, a display of restrained violence against something unidentified for which the cigarette was a symbol. He didn't bother to stand, or even to lower his feet.

"Come on in, Purvy," he said. "Better shut the door." Purvy did both. He sat in the chair beside Lonnie's desk, holding his hat in his lap. Lonnie's expression, still sour, seemed to imply that Purvy was something of a trial, to say the least, which was an attitude on Lonnie's part that Purvy could in no way understand, since he had been helpful and had put Lonnie on the track of something.

"Purvy," Lonnie said, "has it occurred to you by any chance that you sometimes talk too much?"

Since it had, Purvy was forced to admit it.

"As a matter of fact, it has," he said, "and if you mean about seeing someone in the little park at the station, it's been on my mind and worrying me."

"That's good, Purvy. You just keep on worrying. If you recognize something and worry about it enough, chances are you keep ready to take care of it, if necessary."

Lonnie took time at that point to start the construction of another roll-you-own, and it was Purvy's opinion, not expressed, that if Lonnie wanted him to worry, he had sure as hell made a good start toward accomplishing what he wanted.

"You trying to scare me or something, Lonnie?" he said. Lonnie didn't answer immediately, and when he did answer, not directly. He finished his cigarette and lit it and looked at it for a moment as if it were offensive.

"I took a little trip yesterday, Purvy," he said. "Up to Twin Springs."

"Twin Springs? Why'd you go to Twin Springs?"

"Because that's where this girl who was murdered got on the train. I learned that from the conductor, who happened to remember her, and I went up here to find out who she was. Her name was Avis Pisano."

"Avis Pisano," Purvy said.

After saying the name aloud, he repeated it three times silently, fashioning the shapes of the sounds with his lips so carefully that Lonnie was able to read them clearly. And to Purvy, as it had to Lonnie, the name gave substance to the one who had used it, making her real and her death a real death, the sad bad end to which she had come in Rutherford.

"Last summer she worked as a waitress at Sylvan Green," Lonnie said. "I went out there, too. I checked all the registrations for July and August."

"Why for then? I mean, why just pick out July and August?"

"Because it was about that time, somewhere along there, that Avis Pisano became pregnant."

"Pregnant? Who said she was pregnant?"

"The doc says it. Haven't you ever heard of a post-mortem, Purvy?"

Purvy had heard of it, all right, but he didn't want to think about it now. The truth was, he was wishing desperately that he hadn't been on the station platform that night. It was the first time in his life that he actually regretted having seen a train come in and go out.

"You think she was murdered because of that?" he said.

"I think it's possible. Even probable."

"Well, it doesn't seem likely to me. It happens all the time without anyone getting murdered because of it."

"You're right there, Purvy. Every girl who slips sure doesn't get murdered. So I figure it must have had a kind of extra meaning in relation to something else. It *threatened* something."

This made sense, which Purvy had to admit to himself, although it amounted to nothing more, really, than a guess. Purvy didn't want to make any guesses about anything, so he was silent.

"You want to know what I found in the registrations at Sylvan Green, Purvy?"

"No."

"I can understand how you feel. I didn't want to know myself, as a matter of fact, and I wouldn't blame anyone else for not wanting to. It was necessary in my case, though, because of my job, and it's necessary in yours because you're in a spot and ought to know what to watch out for. Besides, you might be able to help me. You helped me once, and you might be able to do it again."

"I don't see how I can help you any more than I already have."

"Maybe you'll see after I tell you. First, though, I've got to tell you what I found out at Sylvan Green. Who was there during the time I checked." Lonnie leaned back and closed his eyes, as if it were easier to say in the dark what needed saying. "Guy Butler," he said, "Rex Tye. Ellis Kuder." Purvy felt an instantaneous and hysterical compulsion to scream a protest, to dispel at once from the mind of Lonnie Womber any suspicion it might hold of the three whose names were mentioned. It was untenable, that was all. It was a monstrous distortion of the way everything had always been and ought always to be. Fellows you knew and liked sometimes got into trouble, and might even have the bad luck to get a girl pregnant, but they didn't murder her for that reason, or for any reason, or anyone at all for any reason whatever.

"Lots of people from Rutherford go to Sylvan Green," he said. "It's good bass fishing there."

"I know. I was there myself a couple years ago. I found another name I recognized, to be truthful, but it was a fellow who doesn't fit. No use mentioning him or considering him, in my opinion. He's got kids older than you or me, must be close to seventy himself, and had his wife with him besides."

"Just the same, I don't believe it was Guy or Rex or Ellis."

"What you mean is, you don't *want* to believe it, and neither do I. The point is, Purvy, you and I aren't in a position to be generous. Not I because I've got a job. Not you because you talked too much. There's a murderer around here, and he's watching and listening, and he's probably filled with a bigger fear than we can imagine, and he knows that you got a glimpse of him in that little park, something distinctive that sticks in your mind and may mean something to you if you ever get it straight, and he keeps wondering if you ever will. He wonders and wonders, and he wishes you were dead, and he may try to arrange it for you."

Purvy squirmed and wanted again to scream.

"Goddamn it, Lonnie, I wish you wouldn't try to scare me."

"You ought to be scared, Purvy. You ought to be running scared until this is settled. I admit running scared gets wearisome after a while, and so I thought you might be willing to do something for me that could hurry things up, if we're lucky."

"What could I do?"

"It's simple. You could tell a little lie."

"A lie about what?"

"You could make out that you've remembered what it was you saw in that little park. The thing that's been itching you. You could spread it around that you're damn well sure who it was that met Avis Pisano there the night she was murdered, but you'd have to make it plain at the same time that you hadn't told me or anyone else, and hadn't made up your mind to tell. You could say that it's just impossible for you to believe that this person would do a terrible thing like murdering the girl, and you don't want to make a lot of trouble for him that he doesn't deserve."

"No!" Purvy jumped to his feet, and this time his voice did skid upward until he was close to screaming. "Damn it, Lonnie, I won't do it, and that's all there is to it!"

"Well, it would probably make the murderer take a crack at you, and I don't blame you for being afraid to do it, even though I'd have you watched all the time to prevent his getting away with anything."

"All right. I'm afraid, and I admit it, but it's not only that. Guy and Rex and Ellis are friends of mine, and I don't intend to play any dirty tricks on them."

"One of them may not be your friend, Purvy. One of them may be the deadliest enemy you've ever had or are likely to have."

"Well, you're just trying to mix me up so I'll agree to do it, and I'm not going to listen to another damn word."

"All right, Purvy." Lonnie sighed and stood up. "You're not obliged to do it, and there's no way I can make you if you don't want to. I intend to find out which one it was, one way or another, but I just thought this might be a good trick to do it faster. Bear in mind what I told you, though, Purvy. Run scared. Keep running scared."

Purvy didn't answer. He got out of the office, out of the jail, and headed for town. He was scared, all right, and he was all mixed up besides, and the whole world seemed like that dark room at night when he was a kid.

CHAPTER 15

Guy Butler slept and later wakened. He had not slept long or heavily, and no time seemed to have passed. The soft light still burned beside the bed. Phyllis Bagby, raised on one elbow, looked down at him with tenderness in her eyes and a kind of conflicting bitterness tucking the corners of her mouth and turning them down. Even so, her face was lovely, with a thin, fastidious sensuality in it.

"I ought to hate you," she said.

"So you should," he agreed.

"You treat me like a whore."

"I make love to you, and you make love to me. We treat each other like whores."

"It's different with me. I *feel* love when I make it. You don't."

"All right. Have it your own way."

"You're very agreeable, aren't you?"

"I don't want to quarrel with you, if that's what you mean."

"Why do you treat me with contempt?"

"I'm not aware that I do. Is making love to you contemptuous?"

"Perhaps not. It depends. At least, the way things are, it's contemptible."

"In that case, I'd better quit. If you don't want me to make love to you, you only have to say so."

"I do want it. That's why I accept it, even though I know you despise me."

"I don't despise you. I like you better, I think, than anyone else on earth."

"That's very nice to hear, but I don't believe it."

"All right. If I tell you the truth, you don't believe it, so there is obviously no use in saying anything at all."

"If you cared anything about me, you wouldn't have stayed away so long."

"I stayed away because I didn't think it was wise to come."

"Why did you come tonight, then?"

"I didn't intend to. I came because I needed you, and felt compelled."

"Now that I have satisfied your need, I suppose you will stay away for another long time."

"Maybe a long time. Maybe forever."

"Depending on whether you can make that rich little bitch up on the ridge. Is that it?"

"I don't want to make her. I want to marry her."

"Get out! Goddamn you, Guy, get out of my bed!"

"Do you really want me to?"

"No."

"I didn't think so."

"God," she said. "Oh, God."

She lay down on her back beside him and stared up at the ceiling with hot, dry eyes. He reached over and placed his left hand flat on her belly, and she trembled for a moment and grew rigidly still.

"You're a rotten bastard," she said.

"That's right," he said. "I am."

"It gives you pleasure to tear my insides apart."

"I don't know. Maybe it does."

"Bastard. Rotten, sadistic bastard."

"Maybe worse," he said. "Maybe murderer."

Her body trembled again, a sudden spasm that shook her and sickened her and left her lying rigid as before.

"Guy! What are you saying?"

"You sound frightened, Phyll. Do you think I could commit a murder?"

"I don't know. Sometimes I think you might do anything."

"What do you think a murderer feels when he murders? Terror? Anger? A kind of enormous exhilaration and assurance of immunity?"

"I don't know. I don't want to talk about it."

"But I do. I want to talk about it, Phyll. I want you to tell me if you think I might have killed the girl who was found outside of town in the slough. Lonnie Womber thinks so."

"Why in God's name should he think you killed her?"

"I didn't say he thinks I did. I said he thinks I might have."

"You're joking. This is another one of your damned distorted vicious jokes."

"No. No joke. Lonnie thinks so, and he has reasons. He found out that Avis Pisano worked at Sylvan Green last summer. He found out that I was there. Avis was pregnant, and she came to Rutherford, and someone killed her here, or near here, and even Lonnie can add that up and get an answer."

"Was it yours, Guy? Was the child yours?"

"If there were a possibility, do you think I would tell you the truth?"

"No. I think you would lie and lie, but I would believe you anyhow, because I'd want to."

"Then there is no point in your asking or my answering." She did not move. How could one be so quiet, she wondered, with such terror and anguish within? And what kind of woman was she whose terror sprang, not from what he was or might have done, but from his deadly peril? Whose anguish issued from the knowledge that he had possibly given a child to someone else, and not to her?

"You and your goddamned crippled hand," she said. "You think, because you have lost something, that you have the right to destroy everyone else."

He didn't answer. From his face, which did not change, there was no way of telling that he had ever heard. After a minute, perhaps two, he sat up on the edge of the bed with his back to her and lit a cigarette, which he took from a pack on a table beside him. She sat up also, leaning forward and laying her cheek against his back.

"I'll tear my tongue out," she said. "Say the word, Guy, I'll tear my rotten tongue out."

Rex Tye came downstairs quietly and would have gone directly out the front door if his mother had not spoken to him. He turned and saw her standing in the entrance to the living room.

"Yes, Mother?" he said.

"Are you going out?"

"If you don't mind."

"Of course not, darling. I should have thought, however, that you'd tell me good-bye."

Against the brighter light of the living room, she looked impeccable and gracious, the light glancing from her hair. In spite of the substance of her words, there was not the slightest sound of reproach in her voice. In his, when he answered, was no tinge of animus. They were both controlled, beautifully mannered, meticulous experts in making things seem other than they were.

"I'm sorry, Mother. I was thinking of something else."

"Yes. Poor darling. No wonder that you're distressed. Are you in a hurry?"

"Not particularly. Why?"

"I thought you might come into the living room and talk with me for a few minutes."

"All right, Mother. If you wish."

He followed her into the living room and sat down on a period chair with tapestry covered seat and back. He sat forward on the chair with his knees together and his hands resting on his knees. In his prim posture, his pale curls reflecting the light, he looked, she thought, like a young boy who had miraculously retained his grace while growing much too fast, and she felt, looking at him, a cold intensification of anger that in no way showed, not for him, but for those who transgressed against him. She thought of it as precisely that. Transgression. She wondered if he could possibly have been seduced and soiled by the vile girl who had come here to Rutherford to die, which was execrably bad taste on her part, and she had vividly a sudden revolting vision of hot entangled flesh. Closing her eyes, as if the vision were external and could thus be evaded, she surrendered herself, without ever knowing if the vision were valid or not, to a delicately savage satisfaction that the girl was dead. She did not feel for an instant, however, that Rex might have killed her. More than that, she did not for an instant feel that anyone else could seriously entertain such a suspicion.

"If you're in trouble," she said, "I wish you would let me help you."

"Trouble, Mother? I'm in no trouble."

"Please don't try to evade me, darling. Sheriff Womber has been talking to you, hasn't he?"

"He wanted to ask me a few questions, that's all. This girl who was killed worked as a waitress at Sylvan Green last summer. I knew her slightly, of course, as did practically everyone there. It's simply routine in these things to ask questions of everyone in the least connected, Mother."

"Nevertheless, it is not fair of Sheriff Womber to involve you publicly. People talk, you know. They imagine all sorts of things that are not true."

"I don't think I've been harmed, Mother."

"No? Perhaps you are far too innocent and generous. After all, this girl was pregnant."

"I know that. Everyone does."

"Then you must know, as everyone does, that you are contaminated by the least contact with this sordid affair."

"I don't feel contaminated, Mother."

"I wonder if you are fully aware of its significance. Don't you care at all if you are suspected of having been responsible for the miserable girl's condition?"

"The truth is, I don't."

"Really? That's very admirable, I'm sure. Are you also indifferent to being virtually accused of murder? Surely you understand the line of thinking that connects the two."

"Damn it, Mother. I've been accused of nothing."

"You needn't swear, darling." Just perceptibly, her mouth turned down in the briefest, slightest expression of distaste. Her selective mind was violated again by the intrusion of the vision of passion. "How do you expect to be accepted by a family like the Haigs when you permit yourself to be associated, even innocently, with such a vile crime?"

"I didn't permit it, Mother. It just happened. One can't really be expected to anticipate the result of every casual relationship or meeting, and I'm sure my innocence is apparent to the Haigs. Especially to Lauren. They are not nearly so bigoted as you seem to think."

"Am I to infer from this that *I'm* considered bigoted?"

"Not at all, Mother. You know I didn't mean that."

"I'm relieved." She smiled at him coolly, again disturbed by the fleshly vision, and she said suddenly, quite casually, "Tell me truthfully, darling, did you take that dreadful girl to bed?"

If he was in the least disconcerted by the blunt question, which was unlike anything he might have expected from her, he did not show it. He was, as a matter of fact, so used to lying to her, living the lies when they were unexpressed, that he was able to tell promptly and naturally the one now necessary.

"Of course not," he said. "I guess that's why I'm unable to feel especially concerned."

He stood up then and crossed to the chair in which she sat facing him. Bending, he kissed her cheek.

"Good-night, Mother. I'm sorry if I've caused you any distress."

"Where are you going?"

"I don't know, really. Just out. I may go to the hotel for a while."

He went out into the hall then, and she sat unmoving and listened for the sound of the front door closing behind him. It was her special terror that every closed door between them was a symbol and a prophecy. Hearing the sound, the door closing, she began at once to listen for its opening.

Bernie Huggins wondered how far it would be advisable, or safe, to go with Ellis Kuder. Bernie was naturally curious and would have been willing to set up a couple of drinks on the house in exchange for a little inside info, but Ellis was so withdrawn and sullen that chances for any kind of understanding didn't look so good, and as a matter of fact, in Bernie's opinion, Ellis was a mean son of a bitch by nature and a fellow you couldn't afford to trifle with. He'd been sitting at the bar for all of a half hour now, and in all that time he hadn't said a word except the name of his drink when he wanted service, and when Bernie had lingered a few minutes across the mahogany to indicate that he was receptive to any friendly gesture, Ellis had ignored him and made it pretty plain that he wished Bernie would get the hell about his business. Well, if that was the way Ellis wanted it, it sure wasn't any skin off Bernie's tail, but Bernie knew one thing, all right, and what he knew was that if he was on the spot Ellis was on, suspected of getting a girl in trouble and then killing her to avoid the consequences, he'd damn well be trying to give a better impression of his character than Ellis was giving.

Of course, there wasn't anything certain about Ellis and the girl. He'd just been at that lousy resort hotel at the right time, or wrong time, that was all, and apparently Guy Butler and Rex Tye had been there, too. Bernie understood that, all right. From what he could learn from the talk going round, the girl hadn't been very choosy, round heels and all that, and probably it could have been any one of a number of guys who fixed her up, but what made it look bad was that she had come to Rutherford on the train, and had been met by someone here, and, well, it simply looked like a local hero, and that's all there was to it.

The way Bernie got it, neither Guy nor Rex nor Ellis could establish any alibi for the full period of time in which it was figured the murder was done, and if anyone cared for his opinion, which was free, any one of the three snotty bastards was perfectly capable of doing it if the chips were down. It wouldn't be smart to express an opinion like that, of course, because most people thought it was absolutely ridiculous to suspect Guy or Rex or Ellis of murder, though fornication might be allowed, but Bernie had been around and had seen what he had seen, and as a result he had a lot of good opinions that he was forced to keep to himself for sagacious reasons.

Another thing you had to consider, though, to be perfectly honest about it. You only had the word of Purvy Stubbs that this girl, this Avis Pisano, was met by someone at the station, and Purvy, it was well known, didn't have brains enough to pour pee out of a boot with the directions on the heel. He told this wacky story about seeing a shadow in that little park at the end of the platform, and how the girl went down there and disappeared, and it sounded a hell of a lot like a good story, or a damn lie, which Purvy wasn't above telling for effect, but in Purvy's favor was the fact that he'd told the story before the murder was discovered, when there didn't seem to be any point in telling it unless it was true. Purvy was an odd nut and might be guilty of concocting a good story after the fact, just to get a little attention, but no one could possibly contend that he was psychic or something, and able to anticipate a murder that hadn't happened. Psychic? Hell, he was barely conscious. You could just look at him now and make up your own mind, if you had any doubts. He was sitting down there at the bar, four stools from Ellis, and he was stewed to his lousy gills. He'd been getting that way the last few days, and it was unusual and peculiar, because Purvy'd always been a light drinker, just a little beer for sociability, but now he'd started drinking whisky and was about as sociable as a muskrat. You might think, to watch him, that he was the one who was on the spot, except that it was doubtful that the simpleton could whip a girl in a fair fight, let alone kill her, and it was even more doubtful, if possible, that he could put one in a condition.

Just then, as Bernie examined Purvy and reflected on his inadequacies, Ellis lifted his empty glass and set it down with a thump. Bernie jumped and cursed silently. Picking up the cue, he moved down opposite Ellis.

"Another?" he said.

Ellis nodded. Bernie fixed another and set it out. Ellis paid, and Bernie rang it up. After registering the sale, he decided that he'd give Ellis just one more chance to be sociable, just refer sort of jokingly to Ellis being inside the excitement, something like that. He tried to think of the best way to put it.

"Well," he said, "I hear you and Lonnie Womber been working together on Rutherford's murder case."

Ellis looked at him. "Do you?" he said.

"That's what I hear. Guy Butler and Rex Tye, too, for that matter. Seems like half the young guys in town knew this Avis Pisano, one way or another. Must be a shock to have someone you knew, maybe talked with and had a drink with or something, turn up murdered. What kind of girl was she, Ellis? Pretty good kid? Lot of people condemn her out of hand because of the condition she was in, but I'm not that way myself. No justice in just blaming the ones that get caught if you want my opinion."

"She was a cheap little bitch," Ellis said.

Well, Bernie was no sissy. He'd been tending bar for a long time, after all, and bartenders don't generally get softer as they get older, but it gave him a jolt, just the same, to hear Ellis come out with it like that. It was brutal, that's what it was. Whatever the girl had been, it was time to forget it now, and maybe even to tell a few lies in her favor. It didn't do any harm to lie a little for someone who was dead, and the least you could do, if you had scruples or something, was to say nothing at all.

Bernie thought all this, but he didn't say it, and consequently he said nothing. Down the bar, Purvy Stubbs had come to life. He turned his head slowly and looked up at Ellis. He seemed to be working very hard at focusing his eyes.

"I'll tell you something, though, Bernie," Ellis said. "Whoever made her, it wasn't me, and whoever killed her, it wasn't me. Remember that. I'm just telling you so you'll have it straight when you pass it over the bar."

This made Bernie hot, the implication that he was a lousy blabber-mouth, and he was fumbling around in his brain, trying to sort out the right words to tell Ellis to go to hell indirectly, when Purvy Stubbs spoke up suddenly, enunciating carefully and getting his words out with only the slightest fuzz on them.

"I remember," Purvy said clearly. "I remember what it was about the one who was waiting in the little park. What was familiar about him, I mean."

Bernie and Ellis turned to stare at him. Slowly, after adjustment, the significance of Purvy's words sank in.

"The hell you do!" Bernie said.

Purvy nodded, and Bernie and Ellis waited. Purvy's eyes still didn't appear to be focused quite properly, and he rubbed the back of a hand across them.

"Well, damn it, Purvy, speak up!" Bernie said. "Who was it?"

Purvy rubbed his hand across his eyes again. Turning his head, he looked into his glass and spoke to it.

"I don't think I ought to tell," he said. "I don't think I ought to tell anyone."

"What do you mean, you don't think you ought to tell?" Bernie sounded almost frantic. "Damn it, Purvy, do you think this is a game of button, button, who's got the button? This happens to be a murder, and you're obligated to tell anything you know that might help. Lonnie Womber gets ahold of you, you'll damn well tell, all right."

"No." Purvy still talked to the glass. "This is someone who wouldn't commit any murder, and I know it. It wouldn't be right to get him into a lot of trouble he doesn't deserve. I'm determined not to tell, and Lonnie Womber or anyone else isn't going to get me to do it."

Suddenly, he pushed the glass away and stood up and walked out of the bar. Bernie, watching him go in amazement, was about to deliver an opinion on lubberly fools in general and one in particular, but he got at that moment a glimpse of Ellis Kuder's eyes, and his mind went coldly blank to everything else.

He had seen friendlier eyes, he thought, in the head of a snake.

Walking down Main Street, Purvy wondered why he'd done it. He hadn't intended to, but he suddenly had and now it was done. Maybe he'd done it because it had become imperative to get the whole thing over with as quickly as possible, and this seemed like the quickest way, and maybe the only way.

In the residential streets, beyond the area of light, he became aware of someone following him, and he began to trot. The one who followed began to trot also. Together, a particular distance apart, they trotted through the streets and all the way up the long slope to the ridge. Purvy had been told that people who didn't exercise much sometimes grew a kind of fatty tissue around the heart, and that it could be dangerous for that reason for them to exert themselves excessively too suddenly, and as he began to feel a developing pain in his chest, he visualized himself dropping dead, his heart smothered and stopped by the enveloping fat, but his fear of the one who followed was greater than his fear of death, and so he kept on trotting.

When he reached home at last, he closed the door behind him and locked it, but it was no barrier. The one who followed came right through the door and followed him upstairs and stood all night at the foot of his bed.

CHAPTER 16

"Darling," he whispered. "Darling, darling."

His voice lingered and faded in Lauren's mind, repeating and repeating itself on the breath of a dying sigh. She lifted her face from the soft hollow of his throat and sought blindly for his mouth with hers. She found it and was drawn in and in to the heart of a giant heart that beat like thunder in an agony of aggressive submission. His hands were at once transgressors and supplicants, eliciting a pleasurable pain.

"Now, Curly," she said. "Now, please."

And so it was reached at last, the delicate and perilous point in the methodically projected and executed seduction at which everything was finally committed. It was the tenth night after the night Avis Pisano was murdered, and they were on a leather sofa in front of a fire in the library of the biggest house on the ridge, where the rich of Rutherford lived, and afterward they lay quietly in a suddenly shrunken world that seemed to expand and contract with the rhythm of their own deep breathing, and he was afraid. Now he must wait to see if it was consummation or abortion, lie in the shrunken world and wait for the sign, and after a while, with a kind of dreamy and assured validity in the recession of passion, she laid her fingers on his cheek and said, "I love you," and he knew that it was all right and that he had won. The world assumed again its vast design, and he in the world again his giant size. Twice he had committed himself and twice he had won, and he felt now, after the second commitment, the same sense of singing power that he had felt after the first. He was somehow removed from the measures of good and evil. He was briefly and grandly immune to danger.

Her fingers trailed away, leaving his face, and she was immediately so still, her breathing so regular, that he turned his head to look at her, thinking that she was asleep, and she had indeed the appearance of being asleep, but she wasn't. Her lashes lay in their own shadows, and a lighter shadow of sadness was on her face, and this, though he didn't know it, was because she was saying good-bye to herself, to the cool and lovely girl she had solely possessed, and now did not, and would never again. But in the sadness there was also pride, an exorbitant sense of accomplishment in having boldly done something she could not have done a little while ago, and in feeling now no other regret than the sadness itself, which was really not regret at all.

"Are you asleep?" he said.

"No."

"Are you sorry?"

"No."

'What are you thinking?"

"I'm thinking that I would like to be married. I'd like to be married very soon, if you don't mind."

"When?"

"Tomorrow. It's all in my mind, the way I want it. We will drive up to the city tomorrow evening and be married there and spend the night in a hotel, and it will be impossible for anyone to do anything to prevent it or change it."

"Who would want to prevent it?"

"Father will be angry for a while, of course, but it won't matter."

"I didn't know that your father was so opposed to me."

"He isn't, really. It's just this horrible business about the murdered girl."

"Why? Does he think I murdered her?"

He said it lightly, with an edge of bitter humor that was just sufficient to imply tolerance of a monstrous injustice, and he felt a surge of great pride that he was able to accomplish the effect so perfectly. Oh, he was enormously daring and clever, and he was perfectly capable of manipulating to the attainment of his own triumph the very threats of his own destruction. Only a very exceptional person, of course, could refer so quietly, with such an admirable implication of absurdity, to his own engrossing guilt.

"No, of course not," she said. "Please don't joke about such a terrible thing. You know how fathers are. It's just that you are innocently involved, however slightly, by the fact that you knew her, or at least had some contact with her, at Sylvan Green last summer. It's perfectly ridiculous, darling, but I'm afraid you must consider yourself tainted."

"Well, I can't blame your father, actually. After all, the damn girl was pregnant, and I was at Sylvan Green at a time to have accomplished it. Considering that she came here to see someone and was apparently killed here by that someone, this is at least enough to make me a subject of suspicion."

"Don't talk like that. Father only takes the foolish position that you were unpardonably indiscreet in not avoiding something you could not possibly anticipate. After a while he will see how absurd he has been."

"I'm surprised that he permits me to come here now."

"To tell the truth, he did make something of an issue of it, and I became quite angry. When I became angry, he conceded at once. I am hardly ever angry about anything, and I think it actually frightened him a little. Do you want me to tell you something strange? Before Father took such an intolerable position, I was not at all convinced that I loved you or wanted to continue seeing you, but then, almost at once, I was absolutely certain and was determined to have you in spite of any opposition."

He had an almost irresistible compulsion to laugh, to laugh and laugh in high, hysterical glee at the perversity of factors that might have ruined him but worked in his favor instead. He was truly the beneficiary of an incredible collaboration of daring and ingenuity and miraculous luck.

"Are you sure?" he said, inviting with a kind of arrogant bravado a retraction of the cardinal commitment upon which everything depended.

"Yes," she said. "I think I've never been so sure of anything before."

And this was true. She had never before made a significant decision which required on her part the assumption of a positive position, and now that she had made one, she was filled with a strange assurance and a disproportionate sense of excitement. Twisting on the leather sofa to face him, she held him tightly in fierce possessiveness, her mind and body responding again with aggressive submission to the resumed stroking of his hands.

"When shall we leave?" he said. "For the city, I mean."

"It had better be late. Come for me about eight. Mother and Father have a dinner engagement and will be gone then. I'll have to take a bag, and it will be much easier to get away if they're not here. It should only take about an hour and a half to get to the city."

"Eight," he said. "Eight o'clock."

The name of the hour was like a pulse, beating in time with his stroking hands, as if the name and the hands were themselves measuring seconds. Somehow, now that the time for their departure was established, the short stretch of hours between now and then became in his mind a cumulative threat, a space of time in which all danger and all possibility of disaster were gathered. Now the remaining perilous imperative was to survive by courage and cleverness for less than one more full day.

And in that diminished day, in order to secure the future, it would be necessary to kill a clown. He had thought and thought about it very carefully, and he had been deterred only by the added danger to himself, but there was surely greater danger in trusting the silence of the clown, who had seen too much by chance, which was the clown's bad luck, and even in waiting this long there had been an appalling calculated risk.

He was conscious of Lauren's quickened breathing. Her body was beginning to tremble again. Stroking her gently, he reviewed in his mind the way he would kill Purvy Stubbs.

CHAPTER 17

By six o'clock the next evening, Purvy was drunk. He was not obviously or offensively drunk, but had merely achieved a sufficient degree of absorption to reconcile him to his problems and to enable him the better to tolerate them, if not to cope with them. At that time, at six o'clock, he went into the dining room of the Division Hotel and ordered baked pork chops with whipped potatoes and applesauce for dinner, but he was not hungry and only picked at the food. After twenty minutes had passed, he got up and went out of the dining room and across the lobby into the taproom. Established on a stool, he ordered whisky.

"Purvy," said Bernie Huggins, "what the hell's the matter with you?"

"There's nothing at all the matter with me, Bernie," Purvy said. "Why do you ask?"

"Well, you came in here and got plastered before dark, which is too early in the day in the winter for anyone to be plastered, and it's something, besides, that you've never done before. All the time I've known you, you never drank anything but beer, and damn little of that, and now all of a sudden you switch to whisky. In my opinion, something's on your mind, and I know what it is."

"If you know what it is, why the hell are you asking?"

"All right, all right. Be as pig-headed as you please."

"Well, I know what you're after, Bernie. Maybe I'm not as dumb as you think, or as drunk either. You're trying to get me to tell you what I saw down there in that little park at the station, and I'm determined not to do it."

Bernie took a deep breath and a swipe at the bar. He looked at Purvy for several seconds with an expression that was meant to be disconcerting, and was. Purvy squirmed on his stool and drank some of his whisky.

"You want to know what I think, Purvy?" Bernie asked.

"Not particularly," Purvy said. "I can't say I've got a hell of a lot of interest in what you think."

"Is that so? Well, I'll just tell you, anyhow, Purvy, and I'll give you a little tip besides, which is that a lot of other fellows think the same thing, and it's been getting passed up and down the bar. What I think, I think you didn't see anything at all in that little park, not a single solitary damn thing, and you just told that cock and bull story to get a little attention for yourself."

"Why would I do a crazy thing like that?"

"I just told you. To get attention. Lots of nuts do that sort of thing, and you can read in the papers almost any day where some nut somewhere has done it. Especially in the big cases. People seeing things and making fake confessions and all sorts of things like that, just to cash in on the excitement and publicity and all. It's psychological, that's what it is."

Purvy's indignation was impressive. Even Bernie was impressed. As Purvy swelled slowly, like a frog about to burst into song, Bernie had for a moment an uneasy feeling that he might actually explode and splatter all over the taproom.

"By God, Bernie," he Said, "I've never had such big lies told about me in my life before, and that's the truth. You ought to be ashamed of yourself. Here I've been, sweating this out, and worrying myself sick over it, and wishing and wishing I'd never been near that damn station platform that night, and all the time you and a lot of other guys been thinking and spreading around that I just made it all up to get people to look at me and listen to me and crap like that. Well, I don't mind telling you I don't care if you never look at me or speak to me again, Bernie Huggins, and the truth is, the way I feel now, I'd a lot rather you wouldn't."

Purvy finished his whisky in a gulp, and slipped off the stool. His knees buckled a little, and he grasped the edge of the bar and pulled himself erect. On the other side of the bar, Bernie watched him with some evidence of concern. As a matter of fact, Bernie had a sort of soft spot for Purvy and was feeling contrite for having insulted him. He didn't object to making Purvy sore, so far as that went, but he didn't want to make him sore *permanently*, that was the difference, and he'd only accused Purvy of being a damn liar and publicity hog because Purvy had been so pig-headed about keeping to himself whatever it was he knew.

"Look, Purvy," he said. "You don't need to go off in a huff. Chances are I've exaggerated things a little."

Purvy turned carefully away and got himself pointed, after a moment, toward the entrance to the lobby.

"You said what you said, and I heard you," he said. "Kindly do me the favor of going to hell, Bernie."

"Okay, Purvy. If that's the way you feel about it. Incidentally, where are *you* going?"

"None of your business," Purvy said. "None at all. I only tell my business to my friends."

"Don't be like that, Purvy. I'm your friend, and you know it."

"I'm damned if I do. My friends don't call me a liar directly and a nut by inference."

"I didn't infer that you're a nut."

"Yes, you did, Bernie. It was perfectly clear what you meant, and it's too late to try to wiggle out of it now. I may never come into your crummy taproom again."

Having delivered himself of this threat, which was not particularly alarming to Bernie or anyone else, he went out through the hotel lobby onto Main Street and turned in the direction of the railroad station. It was very cold, probably about ten degrees below freezing, and he walked along at a pretty good clip for someone carrying a load of whisky, his hands shoved into his topcoat pockets and the too-short skirt of the coat flapping around his knees. The cold air sobered him some, which was good in a way and bad in another. It cleared his head and permitted him to think better, which was good, but it also made him conscious again of someone following him, which was bad. It didn't do a bit of good to tell himself that it was all his imagination and nothing more, that it was simply impossible for someone to follow him every place he went and stand all night at the foot of his bed, for it was precisely his imagination that made the follower so frightening and so perfectly capable of the impossible.

What Purvy intended to do now, first thing, was watch the seven-o-five come in and go out. Not really first thing though, because it was only a little past six-thirty, maybe six-thirty-five, and the really first thing he'd do would be to go down to the restaurant and have a cup of coffee with Pheeb Keeley. Maybe Pheeb poked a little fun at him about girls and trains, but he liked her and got a kick out of talking with her just the same, and she certainly wasn't any god-damned smart-aleck like big-mouth Bernie Huggins, who'd accused him of being a liar and a nut. It was true that she sometimes referred to him as an odd ball, but that was different, the way she said it and the meaning and all, and the fact was, she seemed to have a kind of admiration for him.

Well, he'd have a cup of coffee with Pheeb, and watch the seven-o-five come in and go out, and after that he'd wait around in the restaurant, or go read the magazines at the newsstand in the main waiting room, until the seven-thirty-eight freight came through. The freight was one of the trains he liked best, a big 4-8-4 steam job, and it didn't stop at the passenger station, of course, but went thundering right past on the farthest pair of rails over from the platform, the very last pair, with ten other pairs between. This was too far removed to suit Purvy, and it was his habit to walk across the rails, a few minutes before the freight arrived, clear across beyond all the tracks, and it was then the most exciting experience it was possible to have, standing beside the rails as close as he dared in the great white glare of the headlight as the engine swept down upon him and past him with pounding drives and thunderous wheels in an overwhelming assault of sound that filled and rocked the world. It was especially exciting in winter, when it was dark early, best of all as the great light passed and the night closed in upon him and the rushing cars. By thunder and darkness deified, he was Lord God Stubbs astride a spinning sphere.

Phyllis Bagby saw him when he left the hotel. She could tell that he was drunk, and she knew that he was drunk because he was afraid. Perhaps she knew this so surely because she was afraid herself, and was therefore sensitized to the look and feel of fear in others. She had been waiting for quite a long time for Purvy to leave. Having seen him enter the hotel over an hour earlier, she had been sitting very quietly ever since in a straight chair by the door of her beauty parlor, waiting and watching and thinking of things she did not wish to think about. It was quite chilly in the room in which she sat, for she had turned down the thermostat for the night, but she was not aware of the cold. Wearing a mouton coat and matching mouton hat, she sat in the chair and looked down and across the street at an angle to the door of the hotel.

She did not know exactly why she waited, except that it was imperative. Purvy Stubbs was in danger, of course. Deadly danger. This was a feeling that had grown within her to the stature of conviction, and her own fear had grown in ratio to her certainty of Purvy's danger. It was peculiar, the quality of her fear, something she had not analyzed and had not really wished to analyze, but she knew that it was somehow a perversion and unclean. And now, sitting in the dark cold room in the straight chair, she deliberately considered it and tried to understand it, and the perversion was, of course, that she was not so much afraid for Purvy, for what might happen to him, as for what might happen as a consequence to one who possibly threatened him.

Guy, she thought. *God, don't let it be Guy*!

She was not accustomed to praying, and she was not really praying now. It was merely a blind and undirected cry for help in traditional terms. Anyhow, she did not really believe it was Guy. Not Guy who had killed the girl and left her body in the dry slough and was now a threat to the bumbling, kindly fellow who had seen him by chance in damning circumstances and was too loyal, or too stupid, to relieve himself of danger simply by telling what he knew. She did not believe it was Guy, but she didn't *know*, and the doubt was there in her mind, the perverted fear.

Phyllis was no fool. She had been thinking for herself and doing for herself for more years than she liked to remember, and in the conduct of her affairs, sometimes questionable by proper standards, she had developed a shrewdness that was based essentially upon a sure feeling for character, the ability to judge what someone else might or might not be capable of doing. Her judgment was not infallible, of course, as she had learned empirically, but it worked on the whole with satisfying accuracy. This shrewdness, the feeling for character, she had applied to the murder of Avis Pisano, who had killed her, and this was the problem primarily of the three young men of Rutherford who had been incriminated by circumstances. Guy and Rex Tye and Ellis Kuder. In her mind she examined with a kind of fearful thoroughness every slightest thing she knew about them, each in turn and over and over again, and after a while, though any one of the three was capable of his own atrocities in his own way and own time, she began to believe that *only* one of them was capable of this particular atrocity in the time and circumstances of its commission. Only one.

This she believed, but she did not *know*.

So she thought the prayer that was not really a prayer.

So she sat in the cold room of her beauty parlor and waited and watched, and Purvy Stubbs came out of the Division Hotel, drunk with fear and bourbon.

Getting up at once, she went outside and started after Purvy, about a half block behind and on the opposite side of the street. Purvy walked rapidly, in spite of his condition, his topcoat flapping around his knees. It was soon apparent that he was going to the railroad station, which she had anticipated, as anyone would have anticipated who knew Purvy at all, and she wondered again why she had waited for him to leave the hotel, why she was now following him, and all she knew, as she had known before, was that it was somehow imperative and must be done. Perhaps in her mind, below compulsion and reason and perverted fear, was the obscure understanding that the time for the attack on Purvy was necessarily now, or very soon, and that the place was logically the dark surrounding area of the station, where he went by habit, in strange and tenacious desire, to watch the trains come in. It was not in the hope of saving him that she followed, nor in the positive need to know the identity of his danger; it was in the greater hope and darker need to know for once and all who his danger was not.

Ahead of her, Purvy turned the corner onto the dark, narrow street that ran in front of the station, and she increased her pace in pursuit, but when she reached the corner and turned it herself, Purvy had already vanished. Accelerating her pace still more, rising on her toes to keep her high heels from rapping too sharply on the rough walk, she hurried down to the entrance and looked in through the high window in the door just in time to see Purvy going out the exit onto the platform on the other side of the building. She stood quietly in the narrow street, wondering what she should do. Purvy was going down the platform, she assumed, to the station restaurant. She did not want to follow him there, nor would it be advisable to wait in the waiting room, and so she went, after considering the problem, along the front of the station to its southeast corner, turning there and walking toward the south end of the platform. Slipping quickly along the edge of yellow light, she entered the little park and sat down on the bench among the whispering Junipers.

Now she began to feel the cold. Clenching her teeth to prevent their chattering, huddling in her mouton coat, she stared at the door of the restaurant into which Purvy had gone, and she thought that she was truly engaged in incredible idiocy. Obviously she could not follow Purvy indefinitely, watch him constantly, and chances were that she would gain nothing from her vigil tonight except a bad cold, or possibly pneumonia. It would be more sensible by far to tell Lonnie Womber of her suspicions frankly, which would relieve her of whatever guilt might be assumed in silence, and Lonnie could then do as he pleased about it, something or nothing according to his judgment.

Thinking of Lonnie, she knew for an instant the greatest terror of her life when he spoke to her suddenly. When the terror subsided, leaving her weak and near hysteria, she was aware that she was standing, ready to run, but she could never afterward remember rising from the bench.

"Oh, Christ!" she said.

"I'm sorry if I frightened you," Lonnie said. "I was here when you came. I've been standing behind you and wondering what in hell you could possibly be up to."

"I followed Purvy Stubbs here. He's in the restaurant now. At least I assume he is."

"He's there, all right. Went in just before you came. Why are you following Purvy?"

"I don't know, really. It just seemed imperative."

"Because he talked out of turn? Because you think a murderer may take a crack at him?"

"I suppose so."

"What could you possibly do about it if he did?"

"I don't know. Scream, perhaps. Frighten him off."

"Possibly. Possibly get yourself murdered, too."

"I hadn't thought of that."

"It's something to think of. You'd better let me handle this, Miss Bagby. It's my job. Believe me, I'm fully aware that Purvy may be attacked. I've even got a good idea of where and when it may happen."

"Where? Here at the station?"

He looked at her for a while without speaking, plainly considering the wisdom of answering her directly.

"If I tell you," he said finally, "will you go home and mind your own business?"

"Yes."

"All right. See that last pair of rails over there? Within the next hour a freight will pass on them. Purvy has a habit of crossing the tracks and standing on the other side to watch the freight pass. God knows why. God knows why Purvy does half the crazy things he does when it comes to trains. Anyhow, the freight itself will be between Purvy and the station. Behind him will be nothing but a few old sheds and a high board fence. Everyone who knows Purvy knows he does this regularly. Including the murderer. I figure it will happen there and then, if it happens at all. On the other side of the freight when it passes through."

"How can you be sure?"

"I can't. I just think so because it seems to be the best possible time and place."

"If you think so, why don't you tell Purvy not to go across the tracks?"

"Because I want him to go. I need him for bait. If you think that's pretty risky, you're right. It is. If you think I'm a heel for letting him, you may be right, too. I won't argue the point. Incidentally, would you mind telling me why you've concerned yourself with Purvy's trouble?"

"I know Purvy. He comes to talk with me. I like him."

"Is that all?"

"What else could there be?"

"You're frightened, Miss Bagby. I'm willing to bet that it's not entirely for Purvy. Or even mostly."

"I don't see how you could possibly get such an idea."

"Don't you? Well, it doesn't matter. You better go away now. Go home, or to a movie, or anywhere at all that's away from this."

She stared at him for a moment, at the pale blur of his face in the darkness, and then she turned and walked away, colder under the mouton than even the cold night could make her.

Lonnie stayed on in the little park until the seven-o-five had arrived and departed. Then he crossed the tracks and stood in pitch darkness inside one of the old sheds on the far side.

At the station, Purvy went through the waiting room, as usual, and down the platform to the restaurant. Ahead of him was the dark little park of whispering Junipers, but now he saw no shadow among shadows, and this was now to be expected, of course, for the shadow was behind him. He hurried into the warmth behind steamed windows and sat on a stool at the oval counter. Inside the oval, Phoebe Keeley approached, sniffing audibly the last few steps.

"Purvy," she said, "are you drunk?"

"No, I'm not, Pheeb," Purvy said. "I had a few drinks at the hotel, but I'm not drunk."

"I didn't know you drank, Purvy."

"I don't much, to tell the truth. Usually I just take a little beer to be sociable."

"It sure as hell isn't beer I'm smelling now."

"Well, I've got onto whisky lately, for some reason or other."

"If you want to know the truth, you smell like you'd been taking a bath in it, and what's more, if you aren't drunk now, you have been, and there's no use denying it."

"All right, Pheeb, all right. Let up on it, will you? If you're bound and determined to have your own way, I don't intend to argue about it."

"No need to get huffy, Purvy. It's your own business if you want to have a few drinks, and what I don't see is why you feel like you've got to deny it or be so damn sensitive about it. You like a cup of coffee?"

"I sure would, Pheeb. Thanks."

She drew the cup from an urn and put it in front of him. It was too hot to drink right away, so he spent a while smelling it. Phoebe spent the same while waiting on a couple who were waiting on the train. The service completed, she returned to Purvy.

"How's the murder coming, Purvy?" she said.

"What?" Purvy said, slopping over into his saucer. "What you mean, Pheeb, how's the murder coming?"

"Just what I said. How's it coming?"

"Damn it, Pheeb, I don't know any more about it than anyone else. Why ask me?"

"Well, that's not the way I heard it. I heard you saw something down at the end of the platform that night that's going to help Lonnie Womber turn up the one who did it in no time. It's all over about how you recognized someone who met her or something."

"I haven't told Lonnie Womber a thing, and I don't intend to."

"Why not?"

"Just because someone met her doesn't mean he killed her. Damn it, Pheeb, there's no law against meeting someone at the station."

"That's not your worry. Let him explain it to Lonnie."

"That's the trouble, Pheeb. Maybe he couldn't explain it to Lonnie's satisfaction. I've read how it happened lots of times how an innocent person couldn't explain away something that looked bad for him. Besides, to tell the truth, I'm not absolutely sure who it was. I think I know, but I'm not absolutely sure. Anyhow, I couldn't prove it."

Phoebe was looking at him with incredulity in her face, and maybe just a touch of the admiration he thought he sometimes detected.

"For God's sake, Purvy, haven't you got any sense whatever? You can't keep something like this to yourself for such a crazy reason as that. You ever stopped to think it might be dangerous?"

Her expression changed, and she started looking at him as if he were already dead, a compromise between horror and pity. Suddenly her eyes slithered uneasily to the door to the platform, and he had a terrified feeling that the murderer had come soundlessly into the room from out of the yellow light, bearing upon himself some terrible mark of identification, and was at that moment standing motionless behind him.

Purvy's head swam, and he had a sensation of falling. The warmth of the restaurant was restoring the effect of the whisky, that's what it was. Putting his head in his hands, he held it.

Phoebe, watching him, was beginning to feel apprehensive. She wondered if the poor guy was going to pass out in the restaurant, and she was about to suggest that he step outside onto the platform and breathe some fresh air when half a dozen fellows from town came in and sat down in a row at the counter. They were fresh guys, the kind who were always making wisecracks and these remarks with a kind of double meaning that they thought were just too damn clever, and they started in at it right away, one after the other, and it required all of Phoebe's attention and skill to handle the situation. She knew how to handle cheap guys like these, though, guys who couldn't have raised ten bucks among themselves, and she did it with a fine and scornful thoroughness. In the meanwhile, Purvy held his head and breathed the hot scent of coffee and was forgotten.

At seven-o-five, the local arrived on time, and he got up and went out and stood beside the door. The conductor came down and stood beside the porter at the bottom of the steps to one of the coaches, and Purvy had a crazy notion all at once that this was the beginning of something that had already happened, that Avis Pisano would descend in a moment to the rough bricks washed with dirty yellow light, while in the park among the Junipers a shadow waited and cursed his luck. But no one at all actually descended from the coach. Two passengers came out of the station and boarded it, and the local labored on. Purvy, his head clearer again in the cold, could hear the loud voices of the wise guys in the restaurant. They ought to be ashamed, he thought, to talk to Pheeb the way they did. He didn't think it was right and didn't want to listen to it, and so he decided he'd go up to the waiting room and take a leak and look at the picture magazines at the newsstand.

Relieved, thumbing slick pages, he began to feel sleepy. He wished he could take the magazines over to one of the hard oak benches, but the newsstand operator didn't permit anyone to take the magazines away, and in fact he sometimes got snotty about anyone's looking at them at all. Replacing the magazine on the rack, Purvy went over and sat down on a bench near the doors to the platform, and it was quite warm in the waiting room, though not so warm as it had been in the restaurant, and the soft clatter of the telegraph in the agent's office was a musical and lulling sound, like the sound of a summer day, and even the stern oak bench was magically affected and wonderfully soft.

With a start, some time later, Purvy awoke to the long whistle of the seven-thirty-eight freight. He was on his feet in an instant, his rising accomplished with the opening of his eyes, and seconds later he was on his way across the platform and the ten pairs of shining rails. His response to the whistle was reflexive and excessive. When he crossed the last rail and stood waiting, facing north, the big light of the 4-8-4 was still far up the line.

The light swept down. He was assailed and blinded by the great white light. In a maximum of exhilarating thunder, with flashes of fire and roar of steam, the giant locomotive passed. Darkness rushed in where light had been, and suddenly Purvy was caught in the suction of the spinning wheels, possessed and drawn toward the center of sound and terror. Sickened and strengthened by fear of death, he set his bulk and heaved it back and around and forward again in a powerful continuity of motion that he would not ordinarily have been capable of. Through the coarse thick sound-fabric of rattle and roar ran the brief bright thread of a scream.

The cars ran by into the night. Box cars, flat cars, gondolas. Eventually the caboose. In the vast comparative silence that settled, Purvy kept company with the lifeless substance of the shadow that had stood by his bed and had tried to push him under the train.

With the murderer, and with Lonnie Womber.

Lonnie's shout had gone unheard in the thunder of wheels and the nearer piercing scream. His gun, which was in his hand, he had not needed to use. Unable to save Purvy, who had saved himself, he was at least immediately present to give comfort.

Putting an arm around Purvy's shoulders, he said softly, "It's all right, Purvy. It's all right."

But it wasn't. Purvy knew this perfectly well. It would never be all right.

Now, he thought with a clear and definitive sadness that would never quite end, *it is entirely ruined. I shall never feel the excitement and godliness again.*

CHAPTER 18

As the evening passed. Time changed its pace. After seven it quickly became eight, and after eight it eventually became eight-thirty.

At first she was not excessively disturbed. She assured herself in the beginning of the long drag between the hour and the half-hour that he had certainly only been delayed and would arrive at any moment, but then, as she waited and waited and he did not come, she became slowly convinced that she had been seduced and jilted in the perpetration of a monstrous joke, and that he would not come at all. She felt for herself a great pity, for her corrupted and abandoned body a terrible grief.

But these did not last either, neither the pity nor the grief, and she was possessed instead by anger and shame and hatred, the easily attained antitheses of love. Standing in the hall beside the packed bag that she had carried downstairs immediately after the departure of her parents, she watched the long hand of the clock move interminably toward twelve in the indication of nine, and she thought once that she would call him on the telephone, that something might simply have delayed him after all, but she did not believe this, not in the least, and even so small a thing as the call was by now an impossible concession. Still staring at the derisive face of the hall clock, she began to curse him with a kind of cold and venomous clarity, which was the quality and character her anger assumed, and her mind adopted naturally, as if he were there to hear it, the frontal violence of the second person. Afterward, her invective exhausted, she began to think of ways to make him sorry, of all the things that she could do to make him suffer, and she wished and wished with all her heart that he should die. That she should stand and watch and smile as he lay dying.

But this would not be possible, of course, for he was already dead, and had been dead, though she didn't know it, for over an hour.

By nine o'clock, when he was a full hour overdue, longer dead, her anger and shame had grown too great for the house. It filled the rooms and pressed back upon her from the walls, a tangible and noxious density in which she moved with a great effort and breathed with tremendous difficulty. It was quite apparent that she was being slowly smothered, that she must certainly get away from the house at once in order to survive, and so she got a coat from a closet in the hall and went outside. It was very cold, but she walked with the coat hanging open, and she walked neither fast nor slowly, but with a carefully controlled and imposed gait, as if it were somehow critically important now for the sake of dignity and self-esteem to move and behave in the smallest respects, whether observed or not, precisely as she had always done. Walking in this way, her coat open and her stride measured, she descended the slope from the ridge to the lower level of town, and after a while she came to Main Street and then to the business area and then to the Division Hotel.

Outside the entrance, she became aware that she was cold and tired and desperately in need of a cigarette, and the lobby was suddenly a wonderfully desirable haven that could supply all her needs at once—warmth and smoke and a place to rest. Turning in, she crossed the lobby to the magazine and tobacco counter, and the night clerk, recognizing her, came over at once from the registration desk.

"Good-evening, Miss Haig," he said. "May I help you?"

"I'd like a pack of cigarettes," she said. "Parliaments, please."

He handed her the thin box, and she was reminded then for the first time that she had come off without a purse, and consequently without money.

"I'm sorry," she said. "I seem to have forgotten my purse."

He smiled and made with his shoulders a small gesture of unconcern. "It's quite all right. You can take care of it anytime."

"Oh. Thank you very much."

Standing by the counter, she opened the box and removed a cigarette, leaning forward to accept the light offered by the clerk. Drawing the smoke deeply into her lungs and expelling it slowly, she turned and started back across the lobby toward a cluster of chairs, and then, looking left into the taproom, she saw two young men of some significance in her life sitting at the bar, separated by a vacant stool, and she immediately felt the imperative need of a drink in addition to the needs of warmth and smoke and a place to rest. Changing direction, she went into the taproom and got onto the stool between the two. Her face in the mirror, she noticed, wore a bright and brittle smile, which was rather surprising, for she had not been aware of it, and it was really rather admirable, she thought, to be able to smile so brightly under the circumstances. To rest and warmth and smoke and alcohol was added a final need of flagellation.

"Friends," she said, sustaining the bright smile, "I have been seduced and scorned and left in shame, and I badly need a drink. Who'll buy?"

"I shall," said Ellis Kuder.

"My pleasure," said Guy Butler.

Bernie Huggins supplied it, and the three sat silently side by side in a suggestion of worn expectancy, as if they were waiting for something that might happen or might never happen but must, nevertheless, be waited for.

THE END

TAKE ME HOME
by Fletcher Flora

CHAPTER 1

Henry Harper was a young man who lived in two rooms above a secondhand bookstore. All he wanted to do in the world was to write, but he was forced by circumstances to do other things besides. He was naturally forced by the same circumstances to do most of his writing at times when sane and sensible men are sleeping or making love or getting drunk or expressing their sense and sanity in some other accepted way.

That's what Henry had been doing this particular night, which was the night of a Saturday. He had been writing a book that he had hoped someday to finish, and he had been, in a way, a little drunk himself. He had been drunk for hours on words, but now he was sober, and nothing he had done was good, and nothing would be good that he would ever do. His head ached, and he was filled with sodden despair. It was, he saw, three o'clock in the morning. Since it was impossible to sleep, he went down the street to the Greek's for a cup of coffee.

He felt better in the street. A sharp wind was blowing down the narrow way between old buildings. It slashed his face and blew from his brain the stale litter of leftover words. In the Greek's, behind steamed windows, there was only one customer besides himself. A girl. She sat huddled over a cup at the counter, wrapped closely in a black wool coat as if she were very cold. The cup was empty, drained of what it had held, and so was her face. There was something imperiled in the emptiness, a precarious adjustment to the brief sanctuary of an all-night diner. The Greek himself was behind the counter.

"Hello, Henry," the Greek said.

His name was George. He had a last name too, but it was too difficult to say comfortably and had fallen in disuse.

"Hello, George," Henry said. "Black coffee."

"You don't need to say it, Henry. It's always the same. Always black coffee."

"Don't make a moral issue of it, George. Just draw the coffee."

"It's three o'clock in the morning. It's no time to be drinking coffee."

"Any time's a time to be drinking coffee."

"Sure. Coffee and cigarettes. Cigarettes and coffee. A man lives on them, but not for long. You look bad, Henry. You'll die young."

There was that about George. He was compassionate. He was filled with concern and pity. He was an olive-tinted mass of fat compassion with an oily, earnest face. He grieved in his large and limpid, black eyes for all young men who died young from smoking cigarettes and drinking black coffee.

"A man can't sleep after drinking black coffee," he said.

"I don't want to sleep."

To secure his position, Henry lit a cigarette that he didn't want. George picked up a cup and turned to the shining urn behind him.

"How does the book go?" he said.

"It goes badly."

"You always say it goes badly."

"Because it always does."

George was very interested in the progress of the book. He didn't believe it when Henry said that it was going badly. One of his greatest concerns was that Henry would die from cigarettes and black coffee before the book was finished.

Henry buried his nose in the rich vapor rising from his cup. He was feeling gradually a little better. What he had accomplished didn't seem so bad now, although not so good as he wished. It was never so good.

"You should take better care of yourself," George said. "Why don't you get a haircut?"

Half a dozen stools away, the girl moved. She lifted her eyes and stared for a moment blindly at bright labels of canned soup on a shelf behind the counter. Then she lowered them slowly and began staring again into the empty cup. Henry glanced at her briefly and back to George, and George lifted his heavy shoulders in a small confession of ignorance and impotence. There were far too many troubles in the world even for a compassionate Greek.

"Off the street," he said. "She has no place to go."

"How do you know?"

"Who sits and looks into an empty cup when there is a place to go?"

"Maybe she has a place but doesn't want to go there."

"It's the same thing."

The girl stood up abruptly and came toward them. She was wearing nothing on her head, but her brown hair fitted like a ragged cap around her thin and empty face. "Pay for my coffee," she said to Henry.

"Like hell I will," he said.

"Why not?"

"Why should I?"

"Because I don't have any money."

"Too bad for you."

"Is a lousy dime so important?"

"It's all right," George said. "It's on the house. Compliments of George."

The girl turned her head and looked at the Greek for a moment without speaking, as if she were considering whether or not it would be proper to accept his offer. She didn't appear to be grateful. As a matter of fact, she gave the impression of feeling that he was meddling in a matter that did not concern him.

"It wouldn't hurt the son of a bitch to pay for my coffee," she said.

"Look out who you're calling names," Henry said.

"He's a poor writer," George said. "He has to watch his dimes carefully."

"What does he write?" she said.

"He's writing a book," George said. "He'll be famous." She stared at Henry as if she had caught him in the worst kind of perversion. It was a relief, however, to see an expression, even an unpleasant one, invade the emptiness of her thin face.

"It'll be a lousy book," she said. "No one will buy it."

"Not at all," George said. "It's going badly at the moment, but later it will go better."

George had become an authority on writers and understood that they had to be handled with care. His air of authority was plainly not acceptable to the girl, however. She inspected him with a faint expression of revulsion.

"You're just a fat, greasy Greek," she said. "Why don't you mind your own business?"

"Say," George said, "I give you a good cup of coffee and you call me names. What's the matter with you, anyhow?"

"Maybe you think I ought to kiss your fat tail for a lousy cup of coffee," she said.

Turning, she walked up along the line of stools at the counter and went outside into the narrow street beyond the steamed glass. George watched her go with his large, limpid eyes. For a moment, when she opened the front door, he felt compassionately in his own warm flesh the cold cut of the wind.

"She has troubles," he said. "That's apparent."

"She's crazy," Henry said.

"Because she has troubles, she hates everyone. That's the way it happens. When my wife left me for an Italian acrobat, I hated everyone for months. It was impossible to get along with me."

"I didn't know you ever had a wife."

"It was a long time ago. She came from Salonika as a girl. I seldom think of her."

Henry didn't answer. He lifted his cup in both hands and drank some of the hot coffee.

"She was very young," George said.

"Naturally," Henry said. "As a girl, she couldn't be anything else."

"Not my wife. The one who was here."

"Was she?"

"Under her coat, she was very thin. Did you notice?"

"No, I didn't. Anyhow, it's better to be a thin, young girl, even with troubles, than a fat, greasy Greek or a son of a bitch."

Henry finished his coffee and stood up. He put two dimes on the counter beside the empty cup.

"You have given me one dime too many," George said.

"I know how many dimes I gave you," Henry said.

He walked to the door and paused to turn the collar of his coat up around his neck.

"I hope the book goes well," George said.

"It will go lousy," Henry said, "and no one will buy it." He opened the door and went out, and there at the corner, leaning against a lamp post in dirty yellow light and a kind of arrogant indolence, was the girl. He started past here without speaking, but at the last moment he discovered that it was something he couldn't do, even though he had a strong feeling that it would probably be a mistake to do anything else. Stopping a step or two beyond her in the yellow light, he turned and stared at her, and he saw that the Greek was right, that her body under the coat was very thin, but it seemed somehow to be a natural thinness appropriate to her character and chemistry, and not the thinness that would come from not having enough to eat for too long a time.

"Where are you going?" he said.

"As you see," she said, "I'm not going anywhere."

"Don't you have any place to go?"

"That's a reasonable conclusion, isn't it? If I had a place to go, I'd go there."

"Don't you have any money at all?"

"I have a little, but not with me."

"Where is it?"

"At the place I came from."

"Why don't you go there and get it?"

"Because I don't want to. I don't suppose a chintzy son of a bitch like you would give a girl a cigarette."

"I might if she asked me properly."

"Really? What would you consider properly?"

"With a little respect and courtesy."

"Will you please give me a cigarette?"

"That's better."

He gave her a cigarette and struck a match for her, holding it cupped in his hands against the wind. The tiny light flared up from the protective bowl of flesh and spread across her thin face as she leaned down to suck the flame. He was surprised, and somehow touched, as if it were a special concession to him, to see that she was rather pretty in a taut and sullen way.

"I paid for the coffee after all," he said.

"Actually?" She straightened, drawing smoke deeply into her lungs and releasing it to the wind on a deep sigh. "Thanks all to hell."

"All right. Now that you've got your cigarette, there's no need to behave decently any longer. I can see that. Why don't you go find a nice warm alley to spend the rest of the night in?"

Crossing the intersection, he started down the block, and it was not until he had gone almost halfway to the next corner that he became aware that she was following him. She had moved so silently behind him that he never heard her at all, not the least sound above the wind of her heels striking the concrete walk, and it was only the sudden leaping of her shadow in a small island of light that told him she was there. He stopped and wheeled around, and she also stopped in the same instant, and be thought in that instant that he could detect in her a kind of wariness and apprehension. She was abusive and insolent, the Greek had said, because she was filled with hate for everyone on earth. These attitudes could also be, he thought, a front for fear.

"What do you want?" he said. "Why are you following me?"

"I want to go with you."

"Go with me where?"

"Take me home with you."

"No. That's impossible. It's a crazy idea."

"I wouldn't be any trouble to you."

"The hell you wouldn't."

"I promise I wouldn't."

"No, thanks."

"You'll be sorry if you don't."

"I'd damn well be sorry if I did."

"It wouldn't hurt you to give me a place to sleep and stay warm."

Staring at her in amazement, he had a sudden odd sensation of gaseousness, of being lighter than air and in imminent danger of rising through the dirty light into upper darkness.

"Well, by God," he said, "this is a switch! You abuse me and curse me and behave in general like a bitch, and now you want to move in with me."

"If I say I'm sorry for the way I acted, will you let me come?"

"No."

"Why not? I tell you I wouldn't be any bother. I promise."

"You're pretty good at making promises, aren't you? At breaking them too, I'll bet."

"All right. It's apparent that you're determined to make me sleep in an alley. If I die of the cold, it's no skin off your tail."

She started back the way they had come, and there was a display of desperate pride in the rigidity of her thin back, in each carefully measured and conscious step. He felt himself choke with pity, and he softly cursed the pity and himself and his bad luck in meeting her.

"Wait a minute," he called.

She stopped and turned toward him, waiting beyond the perimeter of light, a pale shadow against the dark street stretching out behind her.

"You'd have to get out tomorrow," he said.

"All right."

"Don't get the idea that you're going to hang around and live off me until you're damn good and ready to leave."

"Don't worry. You said I'll have to leave tomorrow, and I will."

"Later today, I mean. Sunday. Not tomorrow."

"I know what you mean."

"Come on, then. Let's go."

He started walking on at a quickened pace, not looking back, but aware of her behind him just the same, matching steps, measuring and maintaining between them the distance that had existed at the start. And then, after crossing another intersection and moving perhaps fifty feet along the block, he suddenly knew that she was no longer there. Turning, he saw her standing quietly under the lamp at the corner. They stood staring at each other for half a minute before she began to advance very slowly, almost reluctantly, stooping again at the distance from him that she seemed to have established in her mind as being appropriate and proper.

"I don't think I'll go home with you after all," she said.

"Well, for God's sake, make up your mind. Don't imagine for a minute that I'm anxious to have you come."

"If I were to come, what would you expect of me?"

"I'd expect a little civility and gratitude, that's all, but I doubt that I'd get any."

"I thought you might expect me to sleep with you."

"Don't make me laugh."

"Why should it make you laugh? I suppose you'd be justified in expecting it under the circumstances."

"Listen to me. I've been working all night, and I'm tired. I wouldn't sleep with you if you were the last female on earth and it was my last chance. Besides, you're not my type. You're too skinny, and you've got a nasty disposition, and you'd probably accuse me of taking advantage of you. Go sleep in an alley if you choose."

"I'd prefer to go with you and be warm."

"In that case, stop standing here in the cold."

Once more under way, he felt her following at the established interval. Stopping, he felt her stop.

"Why are you walking behind me?" he said. "If you're coming, walk beside me. It makes me uncomfortable to have you walking back there like a servant or something."

"I thought you might prefer it."

"I don't. I prefer to have you up here. If it's not too offensive to you, that is."

"I don't mind walking beside you."

She came even, and they walked on, a distance by this time of slightly more than another block to the second-hand book store with his rooms above. Using his key, he unlocked the street door to the stairway leading up, and using the same key on the landing at the top, unlocked the door to the first of his two rooms, which was the living room. She went past him into the room and stood waiting a couple of steps inside while he closed the door behind them. He had left a lamp burning on the table where he had been working. His typewriter stood in position, loaded with a yellow second sheet on which several lines had been typed and x-ed out, and the top of the table surrounding the machine was littered with two hundred more of the yellow sheets covered with words and words and inexorable x's where words had failed. Additional sheets were crumpled and scattered about the floor.

"Here we are," he said.

She looked at the scant furnishings, old and worn and ugly, the stained and faded walls. She reeked, it seemed to him, of an irritating air of disdain.

"It isn't much," she said.

"It suits me."

"You must be easily pleased."

"It's a place to go, at least. That's more than you've got."

"It's warm, I admit. That's something."

"It seems to me that you're mighty goddamn particular for a beggar."

"Well, you needn't get so angry about it. You're surely aware that it's nothing to be proud of."

"If you don't care for it, you don't have to stay. No one asked you in the first place."

"Under the terms of our agreement, I'm willing to stay."

"Thanks a lot. It's very generous of you."

"You must be very poor."

"I'm not rich. If you thought I was, it was your mistake."

"I should think a writer would make quite a bit of money."

"Some writers don't make any money at all."

"Why don't they quit writing, then?"

"Because they're writers."

"Don't *you* make any money at all from writing?"

"I've made a little in the past, but not for quite a while."

"Why not?"

"Because I've been writing a novel and haven't had anything to sell."

"If you ask me, you'd better quit writing the novel and write something to sell instead. Then you might be able to live in a little better place."

Abruptly, as if she were acting suddenly upon a decision slowly reached, she unbuttoned her coat, removed it, and tossed it into a chair. Walking across to a ratty, brown, frieze sofa, she sat down and stretched her legs in front of her. She was wearing a gray wool dress that did not look shabby or cheap, although not new or expensive, and the thinness of her body, which had been a suggestion under the coat, was now clearly apparent.

After stretching and yawning, she kicked off her shoes. She did look very young, as the Greek had said, and he wondered for the first time what her age was.

"How old are you?" he said.

She yawned again, stretching, and looked up at him from the corners of her eyes with a sly expression. Her hair had a soft luster, gathering the light. It was a soft golden color, thick and full, brushed back over the ears at the sides. At the moment it was badly tousled by the wind, but it was palpably clean, and he had a notion it would have the smell, if he were to bury his nose in it, of scented soap.

"I'm twenty-four," she said.

"You don't look it."

"Don't I? I feel at least three times that."

"Are you in trouble of some kind?"

"If I am, it's my own."

"That's right. I only hope you keep it to yourself. Why don't you want to go back to the place you came from?"

"I'd rather not talk about it, if you don't mind."

"You've run away from home, haven't you?"

"Run away? I told you I'm twenty-four, and that's the truth. I'm old enough to go where I please."

"You do have a home, don't you?"

"I used to have one, but not any more."

"What happened to it?"

"Nothing happened to it, except that it's not mine any more. My family doesn't want me. They consider me a disgrace."

"Are you?"

"I suppose I am. At least they think so."

"Do you have a husband?"

"No, God, no! Why do you keep asking questions? You tell me to keep my trouble to myself, but at the same time you keep trying to get it out of me. It's not sensible."

"Oh, hell. There's no use whatever in trying to come to terms with you. That's plain enough."

Before she could respond, he turned and walked out of the littered living room and through the bedroom into the tiny bathroom that had been built, as an afterthought, in one corner. After turning on the light above the lavatory, he splashed his face with cold water and tried, with a brush and paste, to wash some of the feverish night out of his mouth. He was drawn tight, his nerves on edge, and although he was tired, it was still impossible to sleep. It occurred to him that he didn't even know the name of his guest, and that it had not, in spite of their unusual arrangement, seemed important enough to compel him to learn it. There was no assurance, of course, even if he asked, that she would tell him, or tell him, at any rate, the truth. When he went back into the living room, she had stretched out on the sofa with her arms folded up and her fingers laced beneath her hand.

"It has just come into my mind that I don't know your name," he said.

"Has it? I don't know yours either, for that matter."

"It's Henry Harper."

"Mine's Ivy, if it makes any difference to you. Ivy Galvin."

"Do you know something? I believe it really is."

"Of course it is. Did you think I'd give you a false name?"

"I thought you'd probably either give me a false one or none at all."

"You're suspicious of everything, aren't you? Well, I'm warm now, and I'm getting sleepy. I believe I could sleep for a while. Would you mind letting me alone?"

"Not at all. It would be a pleasure."

"Thanks very much."

She shut her eyes, as if by this small act she could achieve seclusion, and her breathing assumed with completion of the act an added depth and rhythm. In the posture and semblance of sleeping, she looked exposed and terribly vulnerable.

"I'll get you a cover," he said.

"I don't need a cover. It's warm enough in here without one."

"At least you'll need a pillow."

"I'll take a pillow if you have an extra one, but what I'd like more than anything else is a drink of whiskey. Do you happen to have any?"

"I have some bourbon in the bedroom."

"I think, if I had a drink of whiskey, that I could go right off to sleep."

"I'll get it for you."

He went into the bedroom to a chest of drawers, where the piece of a bottle stood in the midst of several tumblers. He poured about three fingers into two of the tumblers, got a pillow from the bed, and carried the tumblers and the pillow back into the living room. Ivy Galvin, or whoever she was if she was not Ivy Galvin, opened her eyes and sat up immediately on the edge of the sofa, her knees and ankles together in a position of unconscious propriety. She took the tumbler he offered and drank the whiskey in two swallows with only the briefest interval between.

"Thank you," she said. "Are you going to work some more?"

"No."

"It's all right if you want to. Don't let me interfere."

"I won't. It's just that you reach a point when it goes bad, or seems to go bad, even if it doesn't really, and there's no use trying any longer."

"That's true in everything."

She set her empty glass on the floor beside the sofa and lay down again with her head on the pillow. Her eyes closed, she began to breathe, as she had before, with depth and rhythm. He drank his own whiskey and sat down in the chair at the table and began to gather the scattered yellow sheets of his manuscript, putting them in order. This done, he began reading, but reading at this time was a mistake, because he was tired and satiated with words, and everything seemed worse than it was. The whiskey began to work on him a little, making him slightly drowsy, and he pushed his typewriter back and lay his head for a moment on the edge of the table where the typewriter had been, and the moment stretched on and on and became nearly an hour, and he wakened abruptly with his head splitting and a dull pain between his shoulders. Standing, he turned off the lamp on the table and walked in darkness into the bedroom and sat down on the edge of the bed and removed his shoes. He thought that another swallow of whiskey would do him good, and so he got up and took the swallow from the bottle and then lay down across the bed for a minute, for just a minute before undressing and getting into bed properly, and this minute across the bed, like the moment at the table, stretched on and on into the day, the particular Sunday that this day was.

CHAPTER 2

She was really Ivy Galvin. That was her name.

She lay quietly on the worn sofa, one hand holding the other beneath her small breasts and her ankles touching in a position that was the prone equivalent of the one in which she had sat erect, a few minutes ago, to accept her whiskey. Except for her deep and rhythmic breathing, a technique she had developed in the methodical seduction of quietude, she had the appearance of having been laid out neatly for burial. She was feeling relaxed and at ease now, not so much from warmth and whiskey as from the assurance, at last clearly established, that Henry Harper, the odd young man she was using in her exigency, was not in the least interested in what she could not possibly give.

It was not true that she wanted to sleep, for she had found that sleep was treacherous. What she really wanted was to achieve and sustain for as long as possible the marginal twilight area between waking and sleeping in which she felt absolutely detached and inviolate, removed alike from the hard, bright threats above and the symbolisms of the same threats in the stirring darkness below. She wished that she could live in this twilight always, and she had become quite expert, as a matter of fact, in sustaining it precariously for long periods of time, but it was impossible, of course, to sustain it, as she wished, forever. Sooner or later she would descend in spite of herself into the waiting darkness of hostile symbols, which were very bad, and sooner or later after that she would rise inevitably to the shapes and names and terms of reality, which were never any better and usually worse.

Her eyes were not completely closed, although they appeared to be. Through her lowered lashes she watched Henry Harper with a kind of dreamy intentness upon the smallest details of what he did. She did not watch him because she was interested or concerned, but only because he was useful as a neuter distraction that helped her remain a little longer in her interim twilight. She saw him drink his whiskey and sit down and gather his papers. His head in the light of the lamp had a massive and shaggy look, and she thought with the detachment that was now possible to her that he looked completely spent and almost pitiable, committed to his own aberrations, whatever they were, and his own consequent loneliness. After a while he lay his head on the table and did not move for a long while.

Realizing that he had gone to sleep in his chair, she wondered if his sleep was sound and deep, as hers was not, or if it was disturbed by symbols, as hers was. This was something that did not bear thinking about, however, because it threatened the detachment she wished to sustain, and she began, as another distraction, to count slowly to herself, forming without sound with her lips the shape of the numbers, to see how high she could go before she stirred, but the time it took was too long to survive, and she was asleep a full quarter of an hour before he got up suddenly and turned out the light and left the room.

For a while she was neither more nor less than she appeared to be, a girl asleep in a posture of primness on a worn sofa, but then, as the windows on the street side of the room began to lighten, which was about seven o'clock in the morning of that day, she wakened in her sleep to another morning of another day in another place, and she was, in the time and place of her waking, another person.

She was, for one thing, much younger. She was much younger, and the day was soft and bright and beautiful, and she thought for these two reasons, because she was young and the day was beautiful, that she would put on a beautiful dress. She selected one from her closet and examined it, and it was just the kind of dress for that kind of day, pale blue and silken to the touch, although it was really polished cotton. It had a short bodice with a full skirt of yards and yards of material flaring out from a tiny waist, which would make a stiff petticoat necessary underneath, and so she selected the petticoat to wear also, and around the hem of the petticoat there was an inch of real lace that was supposed to show, just slightly, beneath the hem of the skirt of the dress.

She laid the dress and the petticoat side by side on her bed and went into the bathroom and bathed with scented soap, and then she put on a white bathrobe that had tiny blue roses scattered all over it, which was rather ridiculous when you came to think of it, inasmuch as there was no such thing as a blue rose, so far as she knew. Wearing the white robe and thinking of the pale blue dress and feeling clean and perfumed and almost as beautiful as the morning, she went back into the bedroom to the dressing table that had a mirror as big as the one her mother used. With the silver-backed brush that had been given to her by an aunt, she began to brush her hair. She pulled the brush through her hair and lifted it above her head to begin a second stroke, and then she stopped, the brush suspended in the beginning of the stroke, and stared in amazement at the reflection of her face in the glass. It was really rather funny, almost ludicrous, for there were three large brown stains on her face, and she began to laugh at herself and watch herself laughing back from the glass, wondering how in the world she could have bathed so carefully and still have failed to remove the stains. She couldn't think where she might have acquired the stains, but it didn't really matter, since they were there, as she could clearly see, and there was nothing to do but wash her face again.

She washed it in the lavatory, using very hot water and a stronger soap, but the stains were stubborn and refused to leave, and all of a sudden she understood that they were never going to leave, never in the world, even if she scrubbed herself every hour of every day for the rest of her life. Filled with terror and monstrous grief, she threw herself on the bed beside the blue dress and the petticoat, and at that instant her Cousin Lila came into the room and began to stroke her hands and arms in an attempt to comfort her, and everywhere that Lila's fingers touched there was instantly another stain that would never leave. Pulling away with a cry of anguish, she sprang to her feet and began to run across the room to the door, and she was wakened by the cry and the action in the middle of a strange room that she could not remember ever having seen before.

And then she remembered that it was the room of Henry Harper, an odd and antagonistic fellow who had agreed to let her sleep here until tomorrow, or today, which it now was. The last she'd seen of him, he'd been sitting in a chair with his head on the table, the one right over there, but now he was gone. In the gray light that filtered through the dirty glass of the front windows, she could see the empty chair and the table and the typewriter and a stack of yellow sheets beside the typewriter, but she could not see Henry Harper anywhere, and she wondered where he was. There was another room, of course, a bedroom with a bath built into the corner, and it was probably that he was in there, in the bedroom, where he would naturally have gone if he wanted to sleep. She walked over to the door of the bedroom and looked in, and there he was, sure enough, not lying properly in the bed, as he should have been, but lying sprawled across it on his face, fully clothed, as if he had simply fallen there in exhaustion and had failed to get up again.

Turning away, she crossed the living room to one of the front windows and stood looking down into the street. The street was narrow and dirty and utterly dismal in the gray morning light. Across the way, in the recessed doorway of a pawnshop, over which hung the old and identifying sign of the Medici, were several sheets of a newspaper that had been driven there in the night by the wind. Just below her and a little to the right, attached at a right angle to the face of the building in which she stood, was a sign that said "USED BOOKS" in large white letters, and in smaller letters underneath, "BOUGHT AND SOLD." She could read the words clearly from her position, and they seemed to her in their innocence to be a gross obscenity, a tiny part of the monstrous distortion of all things that was effect of her depression. She had no watch, but she could tell by the quality of the light that it was still early, which left ahead of her the most of an interminable day, and she wondered in despair how she would live it, and if she did, how she would then live the one that would surely follow it.

She wondered if Henry Harper had any cigarettes. He must have some somewhere, because she remembered that he had given her one on the street outside the diner where they had met. She looked around the room and could not see any, and so she walked softly into the bedroom and found part of a package lying on his dresser with some loose change and a pocket knife and a folder of paper matches. She helped herself to three of the cigarettes and the folder of matches and went back into the living room and sat down on the sofa. The smoke did not taste good, mostly because she had been unable to brush her teeth for quite a while, but she accepted this as being appropriate, natural enough in a life where nothing at all was any good, and it amounted to nothing more than another minute factor in the grand sum of her depression and despair. She had lived in her depression now for far too long, and it was nothing she had been able to do anything about, she had tried, and it had made Lila furious. It was, she supposed, one of the reasons Lila had tried to kill her.

Now she had deliberately thought about it, after trying so hard not to think about it at all, and it seemed like a long time ago that it had happened, far back in the remote and incredible past of yesterday. Something so remote could surely be thought of without particular trauma, could be considered calmly, or at least without excessive emotion, in the hope that something beneficial might come of it, something recovered that had been lost, something learned that had not been learned before, or had been forgotten. She was not actually optimistic that any of these things would result from her thinking, however calmly, or anything good at all, but anyhow it was sometimes easier in the long run to think than it was not to think, and it was a kind of relief for a while, even though it did not last.

So Lila had tried to kill her. There was no question about that. It was only by the merest chance that she escaped, and if she had not escaped, no one would ever have known that she had been deliberately killed, for Lila was far too clever to be found out, and it would have been considered either an accident or suicide, whichever under the circumstances seemed most likely. Her relationship with Lila had started going bad ages ago, long before remote yesterday, and it had gone steadily from bad to worse, and the most terrible part of it was that it had been, until yesterday, all kept carefully under the surface of a terrifying cordiality. So far as she could understand it, for this deterioration of a relationship that had once seemed the only true and possible one in her shrunken world, there were two reasons, and neither was a reason that she could change.

In the first place, she had not been a cheerful or pleasant companion. She admitted that. It's difficult to be cheerful or pleasant when one is burdened constantly, more and more heavily as time goes on, by a complex feeling of guilt and danger and loneliness, and it is impossible not to have such a feeling, or to hide it forever, when one is insecure in one's position. She was like an apostate who, having no longer any belief in God, still fears God's judgment. And then, in the second place, Lila had simply grown away from her and wished to be rid of her, but there was danger in this for Lila, or Lila thought there was, for she did not trust her little cousin any longer, and there was no telling what harm the cousin might *do*, in ignorance or fear or malice or all together, if she were deserted and left to her own devices. Lila was beautiful and talented and ambitious, and if it was compulsory for her to be one thing, it was imperative for her to appear to be something else. Therefore, she had tried to kill, and it was something, after all, that could be thought about afterward in the room of a stranger without grief or anger or exorbitant sense of loss.

Ivy Galvin lit another cigarette and closed her eyes and saw herself clearly. She was standing at the glass doers of their bedroom, hers and Lila's, staring across the small terrace outside and down into the interior court of the apartment building in which they lived, and Lila opened the door behind her and came into the room. Lila was wearing one of her beautiful tailored suits, the silvery-gray one, and she was, in spite of her day's work, which must have been arduous, as perfectly groomed in detail as she had been when she left in the morning.

"Hello, darling," Lila said.

"Hello, Cousin Lila."

Ivy did not turn away from the glass doors. She continued to look out across the terrace into the interior court. Lila, for an instant, looked annoyed, the thinnest shadow of an expression on the smooth cameo of her face. She removed the tailored jacket of her silvery-gray suit and began carefully to remove her wrist watch and the sapphire ring she wore on the third finger of her left hand.

"I wish you wouldn't call me Cousin. I've told you and told you that I dislike it."

"I forgot. I'm sorry."

"Considering everything, it's rather ridiculous, don't you think?"

"I suppose it is?"

"Sometimes I think you do it purposely to annoy me."

"No. I just forget, that's all. I always called you Cousin at home."

"Well, you're no longer home." Lila stared at Ivy's back, and now the shadow on the cameo was a suggestion of slyness. "Perhaps you *don't* do it purposely. Perhaps it's an unconscious expression of hostility."

"I don't think so. It's only a habit."

"Are you feeling hostile, Ivy?"

"What makes you think I am?"

"Never mind. I see we are about to get into a session of answering questions with questions, which will get us nowhere at all. Have you had a good day?"

"It's been just an ordinary day."

"Meaning that it has been a bad one. You have many bad days, don't you, Ivy? I wish I knew what is the matter with you."

"There's nothing the matter with me."

"Obviously there's something. Do you think you ought to see someone?"

Lila removed her blouse and skirt and sat down on the bed to remove her shoes and stockings. She did not look at Ivy now, but she somehow gave the impression of doing so. In the room, suddenly, there was at atmosphere of urgent waiting.

"What do you mean, someone?" Ivy said.

"A doctor."

"No. I don't need a doctor."

"You needn't be so intense about it. It was only a suggestion."

"I don't want to see one."

"Don't, then. It's entirely up to you. As a matter of fact, I agree that it's not necessary and possibly wouldn't be very wise. Haven't you dressed today?"

"No. I didn't see any use in it."

"You should dress and go out more often."

"There's no place to go."

"On the contrary, there are many places to go."

"Anyhow, there is no place to go that I *want* to go, and therefore there's no sense in going."

"Perhaps if you tried it, you'd think differently. You should develop an interest in something to keep your mind occupied. You never read a book or look at pictures or listen to music or do anything at all that might divert you and give you pleasure."

"I'm not clever like you. I'm no good at such things."

"It doesn't require a very clever person to read and look at pictures and listen to music. At least you're not illiterate."

"That's something, isn't it? Thanks for reassuring me."

"Oh, please don't imagine slights where none was intended, Ivy. I'm only trying to be helpful."

"I don't need any help. I only need to be left alone."

"Pardon me. If that's what you need, we should be able to arrange it with no difficulty whatever."

She stood up in her shimmering white slip at the same moment that Ivy turned from the door. Lifting her hands to her head, she began to remove the pins from the black bun on the back of her neck, and the bun became fluid under her fingers and spilled down between her shoulders in a dark stream. In the movements and features of her body there was the hard and disciplined grace of a ballerina. Watching her, Ivy experienced again the intense and tortured reaction of adoration and submission that she had felt almost the first moment of their meeting.

"I didn't mean it that way," she said.

"Didn't you?" How, precisely, did you mean it?"

"I didn't mean anything precisely. It's only that I'm always depressed and afraid of something."

"Afraid? Afraid of what?"

"I don't know. I guess I'm afraid of what may happen to me."

"Would you like me to tell you what your trouble is?"

"I don't think so. I'd rather not hear it."

"Nevertheless, I think I'll tell you. Your trouble is, darling, that you have neither the courage to be what you are, nor to become what you are not. You would, I think, be better off dead. When you are like this, which is now almost always, you are not tolerable to yourself or to anyone else. I'm really getting rather sick of you. Did you know that? I'm sick of your moods and your whining and your sad, sad face. You are no longer a pleasure to me, and so far as I can see there is no other excuse for your existence, and certainly none for your living here. Why don't you go home?"

"You know perfectly well that I can't."

"Why can't you?"

"They wouldn't have me."

"Oh, I'm not so sure. They might. They could lock you in your room and pretend to everybody that you had a lingering and fatal illness of some sort. And perhaps you have. Anyhow, it would be just like them."

"I'll not go back to them. I'll go away from here, if that's what you want, but I'll not go back."

"You'd never survive on your own. You're too ineffectual."

"I could find a job and another place to stay. I may not be so helpless as you imagine."

"What kind of job? As a waitress? As a clerk in a store? Don't be absurd. You are incapable of doing anything worthwhile. In the end, you'd have to find someone else to keep you, if you didn't get yourself into serious trouble first, and where would you be then? Worse off than ever, I imagine. You would go on and on getting worse and worse off, until you had destroyed yourself and possibly others. If you won't go home, you will have to stay with me, that's all there is to be said about it."

Lila walked over to her dressing table and dropped the hairpins from her black bun into a glass tray and went on without stopping into the bathroom, closing the door behind her. After a minute or two the shower began to run behind the door, and Ivy sat down stiffly on a frail brocaded chair and folded her hands' in her lap and looked steadily at the hands. It was beginning to get dark in the court outside the glass doors, and darker in the room than out. Between five and six, that meant. Closer to six. It was true, she thought, what Lila had said. It was true that she, Ivy, could do nothing worthwhile and would surely come to a bad end if she tried. It was for her, after all was said and done, only a question of which end of possible ends was a little less bad than the others. The truth was, she wished nowadays only to sit quite still, as she now was, and do nothing whatever. The sound of the shower stopped, and she sat and listened to the silence where the sound had been. Pretty soon Lila came back into the room and turned on a light above the mirror of the dressing table and began to make a selection of clothing from drawers and a closet.

"Where are you going?" Ivy asked. Her attention locked upon Lila's naked figure—the white, glowing flesh, the smooth curve of breasts that had known the touch of her fingers, the wide sweep of hips, the enticing length of thigh and calf.

"Out," Lila said, turning to face Ivy so that the lush richness of her breasts were exposed to Ivy's feverish glance. There was an odd, taunting look in Lila's knowing eyes which informed Ivy that Lila was completely aware of the effect of her nudity upon her.

"Are you going to dinner?" Ivy asked. Her voice was a hoarse whisper and there was a dryness in her throat that came from the memory of all the times she had been together with Lila. She felt her breathing quicken and had to fight down an urge to run toward Lila and gather her soft, perfumed flesh in her arms. There was an ache deep inside her, an ache of remembrance of things past, a longing for the sure touch of Lila's fingers on her body, a pulsating wish to lose herself in the perfumed mystery of Lila's flesh.

"Yes," Lila answered curtly.

"Who is taking you?"

"A man. Someone at the agency. I'm meeting him at a cocktail lounge."

"Have you been with him before?" Ivy asked, forcing herself to stare at her hands, hoping in that manner to quiet the emotional disturbance in her.

"Yes. Several times."

"Why do you go?"

"Because he's useful to me. He's been useful before, and he'll be useful again."

"I don't understand how you can do it."

"I know you don't. You'd be better off if you did."

"Is it possible to be two persons?"

"I'm not two persons. I'm one person who can adjust at different times to different conditions."

"Is it necessary for you to go tonight?"

"Not absolutely. I'm going because I want to."

"Please don't."

"Why shouldn't I?"

"Because I want you to stay here with me."

"No, thank you. You're not very entertaining company these days."

"I don't feel like staying alone."

"Only a little while ago you were saying that it was exactly what you needed."

"I said I didn't mean it. Sometimes when I'm alone too long. I begin thinking about killing myself. I'm afraid I might do it."

"I don't think there's much chance."

While they were talking, Lila was dressing, and now she slipped her dress over her head and stared at Ivy levelly across the distance that separated them. Her face softened, and she seemed suddenly to regret her words.

"Oh, well," she said, "it's not so bad as you imagine, and I don't wish to be cruel. Just zip me up, darling, and I'll make you comfortable before I leave."

She walked over to Ivy and turned her back, and Ivy, standing, pulled up the zipper and locked it. Lila's shoulders above the dress were as smooth and flawless as her cameo face.

"What do you mean?" Ivy said.

"About making you comfortable?"

"Yes."

"I'll put you to bed and give you a sedative. Something to make you sleep. It will prevent you from dreaming, and you'll feel better in the morning. Tomorrow's Sunday, you know. I'll be home with you all day."

"I never take sedatives."

"It won't hurt you this once. It's the kind I take all the time. You have the most fantastic ideas about what's harmful.'

Lila went to the dressing table again, where she brushed her hair a few strokes and restored the luxurious, dark bun. Then she fixed her face and moved on into the bathroom. Ivy got into bed, sitting erect with her back against the headboard. She heard water running, and the brittle sound of glass against glass. Lila returned with a crystal tumbler half full of a deep pink liquid.

"Here you are," Lila said. "It will be a little bitter, but not too bad. Just drink it quickly."

Ivy drank the liquid and slipped down under the covers with her head on her pillow. The bed and the pillow were wonderfully soft, and it would be, she thought, a kind of minor and healing miracle if she could only sleep deeply and quietly through the night, as Lila had promised, without dreams.

"Will you be late?" she said.

"Probably. I may not be back until morning."

"If I'm asleep when you come, wake me up."

"We'll see. Don't worry about it."

Lila got her fur coat from the closet and turned off the light above the mirror. In the total darkness that followed for a few seconds the extinction of the light, she spoke again.

"I'll put some records on the phonograph in the living room."

"It doesn't matter. You needn't bother with it."

"No. I'll put them on. I know you're indifferent to music, but it will soothe you and help you get to sleep sooner. The phonograph will shut itself off when the records are finished."

She went past the foot of the bed and across the room in the darkness. In the living room, she turned on a table lamp, and the light of the lamp approached the door between the rooms and entered a little way into the darkness. The phonograph began to play softly, the hall door opened and closed, and Ivy, lying alone and sedated in the suddenly enormous apartment, did not know what the music was, its name or its composer, but she knew that it lifted on strings a little of the weight of the night and what the night held, and that Lila, who had been cruel, had in the end been kind.

She lay utterly motionless, except as she moved to breathe, listening to muted strings from one record to another, and the strings no longer seemed to be in the living room, where they had been in the beginning, but above her in the darkness near the ceiling, and they seemed to keep rising and rising, or she kept sinking and sinking, the distance between her and the receding strings becoming vast and incalculable, like the distance to a star, and then all of a sudden the sound of the strings was gone entirely, leaving a profound and terrifying silence, and someone leaned over the foot of her bed in the darkness and silence and terror and said quite clearly: *You would, I think, be better off dead.*

Lila had said that. She had said it with calm, unequivocal cruelty, and later she had become inexplicably kind and had mixed a sedative, which Ivy had drunk, and had gone away casually to meet a man for dinner so that Ivy could go quietly to sleep and die sleeping quietly. It was revealed to Ivy in a blinding flash of insight a sudden rising into consciousness of a pattern of truth that had formed and cohered without conscious thinking in a deep and primitive part of her brain. In the morning, after enough time had lapsed, Lila would return and find her dead, or nearly dead, and Lila would tell how she had been depressed, had talked of suicide, and it would all be very logical and acceptable, and there were certain people who would receive the news with relief and thankfulness.

The bottle of sedative was in the bathroom, in the little medicine cabinet above the lavatory. Or the bottle in which the sedative had been. Ivy had seen it there only today, when she had found the initiative, somehow, to go and brush her teeth, and she had noticed specifically that the bottle was nearly full, and had wondered vaguely why Lila used the sedative in liquid form when it would have been so much simpler to take as capsules. Anyhow, it was now imperative to go and look at the bottle, to see if it was still nearly full or not, and Ivy swung her legs over the side of the bed and stood up. The darkness shifted and swayed treacherously, but at the same time was a kind of fluid and tangible mass that pressed upon her and served to hold her erect. Walking very carefully, with one arm stretched ahead of her to feel the way, she went into the bathroom and turned on the light above the little mirror which was also the door of the medicine cabinet, and the bottle was in the cabinet, and it was empty.

There, there, there. That was the proof of it. She had taken enough of the sedative to kill her, and if she did not wish to die it was necessary to take some kind of action against it. Her mind, for some reason, in spite of the sedative and unreasonable fear of death, was working quits well. It would never do to call a doctor, and it would do even less to call the police. It would not even do to go for help to another inhabitant of the building. It was perfectly clear, if she was to be helped at all, that she must help herself, and the first thing that must clearly be done was to get rid of the sedative inside her. She had no idea how fast it might work, how quickly be absorbed into her blood where it could not be retrieved, but it was certain that it would work more quickly as a liquid than as a capsule, and even now it might be too late. She went over to the commode and got down onto her knees in front of it and gagged herself with the first two fingers of her right hand, and quite a lot of bitter pink fluid came up through her throat and out her mouth to stain the clear water in the porcelain bowl. She knelt there for two or three minutes, retching, and then she stood up and pressed the fingers of her hands against her temples and tried to think what she should do next, if there was anything at all to be done.

But of course there was. It was imperative to keep moving. She had read or heard that somewhere. It was imperative to fight off sleep with physical action, and it would help, also, if the air was clear and cold and not smotheringly warm, as the air in the apartment was. Her stomach settled, she went back into the bedroom aid stripped and began to dress for the street in the first necessary articles of clothing that came to hand. Finally dressed after what seemed an interminable time, although it was no more than a few minutes, she went out of the apartment and down by the stairs to the street, and she was feeling oddly remote and detached from all things around her, which had no shape or character, as if she were floating just out of contact, or were, perhaps, simply going to sleep on her feet.

She began walking the streets without conscious direction, and she did not know how long she walked, or how far, except that it was a great distance and a long time. In the beginning the streets seemed to be broad and brightly lighted with many people on them, but later they became narrow and dark with hardly any people at all. Fragments stuck in her mind, places she had been and things she had seen, and she especially remembered afterward a very tall man in a blue and red uniform outside a swinging door, a bridge lighted at intervals by yellow bulbs above a giant whispering of black water, a stone bench in front of a cast-statue where she wished to sit and rest for a while but did not because she did not dare. And finally, after ages, she was on a narrow street outside an all-night diner, and she was absolutely too exhausted to walk any farther, and she desperately wanted something hot to drink.

There was a dark, fat man behind the counter in the diner. He looked like a Greek, she thought. He put a cup of coffee in front of her and walked away down the counter, where he stood idly, and after a while a young man came in and sat down and began to talk with the Greek. She had finished her coffee by this time and was thinking that she would have to go, although she didn't know where, and then, for the first time, she realized that she had no money, not even enough to pay for the coffee she had drunk, no money at all. Oddly enough, considering what had happened to her and what might yet happen, her inability to pay for the coffee assumed the dimensions of an enormous problem. It was somehow essential for the coffee to be paid for, and perhaps it was because she must demonstrate that she was clever enough to take care of herself after all, in spite of what Lila had said. She looked from the corners of her eyes at the young man sitting on the stool down the counter. He was a shaggy, unkempt young man, his black hair growing on his neck, but there was a lost and dogged quality in his rather gaunt face that seemed to suggest his own aberrations at odds with the world, and she had the strangest and most incredible feeling that it might be possible to be his friend.

Acting with compulsive abruptness, she went down and asked him to pay for the coffee, but he was mean and chintzy after all, the son of a bitch, although he did claim later, after she had waited on the street for him to come out, that he had paid.

She waited for him for two good reasons. She needed a place to rest and get warm, which he might have and share, and she continued to feel strangely, regardless of his meanness about the coffee, that the two of them, she and he, had a common denominator in a general way, although certainly not exactly. And so she had waited, and she had come home with him, and here she was, and the crazy part of it, the monstrous and ugly joke of it, was why in the world she had gone to all the trouble.

Thinking she was dying, she had made herself live and had forgotten that living was not something she really cared to go on doing. Yes, it was funny, a great joke she had played on herself. Sitting on Henry Harper's sofa, she lit the third of Henry Harper's cigarettes and began to laugh at the joke. She laughed and laughed with a hard, internal laughter that shook her body and made her bind, but then she quit laughing and began to think calmly and rationally to determine if the joke might not yet be turned in her favor, the mistake of living corrected. What she should have done, of course, was to lie sensibly in her bed and let death come to her gently as it started, thanks to Lila, and it would have been all over by this time, the dying done, and she would not now have this day to live, nor any of the days after, but it was too late to think about that, what she should have done. What she had to think about now was what could yet be done, and it might be done very simply if only Henry Harper kept sedatives.

It seemed reasonable to assume that he might, a fellow who worked all hours and clearly had trouble sleeping. There was time enough, too. Plenty of time. It was still very early, Henry Harper had not slept more than three or four hours at the most and would certainly go on sleeping hours longer, and by the time he wakened it would have been time enough. Even if it hadn't, even if he wakened too soon, he would probably think that she was only sleeping naturally and would let her go on sleeping until it was too late. If only, to begin with, he had the sedatives.

She got up and went into the bedroom. Henry Harper was lying as he had been before, face down across the bed with his arms outflung as it he were reaching in his sleep for the horizontal extremities of a cross. She went on into the little bathroom in the corner, where she looked carefully among other items for a bottle or a box that might contain what she wanted, but there was none. Sitting on the edge of the tub, she thought about using a razor blade on her wrist, for she understood that it could be done under water with little or no pain, but the idea was revolting and impossible, and then she saw the old-fashioned water heater in a corner with the gas ring underneath. She went back into the bedroom and opened its single window, and then she went in to the living room and opened its two, both of them overlooking the street, after which she returned to the bedroom and covered Henry Harper with a blanket that was folded at the foot of the bed. She did not think it was necessary, since time would not now be so important a factor, but she feared, nevertheless, that the cold air might waken him before she was ready, and it was just as well to take every precaution. In the tiny bathroom, she closed the door and stuffed toilet paper tightly in the cracks around it. This was meticulous work and took quite a bit of time, and it was with vast relief and satisfaction that she finally sat down on the floor beside the water heater and listened to the sound of gas pouring from two dozen holes into the room.

It did not enter her mind, not once, that she was doing Henry Harper a very bad turn.

CHAPTER 3

It was determined by a distended bladder that she should not die. The bladder belonged to Henry Harper. Waking, he was aware first of the nagging discomfort that had broken his sleep, and then he was instantly afterward aware of the cold air coming in the open window. He could not remember having opened the window, and in fact he could remember, after a moment's consideration, that he definitely *hadn't* opened it. He had taken a last swallow from the bottle, and then he had lain down across the bed for a moment and had obviously fallen asleep, and in the meanwhile, while he was sleeping, someone had opened the window and had covered him with a blanket, which was something else he could definitely remember not having done for himself. Then he thought of the girl in the other room who called herself Ivy Galvin and who was clearly in some kind of trouble, and he hoped that she didn't start trying to be ingratiating about windows and blankets and things like that, for it would only make it more difficult to kick her out when the time came, which was not long off, but first, before doing anything else, he would have to get up and relieve the distension of his bladder.

He threw the blanket aside and sat up on the edge of the bed and held his head for a moment in his hands. His temples throbbed, and his eyes felt sore and hot under granulated lids. With the index finger of each hand he pressed against his eyes until the pain became unbearable, and then he removed the pressure and felt for a moment afterward, in the abrupt departure of pain, an illusion of clarity and well-being. Rising in the moment of illusion, he went over to the bathroom door and tried to open it, but the door seemed to be stuck, resisting his effort. He turned the knob as far clockwise as it would go and pulled again, and the door snapped open suddenly in a thin shower of tissue before a gust of gas. He saw Ivy Gavin sitting on the floor with her back against the tub in attitude of definitive peace, and in an instant the stuck door, the tissue, the gas and the girl all slipped into position in a significant relationship. He was always a little proud afterward, thinking back, of the decisiveness of his reaction. Lunging across the room, he closed the tap of the ring beneath the water heater, and almost in the same motion, with hardly a break or change of direction, he gathered up the girl and carried her into the bedroom. In his mind with fear and incipient anger was a small entity of compassion, the thought that she was so light, so very light, hardly anything at all in his arms.

Laying her on the bed in the cold air from the window, he listened with sickening relief to the ragged and reassuring sound of her breathing, and as his fear diminished with the evidence that she was not dead and would not likely die, he became proportionately furious that she had, with no consideration of him whatever, placed him in a position that would have been, without the sheerest good luck of a distended bladder, extremely difficult if not disastrous. He wondered if there were anything more that he should do to help her, but he couldn't think what it would be, unless it were to loosen her clothing so that she could breathe more freely, and after thinking about it for a few seconds, in a kind of deliberate retaliation to the dirty trick she had played on him, he removed her dress and slip entirely, holding her with one arm in a sitting position as he pulled them over her head. The thinness of her body, he saw now, as he had guessed last night on the windy street, was truly the thinness of small bones. She was incongruously delicate and strong, childish and mature, and there was in the center of his anger, as he looked at her, an aching core that was not anger at all. Reluctantly, he covered her with the blanket and sat beside her to watch and wait until she recovered consciousness.

It seemed like a long time. It was very cold in the room because of the open window, and pretty soon he got up and put on his overcoat and sat down again. Later, when he felt that the gas was gone, or nearly so, he went over and closed the window, but the room stayed cold, although the radiator was hot, and so he went out into the other room and found the two windows there open also. He closed them and returned to the bed and sat down once more on the edge, and Ivy Galvin stirred and made a soft, whimpering sound and opened her eyes and immediately closed them again.

"I'm sick," she said.

"It damn well serves you right," he said.

She retched and rolled off the bed onto her feet and started for the bathroom. After three steps, she sank slowly to her knees with her arms reaching blindly for support.

She remained in that position, on her knees with her arms spread, and when he reached her and picked her up, her eyes were shut and her face reposed and her sickness apparently past. She was breathing quietly and deeply. Laying her on the bed and covering her again with the blanket, he stood looking down at her with a feeling of desperation. "Are you all right?" he said.

She shook her head, not so much, he thought, in answer to his question as to indicate that she wanted him to leave her alone. Well, he would leave her alone, all right, if that was what she wanted. He would leave her alone gladly until she had recovered sufficiently to dress and get out and go wherever she had to go, and that would be the end of her, and good riddance. Turning away, he was reminded by his bladder that he had not yet done what he had got up to do, and so he went into the bathroom and did it. Then he went back through the bedroom into the living room and sat down at the table and looked at his stack of manuscript. He wondered dully if he would ever in the world get it finished, and if he did, in time, if it would be worth the finishing. After half an hour, he went back into the bedroom and found Ivy Galvin lying quietly on her back with her eyes open. Turning her head on the pillow, she stared at him with undisguised malice.

"I suppose you think I ought to thank you," she said.

"Not at all," he said. "You've made it perfectly clear from the beginning that you don't believe in thanking anyone for anything."

"Why can't you mind your own business?"

"Well, I'll be damned if you aren't the most incredible female I've ever been unlucky enough to meet! I'd like to remind you, in case you've forgotten, that you've been imposing yourself on me in every way that suited you, and I don't mind telling you that I've had enough. What the hell do you mean by trying to kill yourself in my bathroom?"

"I can do as I please with myself. It's not your affair."

"The hell it isn't! And what was I supposed to do with you after you were dead? Dump you in the alley? Simply call the morgue to come and get you? By God, do you suppose a body is something that can be disposed of without any explanations or any trouble at all?"

The malice in her expression was replaced by a kind of surprised acceptance of his point, and he had the impression, fantastic as it was, that she had not considered previously for a single instant the enormity of the consequences to him of what she had tried to do to herself.

"I didn't think of that," she said.

"Of course you didn't. You never think of anyone but yourself."

"Well, don't feel so abused about it. I'm not dead, thanks to your meddling, and it's apparent that I'm in no danger of dying."

"Not because you didn't try."

"Perhaps I'll try again."

"All right. Better luck next time. Don't think for a minute I care if you die or not, just so you do it somewhere else. When you get away from here, wherever you go, you can do as you like with yourself, whatever it may be."

"You're a mean bastard, aren't you?"

"I don't like women who try to leave their dead bodies in my bathroom, if that's what you mean."

"All you can think of is the little bit of trouble it would have caused you. You don't care in the least what may happen to me."

"That's right. Not in the least."

"In that case, I'd better go away at once."

"The sooner the better."

"I'm sorry I ever came."

"So am I."

"It would have been better to sleep in an alley."

"You can sleep in an alley tonight."

She had been lying quite still, only her eyes and lips moving, but now she sat up abruptly and turned back the blanket. Instantly she was still again, caught and fixed in rigidity as she stared down at her nearly naked body. After a few frozen seconds, she lay back, covering herself, and he realized from the harshness of her breathing and the crimson stains in her cheeks that she was exorbitantly furious.

"Where are my clothes?" she said.

"On the chair over there."

"Hand them to me."

"Why should I? Get them yourself."

"You'd enjoy that, wouldn't you?"

"Not at all. You're nothing much to look at, you know."

"If you know what's good for you, you had better get out of here."

"It's my room, and I'll get out when I'm damn good and ready."

"I suppose it gave you a cheap thrill to take my clothes off when I couldn't help myself."

"Don't be ridiculous. I've had more pleasure taking the panties off a lamb chop."

"If you ever put your filthy hands on me again, I'll kill you."

"No danger. I never want to see you again, let alone touch you."

His anger was at least equal to hers. She had imposed on him and put him in danger and was now accusing him unfairly of motives he hadn't had, and he was confused, as well as angry, and desperately sick, besides, of her and her troubles, whatever they were precisely, and all he wanted was to be rid of her forever as quickly as could be. Retrieving her dress and slip, he threw them across the bed with a violence indicative of his anger.

"Let me tell you something," he said. "I've only tried to help you when you needed it, which was a bad mistake, for all I've had from you is abuse and trouble and nasty allusions to your precious virtue, for the love of God, and if you want to do me a good turn for the one I tried to do you, you will get dressed and go find a place to kill yourself where no one else will be involved."

He went out into the other room and sat down on the worn frieze sofa. He noticed in an ash tray the crushed butts of the three cigarettes Ivy Galvin had smoked, and he wondered if she had got up to smoke them in the night or if she had smoked them this morning after waking. He thought, wrongly, that she had probably smoked them in the night when she could not sleep for thinking about whatever it was that made her want to die, and he saw her suddenly with extraordinary vividness in his mind as she had not actually been, huddled alone in the dark in the room of a stranger that was the only place she could find in the end to go. Seeing her so, he felt his anger drain out of him, and he began to wish that he had not spoken to her with deliberate cruelty, or that he could, having spoken, take back what he had said. He cursed and closed his eyes and waited for her to come in, which she did about ten minutes later.

"Could you give me a little money?" she said.

"No," he said.

"You could if you would."

"All right, then. I won't."

"Why not?"

"Because I only have a little, and I need it for myself."

"I suppose that's so. You're obviously very poor."

"You said last night that you have some money at the place you came from. Why don't you go there and get it?"

"I don't want to."

"You mean you're afraid to?"

"No. Not exactly. I just don't want to."

"Where are you going?"

"When I leave here?"

"Yes."

"I don't know. Somewhere."

"Jesus Christ," he said with quiet despair. "You don't know where you're going, and you don't have any money to get you there. What's going to happen to you?"

"I don't know that, either. Something."

"Well, it's not my fault. I'm not responsible for what you are, or what you've done, or anything that may happen."

"That's true. You're not. I don't blame you for not giving me any money, and I don't blame you for being angry."

"I'm not angry. I was angry in the bedroom, but I'm over it."

"You were right to be angry. You've been very kind, and I've been a perfect bitch. I'm ashamed of myself."

"I wish you wouldn't be."

"I am. I'm grateful and ashamed. Thank you for giving me a warm place to stay."

"It's all right. It was nothing."

"I think I'd better go now. Good-by."

Looking at her, his despair mounting, he knew already, although he was not ready to admit it, that he could not send her off to somewhere with nothing. He wondered, if she would try again to commit suicide, and if she would succeed if she tried. It did not seem possible that she could go on and on failing. He had a mental picture of her in the city morgue, a slim and childish body in a stark box that pulled out of a wall like a drawer. He had never been in a morgue and had no clear idea of what one was like, but he was certain that it would be bleak and cold and inhospitable to the dead.

"Look," he said. "There's no hurry about leaving. Sit down for a while."

"I thought you wanted me to leave as soon as possible."

"I was angry when I said that. I told you I've got over it."

"Nevertheless, I ought to leave at once. It will only be harder to go if I delay."

"Are you hungry?"

"No."

"How long has it been since you've eaten?"

"I don't know. Quite a while. It doesn't matter, though. I'm not hungry."

"I might be able to spare you a little money after all."

"I wouldn't want to take it. I'd be ashamed."

"Oh, nonsense. I wish you'd sit down and stay a little longer. I'd like to talk with you."

She shrugged and sat down in a chair facing him, smoothing the skirt of her wool dress over her knees. Her legs, he saw, were quite good, with slender ankles and clean lines curving nicely to the calves. She was, in fact, a pretty girl altogether, and she would be, he felt, even prettier if only she would take the trouble to make the most of what she had. It would be a pity if she were actually to come, sooner or later, to the bad end she seemed to be looking for. As he watched her, he was reminded suddenly of someone else he had once known.

"What is there to talk about?" she said.

"Tell me about yourself."

"There's nothing to tell."

"There must be something."

"Nothing interesting. Nothing you'd care to hear."

"If you want me to give you some money or try to help you, you could at least tell me the truth."

"What makes you think I'm not?"

"It's pretty obvious."

"I don't see why."

"Because you tried to kill yourself, and almost did. No one tries to kill himself over nothing."

She folded her hands in her lap and sat looking at them. He thought at first that she was considering an answer, but after a long period of silence it seemed that she had merely decided not to make any answer at all.

"All right," he said. "If you don't want to talk, there's nothing I can do about it."

Then she looked up from her folded hands, and he saw that his first impression had been right, that she had been considering an answer all the while.

"It's evident," she said, "that I tried to kill myself because I didn't want to go on living. The truth is, someone I loved tried to kill me last night, and I saved my life by walking and walking and refusing to die, and then later, this morning, I decided it would be better to die after all, and so I tried, as you know, but it was no use. It's rather silly, isn't it, when you stop to think about it?"

"Who tried to kill you?"

"It doesn't matter. I'd rather not tell you."

"Because no one did?"

"No. It's true. Why should I lie about it?"

"Why should you lie about anything? I've got a notion you're pretty good at it. Maybe you think it's fun. Maybe it's essential to your ego."

"If I tell you what happened, will you believe me? There's no point in telling you if you won't."

"I'll do my best."

"All right, then. I've been living with my cousin. Her name is Lila Galvin. Her father, who is dead, was my father's brother. She's very beautiful and clever, and I loved her, and for a long time she loved me, but then I began to bore her and become a nuisance, and she doesn't love me anymore. I don't think she trusts me, either, and she's afraid that I may destroy her. Or destroy, at least, the kind of life she has made for herself. It isn't true, I wouldn't do anything deliberately to hurt her, but she thinks I might, and that's why she tried to kill me. Because she wants to be rid of me and is afraid of what I may say or do. Do you understand?"

She was looking at him levelly, holding his eyes, and he saw in hers an expression that he thought was composed of the pride and pain of masochism. He was convinced that she was deriving, now that she had begun to talk, a kind of intense and morbid pleasure from exposing in herself what he would surely consider shameful, even if she did not. And it was true that he did. He considered it shameful, and it made him sick. Not the aberrance itself, which was common enough, but the specific existence of the aberrance in this particular person—this thin girl with folded hands and pained eyes who was beginning to be someone he liked, and who might have become, with better luck on different terms, someone he could have loved.

"I think I do," he said.

"Well, then," she said, "that's the way I am, and that's what happened, and now I hope we needn't talk about it any more."

"How do you know she tried to kill you? Your Cousin Lila. What did she do?"

"Oh, it was very clever and almost worked, and it would probably have been much better if it had. It would have been so easy, simply a matter of going to sleep and never waking, and there was even music to die by. I wasn't feeling well, very depressed, which is the way I often feel, and she put me to bed and gave me too much sleeping medicine and went away. You see how it would have been? She'd have come back and found me dead, and it would have seemed like suicide, and that's exactly what everyone would have thought it was."

"How do you know she gave you too much sleeping medicine? How did you discover it? Are you sure you didn't imagine it?"

"No. I didn't imagine it. She had been angry with me and had said that I would be better off dead, and later, after she had gone and I was lying in bed in the dark with the music playing. I suddenly remembered what she had said, and I was certain that I would die if I didn't do something to prevent it. I got up and looked at the bottle the medicine had been in, and the bottle was empty, and I had seen earlier that it was almost full. There was no question about it. None at all. She had given me too much, and I was dying painlessly, as she wished, and when I knew this, although I had no particular desire to live, it was somehow imperative that I not die. It makes no sense at all, does it? Anyhow, that's the way it was, and I had heard that the thing to do was to keep moving and not, above all, to go to sleep, and so I dressed and started walking in the streets. After a long time I was too tired to walk any farther, and that's when I went into the diner where we met. You were nasty and chintzy about the coffee."

"Never mind the coffee. If all this is true, what do you intend to do about it?"

"Nothing. What is there to do?"

"Well, if this cousin of yours tried to kill you, you should at least report it to the police."

"No, no. That's not possible. Surely you can see that. Anyhow, it would do no good, and possibly a great deal of harm. I don't want to cause Lila any trouble."

"By God, if she tried to kill me, I'd want to make all the trouble for her that I could."

"You don't understand. You're just like all the others I've known. You're ignorant and bigoted and don't understand in the least how things can be."

"Look, now. Don't start abusing me again. I have trouble enough getting along with you as it is. If this lovely cousin of yours tried to kill you, as you said, we've got to do something about it, and that's ail there is to it. Would you like me to go and see her?"

"God, no! Why should I want that? What could you do?"

"I could scare the hell out of her, at least. I could give her as bad a time as she's given you."

"You leave her alone. Do you-hear me? Leave her alone. If I'd thought you were going to have a lot of crazy ideas about doing things, I wouldn't have told you what happened."

"Oh, all right. She's your cousin, and it's your life she tried to take. If it pleases you to be generous with a murderous queer, go right ahead."

"And don't call her names. Just keep still about her if you can't speak decently."

"I didn't call her anything she isn't. You'd better start learning to face the truth. And you'd better start learning to know who wants to be your friend and who doesn't"

"Do *you* want to be my friend? Is that what you mean?"

"I doubt that anyone could be your friend. You wouldn't allow it. You're so damned abusive and offensive that you'd alienate anyone after a little while."

"Is that so? I was just thinking the same thing about you."

He grinned suddenly, and she grinned back, her small face lighting and assuming a loveliness that almost made it another face altogether, and then all at once they were laughing and laughing, together and at each other, and when they were done and quiet again, they felt relieved and much better and nearly comfortable.

"If we're both difficult and offensive," he said, "we at least have something in common."

"Is it possible to be friends with a man? I hope so. It would be nice to be friends if he didn't eventually want to be something more."

"Maybe if you were good friends long enough you would begin to feel different about being something more."

"Do you think so? It would make everything so much simpler and better if I could."

"It might be possible. I don't know. It seems reasonable to me that you learned to be what you are, and it's just as reasonable, though probably harder, that you could learn to be something else."

"It's encouraging to hear you say so. I like you very much, and I'm sorry I've been so bitchy, even though I know very well that I'd be bitchy again and again if we were going on knowing each other."

"Would you like to go on knowing each other?"

"I think so. I think I'd like to try. Would you?"

"Whether I would or not is beside the point. The point is, you don't want to leave, because you have no place to go, and I'm not going to kick you out, because I'm not tough enough or mean enough or smart enough, whatever it would take to do it, and so you will have to stay here with me, and later we may be able to work something out. There's one thing you've got to stop, however, and that's thinking all the time that I'm about to ravish you, or some damn thing like that. I may want to, and probably will want to under the circumstances, but I won't."

"Do you really want me to stay?"

"Let's not press the point. I'm willing to have you if you behave yourself and quit giving me hell for every little thing I do, or that you imagine. I haven't enough money to buy you clothes or other things you'll need, however. One of us will simply have to go and get what you have in the place you came from."

"All right. I'll go myself tomorrow. I'll go and come right back. I'm determined not to be a coward about it any longer."

She got up suddenly and sat down beside him on the sofa. Leaning toward him, very carefully not touching him the least bit more than she intended, she brushed her lips softly across his cheek, and he was aware of the enormous effort it required and the exorbitant concession that it was.

"Thank you," she said. "I hope we can be friends. I'll try very hard, honestly."

"Oh, hell," he said with quiet despair. "Oh, hell."

CHAPTER 4

The next morning, which was the morning of Monday, Henry Harper was gone when Ivy Galvin wakened. There was a penciled note on his work table, and under the note there were five one-dollar bills. The note said that Henry had gone to work, and it was the first time, reading the words, that she realized that he must surely have a job of some kind, since he was earning nothing from his writing, and that he would have to go to his job today, since it was Monday. The five dollars, the note said, were for breakfast and lunch and taxi fare to and from the place she needed to go, and he hoped that it was enough, for it was, in any event, all he had to spare.

She had slept well in the night for a change, no dreams at all, and she was feeling better this particular Monday morning than she had felt any morning of any day for a long, long while. The note was encouraging too. It made her feel warm and important in a minor way, giving her at least five dollars' worth of significance to someone who was under no obligation to do anything for her that he did not really want to do. She was sorry she had called him chintzy and a son of a bitch and all the bad names she had called him. She resolved hereafter to be as good as possible as much of the time as possible, but she was honest enough with herself to concede that it was unlikely that she could suddenly start being good consistently when she had so little practice at it.

After bathing and dressing, she decided that she would start immediately for the apartment to get her possessions. There was no telephone in the rooms with which to call a taxi, however, and the street outside was not the kind of street on which taxis would ordinarily cruise. Anyhow, surprisingly enough, she was hungry and wanted something to eat before starting. Late yesterday afternoon, after they had settled things between them, she and Henry had gone down to the Greek's to eat a really substantial dinner that Henry had paid for, and here she was already hungry again the morning after. She could not remember the last time she had been hungry in the morning, it had been so long ago, and she thought that her hunger was surely a good sign of things getting better generally.

She went downstairs to the street and down the street to the Greek's. The little diner was beginning to assume in her mind a position of priority. She was fond of it for the part it had played in the changes she had made, or was making, and she was prepared to be just as fond of the Greek himself if he was willing to forgive her for calling him fat and greasy. He came down behind the counter to where she sat, his fat face creased amiably, and it was apparent that either he did not remember her at all or was willing to start over on better terms.

"Do you remember me?" she said.

"To be sure," he said. "You're the girl with trouble and no dime, and I'm a fat, greasy Greek."

"I'm sorry I called you that. I hope you will forgive me."

"It's not necessary to forgive the truth. It's true that I'm fat, and it's true that I'm a Greek. I'd prefer not to be called greasy, however, even though that's also true."

"Nevertheless, I hope you'll forgive me."

"Willingly."

"Fat men are very pleasant, I think, and the Greeks have an honorable history."

"It's agreeable of you to say so. Will you have something to eat?"

"Yes. I'd like some toast and coffee."

"I suggest an egg and some bacon besides."

"No egg. I can't tolerate an egg. Two strips of bacon, perhaps."

While the toast and bacon were being prepared, she sat on the stool at the counter with her sense of acceptance growing warmer and bigger inside her. It was very pleasant to sit there in amiable association with the fat, honorable Greek. It was even more pleasant to know that one had been accepted on reasonable terms by someone who knew the worst about her. The pretense of being what one is not, the sustenance over a long period of time of an enormous deception, is at best difficult, and at worst destructive, as it had nearly been with her. It was such a relief to be honestly understood in one way by one person that she wished now to be understood in all ways by all persons. She wished her young relationship with Henry Harper, for instance, to be clearly understood by this fat, honorable Greek who was at the moment bringing her toast and bacon and coffee. There was also, she saw, a little paper cup of jelly.

"Did Henry come here for breakfast this morning?" she said.

"Henry Harper?" George said.

"Yes. He was gone this morning when I woke up."

The Greek possessed, after all, being the proprietor of a successful diner, his full share of sophistication. He attached naturally to her stark statement an embroidery of details that were not true, but even so, allowing for his ignorance of all the facts, it was creditable that he showed no reaction except a polite interest in her small affairs "Henry's a problem," he said. "He hardly ever eats breakfast."

"Perhaps I can make him understand that breakfast is important."

"It would be a service if you could. He doesn't take proper care of himself. He drinks black coffee late at night and refuses to have breakfast in the morning."

"Well, it's obvious that he's very opinionated. I have learned that already. He's very kind, though, for all that, and has given me a warm place to stay. I'm going to live with him for the time being."

Into the Greek's amiable countenance, despite his reliable sophistication, there now crept an expression of concern.

"Are you convinced," he said, "that it's the best arrangement?"

"We have come to a mutually satisfactory agreement. You needn't worry about it."

"I have a natural concern for Henry, you understand."

"Yes, I do. I noticed it immediately."

"It's really the book. It would be too bad if anything interfered with the writing of the book."

"I promise not to interfere."

"A certain amount of interference arises inevitably from certain situations."

"Distractions, you mean. However, you don't have a full understanding of the arrangement. It's possible that I may even be helpful in the writing of the book."

"Let us hope so," George said.

But it was evident that he was not convinced and was still concerned. He was forced to depart to serve another customer, but he kept glancing at Ivy from the corners of his eyes, evaluating her potential as a distraction as opposed to a help, and when he returned to her after a few minutes it was obvious that he considered the distractive potential, in terms of his own susceptibility to such things in his youth, to be the greater of the two.

"One can only pray for the best," he said.

"As for me," Ivy said, "I've never found prayer to be particularly helpful. It doesn't matter, however, because you are concerning yourself needlessly. Do you have a telephone?"

"Yes. A business phone."

"I wonder if you'd call a taxi for me. I have to go someplace to get a few things."

He called the taxi, which arrived shortly, and she paid for her breakfast with one of the dollar bills and received her change.

"The breakfast was very good," she said. "Especially the coffee."

"I'm famous for my excellent coffee," he said.

"Your fame is deserved. Well, I must go now. Good-by."

"Good-by. I hope you will return."

"It's more than likely that I shall," she said.

Outside in the taxi, she told the driver where she wanted to go and sat back in the seat to watch the streets slip past beyond the glass. She was in much better contact with things than she had been for some time, and everything was, in fact, quite ordinary and dependable, exactly what it was represented to be, and not the distorted and treacherous element of a hostile world that was, incongruously, at once remote and imminently threatening. She felt that she had done quite well with the Greek. She was very pleased with the way she had done. She had been, after apologizing for her previous rudeness, amiable and casual. It would be necessary, if she were to succeed in living normally, to achieve an attitude of amiable casualness with people who wished her no harm, if not actually good, and it was certain that she had made a good beginning with the Greek. Her pleasure and confidence were somewhat shaken when she realized suddenly that they were approaching the apartment building in which she had lived with Lila so long ago, but then she remembered that Lila would almost certainly have a modeling engagement for the day, and that it would not, therefore, be necessary to see her or talk with her, and she felt relieved and again pleased and confident.

But she did not have her key to the apartment. She had come away without it, as she had come away without everything else except the clothes she wore, and so she was forced to find the superintendent of the building and ask him to let her in with his key. He was, fortunately, in his own apartment on the ground floor, and they went up together in the elevator, and Ivy, after thanking him for his help, closed the door of the apartment behind her and leaned against it. She shut her eyes and took a deep, deep breath and waited for the slow recession of the familiar, free-floating fear that had risen within her. When she opened her eyes again, Lila was standing in the doorway to the bedroom watching her.

Strangely enough, Lila did not seem at all angry. If the color was heightened in her cheeks, which was often a sign in her of anger, it was nullified by her lips, which were smiling, and her eyes, in which there was relief. She was wearing, Ivy noticed with an appreciation of detail that was rather remarkable under the circumstances, a soft white blouse tucked into the waistband of a pair of tight lounging pants of a style she always wore so beautifully over her slim and elegant legs. She possessed the same kind of perfection that she did in the sleek, full-page photographs in the slick magazines that Ivy had often looked at with an intense resentment that anyone could see and admire her also for no more than the price of the magazine.

"Where in God's name have you been?" Lila said.

"Away," Ivy said. "With a friend."

"A friend? What friend?"

"No one you know. A man."

"Are you out of your mind? I believe you are."

"You may think as you please about me. I don't care."

"Well, I know I was cruel to you the other night, and I'm sorry. I'm glad you've finally regained your sanity and come back where you belong. I've been sick with worry about you."

"I only came to get my clothes and other things. I'm not going to stay. I'm never going to stay here again."

"Nonsense. Where on earth will you go?"

"Back where I came from."

"To this man?"

"Yes."

"Do you imagine for a minute that I believe such an absurdity? You're lying to me. There's certainly no man at all."

She said this with such an air of conviction that it *was* suddenly imperative to Ivy that the existence of Henry Harper be made absolutely clear and unquestioned as a kind of critical truth from which everything else must develop from this point.

"There is," she said. "His name is Henry Harper, and he lives in two rooms over a bookstore on Market Street. I met him the night I left here. I went home with him, and I've been there with him ever since. He's really very kind, although a little contrary and difficult. He has agreed to let me stay with him until I can make other arrangements."

"You're out of your mind. You definitely are. Are you trying deliberately to destroy yourself?"

"Perhaps you think it would be better to remain here and be murdered."

"Murdered! You must be having delusions. What can you possibly mean?"

"You know very well what I mean."

"I assure you that I haven't the slightest notion."

"Don't bother to deny it. It won't do you any good. You gave me too much sleeping medicine and left me to go to sleep and die, but I discovered it before it was too late. I walked and walked for hours and hours, and I'm still alive, as you see, and now I've come back to get my things and go away again. Don't worry about it, however. I don't wish you any harm, in spite of what you did. I promise that I won't cause you any trouble."

Lila was now looking at her with such an expression of incredulous shock on her face that Ivy, for the first time, began uneasily to question her position, and to wonder if, after all, the sedative bottle had been as full as she had remembered. Thinking back, she realized, moreover, that she had never, that night, become very drowsy after leaving the apartment, except naturally, in due time, as a result of her exhaustion from so much walking.

"I shouldn't have left you alone," Lila said. "I understand that now. I had no idea you were in such a critical state of mind."

She walked over to Ivy and took her hand and began to stroke it, and Ivy was somehow powerless to take the hand away or to halt the disintegration of her conviction and resolution that had begun with the first doubt of Lila's guilt. She felt a compulsion to turn and leave immediately without any of the possessions she had come to get, to run away while there was still time. But the truth was that the time had already passed, and all she could do was to stand and be stroked and seduced.

"Oh, you are much more clever and talented than I," she said, "but I know what you did, or tried to do, and there is nothing you can say or do now that will change it or make any difference. I'm going away, whether you want it or not. Please let me get my things and leave."

Lila kept stroking her hand. Her eyes were soft, and her voice was softer.

"Of course you shall go, if that's what you want. You are perfectly free to do as you please, but surely it will do no harm to talk with me for a while and try to understand that I never attempted to do such a terrible thing to you. Come into the bedroom and sit down, and we'll have a quiet talk together, and you will surely see how wrong you are. Do you seriously believe that I could wish to harm you? Do you remember, when you were at home, how we used to sit under the tree in the yard, and walk together in the country, and lie on the beach, and all the things we said to each other, and were to each other, and meant to each other? Do you think, after all this, that I could do you the least harm or wish, you anything but good? Come now. We'll have a quiet talk, and everything will be as it used to be, and afterward, if you still wish it, you can go wherever you please."

She began to pull gently, leading Ivy away from the door and across the room, and Ivy followed as she had followed in other places and at other times, knowing that she should not and desperately wishing that she would not, but following, nevertheless, because Lila was Lila, the way and the life. She tried to think of Henry, of his kindness and the hope for which he stood, but Henry was at the moment no more than a rather fantastic creature in an impossible world that she had surely dreamed about in a bad dream in a bad night. Now, after the bad dream, there was no one left in the bright and shattering world as it truly was except her and Lila, ineffable Lila, and the world was all green and blue and glittering crystal, above and beyond an expanse of hot, white sand, and they were lying on the beach in a secluded cove at home, not on this bed where she had almost died to music. That was the way it had been in the beginning and still was and would always be.

Lila was stroking her now, speaking in her ear the softest words. Ivy's strength—what was left of it—was drawn from her body like fluid by the insidious caress of Lila's fingers. Then Lila's soft, moist lips were upon hers, hungry and demanding, and the old, familiar sensations rolled through Ivy in a tempestuous tide.

Lila's full-breasted body was locked closely to her own aching flesh. Lila's lips moved from Ivy's mouth, to her cheek, her throat, the soft valley between her breasts. Lila's hands and body were vitally, excitingly alive against her and Ivy began to lose all sense of time. For this little while nothing mattered but Lila—the savage pressure of her writhing flesh against her own slender body, the touch of Lila's sure hands on her breasts and flanks, the sweet and tormenting caress of her feverish mouth.

Then, suddenly, through the seething sea of sensation that enveloped Ivy came a random thrust of fear and with it a fleeting thought of Henry and what Henry could mean to her—if she so willed it. Deep inside her a warning voice—faint but insistent—whispered that if she were to lie any longer in submission to Lila's calculated seduction she would be forever lost.

With a strangled cry that tore at her throat like a claw, Ivy jerked herself free of Lila's warm, intoxicating embrace. She rose, staggering, to her feet, her vision blurred, all her senses hammering, and stumbled to the closet. She jerked open the door, swung it back so that it banged against the wall, then began pulling clothing from the rack in a kind of frenzied abandon.

From the back of the closet she took a large bag. Opening the bag on the floor, she began to throw the clothing into it without the least care. Lila, sitting up on the edge of the bed, her features flushed watched her with eyes that were slowly, after a moment of wonder, filled with the venom of hatred and icy rage.

"What are you doing?" she said.

Her voice was like the edge of a razor. She might have been, from the sound of it, speaking to a guest who had been intolerably vulgar.

"You can see what I'm doing," Ivy said. "I'm taking my things, and I'm going away, as I said I was."

"Go, then. I thought I could stop you from making an incredible fool of yourself, possibly from destroying yourself, but I see now that I can't, and I'm not certain, since you have become such a bore, that I even want to, or would if I could. It will be a satisfaction to me to be rid of you."

Ivy continued her abandoned packing, and Lila continued to sit on the bed and watch. After a while, Lila got up and went over to the dressing table and got an emery board and returned to the bed. She began shaping her fingernails carefully with the emery board, now paying absolutely no attention to Ivy, who had closed the large bag and was filling a smaller one with toilet articles and other small possessions. Lila did not look up from her meticulous work until Ivy had finished at last and was standing erect beside the large bag, the smaller one in her hand, strangely irresolute in the end, as if, now that the time had come to go, she could not quite believe in her ability to take such definitive action.

"Do you have everything?" Lila said.

"I'm not sure. I think so."

"Please be absolutely sure to take everything. I want nothing left to remind me that you were ever here, or that I ever knew you."

"Do you hate me so much?"

"I don't hate you at all. I despise you, which is something quite different. I despise your whining and your eternal, sickly depression. You may call your moods and attitudes by whatever euphemisms you may choose, but the fact is that you are simply a coward, and that's your whole trouble. I can't understand how I've tolerated you so long. It's much better that you are leaving, since you insist, for sooner or later I might have felt compelled to send you away anyhow."

"I'm not such a coward as you think. You'll see."

"Oh, you'll come crawling back when you reach the miserable end of whatever stupid arrangement you've got yourself involved in. I suppose, since I have some responsibility for you, that I'll take you in again."

"I won't come back."

Lila stood up slowly. She made no threatening gesture, no overt sign at all of violence, and her voice, when she spoke, was rigidly restrained. But the quality of her fury was all the more deadly for its restraint.

"For God's sake, then, will you kindly quit talking about it and go? Go at once. I want you to get out of my apartment and out of my sight and out of my mind. Before you go, however, I want you to understand one thing clearly. If you do anything or say anything to harm me, I'll find a way to make you regret it."

"I have no wish to harm you," Ivy said. "I've told you so before, and it's true."

The room was menacing, a place of danger in which all objects were in a conspiracy against her. Bending at the knees, holding her body rigid in precarious balance, she picked up the large bag and walked carefully out of the bedroom and through the living room to the door. She set the large bag down, opened the door, picked the bag up again, went through into the hall, once more set the bag down while she closed the door firmly behind her. She did all this with an air of conscious calculation, as if it were terribly complex and difficult, and afterward, standing safely in the hall at last, she had a sense of exhilaration that she had actually done under the most difficult circumstances, after being subjected to the most seductive influence, what she had come to do.

Carrying the bags, she walked downstairs, preferring not to use the elevator. There was no taxi in sight on the street outside, and so she began to walk and had walked several blocks before a taxi came along and stopped at her signal. This also seemed to her a major and significant accomplishment, stopping the taxi so easily, and she got into it and gave the address on Market Street with a feeling of authority that was quite satisfying. She had one bad moment when she saw that the meter registered an amount larger than the balance of what Henry had left for her, but then she remembered her own money in the small bag, and she got safely to where she was going and paid the fare fully and everything was all right, or nearly so.

CHAPTER 5

In the following days of their chaste cohabitation, Henry became accustomed to having Ivy around the place and would have missed her if she had gone away. Most surprisingly of all, he discovered that he worked better when she was there, somehow supported and sustained in his efforts by the slight sounds of her movement, her breathing, the occasional remarks she made aloud to herself without any expectation of a response from him. When he came back in the evenings from his small job with a minor publisher of three obscure trade journals, he came with a sense of expectancy that was never quite sure of fulfillment, and he always discovered her presence with mixed feelings of relief and astonishment that she had not, while he was gone, packed her things and departed without a sign or word.

Now, on a night in December, he looked up and around from his work at the table and saw her lying on her belly on the sofa with a thick book propped against the sofa's arm in front of her eyes. It was a childish and appealing position, her knees bent and her heels waving back and forth above her narrow stern. He got up suddenly and walked across the room to one of the windows overlooking the street. Christmas was coming on, and the street lamps spaced along the curb were decorated with large red-and-white striped candy canes. The windows of the shops across the street had been dressed for the season with monotonous similarity in bright tinsel and piper above cotton and glitter in the semblance of snow. It had snowed in reality for a day and a night, but the snow was now slush on the sidewalk and street. On the nearest corner, seen at a sharp angle from the window where Henry stood, a large black pot of the Salvation Army hung from a tripod to receive alms for the poor. A soldier of the Army stood beside the pot and rang his bell in largo tempo, calculated to survive the long hours of supplication. The sound of the bell did not reach Henry, but he imagined, each time the soldier's arm rose and fell, that he could hear the clapper strike.

"We ought to have a tree," Henry said.

"A Christmas tree?"

"Yes. Of course."

"They're very expensive. Do you think you can afford it?"

"Certainly I can afford it. I'm not so poor that I can't buy a tree if I please."

"Well, it would be nice to have a tree, but I don't think you ought to buy one."

"Nonsense. Go out and buy one tomorrow. You'll have to get some lights and ornaments for it too."

She closed her book, which was the third one of several that she had decided to read in a program of self-improvement in several areas. Rolling over and sitting up on the sofa, she glared at his back with a kind of sulky resentment.

"I was going to buy one Saturday as a surprise," she said, "but I see that you're bound to spoil it."

"Why wait until Saturday?"

"Because I'm being paid Saturday, that's why. I was going to buy the tree as a surprise with my own money."

"What the devil do you mean? Are you actually working somewhere?"

"That follows, doesn't it? If I'm being paid, I must be working. Sometimes I think you like to be purposely obtuse."

"Never mind abusing me. I'm not in the mood for it. Where are you working, if you don't mind saying?"

"I'm working downstairs in the bookshop."

"For old Adolph Brennan?"

"Yes. I went down to talk with him and to explain our arrangement, that I'm staying with you for a while, because I thought he had a right to know, being the landlord and all, and after talking with him and explaining the arrangement, I asked him if he needed any help during the Christmas rush, and he said it happened that he did, though I can't say I've noticed any particular rush. I guess there aren't many people who give secondhand books as Christmas presents. Anyhow, what I intended, really, was to work for nothing in return for being allowed to stay here, but he insisted on paying me a little besides. He's a very sweet old man."

"You say you explained our arrangement?"

"Yes. I wanted it clearly understood, and I thought it was only fair."

"Exactly how clear do you suppose his understanding is? It seems to me that the reasonable implications of the arrangement would seem to be very different from the truth."

"Well, it's not my fault if he jumps to wrong conclusions. The important thing is, he was kind and considerate and felt that it was our business entirely, just as the Greek did."

"I'll say one thing for you. You're certainly building up quite a reputation for me in the neighborhood."

"You shouldn't be so egotistical. You imagine that everyone is paying attention to what you do, but it's very doubtful, in my opinion, that anyone cares in the least. Besides, writers are supposed to be rather immoral. It's expected of them."

"Is that so? It's interesting to know that you've suddenly become an authority on writers."

"Are you beginning to feel quarrelsome? You sound like it. I only wanted to surprise you with a Christmas tree that I paid for with my own money, and now you're behaving as if I'd done something wrong. I think it's very small of you, if you want to know the truth. It's rather depressing, you know, when everything you do turns out to be wrong."

"I didn't mean that at all, and you know it. I wouldn't think of depriving you of the right to buy a Christmas tree with your own money. I suppose it's only fair that you should contribute something now and then. We'll decorate the tree together Saturday night."

"I'd like that. Really I would. It's been a long time since I've helped to decorate a Christmas tree. Perhaps it hasn't been so long, actually, but it seems like a long time, so much has happened since, and so it comes to the same thing."

"You're right there. Something may seem a long time ago when it really hasn't been so long at all. It's a kind of perspective. When I was a boy, we had an evergreen tree in the front yard. Every year, a week before Christmas exactly, we strung colored bulbs in the tree and lit them every night until Christmas was past. It wasn't too many years ago, but it seems forever."

"Were you actually a boy once?"

"Of course I was a boy. Do you think I was born a man?"

"It's crazy, I know, but it seems to me that you must surely have been born the instant we met. You must have been born in one instant and have walked instantly afterward into the Greek's for a cup of coffee..."

He had often had, as a matter of fact, the same queer notion about himself. Not that he had, specifically, been born full-grown outside the Greek's on the night of reference, but that he had been born suddenly in various places at various times, and that everything he remembered before that time and place, whenever and wherever it was in a particular instance, was somehow something that had happened to someone else. Now, standing at the window and watching the soldier's bell rise and fall in largo tempo, he began to think of the past, the way from another time to this time, and it seemed to him, as it always did when he tried to review the pattern of his life, that the pattern had color and richness and variety and sense in two places at two times, and these places and times were signified by three people he had loved, of whom one was dead and the other two, so far as he was now concerned, might as well have been.

There was, in the first time and the first place, his Uncle Andy Harper. There was also an Aunt Edna, Uncle Andy's wife, but she was never in Henry's mind more than a kind of shadow of Uncle Andy, existing only because he did and having in recollection only the substance she borrowed from him.

Uncle Andy was a tall man, lean and tough as a wolf, with a long nose projecting downward from between a pair of the softest, most dream-obsessed eyes it was possible to imagine, and many folk thought that his eyes were his most remarkable feature, but these were the folk who had never become familiar with the touch of his hands. His hands were very large, with long thick fingers, padded on the palm side with the thick callus of hard work, and you would naturally have thought, looking at them, that their touch would be heavy, inadvertently brutal, but this was not so. The touch of the hands was as light and as gentle as the most delicate touch of the white hands of a fine lady, and it had the effect of a minor miracle, an impossible effect of its observable cause.

Henry first became aware of the light, miraculous touch of the heavy hands at the age of five when he was ill of influenza, and this was less than a year after the deaths of his father and mother in an accident on a highway six hundred miles away, when he had come to live with Uncle Andy and Aunt Edna on their farm about a hundred miles southwest of Kansas City, Missouri. He had wakened from a feverish sleep with the feeling that his fever was being drawn from his forehead by the soft magic of cool fingers, and he had thought at first that it was his mother who was sitting beside his bed, but it had turned out to be Uncle Andy. From that moment he had understood his uncle's vast depth of gentleness, and he had always afterward loved his uncle completely and quietly, with unspoken devotion, which was the only kind of love Uncle Andy wanted or would accept.

Uncle Andy was a puzzle to his neighbors and the despair of his wife, and this was because he declared himself to be an agnostic and maintained his position against all persuasion and prophecies of divine retribution. Enlightenment had its limitations in the area in which they lived, in the time they lived there, and it was not understood how a man could be so good, as measured by his faithfulness to his wife and his attention to his proper affairs, and at once so contaminated by the devil, as measured by his adherence to the devil's gospel. The truth of the matter was, Uncle Andy's formal education had ended at the eighth grade, but he had continued to read widely in a random sort of way, taking what he could find anywhere he could find it, and after an early experience with Colonel Bob Ingersoll, he had come, in the twenties, under the influence of Clarence Darrow and H. Mencken and Sinclair Lewis, and the greatest of these, because of a communication of gentle pessimism, was Darrow. One of the rare times Uncle Andy had become very angry, which was long before Henry's time, was when a Baptist minister from Fort Scott had tried to argue that William Jennings Bryan, who had just died of gluttony, had been specifically spared by God just long enough to confound the greatest agnostic of his day at the famous Scopes trial in Tennessee. Uncle Andy had pointed out that God had used damned poor judgment in his choice of counsel, since Darrow had made a bigger monkey of Bryan than Scopes had tried to make of man's ancestor.

The years on the farm were good years for Henry, although they later became, in the recollection of them after he had gone away, obscured and unreal with incredible rapidity by events that came between him and them. One of the things Henry learned, which was knowledge that filled him with adolescent sadness, was that Uncle Andy, in spite of being a successful farmer with no problems at the bank, considered himself a failure. He was not a failure, of course, but he considered himself one because he had been unable to do what he wanted most to do, which was to set down on paper some of the things he had seen and thought and felt and done, and he would not even allow himself the consolation of thinking that he might have been able to do so if only he had a better chance.

"The test of a Milton is that he act like a Milton," he said to Henry one summer night on the screened-in back porch off the kitchen. "I read that somewhere. I think it was Mencken wrote it. Anyhow, it's true. If I had it in me to do what I want to do, I'd do it, but I haven't got it. It's a great sadness, but there's nothing I can do about it."

So it was from Uncle Andy that Henry acquired his curiosity and his reading habits and, later, his need and hunger to express himself. He read voraciously, as Uncle Andy had, and for years without discrimination. Dickens and

Charles Alden Seltzer were equally acceptable to him, and if he recognized the superiority of the one, it did not prevent him from enjoying the other, and when he eventually encountered the massive, indiscriminate hunger and thirst and bellowing of Thomas Wolfe, it was like a revelation of divine despair. By that time, he was wanting to write stories himself, and he began to try. It was much more difficult than he had imagined, and it seemed to him unbelievable that it could require so much time and effort to fill a single page of lined paper with words that had never before been set down in the sense and order he gave to them.

In spite of his wide reading and his hunger, which was more emotional than mental, he was no better than a mediocre student at the high school in town. This was not because of inability, but rather because of a stubborn resistance to any kind of direction that was contrary to his natural interests. He read, but he read mostly the things he wanted to read, conceding only enough attention to assignments to get him by without disgrace and without distinction. Literature he loved, and history he accepted, but mathematics and science were barely tolerated. Finally, in due time, he graduated and received his diploma, and in the summer following his graduation Uncle Andy died, and was gone from the earth, and the earth was changed.

The morning of the day of that summer, Henry was up early, and the hours ahead of him seemed bright and clear and filled with the certainty of quiet and rich experience. After breakfast, he was standing behind the barn, looking off beyond the fields and pasture to the stand of timber along the creek, when Uncle Andy drove around the barn on the tractor.

"Where you going, Uncle Andy?" Henry said.

"Down to the far field at the southwest corner of the property," Uncle Andy said. "It's been lying there fallow since plowing, and I intend to disc it."

"Where's the disc?"

"It's already down there. I've only got to drive the tractor down and hook on. You like to come along?"

"Well, not unless you really need me."

"I don't need you, but you're welcome to come along for the ride. You got a loafing day planned out?"

"I didn't plan to do much. I thought I'd go down to the creek."

"You want to take the car and go into town?"

"No. Just down to the creek."

"You go ahead and do what you like. I'll be back around noon for dinner."

"Okay, Uncle Andy. See you later."

This was almost exactly what was said, and the reason Henry remembered it so clearly, the small talk that didn't amount to anything, was because it was the last conversation he and Uncle Andy ever had, and it came back to him word for word afterward with all the importance and enormous significance of being the last of something there would ever be. For quite a while he felt guilty, as if he had somehow deserted Uncle Andy just when he was needed most, but he knew, really, that it probably wouldn't have made any difference if he had gone, because he almost certainly wouldn't have been in any position to prevent what happened, it surely happened so fast. Anyhow, that was later, and this summer Saturday morning he went on down across the fields and pasture to the creek, and he spent the morning down there, lying under the trees and watching the dark water and thinking about what he would do with the rest of his life and wondering if he could ever become a writer, as he wished, or if he would finally have to do something else instead.

He got back to the house a little before noon, and Uncle Andy wasn't there, and he still wasn't there by one o'clock. He and Aunt Edna had planned to go into town for the afternoon, and Aunt Edna was frantic with worry, because Uncle Andy wasn't the kind of man to forget a plan or to go deliberately back on one. Finally, to satisfy Aunt Edna, Henry went all the way across the farm to the southwest corner, the fallow field, and he found the tractor stalled against a post at one end of the field, and Uncle Andy lying back in the field on the plowed earth. The disc had gone over him, and the only thing that later helped a little in the memory of it was the assurance of the doctor that Uncle Andy had clearly suffered a heart attack, which had caused him to fall off the seat of the tractor, and that it was probable he hadn't ever felt what happened to him.

After Uncle Andy was buried and gone for good, except the little of him that could be remembered, Aunt Edna asked Henry if he was interested in working the farm for a livelihood, and he said he wasn't, so Aunt Edna let it on shares to a good man with a wife and two sons. She moved into a cottage in town, and Henry went up to the state university on a shoestring in September, and it was there and then that he met the other two of the three people he had loved most. One was a boy, and the other was a girl, and he met the girl through the boy, whom he met first.

Going to the university on a shoestring the way he was, there wasn't any question of social fraternities, anything that cost extra money, and he found a room in a widow's house that was down the hill a few blocks from the campus. There were four rooms for men students on the second floor of the house, a community bath at the end of the hall, and Henry's room was the smallest of the four, overlooking the shingled roof of the front porch. One night of the first week of his residence, he was lying on the bed in the room with his text on *World Civilization* spread open under his eyes, but he wasn't having much luck in reading his assignment because he was feeing pretty low and wondering if, after all, he shouldn't have chosen to work the farm. The door to the hall was open, and after a while someone stopped in the doorway and leaned against the jamb. Looking up, Henry saw a thin young man with a dark, ugly face under a thatch of unruly, brown hair.

"You Harper?" the young man said.

He asked the question as if there were no more than the slightest chance for an affirmative answer. At the same time he gave the impression of caring very little if the answer was affirmative or not.

"That's right," Henry said.

"Mine's Brewster. Howie Brewster. I live down the hall."

Howie Brewster came on into the room, and Henry got off the bed and shook hands. The hand that gripped his was surprisingly strong in spite of a suggestion of limpness in the way it was offered. Immediately afterward, without an invitation, Howie Brewster sat down on the bed and took a half-pint of whiskey out of the inside pocket of his coat.

"Have a drink," he said.

Henry shook his head. "No, thanks."

"What's the matter? You one of old Bunsen's goddamn heroes?"

"I don't even know who old Bunsen is, and I'm no hero."

"Honest to God? You don't know who Bunsen is?"

"I said I don't. Who is he?"

"Football coach. I thought you might be one of his hired hands. You look like it, if you don't mind my saying so. You're big enough. You got good shoulders. I should have known you weren't, though. If you were, you wouldn't be living in Mrs. Murphy's goddamn Poor House. They take better care of the heroes. How come you *are* living here, by the way? Can't you afford anything better?"

"No. Can't you?"

"I can, as a matter of fact. My old man would stand the tariff of one of the frats if I'd live there, but I wouldn't live in one of those fancy flophouses with all those bastards for a thousand a month."

"Why don't you rent a better room or an apartment or something?"

"I know. You think I'm a goddamn liar. That's all right, though. I don't mind. You can think whatever you please and kiss my ass besides."

"Look. What the hell's the idea of coming in here and talking to me like that? I won't *kiss* your ass, but I may *kick* it if you don't look out."

"Sure. You're just the big corn-fed stupe who could do it, too, aren't you? Well, go ahead. I had an idea you had some brains, just from the look of you, but I guess you've got them all in your hands and feet, if you've got any at all, just like all the other stupes around here. Go on. Kick my ass. Kick the shit out of me."

"Oh, go to hell. I think I'll have a drink out of that bottle after all."

He took a swallow from the bottle and gagged. Howie Brewster watched him with open curiosity and an immediately resumed amiability.

"You ever had a drink of whiskey before?"

"No."

"Honest to God?"

"What do you want me to do, apologize for never having a drink before? I've had beer, out with friends now and then, but I never drank any whiskey."

"Never mind. You'll learn. How old are you?"

"Eighteen."

"You've got plenty of time. I'm twenty myself. If I was a year older, I'd be contributing to the delinquency of a minor."

"Balls. You're a big talker, aren't you? Your old man's rich, and you're a regular rounder."

"It's a defense mechanism. The truth is, I'm neurotic as hell. It's a fact, though, that my old man's well heeled. You can believe it or not."

"How come you can't afford anything better than Mrs. Murphy's, then?"

"Because my old man's a bastard. He's a bastard, and so am I. We deserve each other. When I refused to join his goddamn frat, he put me on a subsistence allowance. He thinks it's good for my soul."

He tipped his bottle and took a long pull and did not gag. Standing, he walked to the door.

"Well," he said, "I've got to read my goddamn economics assignment. Not that it'll do any good. I won't remember the crap. This'll probably be my last year here. Second and last. I'll flunk out sure as hell."

He left, swinging his little bottle openly by the neck with an air of bravado in defiance of Mrs. Murphy's posted prohibition of liquor on the premises, but he was back a couple of nights later, and in the weeks that followed, accumulating to a couple of months, he and Henry became comfortable cronies with a developing taste for beer. By tacit understanding, after the first night, whiskey was dropped as an issue, and the beer was in the beginning a kind of compromise that became quickly a social lubricant, and at the same time the substance of a bond. They discovered a small place downtown near the river where the question of age was not raised against them, and it was here that they habitually spent the nights that they could afford to give to it. The compatibility was supported by a mutual interest in writing and a shared conviction that the novelists of the twenties and thirties, the giants of the middle age between two wars, had never been properly read or appreciated until the two of them came along to do it.

Beneath Howie's pretentious rebellion, his excessive profanity and assumption of decadence, there was in truth, Henry learned, a genuine loneliness and uncertainty. And below these, now and then discernible, a depth of black despair. At first, as their sensitivity to each other increased, the real Howie was no more than a collection of suggestions, a personality merely inferred by some of the things he said and did, but then, one night in Mrs. Murphy's Poor House, there occurred an incident that made him, in one rather terrible minute, perfectly clear.

Henry had been to the bathroom at the end of the hall. On his way back to his room, passing Howie's closed door, he heard from behind the door a dry, rasping sound. Without pausing to think or trying to identify the sound, he stopped and turned the knob and stepped into the room. Just beyond the threshold he stopped abruptly, feeling within himself a rising tide of horror that was excessive in relation to its cause. Howie was lying face down across his bed, and he was crying. The sound of his crying was the arid sound of grief without tears.

"What's wrong?" Henry said.

He knew immediately that he had made a mistake. He should not have opened the door to begin with, but having opened it, he should have backed silently out of the room and left without a word. Howie rolled over and sat up on the bed, and his voice, although quiet, had the brittle intensity of a scream.

"Get out of here, you son of a bitch! Who the hell do you think you are to come walking in here any goddamn time you please without knocking?"

Henry's first reaction was one of simple shock at the violence of the attack. He backed out and closed the door, but when he was in his room again, he began to feel angry and was tempted to go back and give Howie a damn good beating. But this reaction was also short-lived, and shock and anger gave way together to genuine concern and an uneasy sense of shame for Howie's brief emotional nakedness. He wondered what on earth could have happened to disturb Howie so deeply, but he was really aware, even then, that it was nothing specific, no one thing in particular, and that Howie had merely reached, as he had before and would again, a time of intolerable despair.

Thirty minutes later Howie was standing in the doorway.

"May I come in?" he said.

"Sure. Why not?"

"Well, you know. I thought I might not be welcome."

"Oh, to hell with it. Come on in."

Howie came in and sat down, and that was the only reference ever made to the incident by either of them. "I've written a long poem," Howie said.

"Oh?"

"Yes. Two hundred twenty lines."

"That's pretty long, all right. What's it about?"

"Well, it's pretty hard just to say in so many words what a poem is about. Would you like me to read it to you?"

"Go ahead."

"I call it *The Dance of the Gonococci*."

"What?"

"*The Dance of the Gonococci*. You know. Clap bugs"

"Oh, come off. You're joking."

"Certainly not. Why should you simply say that I'm joking?"

"You'll have to admit that gonococci are pretty unusual subjects for a poem."

"Nothing of the sort. If Burns could write a lousy poem to a louse, why can't I write one about gonococci? In my opinion, gonococci are much more poetic than louse. At least, one can have a lot more fun acquiring them."

"What do you know about it?"

"Look, sonny. Just because you're a green and sappy virgin, don't think everyone else is too. You're just retarded, that's all."

"Talk, talk, talk. Talk big, talk loud."

"Oh, God, you're impossible. You don't know anything about anything. A dose of clap would do you good."

"It might do you good too. Then you might not think gonococci are so damn poetic."

"I had a dose once. Didn't I tell you about it?"

"No."

"I was seventeen at the time. I caught it from a girl from one of the best families. Nothing but the best for Howie, you know."

"One of the best families in shantytown?"

"Don't be facetious, sonny. Catching the clap is not a minor matter. Not that it amounted to much, really. It's no worse than a bad cold."

"I've heard that before, too."

"It's the truth. You ought to try it."

"Oh, balls. Go on and read the damn poem."

"No. I've changed my mind."

"Why? Don't think I'm going to beg you."

"Please don't. It's just that I don't think you'd appreciate it. You're obviously not sufficiently cultivated. Besides, I've got another idea."

"Do you think I'm sufficiently cultivated to hear it?"

"Maybe. Time will tell."

"Well, what is it?"

"Let's go see Mandy."

"Who's Mandy?"

"Jesus Christ! You mean I've never told you about Mandy either?"

"If you did, I don't remember it."

"Mandy Moran. Junior. She lives over in the dorm. Honest to God, Henry, I've actually never mentioned her?"

"I don't remember it."

"An egregious oversight, I assure you. You've got a treat in store, sonny. Last year Mandy and I did a lot of knocking around together, but this year we haven't seen much of each other. I guess that's why I haven't thought to mention her. I don't think she likes me much any more, to tell the truth, but I'm still madly in love with her, of course, in spite of being neglected. As a matter of fact, I have a standing project to go to bed with her. Come on. We'll go over to the dorm and see if she's in."

"I don't think so, Howie."

"Why not?"

"Well, damn it, I don't even know the girl, and besides that, you can't go busting in on someone without an invitation or a date or anything at all."

"Are you, for God's sake, telling me what you can or can't do with Mandy Moran? You don't even know her yet, and already you're telling me what you can and can't do with her."

"Oh, all right! I'll go with you, just to get you off my back, but It'll damn well serve us right if she has us thrown out on our asses."

"That's the spirit. Who knows? Maybe this will be the first step in despoiling you of your disgusting virginity. I'd consider it a rare privilege to be instrumental in your first tumble, sonny."

"Oh, go to hell, Howie, will you, please?"

They walked up the hill to the girls' dorm and were told by a superior female senior, the receptionist in the entrance hall, that Miss Moran was not in. Miss Moran was, the superior senior volunteered, working that night on the stage of the little auditorium in Fain Hall.

"We'll go over there," Howie said. "Come on, Henry."

"Do you think we'd better?"

"Certainly I think we'd better. Why not?"

"If she's working, she may not want to be bothered."

"Oh, come on, Henry. You're constantly making excuses. Are you afraid to meet a girl, for God's sake?"

"Don't be a damn fool. Some of us country boys might give a few lessons to a lot of guys with exaggerated opinions of themselves. Not to mention names, of course. What's this Mandy doing in the little auditorium?"

"I'm not sure. Probably painting flats. She's got an idea she wants to be a set designer."

"For plays?"

"Hell, yes, for plays. What else do you design sets for? She's a member of the Little Theater Group."

"That sounds like a pretty good thing. Interesting, I mean. I might like to try something like that myself."

"Well here's your chance. You get on Mandy's good side, she might be able to get you in."

The little auditorium in Fain Hall was dark, but there was a line of light across the stage at the bottom of the drawn curtains. Howie led the way up a flight of shallow stairs to stage level and out of a small off-stage room onto the stage itself. It was a very small stage, really, but it gave the effect of echoing vastness, and there was no one on it, excluding Howie and Henry, but a slim girl in a sweat shirt and slacks. She was holding her chin with the fingers of her right hand and staring disconsolately at a flat on which she had, obviously, been daubing paint. There was paint on her clothes, paint on her hands, paint on her face, and even a little paint in her pale, short hair. Henry thought that she must surely be the loveliest girl in all the world, although she wasn't that, and was a long way from it.

"Hello, Mandy," Howie said. "Long time no see."

She shifted the direction of her gaze from the flat to Howie. She did not change her disconsolate expression in the least. She had, apparently, merely shifted her attention from one unsatisfactory object to another.

"Has it been a long time?" she said. "I haven't missed you."

"Well, to hell with you."

"To hell with you too, you crazy bastard."

"I wanted you to meet my crony, but I can see I picked the wrong time for it."

Her attention shifted again, from Howie to Henry. "Hello," she said.

"Hello," Henry said.

"Don't you even want to know his name, for God's sake?" Howie said.

"What's his name?" she said.

"It's Henry Harper."

"I'm glad to know you, Henry."

"Henry, this is Mandy Moran."

"I'm glad to know you, Mandy."

"How about going somewhere for a beer?" Howie said.

"You drink beer, Henry?" she said.

"All the time," Henry said.

"I've written a long poem," Howie said. "I'll recite it for you."

"I can hardly wait," she said.

"It's better than anything Eliot ever did," Howie said. "It's called *The Dance of the Gonococci.*"

"A shocker," Mandy said to Henry. "Howie's a real shocker. He works at it. You don't look old enough to drink beer."

"Cut it out, Henry said. "You have to be a certain age to drink beer?"

"Legally, I mean. What class you in?"

"Freshman."

"God, I envy you. I really do. I'm a junior myself."

"That's what Howie said."

"I feel like your mother."

"Ask her to nurse you, for God's sake," Howie said.

"Don't be crude, Howie," she said.

"A couple of virgins talking to each other like that," Howie said. "It's disgusting."

"Just because you couldn't get any, Howie," she said, "It doesn't signify."

"For God's sake," Howie said, "are we going for a beer, or aren't we?"

"Wait'll I wash," she said.

She walked off-stage to a lavatory. Waiting, they could hear water running and splashing and considerable blowing.

"She washes like a goddamn porpoise," Howie said.

"She's lovely," Henry said.

"Mandy? Well, so she is, when you stop to think about it. She's so damn irritating, it's hard to realize it most of the time. Crazy too, of course. A real nut if I ever saw one. So am I, however, so it doesn't make much difference to me. Something happened to her as a child."

"What happened to her?"

"I don't know. Something."

"How the hell do you know?"

"It must have, that's all. Nothing's happened to her since that I know of."

"Damn it, Howie, you shouldn't say things like that about her. It's not right."

"Well, kiss my ass! Listen to the virgin freshman leap to the defense of his junior mother."

"All right, all right. Get off my back, Howie."

At that moment Mandy returned, and she had got some of the paint and had missed some. Her short, pale hair looked as if she might have run a comb through it two or three times.

"Where we going?" she said.

"We know a place," Howie said.

"I know the kind of places you know," she said.

"Relax," Howie said. "You must remember that we have your freshman child with us."

She took Henry's arm and pulled it up under hers and held it tight against her slim body. He could feel her small breast against his wrist. She kept his arm clamped under hers, and he kept feeling the breast.

"Never mind what Howie says," she said.

"I don't," he said.

"Where is this place you know?"

"I guess he means the one down on the river. We go there sometimes."

"It's a long walk down to the river."

"Quite a way, all right."

"I have to be in by eleven."

"We could have a couple of beers and come right back."

"All right. Let's go."

"Well, by God, I'm glad you got it settled," Howie said. "Am I included, by the way?"

"Suit yourself," Mandy said. "You can come along if you want to."

It took them almost half an hour to walk downhill from the campus and across town to the river, and it was about nine-thirty when they got there. They ordered three beers and drank them and ordered three more.

"Do you want me to recite my poem now?" Howie said.

"Not particularly," Mandy said.

"Oh, let's hear him recite it," Henry said. "It's better than anything Eliot ever wrote."

"All right, Howie," Mandy said. "Go ahead and recite it."

"I'll be damned if I will," Howie said. "I know when I'm not appreciated."

"Are you going to sulk about it?" Mandy said.

"To hell with it," Howie said. "Nurse your child and leave me alone."

They drank the second round of beers, and it got close to ten. Somehow or other Henry and Mandy got to holding hands under the table. When she drank from her schooner, she lifted it in both hands, and this made it necessary for her to release the one under the table temporarily, and during these times she would lay Henry's hand on her knee and leave it there until she was ready to pick it up again.

"Maybe we'd better have another round of beers," Henry said.

"I'm afraid it's time to go," Mandy said, "If I'm to be back by eleven."

"It only took about half an hour coming," Henry said.

"On the way back, we'll be going uphill," she said.

"That's true," Henry said. "We'd better go."

They walked back across town and uphill. At a corner near Mrs. Murphy's Poor House, Howie turned off by himself.

"Where you going, Howie?" Henry said.

"Home," Howie said.

"Don't you want to go with us?"

"To hell with it," Howie said, and walked away.

"Do you suppose we hurt his feelings?" Mandy said.

"I hope not," Henry said.

"So do I," she said. "You never know what hell do when his feelings have been hurt."

When they got to the dorm, they stopped in the deep shadow of a high hedge in front.

"Would you like to kiss me?" she said.

"I was just thinking how much I'd like to."

"Go ahead and kiss me, then."

He put his arms around her and kissed her, and she put her arms around him and kissed him, and after the first kiss they kissed twice more for a longer time each time. "I'd better go in now," she said.

"I guess you'd better."

"I liked you right away," she said.

"Same here," he said. "I liked you as soon as I saw you."

"It doesn't matter because you're only a freshman."

"I'm glad of it," he said.

He went back to Mrs. Murphy's Poor House and went to bed and thought about her. He didn't see Howie again that night, or all the next day, but the next night Howie came into his room and talked for nearly an hour, and it looked like everything was going to be all right.

It wasn't true, as Howie had said, that he was a virgin, but he had never felt for any girl the strange and disturbing mixture of lust and tenderness that he felt for Mandy. He had felt the former in numerous instances, satisfying it in two, and he had felt the latter for a particular girl in high school for six whole weeks on end, but he had not understood then that they could be compatible components of a single shattering emotional reaction. Mandy possessed, he learned in the weeks that followed, a fine capacity for passion, and it was only now and then that he wondered, for a moment at a time, if she had expressed before, or was even expressing now, the passion as freely with others as she did with him. He never asked, of course, because he was in no position to assume the right and did not, in any case, want to know. His major source of chagrin was that circumstances always prevented her free expression of passion from being quite so free as it might have been if circumstances had been more favorable.

In November, the day before the Thanksgiving holiday was to begin, he went over to the dorm in the afternoon to tell Mandy good-by. Most of the girls had already left, or were packing to leave, and the sitting room in which he waited was deserted except for himself. He felt very sad, as if he wanted to grieve for something unknown and to cry for no good reason. The holiday would be, after all, a very short one, only a few days, but it seemed to him to stretch ahead interminably. He waited and wallowed in his sadness for ten full minutes before Mandy came down from her room.

"Hello, Henry," she said. "Have you come to say good-by?"

"Yes, I have."

"I hoped you'd come, but I was afraid you'd gone without it."

"I wouldn't do that. You ought to know I wouldn't."

"Are you going to your aunt's?"

"I guess so. There's no place else."

"When are you leaving?"

"I thought I'd go this evening. There's a bus at six o'clock. When are you?"

"I? I'm not going anywhere. Did you think I was?"

"You mean you're not going home?"

"No. It's too far away for so short a time. I'll wait until Christmas."

"I'm not going either, then. I'll stay here with you."

"Oh, I wouldn't want you to spoil your holiday."

"I want to stay. Will you see me every day if I stay?"

"Isn't your aunt expecting you?"

"I'll write and tell her I couldn't come. Wouldn't you like me to stay?"

"Yes, I would, and if you do I promise to see you every day and every night."

"It's settled, then. I'll stay."

"We'll have a marvelous time, won't we?"

"Yes, we will. We'll have the best time ever. I will, anyhow. I know that."

"Is Howie going home?"

"He's already gone. He cut his classes and went this morning. Everyone else at Mrs. Murphy's has gone to 3."

"Including Mrs. Murphy?"

"Well, no, not Mrs. Murphy, of course. She's there."

"Will you call for me tonight?"

"Yes."

"All right. Come early. About seven-thirty. I've got to go back upstairs now. I'm helping my roommate pack." They were still alone in the sitting room, and so she kissed him hard and held herself tightly against him.

"I'm so glad you're staying," she said.

"So am I," he said.

When he returned at seven thirty, she was already downstairs waiting for him.

"What shall we do?" she said.

"I don't know. What would you like to do?"

"Do you have much money?"

"About twenty dollars."

"I thought we might go downtown and have dinner. Do you think that would be fun?"

"Yes. Let's do that. While we're having dinner we can decide what we want to do later."

"I already know what I want to do."

"What?"

"I'll tell you when it's time."

"Why can't you tell me now?"

"Never mind why. You keep thinking about what it could be and then let me know if you guessed."

They walked downtown to a good restaurant and sat knees to knees at a small table for two. It was the last time they'd had dinner together in a restaurant, and it made Henry feel special and very rich, as if he had a thousand dollars in his pocket instead of only twenty. It took quite a while to get served, and quite a while longer to finish eating, and by the time they'd finished and had coffee and a cigarette apiece, it was nine-thirty, or nearly.

"Have you been thinking about what I'd like to do?" she said.

"I've been trying," he said, "but I can't think of anything special."

"Shall I tell you?"

"Yes."

"I'd like to buy a bottle of wine and go to your room."

"At Mrs. Murphy's?"

"Yes. It seems to me we ought to have a celebration to begin the holiday, and I'd like to go there and have it."

"We'd have to be careful Mrs. Murphy didn't see us. She's deaf, though. We could probably slip in."

"It would be fun. Don't you think so? Will you take me?"

They went to a package store for the bottle of wine. Henry was afraid the clerk might embarrass him by asking him his age, and he was prepared to lie if necessary, of course, but the clerk apparently thought that he was old enough, or did not care if he was old enough or not. He was not familiar with wines, moreover, and hadn't the least idea of what would be the best kind to buy.

"What kind would you like?" he said to Mandy.

"Dark port would be nice," she said. "It's not so dry as some of the others, and besides, it's stronger than most of them."

"You mean it has more alcohol in it?"

"Yes. Port has around twenty per cent and most of the dry wines have only twelve or fourteen."

"That's a good thing to know. I'll remember that."

"Oh yes. Port is six or eight per cent stronger."

"A bottle of dark port, please," Henry said to the clerk.

"I'd like to suggest a New York wine, if you don't mind," Mandy said. "It may be only imagination on my part, but it always seems to me that New York wines are better."

"A bottle of dark port from New York," Henry said to the clerk.

The clerk put a bottle of Taylor's dark port in a brown paper sack, and Henry paid for it. He was surprised to discover that it was so cheap. He had somehow expected a bottle of wine from New York to be quite expensive. With the bottle under one arm and Mandy holding onto the other, he started uphill for Mrs. Murphy's Poor House.

"Do you think Mrs. Murphy will be asleep?" Mandy said.

"Probably. She goes to bed early usually, but sometimes she sits up and watches television. It's all right, though. Her sitting room is at the back of the house. If we're careful we can get in without her seeing us."

"What would she do if she saw?"

"Raise hell. Report me to the dean."

"That would be too bad. I don't want to get you into trouble."

"In my opinion, it would be worth it."

"Do you really think so?"

"I surely do."

"Well, that was a very nice thing to say, and I promise that I'll do something nice for you in return."

"What will you do?"

"Wait and see. We must remember, after we get upstairs, not to get careless and make too much noise. Isn't this the house?"

"Yes. You wait out here, and I'll see if the hall's clear." He went up across the porch alone and into the hall. The hall was clear, with only a small light burning on one wall, and he signaled Mandy from the door to come on. She came up and into the hall without the slightest sound, except a soft giggle of excitement that was hardly more than a whisper, and they went upstairs together to his room. Henry drew the blinds and turned on a light.

"It's very small, isn't it?" Mandy said.

"Yes, but it's handy. I can lie on the bed and reach damn near everything in the room."

"It's cozy, all right. I think it's very cozy. Do you have some glasses?"—

"Dixie cups."

"Dixie cups will do nicely. Will you please pour the wine?"

He opened the bottle and poured dark port into two Dixie cups. The wine was sweet and strong, and he could feel it almost immediately in his blood. By the time his cup was empty, his head was feeling strangely and pleasantly light, and he sat down on the edge of the bed. Mandy came over and stood in front of him between his knees, and he put his arms around her hips and leaned his head comfortably against her flat belly. After holding her so for a minute or two, he drew his hands slowly down over her hips and flanks and up again under her skirt.

"You're sweet," she said.

"You," he said. "You're the sweet one."

"I promised I'd do something nice for you. Do you want me to?"

"Yes. Please."

"It would be nicer if the lights were off. If you were to turn off the light and raise the blinds, we could still see each other, but no one could see in."

He got up and turned off the light and raised the blinds. Turning, he stood with his back to the window until his eyes had adjusted to the shadows. She was standing in the precise place and position he had left her, and he could sense her excitement and expectancy as surely and as strongly as he could feel his own.

"Shall we have a little more wine first?" she said.

"If you wish."

"I think a little more wine would be nice."

He filled their cups again, and when they had drunk the sweet and heady wine, she turned around and said, "Please unbutton me," and he did so with great difficulty, and then, when he had at last accomplished the unbuttoning, she turned back to face him and unfastened his jacket and the shirt under the jacket, throwing both to the floor. Then she came hard against him, clutching him close so that the hard nipples of her breasts rubbed teasingly across the flesh of his chest. Instinctively their mouths met and fused in a kiss that was filled with hunger and yearning. They remained locked together like that as if they could not get enough of each other.

Finally, Mandy drew away slightly and in the faint, uncertain light of the room he saw the svelte, exciting lines of her nude body. Her skin held a rich, pale glow, her breasts were high and firm, her waist narrow and flat, the hips having a wide flare, then narrowing into smooth, slender legs.

"Darling!" she whispered and drew his head to her bosom. He kissed the mounds of her breasts, his mouth lingering on the pink buds of her nipples, then coursing along her ribs, while desire mounted in a powerful tide in both of them.

Her own hands began a feverish stroking of Henry's body while they kissed and kissed again. Finally, in blind impatience they stumbled toward the bed and fell upon it, their arms and legs intertwining, their hot, moist lips still joined. And afterward the lingering and deliberate revelation of each to the other was mounting and tempestuous excitement that grew to intolerable intensity and shattered at last to the crying of a voice that might have been his or hers or both.

"Was it nice?" she said afterward. "Did I please you?"

"Darling," he said. "Darling Mandy."

"Do you love me a little?"

"No. Not a little. I love you so much that it hurts and hurts and I can hardly bear it."

"I'm so glad you love me, even if it's only a little, and it makes me happy to know that I've been able to please you."

She was then so quiet for so long that he thought she had gone to sleep, and time had passed from one day to another, to the day of Thanksgiving, when she spoke again and asked what time it was.

"After twelve," he said. "About ten minutes."

"Oh, God, I'll have to go. I have to be in by one."

"Even on a holiday?"

"Yes. Isn't it depressing? School nights we have to be in by eleven, but weekends and holidays it's one."

"I wish you didn't have to go."

"So do I. I wish I could stay all night and wake up and please you in the morning."

"Will you come back again?"

"Tomorrow night, if you like. We'll have a wonderful holiday, won't we?"

They barely beat the one o'clock deadline at the dorm, and the next night was wonderful and pleasing, as was the holiday altogether, but in the time that followed from Thanksgiving to Christmas they were sometimes almost in despair, partly because circumstances again made certain things difficult, if not impossible, and partly because it was a time leading inevitably to another period of time when they would be unable to see each other at all in any circumstances whatever. Henry's despair increased as the dreaded Christmas holiday drew near, and then, a few days before it was to begin, something happened to Howie that reduced his own affairs to insignificance and made him feel that he had committed a hideous wrong in having been so excessively concerned with them.

The evening of the day it happened, Henry was in his room, trying to study but not being very successful at it, when Howie came in and sat down on the edge of the bed and stared at the floor between his feet.

"I expect this will be my last semester here," he said suddenly.

"Last semester?" Henry looked up from his book. "Why?"

"Well, I'm not doing so well. I've got behind in all my subjects. I'm sure to flunk at least three of my semester exams."

"Exams aren't until the middle of January. If you worked hard between now and then, you could catch up."

"Maybe. I don't know. Anyhow, I won't do it. I know that. For some reason or other, I can't seem to get interested in anything. The old man will raise hell, but I guess it doesn't make much difference. I've been thinking about not coming back after the holiday."

"I hope you will."

"Why? I'd only be dropped after exams."

"Maybe not. Maybe you're being too pessimistic about your chances."

"No. There's no chance at all of getting by unless I work like a dog between now and then, and there's no use kidding myself that I'm going to do it. I just haven't got it in me."

"I don't want you to leave school, Howie. I'd miss you if you did."

"Oh, balls. You wouldn't miss me as long as Mandy's around."

"Yes, I would. Mandy would miss you too."

"Cut it out. She hardly ever sees me as it is, and she isn't very happy about it when she does. You've heard the way she talks to me."

"Well, you invite it, Howie. You know you do."

"I suppose so. I'm an unpleasant son of a bitch. I don't really want to be, though. It's because I'm afraid of being disliked or something, and so I deliberately try to make everyone dislike me. It gives me a kind of excuse. You've probably figured out for yourself by this time that I'm a goddamn phony."

"You're nothing of the sort, and I've never thought so."

"Well, thanks. I guess maybe you haven't. You've been a good friend."

Suddenly Howie made a fist with one hand and began to beat it with a slow and desperate cadence into the palm of the other. Standing, he walked out of the room without another word, and it was not more than fifteen minutes later when Henry heard him scream. The scream was repeated and repeated in almost the same cadence with which the fist had pounded the palm, and the screams were accompanied by the sounds of objects crashing and breaking and overturning in what seemed a systematic plan of demolition. After recovering from the first paralysis of shock, Henry hurried into the hall and down to Howie's closed door. The student who lived in the room across the hall was already there, staring at the door with an expression of incredulous horror.

"What in God's name's the matter with him?" he said. "Why the hell don't you open the door and find out?"

"I tried to, but it's locked."

"Help me break it down."

They threw themselves against the door together, and the flimsy lock snapped at once. The room beyond was in shambles. Curtains and blinds had been ripped from the windows, mattress and covers torn from the bed, chairs and tables overturned, lamps smashed, books and papers scattered everywhere. In the middle of the shambles, facing the door, was Howie. His shirt was ripped, and his face was bleeding in several places where he had clawed himself. He looked at Henry and saw no one and continued his terrible, cadenced screaming.

"Jesus, Jesus," the student said. "He's gone completely crazy."

"Go call the infirmary," Henry said. "Tell them to send an ambulance."

The student left, and Henry waited by the door. He spoke to Howie once, but he got no response, no slight sign of recognition, and with a kind of instinctive feeling for what was right, he made no effort to force himself upon his berserk friend. He only waited and watched to see that Howie inflicted no more damage on himself, and after a while the student returned, and a longer while after that the ambulance came with a doctor and two attendants from the infirmary. As soon as he was touched, Howie, who had become quiet, was immediately violent again, screaming and cursing and fighting with incredible strength. It required both attendants and the doctor to subdue him and administer an injection of some kind of sedative. When they had taken Howie away at last, Henry went into the bathroom and was sick.

He did not see Mandy again until the night before the day the Christmas holiday was to begin. They met in the sitting room of the dorm and walked from there across the campus to the Museum of Natural History and along a path behind the museum to a campanile on a high point of ground above a hollow with a small lake in it. A wind was blowing, and it was cold there, but they sat for a while in the cold wind on a stone bench, and the cold was like a punishment inflicted, a penance borne. He could feel her shivering and heard for a moment the chattering of her teeth, but when he lifted his arm to put it around her for warmth, she drew away from him a little on the bench.

"No," she said. "Don't touch me tonight."

"All right. I won't if you don't want me to."

"Please don't be offended."

"I'm not. I think I understand."

"I should have been kinder to him. It wouldn't have hurt me to be a little kinder, and it might have helped."

"You musn't blame yourself for anything. It was something more than you or I or anyone else ever said or did or failed to say or do."

"You're right, I suppose. It must have been something in himself that couldn't be helped."

"Maybe now it can be helped."

"I don't know. Maybe. I only wish that I had been a little kinder. He was in love with me, you know. Last year, before you came, he wanted me to run away and marry him."

"I didn't know. He never said anything.

"I couldn't do it, of course. I never even liked him very well, to tell the truth, but it wouldn't have hurt me to be a little kinder."

"Don't say that again. Please don't say it. You couldn't be expected to know how he was or what would eventually happen to him."

"Do you think he will be all right?"

"After a while. Someone will help him now."

"I hope he's all right. I hope he will be helped by someone who is kinder than I."

She stood up, shivering and drawing her coat around her. They walked back along the path to the museum and on to the dorm, stopping in the shadow of the leafless hedge.

"Good-by, Henry," she said.

"Good-by," he said. "Will I see you after Christmas?"

"Yes," she said. "After Christmas..."

CHAPTER 6

...Christmas.

And now, he thought, it was almost another one, and between then and now, that Christmas and this, a great deal had happened and he had been many places, but all that had happened and all the places he had been seemed in retrospect to be more remote in his life than the things and people and places of longer ago. Something had somehow ended with the end of Mandy, a quality of intensity, an impressionability, something that was his that she took away. She had left the university at the end of the next year, and afterward he received several letters from her at longer and longer intervals, and finally the one, which was the last, in which she explained that she was getting married to someone she had known for a long time, long before their time, and in the last paragraph of the letter she said, with a kind of gaiety and bravado that must have been intended as a tear and a kiss and a flip of the hand, that she was so happy she had been able to please him, and good luck, and to think of her, please, sometimes.

Well, he did that. He thought of her sometimes. But after the last letter, which came in the spring of his third year at the university, it no longer seemed quite worth his while to stay where he was and do what he was doing, and so he left in June after taking his examinations and did not return. He pulled his hitch in the army instead, and one day in the hills of Korea, when he was thinking about what he would do next, if he lived to do anything, he decided definitely, like Saroyan, that he must be a writer or be nothing, and although he had worked at it very hard ever since on the side of a variety of jobs in various places, he sometimes thought, unlike Saroyan, that it was nothing that he would turn out to be.

And now it was almost another Christmas. And now he stood at the window and looked down into the street below, and the bell of the soldier of salvation rose and fell, rose and fell, and he felt the striking of the clapper that he couldn't hear. Three people were crossing toward Adolph Brennan's bookstore from the other side of the street. One man and two women. Their arms were linked, the man in the middle, and they picked their way carefully through the slush. One of the women was carrying a paper bag in the arm that was not linked with the man's. "Someone's coming," Henry said.

"Coming?" There was a high note of alarm in Ivy's voice. "Coming here?"

"I think so. Yes, I'm certain of it."

"What makes you think so? How do you know?"

"Well, they're crossing the street in this direction, and they happen to be three people I know, and so I assume that they're coming here."

"Who are they?"

"A man named Ben Johnson. He writes Western stories for slick magazines and makes quite a lot of money. And two women named Clara Carver and Annie Nile."

"How do you happen to know them?"

"Well, damn it, I do know a few people, you know. Do you imagine that you are the only person I've ever met in my life? As a matter of fact, though, if you must know, Ben and I were in the army together. When I came here later, I looked him up. He lives in an apartment not far away. Besides writing Westerns for money, he writes poetry for the good of his soul. Clara lives with him, but they aren't married. She's very pretty and friendly but rather stupid. I like her."

"What about the other one. What did you say her name is?"

"Annie Nile. Her father owns a shoe factory. She lives by herself and paints pictures, but fortunately it isn't necessary for her to sell any in order to live, for she isn't very good at it. Sooner or later she'll give it up and go home and marry someone richer than she is, but in the meanwhile it amuses her, and so do Ben and Clara."

"Do you amuse her too?"

"What do you mean?"

"What do you think I mean?"

"God only knows. I've learned already that it's impossible to know what you really mean by anything you say."

"Why are you so sensitive about it? It was only a perfectly natural question. Do you think I give a damn if you amuse her, or what method you use in doing it?"

She was sitting erect on the edge of the sofa, and he was puzzled and a little concerned by the ferocity of her expression as she looked at him.

"Look," he said. "Will you please behave yourself? There's no need to be offensive, and I'd appreciate it if you wouldn't be."

"Don't worry. I won't say anything to hurt the feelings of your precious friends. It may be interesting to watch their expressions when they discover me here. What do you suppose they will think?"

"They'll probably think the same thing that Adolph and George think, thanks to your admirable compulsion to explain matters."

"Do you think so? It's very funny, isn't it?"

They could hear the trio tramping up the stairs from the street. The sound of their voices in words and laughter rose clearly ahead of them.

"They seem to be gay enough," Henry said.

"Or drunk," she said.

"Both, probably," he said.

He went over and opened the door in response to banging and his name called out. The two women came into the room ahead of the man. Both were wearing fur coats and fur hats to match. One of them was also carrying a fur muff, but the other one wasn't. The one without the muff was carrying the brown sack, and it was obvious from the sounds that came from it that it contained bottles. The one with the muff was prettier than the one with the sack, but you felt almost at once, after the first concession to superior prettiness, that the one with the sack would be more attractive to most men in the long run. The prettier one was a redhead, the deep red known as titian, and the more attractive one in the long run was a brunette whose hair below the fur hat had the color and luster of polished walnut. There was about her, the more attractive brunette, an air of being present by accident in circumstances and company that she accepted in good humor. She leaned over the sack of bottles and kissed Henry on the mouth.

"Darling," she said, "where have you been forever? It's shameful, the way you've been avoiding me, and I ought to be angry, but I'm not. As you see, I've come with Clara and Ben to wish you a merry Christmas."

"He's a genius, Annie," Ben said. "It's impossible to be angry with a genius."

He was a stocky young man with a broad, homely face dusted across a pug nose with freckles. A thin, sandy mustache on his lips was just faintly discernible when the light was favorable. He removed his hat and coat and relieved Annie Nile of the sack.

"Wouldn't it be nice if he could sell something and make a lot of money?" Clara Carver said. "Don't you wish Henry had a lot of money, Annie?"

"Yes, I do," Annie said. "It would make things much more pleasant and simple all around."

"It isn't expected of a genius to sell anything," Ben Johnson said. "A genius is never appreciated until he's dead. Everyone knows that."

"If it's true that a genius never sells anything, then I must be a genius too," Annie said, "for I've painted pictures and pictures and never sold a one."

"Darling," Clara said, "you already have nearly all the goddamn money in the world. You must leave a little for the rest of us."

"Nevertheless," Annie said, "it would be encouraging to sell a picture as a matter of principle."

"The only principal you need be concerned with," Ben said, "is the one you draw your interest on."

While they were talking, they were also disposing of hats and coats and dispersing a little in the room. Ben set the sack of bottles on Henry's work table and sat down in Henry's chair. Annie and Clara sat beside each other on the frieze sofa. Clara stretched her long nylon legs in front of her and stared at them with an air of appreciation. It was clear that she admired them and considered them her most valuable asset, which was a judgment just as clearly shared by Ben. Ben also stared at the legs with an air of appreciation.

Ivy stood quietly in a corner and was ignored. Everyone had seen her there, but no one had spoken or recognized her presence by any sign or word, and there seemed to be a conspiracy instantly in existence among then to establish the pretension that she wasn't there at all.

"Ben," Clara said, "why do you simply sit there staring at my legs? Why don't you open one of the bottles and give us all a drink?"

"I prefer to look at your legs," Ben said. "Let Henry open it."

"It's sparkling burgundy," Annie said to Henry. "I prefer champagne myself, but Clara and Ben insisted on sparkling burgundy. It's a peculiarity of theirs. Do you like sparkling burgundy?"

"I like it all right, but I hardly ever drink it."

"Why don't you drink it if you like it?"

"Because it's too expensive."

"Don't forget he's a poor genius," Ben said.

"I don't object to his being a genius," Annie said, "but his being poor is a great bore. Henry, why must you be so depressingly poor? If you had a lot of money we could go to Florida or someplace for the winter and have fun."

"Why don't you pay the expenses?" Ben said. "Have people quit wearing shoes all of a sudden?"

"I'd gladly pay the expenses if Henry would go," Annie said. "Henry, will you go to Florida with me if I pay the expenses?"

"No," Henry said.

"You see?" Annie said. "He won't go."

"He's crazy," Ben said, "that's what he is."

"No," Clara said, "he's merely proud. Henry, I don't blame you for not going. If Annie wants to sleep with you she can do it right here."

"I'll think about it," Annie said. "In the meantime, Henry, please open a bottle. There are four of them, as you will see. It was our intention to have a bottle for each of us."

This was the first oblique reference to Ivy, who still stood in the corner, and everyone turned his head to look at her in unified abandonment of the conspiracy of neglect. Ivy came out of the corner reluctantly and returned their looks with an expression of somewhat surly defiance. She had been prepared to be compatible if possible, for the sake of Henry, but it was now apparent from her expression that she considered compatibility, if not impossible, extremely unlikely.

"This is Ivy Galvin," Henry said. "Annie Nile. Clara Carver. Ben Johnson."

Each of the three, watching Ivy, nodded in turn. Clara looked curious and rather friendly, Ben looked faintly salacious, as though he were mentally dispossessing Ivy of her clothes, and Annie looked carefully and blandly remote.

"Ivy Galvin?" Annie said in a careful voice that matched her careful expression. "I don't believe I've ever heard Henry mention you. Are you old friends? Are you old friends, Henry?"

"No," Henry said.

"On the contrary," Ivy said, "he picked me up on the street only two weeks ago."

"How interesting," Annie said.

"It hasn't been so interesting, as a matter of fact," Ivy said, "but it has been convenient."

"I should think so," Annie said.

"It isn't what you think," Henry said. "She had no money and no place to go."

"Disregarding your assumption that you know what I think, Henry, darling," Annie said, "it's absolutely unnecessary for you to explain anything. It makes you sound as if you were feeling rather nasty about something."

"Balls," Henry said.

"I think she's pretty," Clara said. "Don't you think she's pretty, Ben?"

"In a famished kind of way," Ben said, "she's lovely."

"Well, you needn't be an extremist about it."

"Damn it, I am not being an extremist. I only said that she's lovely in a famished kind of way. I distinctly qualified my judgment."

"The trouble with you, Ben, darling, is that you are constantly in heat, as I know better than anybody. It's disgusting."

"Heat? Do males get in heat? I thought it was only females who get in heat."

"In your case, an exception has been made. Henry, will you please pour the sparkling burgundy? Ivy, you must sit down here beside me on the sofa where Ben can get a good view of your legs. It will keep him entertained."

Henry went into the other room for glasses. Ivy sat down beside Clara and smoothed her skirt down over her knees. After a minute or two had passed, Henry came back with the glasses. He had been forced to rinse out the one that held the toothbrushes in the bathroom in order to get enough to go around.

"I only have water tumblers," he said.

"I don't believe I care to drink sparkling burgundy from a water tumbler," Clara said.

"Who you trying to kid?" Ben said. "You'll drink anything from anything."

"Are you implying that I'm addicted to alcohol or something?" she said.

"Well," he said, "it's better than dope."

Henry opened a bottle and poured sparkling burgundy into five glasses. He distributed the glasses and sat down on the arm of the sofa beside Annie.

"What have you been doing lately?" he said.

"Painting," she said.

"She's painting a picture of me," Clara said. "It's a nude. I'm absolutely naked."

"It's ghastly," Ben said. "She looks like a skinned mink."

"Are you saying, actually, that I looked like a skinned mink naked?" Clara said.

"Just in the painting," Ben said.

"Ben has no artistic judgment whatever," Annie said. "It's an interpretation. You have to *feel* her."

"I prefer to feel her as she really is," Ben said.

"Besides," Annie said, "how many skinned minks have you ever seen?"

"Well," Clara said, "I think that was a sweet thing to say, just the same. The part about preferring to feel me as I really am, I mean. Ben, that was really a sweet thing to say."

"I only said it because it's true," Ben said. "As you come naturally, you're very feelable."

"Oh," said Clara, looking around, "isn't he the sweetest thing?"

"I think I'd better pour some more sparkling burgundy," Henry said.

He got up and gathered the glasses and filled them and distributed them again. He got them mixed up in the process, but no one seemed to care.

"This party is rather dull," Annie said. "What we need is some music to dance to. Henry, why don't you have a phonograph? If you are so damn poor you can't afford a phonograph, I'll give you one as a present for Christmas."

"I have a phonograph," Henry said.

"In that case, let's put on some records and dance."

"I don't have any you can dance to. They're all symphonies and concertos and things like that."

"Long-hair stuff," Clara said.

"What would you expect?" Ben said. "It's characteristic of geniuses to listen to nothing but long-hair stuff."

"Get off the genius kick," Henry said.

"Why do you object to being called a genius?"

"Because I'm not one, and you don't think I'm one. Just because you're getting fat selling your stuff to the slicks, you don't have to be so goddamn patronizing."

"And you don't have to be so goddamn sensitive either, when you come to that. If you're going to get red-assed over a little joke, you can go to hell."

"Merry Christmas," Clara said. "A merry, merry Christmas."

"Do you have a radio, Henry?" Annie said. "We could find a D.J. on the radio."

"There's a table set in the bedroom.

"A table set will do. If you would be so kind as to quit quarreling with Ben long enough to get it, maybe we could get this dull party on its feet."

Henry got up and went into the bedroom, and Ben followed. Clara watched them go with an expression of concern on her pretty and rather stupid face.

"Do you suppose they will have a fight in the bedroom?" She said. "Ben has such a violent temper. He's perfectly ferocious when he imagines he's been offended."

"Oh, hell. How could you have been sleeping with this man for ages without learning that he's a perfect puppy? All you need to do is pat him on the head, and he starts licking your hand immediately."

"Really? Honest to God, Annie, I admire you tremendously. You are so truly clever at analyzing people and knowing just how they are. What I would like to know, however, is how you know what is to be learned about Ben from sleeping with him."

"What we had better do," Annie said, "is combine our strength and move the furniture back for dancing."

"You would do well," Clara said, "to concentrate on sleeping with Henry and quit thinking about what is to be learned from sleeping with Ben."

"Darling," Annie said, "if you will get off your tail and take the other end of the sofa, I'm certain we can push it back out of the way easily."

"It serves you right that Henry has taken up with someone else." Clara turned to Ivy. "Is it true that you've been staying here with Henry?"

"Yes," Ivy said.

"You see?" Clara turned back to Annie. "While you have been being so clever, Henry has taken up with Ivy."

"She's welcome," Annie said. "Ivy, you are more than welcome."

"It's a practical arrangement," Ivy said. "He has only given me a place to stay for a while."

"Everyone keeps trying to explain everything," Annie said. "It's quite unnecessary."

At that moment Henry and Ben returned with the radio. Ben had said that he hadn't meant to sound patronizing, and Henry had said that it was all right, and everything apparently was. Ben got a D.J. program, the top tunes, and Henry began to push the furniture around. When a space had been cleared, Ben began to dance with Clara, and Henry began to dance with Annie. Ivy sat and watched. Clara danced beautifully, even in the congested area. She was not very bright, but she always did beautifully anything that was purely physical. Between one tune and another, Ben approached Ivy and asked her to dance.

"No, thank you," she said.

"Oh, come on," he said. "If you don't, I'll think you find me offensive or something."

He had been a little drunk when he arrived, and he was now a little drunker on the sparkling burgundy, and she felt for a moment a powerful compulsion to tell him that she did, indeed, find him offensive, though not for the reason that he had been drinking or any reason that would have occurred to him, but she remembered that she had promised Henry to be good, which seemed little enough to be in return for what he had been to her, and she was determined to keep her promise if she possibly could.

"I don't know how," she said. "I've never learned."

"All you have to do is move with the music," he said. "I'll show you."

Rising, she began to dance stiffly, resisting his efforts to draw her close. It was not true that she didn't know how, and she was really rather good at it, with a true sense of time and rhythm, but the dance was, nevertheless, somewhat more unsatisfactory than a simple failure. When the tune ended, she sat down in the place and position she had held before and was ignored again thereafter, except when her glass was filled and handed to her. Covertly, through her lashes, she watched Henry under the influence of the burgundy and the music and the two girls. Her own head was strangely light, and she had the most peculiar sensation of becoming detached from her familiar emotional moorings. It frightened her a little, but at the same time she was acutely aware of concomitant excitement. She wished with sudden intensity that the intruders, this man and these women whom she did not know or wish to know, would go away and leave her alone with Henry. They were drinking, she noticed, the last of the four bottles. Perhaps, when the bottle was empty, they would go.

Although Ivy did not know it, Henry also wished that his guests would leave. At first he had been pleased to see them, especially Annie Nile, but after a while he began to get bored and to feel unreasonably irritated by things that were said and done in all innocence and good humor. He had been, in the beginning, uneasy in the fear that Ivy would say something to offend the others, or that she might, even worse, deliberately and defiantly expose herself for what she was, but then, when she had stepped forward from her corner to be introduced, he realized suddenly that it was really she for whom he was concerned, for she was the vulnerable one, after all, who would certainly be hurt the most by casual affronts or her own inverted cruelty. He felt for her a painful possessiveness, an exorbitant desire for her to come off well, and he was not alienated even by her brazen admission to being picked up in the street, which was, he understood, no more than abortive defiance of anticipated rejection. Later on, after they began dancing, he kept watching her as she sat primly apart with closed knees and folded hands, and all at once her thin and vibrant intensity under a pose of quietude reminded him so powerfully of someone else that he was for an instant in another place: in another time, and the wine in his glass and blood was sweet port instead of burgundy.

The last of the four bottles was empty at last, and he went, about midnight, into the bathroom. He did not go because it was necessary, but only because he wanted to get away for a few minutes by himself. Closing the door, he sat down on the edge of the tub and put his elbows on his knees and his head in his hands. The radio continued to play in the living room, and he heard a shriek of laughter from Clara in response to something that amused her, which would not need to be, for Clara, anything very amusing. He liked Clara, and she could be very amusing herself in certain circumstances, especially in bed, but he wished she would go home. He wished she would go home and take Ben with her, and that Annie Nile would go alone to wherever, leaving here, she intended to go. He knew that Annie had not, when she came, intended to go anywhere, at least not until tomorrow, and he felt in the knowledge a vague regret for something else lost that could not be recovered. He had met her about a year ago at a party Ben had taken him to, and his relationship with her since had been generally agreeable and sporadically passionate, but it could not be, after tonight, anything at all, and he did not care.

But Annie had behaved quite well in a difficult situation, he had to admit that. It was no more than the way he would have expected her to behave, though, and it was certain, aside from a slight sense of shame and humiliation, that she cared less, if possible, than he. She had liked him for her own reasons, and he had amused her and given her pleasure in his turn among other men who had done the same in the same period of time, but she had always considered him, as he knew, quite impossible for permanence or other purposes. She would not have cared in the least if he had made love to a dozen women besides her, for she was fair enough not to deny him what she allowed herself, but she would never forgive him for letting her intrude in a situation that was humiliating. She had carried it off well, though. You would never have guessed, not knowing, that she was a bit humiliated or had any reason to be. She would merely sustain the pretension, which she had already established tonight, that no intimacy had ever existed between her and Henry Harper, and soon it would seem actually incredible to both of them that any ever had.

Well, Henry thought, he had better get back to the others. Standing, he went out of the bathroom into the bedroom and found Ben Johnson in his hat and overcoat seated on the edge of the bed.

"Are you leaving, Ben?" Henry said.

"Yes," Ben said, "you can stop stewing now. We're going."

"Cut it out, Ben. You know I want you to stay as long as you please."

"Do you? I'd have sworn you began itching for us to get the hell out of here an hour ago. Not that I blame you, you understand. I must say, however, that you've played a damn dirty trick on Annie."

"I haven't played any kind of trick at all on Annie. Damn it, this is the first time in weeks that I've even seen her."

"Oh, I know there's never been anything between you and Annie except a night now and then, but that's not the point. The point is, you let her walk into an embarrassing situation. You'll have to admit it's not pleasant to walk in with your shoes off and find someone else in your half of the bed."

"I didn't let her do anything of the sort. Will you kindly tell me how I could have prevented it when I had no idea you were coming?"

"I suppose that's true. It isn't fair to blame you when you couldn't know. I wouldn't be acting like a friend, though, if I didn't say that I consider this a very questionable arrangement."

"Thanks for acting like a friend."

"Well, go ahead and be sarcastic. I can understand your bringing a girl home, and I can't deny that I've done the same thing more than once myself, but do you think it's wise to make an affair out of a pick-up?"

Henry understood that Ben meant well and was trying to be helpful, but he was only irritated by the necessity for making concessions to Ben's good intentions. What he wished was that Ben mind his own goddamn business and not try to give advice in matters where his only qualification was ignorance. He had an urge to employ the shock tactics that Ivy herself sometimes found useful, and he wondered what Ben's reaction would be if he were to spell out his arrangement with Ivy clearly.

"She isn't a pick-up," he said. "You don't understand."

"Sure. I know. She doesn't have any place to go, and you're only being a lousy Good Samaritan. Okay, pal. I'm sorry I mentioned it."

"Look. I'm trying to tell you. She's not like Clara. Not like Annie. You danced with her tonight, lover. Did she act as if she enjoyed it?"

"As a matter of fact, she made me feel that I needed a bath."

"Well, there you are."

"You mean she's queer?"

"That's one word for it. She was living with a girl cousin and ran away. I happened to meet her, and she had no place to go, and I brought her here. That's all there is to it."

"Pal, it may be all there is to it, and it may not be. I always knew you were crazy, but not this crazy. You could get yourself involved in a pretty sticky mess."

"That's not your problem. If you want to do me a favor, you can keep this to yourself."

"Sure, pal. At the moment I don't feel a hell of a lot like doing you any favor, but I doubt that it would make very good conversation to go around telling people I've got a friend shacked up with a queer."

"You can be a pretty bigoted, intolerant son of a bitch when you want to be, can't you?"

"Thanks, pal, and a merry Christmas to all."

"Maybe you'd better finish the line."

"And to all a good night. Good night, pal."

Ben stood up and walked into the living room, Henry following. Clara and Annie were standing near the door in their fur coats and hats, and Ivy still sat on the sofa in the posture of primness. Clara said good night to Henry, kissing him, and Annie said good night also, not kissing him, and Ben opened the door and walked out into the hall and stood there waiting with his back turned.

"Come on," he said. "Let's go."

Henry listened to the three of them go down the stairs, and then he walked over to a window and looked down upon them in the street as they crossed to the other side and moved away toward the corner where the black pot hung from its tripod. Behind him, Ivy continued to sit primly, her eyes downcast. No one had said good night to her, and she had said good night to no one.

"They didn't like me," she said, and her voice had a tone of arid acceptance.

"You didn't give them much reason."

"I admit I wasn't very congenial, although I wanted to be and tried my best to be, but I don't think it would have made any difference, however I was. They wouldn't have liked me anyhow."

"What makes you think that?"

"It's not something I think. It's something I feel. There's a difference between us, and everyone feels the difference and knows that nothing can be done about it, even though no one knows what the difference is exactly,"

"You're exaggerating. Most of what you say is only imagination."

"Is that what you believe? I wish it were true. It's kind of you, at any rate, to encourage me. Is that girl who was here in love with you? The dark one, I mean."

"Annie? God, no. Whatever gave you such a fantastic idea? Annie loves only herself. Not even that. She loves the picture she has of herself."

"I'm not so sure. I could tell that she was angry because I was here. She treated me very courteously on the whole, however. Rather she ignored me very courteously. I shouldn't have been nearly so admirable in her place. I'm sure I'd have made an unpleasant scene."

"Forget it. She isn't in love with me, whatever you think, and never has been."

"Are you in love with her?"

"No."

"Have you ever been?"

"No. Maybe I thought I was for a little while, but I wasn't."

"Have you ever made love to her?"

"Yes."

"More than once?"

"Several times."

"Where? Here?"

"Here and there. Her place, I mean."

"I wish you'd never done it here. I don't mind so much there."

"I don't see why you should mind at all. Besides, you're far too curious. It's none of your business, you know."

"You didn't have to tell me if you didn't want to."

"All right. You asked, and I told you."

"She wanted to stay tonight, didn't she? That's what she intended to do, wasn't it?"

"Possibly."

"Would you have let her?"

"Probably."

"You mean surely, don't you?"

"Yes. Surely."

"And now I've spoiled it for you. Are you angry?"

"No. You haven't spoiled anything that wouldn't have spoiled anyhow, sooner or later. It doesn't matter."

"I'm glad you're not in love with her. Have you ever been in love with anyone else?"

"Yes. Once. A long time ago."

"Who was she?"

"Her name wouldn't mean anything to you."

"I'd like to know. Just to hear it. The sound of it."

"Her name was Mandy."

"Was she very young?"

"We were both young. In college."

"What happened to her? Did she die?"

"No. She married someone else."

"Oh. I'm sorry."

"You needn't be. It got to be all right long ago. I only think of her now once in a while."

"Was she pretty?"

"I guess so. Pretty's a vapid word. You don't think pretty about someone you love."

"Tell me what she looked like."

"I can't. Most of the time I can't see her myself. Only now and then for just a moment."

"You could tell me the color of her hair and eyes. How tall she was and how she walked and held her head."

"That wouldn't be telling you what she looked like. You reminded me of her tonight, when you were sitting by yourself on the sofa with your knees together and your hands folded."

"Did she sit that way?"

"No. It was something else. I thought it was a kind of intensity."

"I wish I could love you. If I were able to love you, would you love me in return?"

"I don't know. I think so."

"It would be wonderful to love you and be loved by you."

"I'm happy that you think so."

CHAPTER 7

Toward morning she awoke on the sofa and lay in the precarious peace between sleeping and waking, while the ceiling receded, and the walls withdrew, and the room became spacious and vaulted and filled with sunlight and music and the scent of flowers. She sat erect on the edge of a hard bench of dark and polished oak in the posture of primness that she would never lose, and the sunlight slanted in through high Gothic windows of stained glass and touched with transparent flame the arrangements of lilies and carnations and white, white roses that were massed in woven baskets before a pulpit.

She was in church, and someone must have died and been buried, for it was only after a funeral, unless it was Easter, that so many flowers were displayed before the pulpit. Yes, yes, she was in church, and the music she heard was coming from the great pipes of the organ, which were concealed by the lattice behind the choir loft, and there was a beautiful man in a frock coat standing below among the flowers in the slanting sunlight. The music was something by Bach that she could never remember, and the man was her father, whom she could never forget.

The music stopped, and there was a long silence disturbed by no more than the merest whisper of movement, and then the man, the minister, her father, began to read from an enormous open Bible, and his rich voice, sonorous and penetrating, was like a golden resumption by the organ that had become quiet, and his head in the soft and shining light was massive and leonine, its tawny hair swept back like a flowing mane.

Blessed are the poor in spirit, for theirs is the kingdom of heaven. Blessed are they that mourn, for they shall be comforted. Blessed are the meek, for they shall inherit the earth.

She sat quietly on the oak bench beside her quiet mother. The beautiful words in the beautiful voice of the beautiful man seemed to reach her from a great distance and a remote time, from the Mount itself and the day they were spoken there. The adoration of the woman beside her, the wife and the mother and the worshiper, was a tangible emanation that could be felt like the air and smelled like the scent of the flowers. Ivy had learned long ago that her mother did not come to church for the same purpose that other people came. Other people came to worship God, but her mother came to worship the minister. This had at first seemed to Ivy a fearful defection, a flagrant incitement of God's wrath, but she had later lost her fear with the loss of her belief, not in God, but in the power of her father to incite in God any responses whatever. Thereafter, in the presence of her mother's adoration of her father, she felt only a terrible sense of inadequacy and isolation, as if she had been excluded from their love by the same passion that had created her.

She listened uneasily, with a feeling of shame, to the text her father read. She always felt, when he talked of meekness and humility, that she was a passive part of an enormous hypocrisy, for he was not meek, nor was he humble, and he was in fact the vainest man she had ever known or would ever know. Not only was he vain in petty matters, the effects of his voice and hair and every studied pose, but also in his utter inversion, a narcissistic absorption in himself which made impossible any awareness of the pain that others might suffer, or any genuine compassion if he had been aware.

He was not really a good man, but he gave the impression of goodness, nor was he a brilliant man, but he gave the impression of brilliance, and so he exploited the illusion of being what he was not, and he was extremely successful in the ministry of God and Church. There was in Ivy's life from her earliest memory a succession of churches in a succession of towns, each of them better than the one before, and so she sat now in the last and best and listened in shame to the golden words of an ancient sermon, but then she was suddenly not sitting in church at all, but was standing before her father's desk in his paneled study at home, and his voice continued from church to study without interruption, although it was saying in the latter place something entirely different in an entirely different tone.

"Ivy," he said, "this is your Cousin Lila, whom we have been expecting. She has come to spend the summer with us. We hope she will like us so well that she will want to come every summer for a long time."

Ivy turned to face her cousin, and her life, which had seemed until that moment to have a certain orderly purpose that could be traced in the past and anticipated for the future, had in an instant no purpose and no past and no future at all. There was only this moment of awakening at the end of an emptiness that had no meaning because it had no Lila. Lila was slim and shimmering, beginning and end, and she held out her hand in an aura of light. The hand was cool and dry and wonderfully soft, and its touch to Ivy was an excitement.

"Hello, Lila,"' Ivy said. "I'm so happy you've come."

"Thank you," Lila said. "I'm sure I shall enjoy my visit very much."

This was, Ivy thought, only a politeness, and she had a feeling that Lila had no certain expectation of enjoying herself, and that she had, in fact, come unwillingly to spend the summer. Ordinarily Ivy would not have been particularly concerned about the attitude of a guest in the house, especially a relative, but now she felt that it was desperately imperative that Lila, this shining cousin, should truly enjoy herself so much that she would never want to leave, or leaving, should long to return.

"I'm sure you girls will find a great deal to talk about," the Reverend Dr. Theodore Galvin said. "If you don't mind, I'll ask you to excuse me now, as I have some work that must be done. I'll see you at dinner, if not before." Ivy and Lila left the study and the house and sat down together in a glider that had been placed under an elm tree on the side lawn. Lila was wearing a white silk dress without sleeves, and her skin above and below the silk was a tawny gold. Her rich, curling hair was black and full of shimmering light. Looking at her, Ivy felt all edges and projections, an awkward assembly of ugly bones. This wasn't true, for she was almost as attractive in her own way as Lila was in hers, but Lila had already, as she would always have afterward, the unintended effect of making Ivy feel plain by comparison.

"How old are you?" Lila said.

"Sixteen," Ivy said. "Almost seventeen."

"Are you? I'm nineteen, almost twenty. I wanted to work this summer until time to return to school, but my father wouldn't allow it. He didn't want me at home either, however, which is why he packed me off out here."

"I'm very glad he did. What kind of work did you plan to do?"

"Modeling. I was promised a place in a shop for the summer. It wasn't a very good job, to tell the truth, but it would have been experience. I think I'd like modeling."

"You'd be certain to be successful, you're so lovely."

"Do you think so? Thank you very much. You're pretty too, you know."

"I'm not really. You're only being kind."

"Kindness is not one of my virtues, and you shouldn't be humble. A pretty girl who knows it, is prettier than a pretty girl who doesn't know it. The knowledge does something for her. It lights her up inside."

"Well, anyhow, I'm pleased that you think I'm pretty, whether I am or not. I wonder why we have never met before. Don't you think it's odd?"

"Not particularly. Why?"

"I mean, your father and my father being brothers and everything. I've never seen your father at all. My father hardly ever even mentions him."

"I'll bet he doesn't."

"What do you mean? Why shouldn't he?"

"They never got along, you know. Uncle Theodore's a minister, of course, and Father's a kind of black sheep. He likes good living and whiskey and women and things like that. One of the reasons he sent me out here, I'm sure, was simply to get me out of the way. With me gone, he can bring a woman to the apartment any time he pleases. I'm too old to go to the kind of camps he used to send me to in the summer, and he had this ridiculous notion that I should not be permitted to work and live alone, and so here I am. I think, besides, that he thought it would be good for me to spend two or three months in the house of a minister. The Christian influence, I mean. Every once in a while, he gets to feeling guilty about the kind of atmosphere he's subjected me to. It's silly, of course, and it never lasts long, but here I am, anyhow, and we shall have to think of ways to make the most of it and enjoy the summer together."

"What do you like to do? Do you like to swim?"

"I love to swim, and I love to lie for hours on the warm sand. Is it far from here to the beach?"

"Not far. We can drive the distance easily in half an hour. I don't drive yet, though. Not without Father in the car. Do you drive?"

"Of course. I had a car of my own, but I smashed it up, and Father is punishing me by making me wait until I'm twenty-one before I get another."

"We'll drive to the beach every day, then, if you wish. I'm sure Father will let us have the car unless he needs it, and he doesn't very often. Not for a whole day at a time, at least."

"Won't I be a nuisance to you?"

"Oh, no. Why should you think so?"

"Well, you're pretty and almost seventeen. I should think in the summer that you'd be wanting to go places with boys. Do you have lots of boy friends?"

"Not many. Father is very strict about such things, boys and dates and such things, but I don't really mind. I'm not very interested in boys anyhow."

"Aren't you? Why not?"

"I don't know. Just not. You're older, though, and may go out as often as you please, I'm sure. After you've been seen, there will be all kinds of boys wanting to take you out. Almost all the college boys are home for the summer, of course."

"I can't say that I'm terribly excited about it. College boys are a bore, mostly."

"Do you like older men?"

"I can take them or leave them alone." Lila looked at Ivy from the corners of her eyes and her lips curved slightly in a strange little secretive smile. "I think I'll prefer to spend the summer with you."

Sitting on the glider, watching with an air of abstraction the patterns of sun and shade on the green grass of the side lawn, Ivy had the most delicious sensation of pervading warmth, as if she were sinking slowly into a warm bath. It was the best of good fortune to have acquired her lovely Cousin Lila to love for a whole summer, but to be granted already the implications of being loved by Lila in return was the most incredible fulfillment. She stirred and lifted one hand to her breast, feeling there a sudden and pleasurable pain.

"Is there anything in particular you would like to do now?" she said.

"Your father said that your mother would not be home until this evening. Is that true?"

"Yes. She had to attend a meeting of one of the women's societies. Of the church, you know. Apparently it was quite important, something she couldn't miss, and she said to tell you she was very sorry she couldn't be here to meet you when you arrived."

"I don't mind. I quite understand. I wonder what it would be like to have a mother. My father divorced my mother when I was a child. Perhaps you've been told about it. I haven't seen her for years, although in the beginning, right after the divorce, she came to visit me once in a while."

"I'm sorry."

"Oh, you shouldn't be. I'm not. I suppose she was unfaithful, since Father got the divorce and custody of me. I'm glad it turned out that way. I doubt that Father would be considered a proper parent, but being in his custody has proved interesting for the most part, even though he has often considered me a bother and sent me away, to school or camp or someplace, to be rid of me."

"Why did you ask about Mother? When she would be home, I mean?"

"I was just thinking that we might go for a walk. It's pleasant to walk along the strange streets of a strange town. They change, somehow, after the first time, and are never the same again. But I wouldn't want to be gone when your mother gets home. She might think it was rude."

"We have plenty of time. We could walk for an hour at least. Would you like to go?"

"Yes. Let's go. Will it be necessary to tell your father?"

"No. He'll never miss us. He pays very little attention to anything unless it is brought directly to his attention."

They had begun to walk, and they continued to walk for an hour under arcs of branches on tree-lined streets, and at some special second in the course of the hour their hands happened to meet and cling, and it was at once a sign of acceptance and a shy beginning of exploration. When they returned to the house, Ivy's mother had not yet returned, but she did soon after, and after another hour, perhaps longer, they all sat down to dinner and sat with bowed heads while the Reverend Dr. Theodore Galvin said grace with subdued sonority. Ivy looked through her lashes at Lila across the table, and Lila was looking at her at the same moment in the same way, and it seemed to both that they shared an ineffable secret, and they smiled secretly.

If there was any symbol of the summer, it was that secretive smile. It seemed to develop a separate and somnolent existence of its own, so that it permeated the atmosphere and became a quality of the sunlight, the whispering rain, and the silent, moonlit nights. It was always present, the quality of the smile, and it had, Ivy thought, both scent and sound. The scent was the essence of a delicate perfume that was caught only now and then in a favorable instant, and the sound was the softest sound of a distant vibration, like the plucked string of a conceit harp, that could be heard only in the depths of profound stillness. Sometimes in the middle of doing something, of reading or making her bed or playing tennis or coming down the stairs, she would suddenly smell the scent or hear the sound in a brief suspension of all other scents on earth, and she could never remember certainly when she smelled and heard the scent and sound of the secretive smile for the first time, but she thought it must surely have been the first night Lila came to her room, which was a night not long after Lila's arrival at the house.

She had been asleep, and she ascended slowly from the deep darkness of sleep into the moonlight flooding the room through open windows, and the smile was in the room with the moonlight, the sense and scent and sound of it, and Lila was there too, beside the bed. Spontaneously, with the ease of instinct, Ivy held out a hand, and Lila took it in hers and sat down on the bed's edge.

"You were sleeping," Lila said. "I've been watching you."

"Did you speak to me or touch me?"

"No. Neither."

"I must have sensed you here to have wakened as I did. Do you hear something?"

"No." Lisa sat listening, her face lifted to the moonlight. "No, nothing. Do you?"

"I think so. Perhaps I'm only imagining it, though, it's so soft."

"What kind of sound? Someone in the hall? Someone outside?"

"No, no. Nothing like that. It's more like music. A string vibrating."

"It's the moonlight. Didn't you know that moonlight makes a sound? Haven't you ever heard it before?"

"No. It's lovely, though. I love the sound of moonlight. Why do you suppose I'm hearing it now for the first time?"

"Because I'm here. I make you aware of things. Isn't that so?"

"Yes."

"I can make you aware of many things you never knew about before. Are you glad I came?"

"Yes, I'm glad, and I'm glad you wanted to. Why did you want to?"

"I was lonely and wanted to be with you. I'd rather be with you than anyone else. I couldn't sleep. I kept looking at the moon through my window and wanting to be with you, and so I had to come. Do you think your mother and father would be angry if they knew?"

"I don't think so. Why should they?"

"Perhaps they wouldn't think it right for us to love each other. We do love each other, don't we, Ivy? Didn't you feel it immediately? Haven't you known it right along? We are the truest of lovers with the best of love."

"Yes. It's true. Our own true love."

The words were spoken with a strange, instinctive ease and they were a prelude to a kind of delirious and sensuous excitement such as Ivy had never experienced. As if in a dream she shifted in the bed to permit Lila to slide in beside her. And in a continuing dream she felt herself enfolded in Lila's arms, and the warmth and intoxicating softness of Lila's body, the sweet pressure of her lips on her mouth and throat transported her into a world of dizzying sensation. For the first time her own body seemed to come fully alive. There was a wild singing in her blood, a delightful trembling in all her nerve ends and suddenly her arms and her lips and her whole body were as eager and demanding as Lila's.

It was not until afterward that Ivy became aware that love had ceased to be one thing in a moment and had become another thing entirely, although what it had been was included in what it became, and neither was he aware until later that there was in her ecstasy the deep and grievous sadness of irreparable loss.

And so for Ivy there was the summer and the symbolic smile, the ecstasy and anguish of what was gained and lost and of learning to know and accept herself as someone quite different from the person she had thought she was, or had thought she could possibly be. There was also in the passing of days and weeks and months an accretion of guilt and unspecific fear that was something quite apart from, and far deadlier than, whatever specific fear of discovery she might have felt in relation to her mother and father. But guilt and fear were still, and would for a long time be, of less effect than love, and at the end of summer, when it was time for Lila to go away to her father and then to her school, everything was of no effect at all in the dreadful desolation and loneliness in which Ivy was left.

"You'll never come back," Ivy said the night before Lila departed. "I have the most terrible feeling that I'll never see you again."

"You're wrong. Next summer I'll come, if your parents will have me. I'm sure that Father will be most happy to dispose of me so conveniently. In the meanwhile, I'll write to you. Does your father or mother ever open your mail?"

"I don't get much mail, but I don't remember that they've ever opened any."

"Nevertheless, I'd better be careful what I write. You'll understand me, however. I'll make allusions to places and times, and you'll know what I mean."

"I wish I could go away with you."

"One day you shall. I'll become a model, and we'll have an apartment together. Good models are paid quite well, and I'll have some money from Father besides, when he dies. He's lived so hard that it's very likely he won't live to old age. I think his liver's gone bad."

"One day. It seems so indefinite and far away. How long, do you think?"

"Maybe sooner than you imagine. You'll be eighteen in a little over a year. I think I may leave school for good next spring. Maybe soon after that. Isn't the moonlight lovely? It's like the first night I came here to your room."

"I can hear it. Can you? You must listen very intently. It makes me so drowsy. I feel as if I were floating away on the sound of the moonlight, right out of the window and away forever."

"I wouldn't want you to float away forever. Then you wouldn't be here when I return next summer."

"Let's not talk about that. About your going away, I mean. I can't bear to think of it."

"Would you like to sleep for a while?"

"I think I would, but I don't want you to go away. Will you stay here if I sleep?"

"I'll stay for another hour and watch you. I love to watch you when you're asleep. You look so incredibly innocent, like a small child."

"Will you wake me before you go back to your room?"

"Yes. I promise. Go to sleep now. Listen to the sound of the moonlight."

She lay quietly in the cradle of Lila's arm and went to sleep to the sound, and all through the fall and winter and spring that followed, lying alone at night, she always listened for the sound and waited in the darkness for it to come, and at first it came quickly and clearly, without delay, but then it began to be more and more elusive and remote, and finally could not be heard at all. With Lila gone, with only an allusive letter now and then to assure her presence on earth, the domination of guilt by love became uncertain, and the unspecific fear, which her father might have simplified as the fear of God, assumed slowly a commanding place and became a constant threat. During the time of the three seasons, Ivy was balanced precariously between one thing and another, standing in the time of decision between two ways to go, either of which was possible. But she made no decision, and the seasons passed, and Lila returned in the fourth season, the summer, and then there was no longer a decision to be made, and no way to go but one. The quality of the secret smile was again in everything, and the sound of the moonlight could again be heard, but there was nevertheless a significant difference between the first summer and the second, and the difference lay in an increased consciousness of an enormous commitment and in the dangerous consequences the commitment might entail.

It is possible to hide from the senses forever something that can only be seen, but it is not possible to hide from the senses forever, or even for very long, something that can be felt. Awareness may come slowly, but it comes certainly, and it carries conviction even if there is no material evidence to support it. And so it happened in the second summer that even so insensitive an egoist as the Reverend Dr. Theodore Galvin became uneasily aware that the emotional climate surrounding his daughter and his niece did not satisfy his conception of the effect of a normal attachment. He reluctantly discussed it with his wife and found support for his suspicions, which were by the support immediately transformed into conviction. They decided between them that something would have to be done to prevent a consummation they did not know had already been accomplished, and their idea of what to do was to institute a kind of police action. They imposed such sudden and severe restrictions and engaged so palpably in surveillance that both Ivy and Lila knew almost at once that they were under unspoken indictment.

"They know," Lila said.

They were sitting on the glider under the tree on the side lawn. To Ivy the familiar patterns of sun and shade were the shapes and signs of a corporate threat. It did not occur to her, however, that there was any escape from it by retreat, or any choice left to her except the one that had been set. There was Lila, or there was nothing. There was hope, or there was hopelessness.

"Yes," she said. "What can we do?"

"There's nothing we can do. Not now. They'll surely send me away."

"If they do, I'll go with you."

Although Ivy was not clearly conscious of it, the *they* was not used in simple reference to her father and mother, for already the specific had been absorbed by the general, the smaller overt threat no more than a sign of the greater and deadlier one of which it was a part. *They* were the enemy in an ancient conflict, the accusing host.

"You can't," Lila said. "It's not time. We'll have to wait."

"I can't stand it if they send you away. I think I'll die."

"You won't die. You'll wait. In a few month you'll be eighteen, and then you can come to me if you wish. In the meanwhile, I'll prepare for it. Father knows a man who runs a model agency, and he's promised to take me on. When I leave here, I'll go to work immediately."

"Suppose they try to stop me from coming. Do you think they could?"

"Your father and mother? They may try, but there's a limit to what they can do. They won't make an open issue of it, you know. They couldn't bear the disgrace if the truth became known, and so, after all, you will be able to control the situation. As a matter of fact, I suspect, whatever they do or say, that they'll be relieved to have you go. They'll pretend afterward that you are dead."

"How will you let me know when and where to come? It wouldn't be safe to write."

"Not here, of course, but I can send it to another address. To someone you know who will pass the letter on to you. Write to me when I get home and let me know where."

Lila was right in assuming that she would surely be sent away, but it was done indirectly with no open reference to the reason for it, and indeed with the pretension that it was not being done at all. The Reverend Dr. Theodore Galvin, a master of indirection, simply wrote to his brother, Lila's father, that it had become apparent, for reasons he would prefer not to divulge unless they were specifically requested, that it would be better for everyone concerned if Lila were ordered to come home. The black sheep brother knew his daughter rather well, and he had no wish to know any more than he already did. He wrote Lila to come home and did not ask for reasons. Lila went. She said good-by politely, expressing her regret at having to leave, and the Galvins said good-by just as politely, expressing their regret at having her go, and the pretension was sustained to the end. The Reverend Dr. Galvin drove Lila to the station with her luggage, and Ivy went to her room and lay down on the bed and had for the first time in her life a sincere wish that she would often have later, which was the wish to die quietly and quickly without pain.

The period that followed was an extremely difficult one for Ivy, but she lived it somehow in intervals of days, often certain that Lila would never send for her as she had promised, but finally the letter came that fulfilled the promise. The definitive break, the departure from her home and parents, was accomplished so quietly that its finality was implicit in its quietness.

"Going?" her father said. "Where are you going?"

His face was perplexed and wary.

"I'm going to live with Cousin Lila."

There was a brittle, defiant note in her voice.

"I forbid you to do so."

"You may forbid me if you please, but it won't stop me. I'm going."

"If you leave against my wishes, I shall consider you dead. You will never be allowed in this house again, or in any house of which I am master."

At this moment his face was like a stranger's.

"I expected that. I'm willing to accept it."

"Very well. Go when you are ready, but don't speak to me again. I won't want to say good-by."

Ivy's mother stood with the man she adored, and Ivy could not remember afterward a single thing she did or a single word she said, either of reproach or regret, in the time of parting. Everything was understood, but nothing was expressed.

And so began the life of Ivy and Lila together, and for a while it had gone wonderfully, and for a longer while it had gone well, but then it had begun to go bad. One cause of the growing badness was Ivy's recurring and deepening depression, and another cause was Lila's duality. Unlike Ivy, she was not wholly committed, and she could be one person in one time and another person in another time, depending on the times and their demands. The night of Ivy's flight and meeting with Henry, the bad time getting worse had become as bad as it could be, but in the relationship with Henry, although the time was still bad, it was a bad time getting better. Lying in darkness on Henry's sofa, she believed at last that it would be possible to have with him a saving alliance that would absolve her of the past and secure the future, and there was in her belief a compelling urgency to test it. The possibility was directly contingent, she felt, upon present circumstances, and what could be accomplished here and now and with this man could not be accomplished hereafter in another place with anyone else.

Getting up, she walked through the dark into the bedroom and stood beside the bed on which Henry lay. He was lying on his back on the far side with one arm crossing his chest on top of the covers and the other arm, the near one, stretched out at his side. She could see him only dimly in the dark room, but his breath was drawn and released with the rhythm and depth of sleep.

"Henry," she said.

He didn't answer, nor even stir, and there was no break in the rhythm of his breathing. She got into bed and lay beside him, very carefully not touching him until she was entirely ready, and then she reached for his hand and laid it deliberately on her breast. He stirred briefly, making a whimpering sound and Ivy held her breath. She squeezed his hand with hers, placed it more firmly on her breast and felt a surge of strange emotion in her.

Henry grunted and suddenly turned.

"Who is it?" he mumbled.

"Henry—Henry, I—I—" Ivy's voice broke off in a faint whisper.

"What are you doing here?" he demanded, then in the dim, uncertain predawn light she saw his eyes widen as he became aware of where his hand was resting.

"Do you mind?" she asked.

He laughed uncertainly. "No. Of course, not."

"Henry, would you like to kiss me?"

Instead of answering her, he turned fully toward her and placed his lips on hers. It was a groping, tentative kiss and Ivy could feel a terrible trembling in her body. She was suddenly cold and she wanted to push Henry away, but she suffered the kiss to go on. Then she felt his hand pressing more firmly on her breast through the thin cloth of the nightgown. After a moment he removed it and put both arms around her, pulling her closer. She resisted momentarily, her body still strangely cold, then yielded. He brought her soft, quaking flesh against his lean hardness and Ivy felt panic begin to blossom deep inside her.

She was mashed against Henry now and he was kissing her, this time not so gently. His mouth was urgent and a little rough and suddenly his hand crept under the nightgown and was caressing the bare flesh of her breasts. His thumb and index finger toyed with the nipple of her lift breast, massaging it gently. A wild current of feeling rode like quicksilver through Ivy's veins. She wanted to scream and cry. There was a stirring of desire in her—like the remembered delight of the hours spent in Lila's arms—but there was a difference she couldn't fathom and she couldn't fight down the horrible, crawling fear that suddenly clutched at her vitals.

Suddenly, without conscious volition, she arched against him, pushing against his chest with a terrible frenzy. She withdrew slightly and in that moment she lashed out at his face, raking the nails of her left hand across it. Henry cried out in pain, then cursed.

Ivy scrambled out of the bed, clutching her nightgown to her quaking body. Henry got out the other side of the bed and quickly turned on a lamp. Blood was trickling down his cheek from the gashes left by Ivy's nails. She had hurt him and she was sorry and there was a deep sadness in her for him. She wanted to ask his forgiveness but the fury she saw in his eyes held her back.

"You rotten bitch," he said. "You goddamn queer."

"Henry, please, I thought I could—"

"Shut up, damn you!" he raged

He put his hand to his face, then lowered it and stared at the smear of blood across fingers and palm, and his eyes were suddenly sick with shame. Turning, he walked into the bathroom and she could hear water running into the lavatory, followed by the sound of the door of the medicine cabinet being opened and closed. She wanted to get up and go after him, to heal his wounds by the miracle of her intense desire, but she thought with despair that miracles did not come to pass, and on one moment of irrational fear it had become too late for the healing of anything. She did not blame him for his cruel words, which had been spoken in reaction to her cruel act. He hadn't called her a tithe of the evil things she was, and today, instead of buying a Christmas tree, as she had planned, she would gather her things and go away before she could cause him more trouble and shame in return for his kindness

CHAPTER 8

When he came out of the bathroom he had washed his face and stopped the seepage of blood with a styptic. Without looking at her, he removed his pajamas and stood before her naked, which was something he had not done before, and she thought that he did it now as an expression of contempt or indifference. Which of the two was worse she didn't know, but either was bad enough, and she watched him steadily in his nakedness as a kind of submission. He began to dress for the street, dressing slowly, not speaking, not looking at her, and he did not speak or look at her until he was ready to leave. Then he looked at her levelly, with no discernible animosity, and spoke in the same dry, precise voice with which he had cursed her.

"I'm going to work," he said. "When I get back this evening, I'd be happy to find you gone. I was a fool to bring you here in the first place, and I've been a fool ever since to let you stay, and I hope to God I never see you again. I treated you decently, you'll have to admit that, and I've respected you for what you are, but then you crawl into my bed like a whore when I'm asleep, and you scream and claw me like a goddamn violated virgin when you wake up to find yourself where you came of your own will. You're crazy, that's what you are. You're psycho. I don't believe your cousin tried to kill you at all. Maybe it was just the other way around, and I wouldn't be surprised if it was, but more likely it was just something you dreamed up to try to get someone into trouble. Trouble's all anyone will ever get from you, that's plain enough but I've had enough, thank you, and that's all I've got to say. There's twenty dollars in the top drawer of the chest. You're welcome to take it when you go."

He went out and downstairs and began to walk in the direction of the building in which he worked. It was still dark, and far earlier than he ordinarily left in the morning, and he had plenty of time to walk the entire distance, over three miles, rather than having to take the bus as usual. He was glad of this, for he needed the physical action, and he was grateful for the cold air that stung his face and carried a threat of snow. He could not remember having been angrier in his life than he was now, and his anger was not because of the little pain he had suffered, the scratches on his face, but because of the shame he had felt and was still feeling, almost a sense of degeneracy. Waking to find her sleeping beside him, her slender body warm and lovely and inciting in its thin gown, he had not touched her until she asked for it, and the violence of her repulsion had made him feel irrationally like a rapist at least, although he was not.

Well, he had told her the truth. She was psycho. Queer. Trouble. He couldn't imagine what had possessed him to expose himself to her in the way he had, except that he was a little crazy himself, and if she did not leave voluntarily while he was gone, then he would send her away tonight when he returned, and that would be the end of it. His anger had made him physically ill, on the verge of vomiting, but walking and cold air began to clear his head and reduce the angry fever in his flesh, and when he reached the building in which he worked, he was feeling much better.

As the morning passed, Henry's anger diminished, and he began to wonder if, after all, he had been fair. Reviewing the sordid episode in the clearer climate of his lessened anger, he thought he could understand Ivy's intent, which had been good, and its failure, which was understandable. Last night, after the impromptu party, they had achieved in their conversation a warmth and compatibility greater than any they had achieved before, and they had even mentioned for a moment the chance of love. Waking early, as it must certainly have happened, she had thought of him and wanted him, or had at least wanted to try him, and so she had come in to find him sleeping and had lain down beside him on the bed. She had acted rashly, that was true, but there was in the action, just the same, a kind of pathetic courage.

Once he had considered it dispassionately, this seemed so obviously the truth that he was tempted, when it was time for lunch, to take a taxi home and talk with Ivy again. But perhaps she was already gone, and perhaps it would be better, regardless of the truth, to leave matters as they were. They had established a precarious relationship, and it would be foolishness, maybe dangerous foolishness, to try to save it under the illusion that it might be the saving of her. People like her did not change. The basic fault they shared must be organic and irreparable. The only sensible thing to do with one of them, he thought, was to turn and walk away.

He lunched alone in a cafeteria in the basement of the building. Afterward, upstairs, he could not dismiss a feeling of uneasiness and guilt that had replaced his anger. If he did not regret his position, he at least regretted the brutality with which he had assumed it. For the first time since knowing Ivy, he felt a need to make some kind of personal contact with her past, to meet and talk with someone who had known her before him. It was then, in the development of this need, that he began to think of Lila Galvin, and sometime during the afternoon he made up his mind definitely that he would see her and talk with her that evening if possible.

He left the offices at five and stopped in a telephone booth in the lobby below. Checking the directory, he found Lila's name and address listed, and he considered calling to see if she was at home, but he decided against it. If he were to speak with her on the telephone, she might refuse to see him, which would make his calling on her all the more difficult. If he were simply to appear at her door without an invitation, he would at least not have the disadvantage of an expressed denial of one.

On the street outside, he caught a cab and was driven to the address he gave. The apartment house was impressive enough to exert a kind of preliminary intimidation over most trespassers, but Henry was in no humor to be intimidated, and he paid off the cab and entered the lobby. It was then that he remembered that he didn't know the number of Lila Galvin's apartment, and there was no doorman, no directory, no one in the lobby to answer questions. He supposed that he could check the floors until he came to the door with the right name on it, provided there was a name on it at all, but this did not seem to be a very sensible solution, and he was trying to think of another when a thin, dehydrated man came in from the street behind a Pomeranian on a leash. The man gave the impression of being dragged by the dog.

"I beg your pardon," Henry said. "I have an appointment with a Miss Lila Galvin in this building, but I'm afraid I've forgotten the number of her apartment."

The Pom did not stop, and neither, consequently, did the man. Passing, he spoke over his shoulder.

"Five-o-three. My floor. If you're going up, come along."

Henry followed the dog and the man into the self-service elevator and rode up five floors. As soon as the elevator doors were open, the Pom departed, turning right.

"You're the other way," the man said, again over his shoulder. "Just look for the number."

Henry did and found it. Pressing a pearl button beside the door, he listened to a bell. He was about to press the button a second time when the door was opened without any prelude of sound, and he found himself staring at a young woman whom he took to be Lila Galvin, and who was, whoever else she was, one of the loveliest women he had ever seen. Her hair was a shimmering black cloud, gathering and holding the light, parted cleanly and drawn back sleekly into a knot on the back of her neck. The severe perfection of her face was relieved by a sensual mouth, and her body, in a black wool dress of beautiful simplicity, possessed the lean seductiveness of a high fashion model. Which was, he recalled, what she was.

"Yes?" she said. "What is it?"

"I'm looking for Miss Lila Galvin," he said, certain that he was speaking to her.

She acknowledged her identity and continued to watch him with cool serenity tinged by a faint amusement implicit in slightly arched brows. Her loveliness and serenity and implicit amusement had altogether the effect of making him sound truculent.

"I'm Henry Harper," he said, and waited.

"Oh?" Her brows arched, if possible, a little higher. "Is that supposed to mean something? Should I know you?"

"Probably not. There is someone else, however, whom we know in common. Ivy Galvin, your cousin."

"I see." Her brows descended, and she no longer looked amused, but neither did she look angry or to any degree distressed. "You're the man she told me about when she returned for her things. She's been staying with you."

"That's right. I'd like to talk with you."

"No more than I would like to talk with you. Please come in."

He walked past her into the living room that had a clean, modern look. The furniture, low and heavy but achieving in its simplicity an effect of lightness, was covered with a tweedy material that looked expensive. On the wall that Henry faced there was a good copy of a Van Gogh. Against the wall near a door to another room, there was a bleached console phonograph. It must be the one, he thought, to which Ivy had listened the night she meant to die. If the whole story was not, as he suspected it might be, a lie at the worst or a delusion at best.

"I just got home a few minutes ago," Lila Galvin said. "I was about to fix myself a cocktail. Will you join me?"

"I didn't come on a social call. Maybe, after you've heard me, you won't want to give me a cocktail."

"You sound very grim. Is something wrong?"

"Something's wrong, all right, but I'm not sure what it is. That's what I'd like to find out."

"Do you know what I think? I think you really need a cocktail, and so do I. I like a martini myself. Will that do for you?"

"Whatever you like."

"I'll get some ice. Excuse me, please."

She went into the kitchen, which he could not see, and returned shortly with ice. She mixed gin and vermouth in a tall frosted glass and stirred it briefly with a glass rod. After pouring the martinis and handing him one, she sat down on a sofa and crossed her knees, holding her own glass with the fingertips of both hands so that it brushed her lips below her nostrils, as if it were a snifter of brandy and she were breathing the aroma.

"I wish you would sit down and quit looking so angry," she said. "You look on the verge of attacking me. I imagine Ivy has been telling you the most terrible things about me, however, and so it's quite understandable. Isn't that right? Hasn't Ivy been telling you things?"

He sat down facing her, feeling in his joints an unusual awkwardness. The glass he held seemed so fragile in his thick fingers that he had the notion that he must handle it with the greatest care to avoid crushing it inadvertently. "What do you think she's been telling me?" he said.

"I think, for one thing, that she probably told you that I tried to kill her. Did she?"

"Yes. Did you?"

"Do you think, if I did, that I'd be fool enough to admit it?"

"No."

"Of course not. But, to answer your question, I didn't. Not that there's any point in saying so. You'll believe whatever you wish."

"What made you assume at once that she told me you tried to kill her?"

"Because she accused me of it when she returned. Truly a fantastic story. I was supposed to have given her an overdose of sedative, and she was able to save herself only by walking and walking in the streets until she was exhausted. It was an exceptionally brilliant bit of fiction, even for Ivy. Is that the same story she told you, or did she develop a variation?"

"That's the one."

"Do you believe it?"

"I don't know."

"I shan't blame you if you do. Ivy can be very convincing. I've been deceived myself many times.

"Do you mean that it's only her imagination? That she has delusions?"

"No. I don't mean anything of the sort." Lila tipped her glass against her lips and smiled at him across it. She was clearly in perfectly good humor. "I mean that she's a deliberate liar. She's one of the most accomplished and conscienceless little liars that it's possible to imagine."

"On the other hand, perhaps it's you who are the deliberate liar."

"Think as you wish. I'm only trying to warn you. If you are determined to get yourself involved with Ivy, as you seem to be, you had better know her for what she is."

"Why should she accuse you of trying to murder her if you didn't, or if she didn't at least think you did?"

"Because she's malicious. She wanted to say the most damaging thing about me that she could think to say. I'm trying to tell you that she's a psychopathic liar. A psychopathic personality. Do you know what a psychopathic personality is? If you do, you know what Ivy is. She has no more sense of moral values than a cat. She is absolutely incapable of love or gratitude or responsibility or remorse. She would do anything or say anything without regard for any person on earth, so long as it suited her purpose. She can also be extremely ingratiating when she pleases, as you have surely learned. Would you like another martini? Why don't you mix another for each of us?" He looked with surprise into his glass to see that it was empty. He had not been aware of drinking, and he thought he must have spilled the contents without knowing it, but there was no sign of it on himself or the carpet. He had drunk the martini, all right, and he did badly want another, and so he got up and mixed more gin and vermouth and filled his glass and hers.

"It would make it much easier for us to talk if you sat beside me on the sofa," she said. "Don't you agree?"

"Not particularly."

"Oh, please. There's nothing to be gained by being antagonistic. You obviously didn't come here to accuse me of anything. You can't make up your mind about Ivy, and you think I might be able to help you. If we're going to be confidential, we may as well get into position for it."

He sat down beside her, and she smiled and reacted over with her free hand

and patted him on the knee in a gesture of approval. It seemed to him now entirely incredible that this serene and lovely woman had ever even considered killing anyone, let alone attempting it, and it seemed equally incredible that she had been a partner in a deviant relationship. Quite the contrary, allowing for the influence of his second martini, he thought that he could sense beneath her serenity a readiness to respond to the normal incitements to love.

"Are you willing to tell me the truth?" he said.

"Well, I'm resigned to it. What do you want me to say?"

"I warn you that I'm in no mood for euphemisms."

"Neither am I. I never am. I prefer to speak plainly, and I know very well what's on your mind. After all, you're quite obviously neither an innocent nor a pervert. You could hardly have taken Ivy to stay with you without learning what she is."

"She told me in the beginning."

"Really? How clever of Ivy. And knowing this, you allowed her to stay? You must be either an unusual man or a fool."

"She was in trouble and had no place to go. I felt sorry for her."

"I see. You're compassionate. Genuine compassion is rare in this world, I think. However, don't believe that Ivy will feel any gratitude for what you do for her, or that it will prevent her from hurting you any way she can if you offend her. You've let yourself get into a situation that could become pretty ugly. Or perhaps it already has. I haven't asked you yet what happened to your face."

"I cut it shaving."

"All right. It's your affair. But if you expect me to tell the truth, you should be willing to do the same."

"The truth is, Ivy clawed me. The circumstances were probably not quite what you're thinking, but let it go."

"Whatever they were, she must have been disturbed by them."

"She thought I was trying to make love to her, and how disturbing that would be is something you should know." He thought he saw a glitter of fury in her eyes, but it was so quickly gone, if it had existed at all, that he couldn't be sure.

"Do you think I'm that way? Did Ivy tell you I was?"

"Did she ever actually say? I don't believe she did. Anyhow, it was implicit in your relationship."

"Was it? Is it implicit in yours? Although it's really none of your business. I don't mind telling you that that was the source of our trouble. It's the reason she finally came to hate me. She hates me for rejecting her."

"In that case, why did you let her stay?"

"Why did you take her in? After all, my responsibility is greater than yours. She's my cousin. I knew her as a girl. She had no one else to turn to who could understand her and try to help her, and she was better off here than she would have been in some sordid place with her own kind."

He had eaten little that day, only lunch, and the two martinis were having a strong effect. As if she knew this and approved it, or had perhaps planned it, she got up and mixed a third. When she sat down again beside him, her thigh was brushing his, and he waited for her to move out of contact, but she didn't. She smiled and lifted her glass in a slight salute. He responded, and they drank together.

"Do you know something?" she said. "You're a very attractive young man, and I suspect that you could be very nice if you chose to be. I'm glad you came to see me. It would be too bad if you were to have the wrong idea about me."

"I'm not sure," he said, "what the wrong idea is."

He drained his glass and set it aside, as she did hers. Then, because he wanted to and because her words and expression seemed to invite it, he put his arms around her and kissed her, and her response was immediate and warm. Her body arched inward, her head fell back, and her lips parted slowly under his. When he released her and looked down into her upturned face, her eyes were open and clouded with desire, and she was breathing rapidly with excitement that could not possibly, he thought, be simulated.

"Was that a test?" she said with the slightest inflection of mockery. "Were you trying to find out?"

"Maybe."

"If it was, it's not enough. It proves nothing. Any man can kiss."

"What would be enough?" he asked.

"I can show you. Would you like me to show you?"

Henry grinned. "Yes. Show me."

A dark glint of feeling roiled up the depths of her eyes. Her red mouth curled and suddenly she slid close to him, pressing her body urgently against him. She put her moist, open mouth against his, grinding her lips back and forth in a frenzy of passion, while her hands clawed at his back and his flanks.

Somehow the zipper of her dress was down and she drew away from him long enough to clamber out of it. A twist of her hand behind her back freed her bra so that the burgeoning richness of her full, rounded breasts came free. Then she put his hand to her breast, surging against him. When his hand groped for the elastic of her panties she arched her body to help him so that all of the glowing white riches of her flesh were yielded up to him.

There was fire in her, fire in her hard-nippled breasts, her quivering loins as she pulled him down upon her. He was fumbling to get out of his own clothes now and when he was free of them she crushed her body against him, writhing in a hoarse, panting rhythm. She was all eager, yearning, devouring flesh and her hands upon his chest and thighs and belly were bold and daring, seeking to rouse him to a frenzy that matched her own.

"I'll show you," she breathed once, as she pulled her moist, avid mouth away from his. "This way... And this... And this..."

Her surrender was so complete and so adept that Henry did not fully understand until later that it was not surrender at all, but aggression, and that the suspiciously easy seduction of a practical stranger was hers, not his, and that its purpose was deception, not pleasure.

CHAPTER 9

Ivy lay very still in Henry's bed and stared at the ceiling with bright, dry eyes. There was a large brown stain that began at one upper corner of the room and extended diagonally toward the center. The stain was long and rather narrow, with an irregular perimeter reminiscent of a rough coastline on a map, and it looked, in fact, somewhat like the Italian boot. Tracing the perimeter of the stain with meticulous attention to every salient and recession, an exercise in careful diversion which was helpful in avoiding disintegration, Ivy could hear Henry descending the stairs to the street, the heaviness of his tread being a kind of index to the degree of his anger. In Ivy there was no anger. There was only the deep and acceptant despair that comes with definitive defeat in a moment of hopefulness. She thought that it would be a great relief to cry, but crying was not possible.

She continued to lie in bed for almost another hour, and as she lay there she tried to decide where she should go, but she knew all the while that there was really nothing to decide and nowhere in particular to go, and that all she was doing, or wanted to do, was to delay doing anything decisive whatever. In time, however, the self-deception could no longer be sustained, and so she got up and took a bath and dressed slowly and began to consider what she should take with her when she left. She did not wish to carry both of the bags she had brought, and it required some time and thought to decide which of the two she should take, the larger or the smaller, but finally she chose the smaller with the qualification that she would also pack the larger and leave it here to pick up later.

Having made this decision she felt a sudden urge to hurry, to complete in all haste what must be done. Opening both bags, she gathered her possessions, deciding quickly whether each item was something she would need soon or not, and putting each in the large or small bag according to the decision. Her packing done, she left the smaller bag standing closed in the middle of the room and put the other one out of the way against a wall. Then she made Henry's bed and folded the covers of her own, the sofa in the living room, after which she went systematically through both rooms, putting everything neatly in its place. This done, she took the twenty dollars from the chest drawer and put on her hat and coat and picked up the small bag and went downstairs to the street and walked away quickly without pausing or looking back.

She did not choose her direction deliberately, but she turned out of habit in the direction of the Greek's diner. When she had reached it, becoming conscious of her location, she stopped and looked in through the window and saw the

Greek standing behind the counter beside the cash register. Because she was hungry, and because she wanted to say good-by to George, for whom she had affection, she went inside and set her bag on the floor beside a stool at the counter, and sat down on the stool. George was pleased to see her. Taking a position opposite her, he placed the heels of his hands on the edge of the counter and leaned forward with an air of easy camaraderie.

"Hello," he said. "I'm very glad to see you. Will you have something to eat?"

"Thank you," she said. "I'll have some coffee and toast, if you please. I've not eaten any breakfast."

"How is the arrangement with Henry?"

"Very bad. It hasn't worked out."

"Is that so? I'm sorry to learn it. I thought it was working out well."

The Greek's face wore an expression of grave concern. His concern was, as it were, doubled and divided in equal parts. In the beginning of the arrangement, he had worried only about possible deleterious effects upon Henry and the book, but later, in affection and ignorance, he had begun to worry about the consequences to Ivy. Beneath his overt attitude of sophistication, he considered the arrangement as he understood it to be, if not sinful, surely regrettable, and he did not want Ivy hurt or abandoned.

"It worked for a while," she said. "But now I've been asked to leave. You see that I have my bag, and I've stopped now to say good-by."

"Henry has asked you to leave?"

"Yes, he has. When he left for work this morning, he told me to be gone by the time he returned."

"Henry's hot-headed. No doubt he didn't mean what he said. I advise you to go home and wait until he returns. It will be all right then. You'll see."

"No, no. You don't understand. It was all my fault. It was my fault entirely."

"Where are you going?"

"I don't know. I'll have to find a place to stay for a day or two until I can make other arrangements. I have a little money. Could you suggest a suitable hotel? It must be quite cheap."

"Well, there's a hotel directly down the street. About a mile. It's not so much, but it's cheap and as clean as could be expected. It's called the Hawkins. I lived there once myself for a year and found it acceptable."

"All right. On your recommendation, I'll go there." Resolving to speak sternly to Henry at the first chance, the Greek served the coffee and toast and refused, after she had finished, to be paid.

"You're very generous," she said. "It may be that I'll see you again."

"It may be," he said.

She went out and down the street, carrying the bag. The bag, which was small and light, kept getting bigger and heavier, and at first she alleviated this by changing it from hand to hand, but then it was as heavy in one hand as the other, and the mile to the hotel was surely two at least. She finally arrived, however, stopping to read the vertical sign above the entrance, and she was relieved to see that the building made a somewhat better appearance than she had hoped for, in spite of the Greek's recommendation. It was a narrow building, constructed of brick and pressed between two other buildings that were not so high and consequently gave to it an effect of greater height than it had. It had a revolving door, which she entered, and two shallow steps upward to the lobby, which she climbed. The lobby was small and shabby, but the shabbiness managed to retain a suggestion of respectability, and there were some deep leather chairs and potted plants distributed over a worn red carpet. Some of the chairs were occupied, and she noticed that the occupants were all elderly men who were so in harmony with the general tone of the place that they might have been installed there by design as part of the furnishings. There was also an elderly man behind the desk, and Ivy approached him and spoke with spurious arrogance that was a defensive effect of her uncertainty.

"I'd like a room, please," she said.

The elderly clerk responded as if this were a reasonable and routine request, which somehow surprised her and gave her an exorbitant sense of acceptance. He presented a card, which she signed, and then slapped a bell that summoned a Negro bellhop.

"Six-ten," the clerk said.

He handed the Negro, who was also elderly, a key fastened by a chain to a heavy fiber tag. The Negro took the key and Ivy's bag and started for the elevator, and Ivy followed. They went up in the elevator together and down the narrow sixth floor hall to room ten, and then, after the Negro was gone and the door closed behind him, Ivy was swept immediately by the terrible desolation of being in a strange and unloved place with absolutely nothing to do.

She did not know how she could ever survive the desolate day, and she wished now that she had remained at Henry's until late in the afternoon, just before he was due to return. Then, at that time, it would already be getting dark at the end of the short winter's day, and the gray hours would be past, over and done with, the neons and fluorescents and incandescents burning against the darkness, and if there was a menace in the night that the day did not have, its pulse was quicker, and it passed faster, and it was usually possible, sometime in the course of it, to sleep and lose the consciousness of time entirely. But she had not thought, she had left in the middle of the day, the worst possible of times, and now she was trapped in this deadly room and must either escape it or somehow devise a way to bear it.

She removed her hat and coat and put them in a closet and went over to a window and stood looking down upon the tarred roof of the building next door. The black expanse was bleak and ugly, with sooty patches of snow in the corners at the base of the parapet and against the north sides of the chimney and a metal ventilator. The ugliness of the roof increased her depression, and she turned away from the window and sat down in a chair and began to think about where she could go from where she was and how she could live after the twenty dollars were gone. She could not go home, to the house of her parents, and she would not go back to Lila, and it was very doubtful after what had happened, in spite of the Greek's assurance, that she could go back to Henry. There were places she could go where she would find understanding and help, the allegiance of kind, but she had never gone to any of these places and did not want to go, because going to them was the voluntary acceptance of a kind of segregation that was crippling and degrading.

Well, she would have to go to work and live alone, but what could she do? She had no particular talents and no special training. She could get a job as a clerk in a store, of course, even though she had no experience, and it should be especially easy now, during the Christmas shopping rush, but such a job would be very dull and would pay very little, and it could be considered at best only something to do until something better could be found. Thinking about the necessity for getting a job, she remembered for the first time that day that she actually already had one, that she was committed to helping old Adolph Brennan in his book shop, and that she had walked away without once thinking about it. It would have been only common courtesy to have stopped to explain why she couldn't work any longer, and to say good-by, and she regretted that she had not. He owed her a little money, too, and perhaps later she could go there and get it.

The air in the room was stale and very warm. The radiator against the wall made a soft, whispering sound of escaping steam that was pleasant to hear and soothing in effect. Listening to the sound, she felt herself becoming a little drowsy, and this was good. It would be good to sleep and would solve the problem of how to survive the day. She got up and sat down on the edge of the bed and removed her shoes and lay down. The action dispelled the drowsiness, but she lay and listened to the sound of the steam and slowly became drowsy again, and after a while she went to sleep and slept through the rest of the day and wakened in darkness about eight o'clock. She wakened in terror with a scream in her throat, but she remembered in time where she was and why, and terror diminished as the scream became a whimper. Getting up, she turned on a light and washed her face in the bathroom. Leaving the light burning, wearing her hat and coat, she went out of the room and downstairs in the elevator and across the lobby into the street.

She wasn't hungry, but she thought that she had better eat for the sake of her strength, and besides, eating was something to do that would pass some time. She walked along, looking for a place, and in the next block, or maybe it was in the block after the next, she came to a basement restaurant with a flight of steps leading down from street level to the door, and she descended the flight to the door and went inside. On her right as she entered was a long bar with two men and one woman in front of it on stools and a bartender behind it in a white jacket. The men and the woman and the bartender were all watching a prize fight on an elevated television set at the far end of the bar, and she walked past them down two more steps into the restaurant.

Since she had so little money, she felt compelled to order wisely, to get as much food as possible for what she would have to pay. Considering this, and feeling very sensible and efficient in doing so, she decided that a steak would be best all around, one of the cheaper cuts, and she ordered the steak medium rare and ate it slowly after it was served, cutting small bites and chewing each one thoroughly. From where she sat, she could see at an upward angle, over the top of a low partition, the heads of the two men and the woman at the bar. They were now faced squarely around, no longer looking downbar toward the television, and so she assumed that the fight was over.

The bar seemed all at once a wonderful place, a sanctuary, and she made up her mind suddenly that she would go in and have a drink and sit there for a while in the sanctuary. She couldn't afford it, of course, not even one drink, but she thought of the cost in terms of warmth and casual companionship and the pleasant passage of time, and the price of a drink for all this was surely little enough. The waiter had left her check, and she picked it up and carried it over to the cashier and paid it. With part of her change, she got a package of cigarettes from a machine, another extravagance which she did not even try to justify. She was beginning to feel, in fact, strangely compatible with immediate circumstances, indifferent to matters which had previously, only a little while ago, seemed enormously important and threatening. At the bar, the bartender stood opposite her and smiled politely. He had a twisted nose and a thick ear on the left side, but these acquired defects had the effect of making him more attractive than he would otherwise have been, giving distinction to a face that would have been nondescript without them, and she wondered if he had been a prize fighter or wrestler before becoming a bartender.

"Good evening," he said.

"Good evening," she said. "I think I shall have a double manhattan, if you please."

Double. She had said double promptly and quite naturally, without thinking about it. From a cheap cut of steak to a double manhattan was a long way in terms of economy, but the inconsistency in this was more apparent than real, and there was definitely an underlying sense and purpose in it, although she couldn't immediately isolate it. The bartender brought her double manhattan and left her with it, and an incredibly short time later, lifting her glass, she discovered that it was empty. This would not do. It simply would not do. It was all right to allow oneself a drink, especially if it contributed to survival in a period of time, but such careless extravagances as this was another thing entirely. She had intended to nurse the double manhattan, to make it last, but she had gulped it down at once instead, and now she would have to leave or buy another.

The prospect of leaving being intolerable, there was only one thing to do, and she beckoned to the bartender, who returned, and ordered another double manhattan. With this one, however, she would mind what she was doing. She would drink slowly, in sips, with attention to time. Having made this resolution, she no longer regretted having drunk the first one quickly, for the result had been beneficial. It had increased her sense of compatibility, the capacity to cope, and had given her the beginning of a feeling of pleasurable excitement.

"Excuse me," she said to the bartender. "Would you mind very much if I were to ask you a question?"

"Not at all, lady," he said. "I gets lots of them."

"I was wondering if you were once a prize fighter or a wrestler."

"Both. I was a fighter first and a wrestler later."

"Did you prefer wrestling to prize fighting?"

"No. I prefer bartending to either."

"Really? That's very interesting. Why did you quit prize fighting for wrestling if you didn't prefer to wrestle?"

"I quit fighting because I wasn't any good at it. I kept getting my brains beat out. Wrestling wasn't as tough on a guy. It was all rigged, you see. Just a show. It was always decided in advance who would win."

"Is that so? Were you allowed to win often?"

"Not often. The way it is, you got a hero and a villain. I was always the villain."

"You don't look like a villain to me. In my opinion, you look like a perfect gentleman."

"As a bartender, I'm expected to look like a gentleman. As a wrestler, I wasn't. I made a pretty fair villain, if I do say so myself."

"Then how did you happen to quit wrestling for bartending?"

"I got too old. Too slow and brittle. One night In Dallas a Swede named Igor the Golden accidentally broke my arm. He was the hero and was supposed to win, but he wasn't supposed to break my arm. It wasn't his fault, though. It was all arranged, but I was too slow in shifting my weight in the right direction at the right time. In giving with the hold, you know."

"I see. I'm sorry your arm was broken, but if you prefer tending bar, as you say, it has all worked out all right in the end."

"Yes. It's all worked out all right."

He went away, and she sat nursing her double, but soon he was back to serve a customer who had taken the stool next to Ivy, on her left. The new customer was a man. Ivy knew this by the smell of him, even before she had heard his voice or had seen, looking down at a sharp angle from under lowered lids, a worsted knee against the wall of the bar. He ordered a rye on the rocks in a voice that had a trace of an accent, and she tried to identify the accent, whether it was foreign or sectional or one modified by the other, but she couldn't even be certain that he had an accent at all. Neither could she get a clue from his appearance, which she examined covertly in the mirror over the backbar. He had a narrow face with a scar diagonally across his chin, and although she could not tell in the shadowy mirror, she had an idea that his eyes must be pale blue. The assumption of pale eyes was based, perhaps, on the observable fact of pale hair. He wore a soft hat, but it was pushed so far back on his head that she could see the hair brushed flatly across the front part of his skull. There was, she thought, a peculiar quality in this particular man, something that made him exceptional among other men, but she was no more successful in identifying this quality than she had been in identifying the accent, if any, and she did not learn until later, too late, that it was the quality of danger, the elusive essence of a dangerous man.

"What's your opinion?" he said suddenly in the voice that might have had an accent.

"Were you speaking to me?" she said.

"You were watching me in the mirror, weren't you? What's your opinion?"

"Was I watching you? Excuse me. I really wasn't paying the slightest attention to what I was doing. I was thinking of something else."

"I'm disappointed."

"Are you? I don't see why you should be."

"It's always pleasant to be looked over by a good-looking woman, provided the impression is favorable. My mistake, however. And my apologies. Are you waiting for someone?"

"No."

"In that case, may I buy you a drink?"

"I already have a drink."

"It won't last forever."

That was true, she thought. Even with the most careful nursing, the double manhattan wouldn't last forever, and it would be nice, when it was finished, to have another. Surely there was nothing wrong in allowing a man to buy her a drink, or even several drinks, in a bar that was a sanctuary that she did not want to leave. It was, in fact, kind and considerate of him to offer, and would be a rudeness on her part to refuse.

"Perhaps I'll be ready for another by the time it comes," she said.

"If you aren't," he said, "it won't spoil."

No longer under the necessity of nursing, she drank her manhattan quickly, and he kept her company in rye. In the meanwhile, he had given the signal for duplicates, which were supplied by the attractive bartender with the twisted nose and thick ear.

"My name is Neal," he said. "Charles Neal. My friends call me Chick."

"How do you do, Mr. Neal," she said formally. "My name is Ivy Galvin."

"Oh, come on. Be my friend."

"I don't know. It was nice of you to buy me a drink, and I'm prepared to be friendly for it, but I don't believe I could call you Chick."

"Why not?"

"As a name, I don't like it. Does that offend you? I don't want to be offensive."

He stared at her with his pale, shallow eyes and thought that she was certainly tight, probably a nut, and altogether something nice and easy to be had for the night.

"I'm not offended."

"I'm willing to call you Charles, however. Is that satisfactory?"

"Sure. Call me Charles. I haven't been called Charles since my old man ran me away from home."

"Were you run away from home? I was too, in a way. Not exactly, but in a way. It gives us something in common."

"Maybe we can find other things in common. Let's work at it."

She lost track of the number of manhattans she drank and the length of time she was in the bar, but there were quite a few over a period of quite a while, and in this period, while the manhattans were being drunk, she was aware of the pressure of a knee and the sly and tentative explorations of a hand, the knee and the hand being the property of Charles Neal, whom she could not bring herself to call Chick. She tolerated his trespasses, which were minor, for the sake of the manhattans, which were sustaining, and in fact she was proud of herself for the really competent way in which she was getting along in a strange situation that would once have terrified her, and it just showed again that she could get along quite well in any situation whatever if she only had the confidence.

Someone kept feeding coins to a jukebox, and it seemed to Ivy that the same music was played over and over again, a full-voiced woman singing "Oh, How I Miss You Tonight," and it was that song in that voice that became the night's accompaniment, with power to restore it later, not in the fuzzy details of what happened, which were always vague, but in its emotional quality. After the consumption of a good many manhattans, Ivy felt the need to relieve herself, and she slipped carefully off her stool and said, "Excuse me, please," and started toward the door of the ladies' room that was clearly marked by a little electric sign above it. But the door was animated by a capricious spirit and insisted upon playing jokes on her. Although she had located it exactly before starting and had walked directly toward it, it kept shifting a little to the right or to the left, so that she had to stop and start again each time in a new direction. Moreover, it kept withdrawing slowly, so that she gained on it only about half as much distance as she should have, and therefore required twice as long to reach it.

There was a clock in the restroom, which she was able to bring into focus after a few moments of intent concentration, and she was surprised and delighted to see that it was eleven o'clock and that she had managed to pass several hours of the night with practically no trouble. It was evident to her now, however, that she had drunk quite enough manhattans for one night and had better return to the hotel to which she'd gone after leaving Henry's, and the name of the hotel was, she believed, the Hawkins. Yes, that was it. It was named the Hawkins, and it was just down the street a short way, in the next block or the block after.

Leaving the restroom, she returned to the bar to say good night to Charles Neal. She owed him this courtesy, she thought, for being generous and buying her so many manhattans. She did not attempt to get back onto the stool, a difficult and dangerous exercise, but stood beside him and spoke politely in his ear, forming the shape of each word with care before enunciating it.

"Than you very much for the manhattans," she said, "but I think I had better leave now."

"Where are we going?" he said.

"I'm staying at the Hawkins Hotel. It's only down the street a little way, though, and it isn't necessary for you to come with me. I can get there easily by myself."

A comedian, he thought. *A lush and a nut and a goddamn comedian.*

"I wouldn't think of letting you go alone," he said.

"Really it isn't necessary, and you've already been quite considerate and generous enough. I wouldn't want to put you to any trouble."

"You've got a real sense of humor," he said. "You kill me."

These words surprised her, for she had intended no humor, and they were spoken in a hard, flat tone of voice that did not suggest that he was in the least amused. But her senses had become unreliable, and it was likely that her impressions were distorted. Anyhow, he was definitely determined to see her to the hotel, having already slipped off the stool as a beginning, and it would be ungracious of her to make an issue of it. And so she permitted him to walk out of the bar and down the street beside her.

The sidewalk was unsteady and kept tilting toward the street. This caused her to keep bumping into Charles Neal, who was between her and the curb, and once, at an intersection, the pavement moved so suddenly as she was stepping down from the sidewalk into the street that she stumbled and would have fallen if he had not held her by the arm. After that he continued holding her by the arm, even when it was no longer necessary, and when she assured him that she was perfectly all right and did not need his help, he only laughed and kept hold of the arm, and the laugh had the same hard, flat, disturbing sound that his voice had had at the last moment at the bar.

The lobby of the hotel was empty, except for the night clerk, another elderly man who was asleep in a chair behind the desk, his head fallen back and his Adam's apple working convulsively as he sucked air through his nostrils and blew it out noisily through his mouth. Since she had carried her room key with her in the pocket of her coat, Ivy did not find it necessary to waken him. She walked across the lobby to the elevator and stopped, turning to face Charles Neal with what she hoped was an attitude of decisiveness.

"Thank you for coming with me," she said.

"Don't mention it."

"Good night, then."

"Joke again."

"What?"

"Suppose we have a nightcap in your room."

"I'm sorry. I don't have anything there to drink."

"No? Well, I'll just see you safely upstairs."

She understood then, going up in the elevator, that she had made a wanton commitment to a dangerous man, and when she opened the door of her room and entered she was afraid to try to close it against him. Slowly, with despair, she removed her hat and coat and faced him.

She was horrified to see that Neal too had tom off his own coat and tie, tossing them toward a chair, and was now loosening his belt. Her eyes fastened on the stiff brush of hair at the parting in his shirt, and before she began to shiver with revulsion, she was conscious of a sharp spurt of unwanted excitement within her.

Chick's clothes had been deceptive in the bar. She saw now that he was brutally formed, and that with such a man there would be no mercy. Not knowing what else to do, she backed slowly away, her frantic gaze fixed on his pale eyes, with their shallow glitter of blind lust. Slowly Chick walked after her.

His pointed tongue flicked wetly over his half-smiling lips, and it dawned on her for the first that he thought she was playing his game, teasing him on, building his passion, and a moan of realization formed in her throat.

This whipped him into action, and suddenly he lunged at her, the veins in his neck swollen and pulsating as if ready to burst. One grimy hand darted out and grabbed the collar of her dress, while he shoved her savagely with the other. The dress ripped like paper and Ivy sank helplessly to the floor.

Laughter exploded in his throat, as his hard flanks imprisoned her sides, and he reached down to draw her to him. Slowly, with calculated brutality, he brought her up against his rigidity, the hard length of his male body pressing into hers at every point. Her senses reeled, unable to cope with this strange and terrifying excitement, then took refuge in the paralysis of pure terror.

His searching hands were now taking rough liberties with every part of her, caressing her breasts, massaging her flanks, exploring her thighs, his mouth ravenous on her neck, her ears, and finally sinking between her lips.

It was in her mouth that her paralysis was shattered, and without warning she bit down on his lip, and tasted blood. He cursed and slapped her back-handed across the face. Like a cornered animal, she lunged for his hand with her teeth, and again he cursed and struck her harder, so that she fell to the floor.

There, between sitting and lying, she stared down with mute shame at the exposed pink of her breasts. How much longer would this go on? And did it really matter any more? Was this not, perhaps, the violation she had been unconsciously seeking from the beginning? No, no, she thought, it was the ultimate degradation that she should lose in violence to a stranger what she had hoped to gain in tenderness from a friend.

With a flicker of regained hope, she looked up almost beseechingly into Chick's bleeding face, as if somehow he ought to understand this. But Neal was beyond the reach of such sanities, and this time he made no effort to bring her to her feet, but flung himself down upon her with such force that it drove the breath from her body.

In the desperate moments that followed, she cried out once, not loudly, but in a plaintive hopelessness that she knew no one would ever hear.

CHAPTER 10

Between nine-thirty and ten, while Ivy was enjoying the illusory warmth and security of too much alcohol, Henry was on the way home. He arrived just before ten, and he was already beginning to feel uncertain of a number of things he had accepted as true in Lila's apartment. He was also beginning to feel guilty in proportion to his growing uncertainty, and he was nagged by the suspicion that Lila, in addition to being beautiful, was extremely clever as well. He had been altogether too ready to accept her diagnosis of Ivy, which was a measure of his own cowardice in trying to justify his own injustice, and now that he was away from her beauty and her assured voice and her willing flesh, he thought that he could detect in her remembered words and behavior a pattern of deception that he had not seen before.

He faced the rather humiliating conclusion that he had probably been seduced for a purpose other than pleasure, and this purpose was simply that of making Lila Galvin appear convincingly something that she was not. After all bisexuality was not particularly rare, and certainly had a far greater incidence than was generally known. Lila was, by the nature of her ambition, especially vulnerable to a kind of disgrace that could destroy her life as she wanted it to be, including probably a marriage for money and position, and her fear of Ivy, what she might say and do, was surely commensurate with her vulnerability. He wondered if this fear could actually become murderous. He had never fully believed Ivy's story about the sedative, but he had considered it an effect of feverish imagination, not calculated deception, and he had not doubted until tonight, in Lila's apartment, that Ivy had believed it herself. Now, in his own rooms, where the sense of Ivy's presence was strong and Lila's wasn't, he again began to believe in Ivy's innocence, if not her reliability.

Lila had said that Ivy was a psychopathic personality, a liar and cheat and egoist as well as deviate, but this was not so. It was Lila who lied, and possibly it was Lila who was the psychopathic personality. Henry's knowledge of abnormalities was no greater and no broader than his experience of observation and reading, but he was certain that psychopathic personalities did not commit suicide or seriously try to. They destroyed others, never themselves. And Ivy's suicide attempt had been genuine, there was no question about that, and she had been saved only by the thinnest and most ludicrous of chances, that she could in no way have predicted.

It was Lila who lied. She was very beautiful and very clever and maybe very dangerous. She had lied with her voice and with her body, and he had believed, for a while, both lies.

And where was Ivy? Well, she had gone away, because she had been told to go in anger that was now regretted. The rooms above the bookshop seemed desolate and deserted, and it occurred to Henry that emptiness, against all logic, existed in degrees. He noted the tidiness of the living room, and the tidiness somehow emphasized the absence of the person who had accomplished it. Walking into the bedroom, he saw the packed bag against the wall, and then, looking into the drawer of the chest, saw that the twenty dollars had been taken. The packed bag indicated that she intended to return for it, but this might not be for a long time, or might be never. In the meanwhile, she was gone, because he had sent her away, and where could she possibly be?

Was she, like the night he had found her, roaming the streets? The thought of her doing this was deeply disturbing, increasing his conviction of senseless cruelty and concomitant guilt, and he had a vision of her passing like a lost child through the intermittent areas of light and darkness along the cold streets. She had taken the twenty dollars, however. Having the money, it was unlikely that she would go without shelter and a bed the first night.

Perhaps she would go back to Lila. This thought was in his mind suddenly, and it was the most disturbing possibility of all. If she roamed the streets or stayed somewhere for the night in a cheap room, it was at least a sign of stubborn adherence to rebellion, a refusal to capitulate, but if she returned to Lila it would be a final admission of failure, the definitive submission. She had not been there while he was, that was certain, and he had left late enough so that she should easily have arrived, if she was coming at all. But perhaps it had merely taken her a long while to make a decision, or to be driven to it in desertion and desperation, in which case she might be there at this moment, and it was imperative, now that he had thought of it, to know if it were so or not.

Putting on his hat and overcoat, he went downstairs to the street and turned left toward the Greek's as far as a public telephone booth on the corner. It was very cold in the booth, and the bulb which lighted it was growing dim. He found Lila's number listed in the directory and dialed it. Her phone rang and rang in short bursts at the other end of the line, and he was about to give up and break the connection when her voice came on abruptly. "Hello," she said. "This is Lila Galvin speaking."

"Henry Harper," Henry said.

There was a long pause before she spoke again, and in the pause a suggestion of wariness. Her voice, when she spoke, was so cool and impersonal that it seemed completely unrelated to the voice in which he had heard, a few hours ago, the soft solicitations and gutturals of passion.

"What do you want?" she said. "Why are you calling me at this hour?"

"Is Ivy there?"

"Ivy? Certainly not. I supposed that she was with you."

"She's gone. She was gone when I got home."

"What made you think she came here?"

"I only thought she might have. It was the only place I could think of that she might go to."

"Why did she leave? Was it because of something you did to her?"

He had been made sensitive to inference by his feeling of guilty responsibility, however irrational it might be, and he was, sitting cramped in the cold and dimly lighted booth, shaken of a sudden by a diffused and futile fury that was at once directed inwardly upon himself and outwardly upon both Ivy and Lila.

"Listen to me," he said. "Whatever I have done to her is not one-tenth so bad as what you have done to her, or what she has done to herself. Anyhow, it will do no good to make accusations or call names. She's gone, and where she may go finally and do to herself in the end is something I don't like to think about. Neither do you, I'll bet. You don't like to think about what she may do to herself and, incidentally, to you."

"Are you trying to threaten me?"

"If you're threatened, it's not by me."

"I thought earlier tonight that you might have a little intelligence, but I see now that you're a complete fool."

"On the contrary, you thought earlier that I was a fool, and I was, but you're beginning to think now that I may not be. Never mind that, however. There's no use talking about it. I'll look for Ivy, and if I can't find her I may report to the police that she's missing."

"No! Wait a minute."

He waited, listening to the humming wire, and he could feel in the little booth, as though it came through the wire on the sound he heard, the anxiety and calculation of the woman at the other end.

"Are you there?" she said.

"Yes."

"You're quite right about making accusations and calling names. There's nothing to be gained by it. Where are you now? Are you at home?"

"No. I'm in a sidewalk telephone booth."

"Where can I meet you?"

"I'm not sure that I want you to meet me. Why should I?"

"Because you want to find Ivy, and so do I. I can be of help. You don't have a car, do you?"

"No."

"Do you propose to walk the streets all night? In my car, we may have a chance of finding her. At least we can check the cheap hotels in your area. I don't suppose she had much money."

"Twenty dollars, I think. Not much more."

"That won't last long, and God knows what she may do after it goes. We must find her, that's all, and then she must come back to stay with me. I hope you're convinced by this time that no other arrangement will work. She simply can't be allowed to go on jeopardizing herself and causing endless trouble for others."

"What she does is something she will decide for herself."

"All right. Will you tell me where we can meet?"

"There's an all-night diner down the street from here. The Greek's. You'd better meet me there."

"Give me the address."

He told her how to find the place, and then he hung up and went there to wait for her. George, behind the counter, watched him with a frown as he crossed from the door and sat down on a stool. The customary warmth of his reception was totally lacking, and in the severity of George's gaze there was more than a hint of disapproval.

"It's apparent," George said, "that you are feeling despondent tonight. Could it be because your conscience is bothering you?"

"Why the hell should my conscience be bothering me?"

"One's conscience becomes a bother when one has done something he should not have done, or failed to do something he should have. Provided, of course, one has a conscience to begin with."

It was obvious that George was making some kind of point about something, preferring for his own reasons to be devious instead of direct, but Henry was in no mood for subtleties. It had been, since the bad beginning of the abortive fiasco of the morning, a long and difficult day, coming to a kind of climax in the feverish episode in the apartment of Lila Galvin, and he had an uncomfortable feeling that he had not, on the whole, accounted very well for himself in the day's events.

"George," he said, "I have a notion that you're referring obliquely to something specific in which I seem somehow to be involved. With all due respect for the subtlety of the Greek mind, which is notoriously devious, I'd appreciate it if you'd say directly what you mean."

"Gladly," George said. "I was referring to your shameful treatment of Ivy."

"Oh? Am I to understand from this that you've seen her today?"

"She was here this morning to say good-by and to have breakfast."

"I suppose she gave you a full report on all my qualifications as a son of a bitch. Is that it?"

"On the contrary, she had nothing bad to report. She said, merely, that you had ordered her to leave. Although I had doubts about her in the beginning, especially in relation to you and the book, I confess that I have become very fond of her since, and I don't mind saying that I consider it more than likely that I was worried about the wrong person."

"The hell with that! Did she say where she was going?"

"Not knowing, she couldn't say. But she asked me to recommend a cheap hotel as a place to go for the time being, and I suggested the Hawkins."

"Did she go there?"

"I don't know.

"You going down there and see?"

"I don't know why I should."

"She's a nice girl, Henry. She has her trouble."

"She has a hell of a lot more trouble than you know about."

"I will tell you one thing, Henry. I would never take a sweet girl with trouble into my house for shelter and then put her into the cold street for no sufficient reason. Sometimes I, too, am inclined to believe that it will be a lousy book that no one will buy."

"By God, it looks right now as if it will never even be written. How the hell do you know I had no sufficient reason?"

"In spite of certain foolishnesses, she is a nice girl. It would be too bad if she came to a bad end."

"All right, George. You can get off my back now. I'll go down to the Hawkins and see if she's there. Damn it, I intended to go from the start. Why the hell do you think I'm out prowling the streets, if not to try to find her?"

"In that case, I'll spare you the ignominy of explaining how you got the scratches on your face that look as if they may have been made by fingernails."

"That's right, George. Spare me. And, incidentally, go to hell."

Getting off the stool at the counter, he walked over to the door and stopped, making a pretense of adjusting his collar against the cold outside. He was sick and tired of being unfairly accused by others, and most of all he was sick and tired of being unfairly accused by himself. He wished, however, that it had not come to this between him and the Greek. He liked George and did not wish to lose his friendship, and he waited now inside the door in the hope that George would say a healing word. Having sustained the pretense of adjusting the collar as long as he could, he reached for the door handle and was about to leave when the Greek finally spoke.

"Henry," George said.

"Yes."

"It would also be too bad for friends to become strangers."

"Yes, it would."

"I spoke hastily about the book. It will be good and sell well."

"Thank you, George. And I, for my part, don't really want you to go to hell."

"I hardly thought so."

"Good night, George. I'll see you soon."

"Let us hope so."

Henry opened the door and went out. He felt better after the pacific exchange, but at the same time he began to develop a premonition that grew stronger with each step in the street until it was so strong that he could not dispel it by reason or disregard, and the premonition was that Ivy was dead.

He walked rapidly down the street toward the Hawkins, exercising restraint to keep from breaking into a trot, and his compulsion to hurry was as irrational as his conviction of death, for if Ivy was dead hurrying had no point. But he hurried, nevertheless, and he had covered half the distance to the hotel before he remembered that he had agreed to wait for Lila at the Greek's. Well, she would probably inquire for him there, and George would tell her where he had gone. She could follow if she chose, and if she did not choose, it did not matter. His only concern now was to see as quickly as possible if his premonition was true or not, and he could not doubt that it was.

To give the premonition credence, there was the fact that Ivy had already tried once to kill herself, and had almost succeeded. In addition to this, he attached an ominous significance to the report that she had apparently gone immediately from the diner to the hotel. Hotel rooms were often used by suicides. He had read about such deaths in the newspapers, and there were probably many more that were kept quiet or passed off as being natural. The odd thing about it was that many such suicides could much more easily have destroyed themselves elsewhere, in their homes or offices, for instance, and it was possible that they were trying in a twisted sort of way to remove the shame and sorrow of their self-destruction from the places and people they knew and loved, simply be removing the act to a strange place among strangers. It could be that Ivy had been so motivated. She had had the day alone above the bookstore in which to kill herself, but she had thought of him in the end, as she had not thought of him in her first attempt, and had gone away to a hotel to save him trouble.

He saw the sign of the hotel hanging high above the sidewalk ahead of him. Increasing his pace until he was in fact moving at a kind of awkward lope, he crossed an intersection and was no more than thirty feet from the hotel's entrance when he stopped abruptly in his traces with a gasp, as if he had suddenly been struck a powerful blow to the solar plexus, and he had for a moment an absurd fear that he was going to faint. For there ahead of him, coming from the opposite direction, was Ivy herself with a man. The man had a hand on her arm in casual, public intimacy, and she seemed to be allowing this intimacy with complete congeniality, but whether she was congenial or not, she was certainly not dead.

The absurd faintness having passed, Henry was furious. He felt that he had been made a fool of, as though Ivy had maliciously put into his mind by telepathy the premonition of her death, and it was far too much to bear calmly at the end of a day in which he had been a fool too many times before. But the fury left him, passing only a little less quickly than the faintness, and he wondered in dismay, remembering her in his bed that morning, if she was attempting now with this stranger a kind of radical surgery that had failed with him.

Moving again, he went into the hotel lobby and saw the floor indicator above the closed elevator doors moving upon the number two. He started up the stairs three at a time, staying always a floor behind the elevator, until he found the indicator unmoving on the number six. Looking down the hall to his right, he was just in time to see a door closing.

He stood looking at the door in indecision. He assumed, from what he had seen, that Ivy had willingly admitted the man to her room. He guessed at her motive and feared the consequences of her behavior, but he had no desire, by intruding where he was not wanted, to make a fool of himself again. He was still standing and looking at the closed door, wondering if he should intrude or retreat, when Ivy cried out. It was not a loud and piercing cry. It had more of the quality of a plaintive cry of despair, rising barely above the volume of a normal voice, and he was not certain, after it was gone, that he had heard it at all.

But it was enough to make him act decisively. He went down the hall to the door and tried the knob. The door, unlocked, swung inward before pressure. Ivy, on the floor, was struggling with a man who was trying to pinion her flailing arms, and as he stood fixed in the doorway, she lifted her shame-filled eyes over the shoulders of the man and saw him standing there. Her lips formed the shape of his name, but she made no sound.

Henry, for a couple of seconds, went blind with rage. Everything was obscured by a pink mist deepening through red to black, and he stepped forward into the mist as it began to lift, striking with all his strength at the kneeling figure of the man. The man, Charles Neal, had not heard the door open behind him, but he was made aware of Henry's presence by the direction of Ivy's gaze and the sudden rigidity of her body. He whirled to one side, and this turning saved him from the force of Henry's blow. Henry's fist brushed his jaw, spinning him away and sending him sprawling. He rolled to the wall beyond the bed and came up like a cat onto his feet. In his hand as he rose, apparently by some kind of legerdemain, was a switch knife. The long blade of the knife sprang out of its handle, shining, with a snick of sound. Slowly, with a calculated deadliness of purpose that went oddly with the insane light in his shallow eyes, Charles Neal, feinting and weaving and driving in, brought the knife held low and ready with the blade angled up.

Henry's movement was hampered by his overcoat, which weighed suddenly a thousand pounds, but it was too late now to remove it, and it was luck for him that it was, for it saved him from the shining blade. Charles Neal feinting and weaving and driving in, brought the blade upward in a short, flashing arc. Henry, falling back and aside, felt a dull blow in the belly, a hot prick of flesh above his navel. The blade caught and held for a second in the thick fabric of his coat, and his motion away from the blow pulled Neal off balance for that second. He stumbled, bent over, and Henry brought a heavy fist down like a club on the back of his neck at the base of the skull. Driven to his knees, he remained for another second in the kneeling position, and then he lay down on his face on the floor with a rattle of breath.

Henry looked down at him and drew his own breath with heavy labor.

No one, he realized, had spoken a word or made an unnecessary sound since he opened the door, and except the sound, of breathing, the room was now utterly sill.

Lifting his eyes and looking around, he saw that he was alone with the stranger at his feet. Ivy was gone.

CHAPTER 11

She could never remember leaving the room or descending the stairs or crossing the lobby. She could only remember being suddenly in the street, in her torn dress, in the cutting cold. It did not occur to her that she was doing a cowardly thing in running away to leave Henry, who had looked for her and found her and come to her in time to save her, alone and unarmed against a dangerous man with a knife. It did not occur to her, as it had not previously occurred to her that it was a wicked thing to attempt suicide in his bathroom, because she was blinded to the implications and effects of her action by the one imperative need to escape the circumstances that had closed upon her. She was not, in fact, merely running away from the sordid situation in the room she had left, nor was she running from the danger. Her flight was a symbol and a gesture. She was really fleeing the aberrant and threatening part of herself that made sordidness and danger probable, if not certain.

And so she ran, holding her tom dress together and carrying the constant threat with her, from one place to another. She did not actually run, but walked very fast, and she had no idea where she was going, either immediately or eventually, except that she must, in the first place, cross over at once to the other side of the street, for the street would somehow be a barrier between her and the proximate past. When this came into her mind, she was halfway to the corner of the block, but she turned with the thought, without slowing or thinking further or seeing anything whatever, stepping off the curb between two parked cars and walking blindly and imperiously into the traffic lane. At the last moment, just before she was struck, she looked around and through the windshield of the car, as if in the instant of this new and different danger she was mysteriously compelled to see from where and what it came. She was aware of a white and staring face, set behind glass in lines of virulent hatred, and she had in that final instant, before the bolt of pain and thunderous night, the most fantastic notion that it was the face of Lila...

But it was not the face of Lila at all, and it was absolutely absurd that she had ever thought so. The face was much older than the face of Lila, and set not in lines of hatred but of reassuring and disciplined kindness, and above the face was a foolish kind of white cap that Lila would never have worn. At first sight, the face appeared to be disembodied, hanging above her without support, and this was so clearly impossible that the face itself was impossible, and she shut her eyes and waited for it to fade away, but when she opened her eyes again it was still there. Now, however, there was also a body to support the face and give it credence, but the body was incidental and unimportant; the important thing was that the face was smiling and was obviously trying to say something.

"What did you say?" Ivy said to the face.

She intended to speak normally, and tried to, but her voice came out a whisper, and she couldn't understand why this should be so.

"I've been waiting for you," the face said.

"Waiting for me? Why? Where have I been?"

"You've been unconscious. For quite a long time. Hew do you feel?"

Now that the question had been asked, Ivy realized that she did not feel right in several ways. In the first place, she did not understand where she was or how she had got there, and this was confusing. In the second place, apart from the confusion, she had a feeling of insecure cohesion, as though at any second she might fall into pieces. In the third place, she hurt. She hurt in her head and body, in flesh and bone, and the hurt was worse with her slightest move.

"I feel strange," she said. "Why do I hurt so?"

"Don't you remember? You had an accident. You were struck by a car."

Then she remembered, and remembering, saw it all again in a split second as it had happened over a period of hours. She shut her eyes against it, trying to recover the deep and solacing peace of total darkness, and she lay for so long with her eyes closed that the nurse thought she had gone naturally to sleep, and was about to go away when the eyes opened.

"That's why I thought at first you were Lila," Ivy said.

"Lila? Is she a friend of yours?"

"She's someone I know."

"Well, now that you've recovered consciousness, you will soon be able to see your friends."

"Has anyone been here?"

"Two people that I know of. The lady who was driving the car that struck you, and a young man. The lady is terribly distressed about the accident. She insists on assuming all expenses."

"What does she look like?"

"She's young and lovely. Like a fashion model. She has black hair."

"Then it *was* Lila."

"What?"

"Nothing." She closed her eyes and saw the white face behind glass and opened the eyes immediately to escape it. "Who was the young man?"

"His name is Henry Harper. He comes every evening."

"Every evening? How long have I been here? This is a hospital, isn't it?"

"Yes, it's a hospital. You've been here three days. This is the third day."

"I should like to see Henry."

"You may see him soon."

"How soon?"

"The doctor will decide. Perhaps for a little while in a day or so."

"I want very much to see him."

"I know. I understand. But now you mustn't talk any more. You must go to sleep if you can."

The nurse meant well. She was trying to do the right thing. Obediently, Ivy closed her eyes again and listened to the nurse move quietly away, and then she opened her eyes one more time before sleeping and looked out through a window at a black branch covered with ice, and the ice was like cold white fire in the sunlight, the black branch aflame against a patch of pale sky.

Later that day the doctor came. He was an elderly man with gray and white hair brushed smoothly across his skull from a low side part. He also had a ragged gray and white mustache that needed trimming and had grown so far down over his upper lip that he could hold the ends of the hairs between his upper lip and his lower lip, and he did this abstractedly while thinking. His face and voice had the gentleness that comes from the kind of tiredness that is a final estate. He said his name was Dr. Larson. He told her that she had received a severe concussion and a simple fracture of the right arm, which she had guessed from the cast that was on it, and was lucky that she had, besides these, only bruises and lacerations. She was lucky, indeed, to be alive. He came that day, and the next day, and the third day, in the evening, she was allowed to see Henry. He came into the room looking awkward and shy and sit down in a chair beside the bed.

"How are you feeling?" he said.

"Much better," she said. "I hurt much less than I did. How is the book coming?"

"All right. For some reason I feel confident now that it will be a good book."

"It's very generous of you to come to see me."

"I haven't come out of generosity. I've come because I wanted to."

"It was cowardly of me to run away and leave you when you were in danger because of me. I'm grateful to you for saving me, however."

"It's all right. It came out all right."

"I didn't dream that you were so brave."

"Oh, nonsense. Anyone will fight if it's necessary, I paid your bill at the hotel and took your things home."

"Did you? Thank you very much. I'm sorry that I've caused you so much trouble."

"I also talked to the police about the accident. You'll have to talk to them yourself, when you feel like it, but it will be only a formality."

"It was Lila who did it, wasn't it?"

'Yes."

"She did it on purpose. First she gave me too much sedative, and then she ran me down."

"Listen to me. I doubt seriously that she gave you too much sedative, and she certainly didn't deliberately run you down. There were witnesses to the accident, and they testified that you walked right in front of the car. She couldn't have stopped or missed you."

"It seems to me a great coincidence that it should have been Lila."

"That's what it was. You must believe it."

"Why was she there? That's something I've been unable to understand. She couldn't have known where I had gone."

"I'd arranged to meet her. We were going to look for you together. I'll tell you all about it when you are better."

"Well, I'll believe that she's innocent if you tell me to, but I don't want to see her again. Not ever again."

"That's good."

"If she comes here to see me, I'll have them send her away."

"She won't come. I've told her it would be better if she didn't."

"Do you really want me to come back to you?"

"If you want to."

"I want to, but I don't know if it would be wise. How will it end?"

"I don't know."

"I think it will end well. I think so."

"We'll see."

"How is George?"

"George is fine. He sends his regards. He'll come to see you when you're stronger."

"I'll be glad to see him. I would be glad to see Mr. Brennan too, if he cares to come."

"Perhaps I can bring him one time."

"Did you have any trouble over the fight in the hotel room?"

"No. No trouble. It didn't last long. I knocked the man out, whoever he was, and when he came to, he went away. I took your things, as I said, and paid your bill. I had heard the ambulance in the street, but I didn't know what it was for. When I got outside, they were just putting you into it."

"I'll tell you about the man sometime."

"You don't have to. I don't care about him."

"I've caused you a great deal of trouble, haven't I?"

"Never mind that."

"I can't understand why you bother with me."

"Maybe it's because you remind me, for some reason, of someone else I once knew."

"The girl you told me about that you were in love with?"

"Yes."

"I'm glad I remind you of her. She must have been very nice if you were in love with her. I hope that you get to be in love with me too, and I with you. I'll try to make it come out so."

"You tried once. Remember? It didn't work."

"I'll try again."

"It's a good thing to keep trying."

The hand of her unbroken arm was lying near him on the bed, and he took the hand in his and held it. They sat silently for a long time as the room grew dark in the short and sudden winter dusk.

"I'd better be going," he said at last.

"I don't want you to go."

"I'd better. I was told to stay only a little while."

"I wish you could stay longer."

"Perhaps I can stay longer tomorrow."

"Would you be willing to kiss me before you go?"

"Yes."

He leaned forward and kissed her on the lips and then stood up. She looked very small and frail, he thought, with her head in bandages and her right arm in a plaster cast. The cast gave her a kind of comic touch, an incitement at once to laughter and tears.

"Good-by," he said.

"Until tomorrow," she said.

"Yes," he said, "Until tomorrow."

He went out and she lay quietly in the dark room. She thought for a while that she would surely cry, but she didn't because she couldn't, and pretty soon she went to sleep and wakened only once for a few minutes in the night, and in the morning, when she turned her head on her pillow and looked out the window, she could see the black branch aflame in the sunlight.

THE END